I0762264

The Mysterious Village

The Mysterious Village

Tom Morris

A Journey of Revelation

Book Five

Walid and the Mysteries of Phi

Wisdom/Work
Published by Wisdom Work
TomVMorris.com

Published 2021

ISBN 978-0999352472

Printed in the United States of America

Set in Adobe Garamond Pro
Designed by Abigail Chiaramonte
Cover Concept by Sara Morris

To my good friends Ollie,
Abbey, Odie, and Mister Wes.
Odes, wait for us on the other side.
Woof. Meow.

Contents

I

A Bright Idea

Egypt: Many years ago.

The middle of the nineteen-thirties was a fascinating time in Cairo. And it was about to get much more interesting in some strange and puzzling ways.

In a sense, everything that happens in life is a piece in a very big puzzle. There are some pieces that are blank. Others have only markings that look like random parts of mysterious patterns and can cause the reaction of puzzlement—appropriately enough. Still other pieces display bits of color or overall shapes that you can't imagine fitting anywhere. You may not know at first what to do with any of these. And yet, every one of them will eventually fall into its proper place. In the meantime, now and then and to your great relief, you'll come across a piece that sparks a sense of discovery and recognition and helps you get your bearings: an obvious corner, or a clear part of an easily identified object like a branch of a tree, or the nose of an animal, or the eye of a man. These individual pieces then become little organizing guides for making more progress with the challenge of the entire puzzle.

The door had been left slightly open. And suddenly there was a familiar voice. "Hey! I've got a question for you." Mafulla had just walked into Walid's room so quickly that his words could barely keep pace with his sandals.

"What's the question?" Walid looked up from the king's weekly briefing book he was reading.

"When was the last time you were on a camel, my friend?"

"Almost a year ago."

"Correct."

"And so?"

"And that's too long, especially for a man once almost known as The Desert Viper, before of course I convinced you how golden you are. So, my good buddy, prepare this day to saddle up again. It's time for The Golden Viper to take a ride, old style."

Walid smiled, but looked perplexed. "What are you talking about?"

"It just so happens that I have managed to procure, for our mutual riding pleasure today, two of the kingdom's finest dromedaries."

"You have?"

"Yes. Consider it an early birthday present. Complete camel contentment awaits you."

"Well, that's very thoughtful, but as you'll soon discover, the pleasure of riding on a camel depends a lot on the individual beast."

"Really?" This was clearly news to Mafulla.

"It's not exactly the Rolls Royce of riding animals, guaranteed to be all smooth and silent and relaxing."

"What do you mean?"

"Well, imagine a six foot tall bicycle with long legs rather than wheels, and a sometimes stubborn personality all its own. Bicycles usually obey quite well—camels, sometimes not."

"Hmm. Good points. I did not know that. But you still sort of miss the experience, now that I've mentioned it, right?"

Walid's expression changed instantly. He said, "Yeah, I guess I do. There were days crossing the desert on Cammo that were amazing."

"Cammo?"

"That's the name I gave the main camel that Uncle Ali and I were using the most on our trip here last year. He was lighter in coloration than his fellows, almost exactly the hue of sand, and so, in the desert, he was pretty well camouflaged."

"Oh, so you must have seemed to the uninformed onlooker to be floating several feet above the ground as you made your way toward the capital city, as if you were on a magic carpet."

"That could be so."

"Well then, no wonder they made you prince, and you enjoy such popular acclamation. Magic does it every time."

Walid laughed. "That must be it, but I have to admit, I'd never realized this before."

"Oh?"

"Yeah. It was quite likely that illusory, royal float-across-the sand that secured my exalted position around here."

"No doubt," Mafulla replied. "I mean, in addition to the whole king's beloved-nephew-and-only-heir business."

"I guess that could have helped, too." He looked at his friend and made a face, adding, "You know, you didn't have to get me a birthday present, and especially not something as cool and creative as this."

"Well, when I turned thirteen not long ago, you guys put on such an elaborate party and gave me such great presents, you basically set a standard for celebratory indulgences."

"But that was mostly the king using kingly funds. You don't have to compete with the king."

"No competitive urge, my friend—just appreciation for your worldly arrival. And don't worry, I made it all happen on the cheap."

"Ok, so when do we saddle up?"

"This very morning, if you'd like. I mean, since there's no school today, I thought, why not a little expedition, the Old-School Way?"

"Actually, this is a really good idea," the prince granted. Then he said, "How about we go ride in roughly half an hour?"

Mafulla raised his eyebrows high and replied, "As distinct from riding roughly in half an hour."

"Yeah. As distinct from that."

"Excellent! I would vastly prefer as smooth a ride as possible, in line with your earlier words of caution. You know, I'm not exactly as accomplished as you are in these matters."

"I'm hardly accomplished."

"Well, compared to me, you're a real camel cowboy."

"Ha. Maybe. Look, I'll finish the section of this report I'm reading and come down and get you and we can eat a quick breakfast and take off. But first, I have to know: Where's all this going to happen?"

Mafulla leaned against Walid's dresser and said, while gesturing grandly, "I've had the camels made ready in the royal stables at the edge of town. Darwishi said he can run us over there by car, and then we can travel around a bit in the way nature intended."

"Out in the clean air with no car exhaust," Walid said.

"Exactly," Mafulla replied, "but, of course, perhaps, some camel exhaust."

"I'm not sure which is worse."

"Well, I was careful. I insisted that the primary creatures of conveyance today have no beans of any kind in their breakfast mix this morning," Mafulla quickly explained, punctuating this with a wiggly wave of his hand and his classic double eyebrow jump.

"Oh, good," Walid laughed. "That's certainly reassuring. It would have *bean* different with beans," he said, emphasizing the mispronounced verb in a way that he considered eminently witty.

Mafulla grimaced. "Yes. You're correct, my friend. Well, not to overly extend our current little bout of inappropriate digestive humor, but I'll *slip out quietly* now and let you return to your previous comfort. Just make it down to my room when you're ready. I promise you that on this day, we'll have an *explosively* good time!"

Mafulla scooted out the door as quickly as he had entered and Walid sat for a moment just gazing blankly at the door, seeing in his mind's eye a camel and sand all around. He had been up early reading a report given to the king and then passed on to him. It was about educational needs in the kingdom, and potential plans for building new schools. Since the recent attempted take-over of the palace by the now-deceased industrialist Farouk al-Khoum and his equally deceased brother Faraj, King Ali had been sharing more information and governance duties with Walid. It was almost like the dangers of those events had convinced the king that it might be time to prepare Walid more fully for his future role in guiding the kingdom. So there were more meetings, more reports to read, and many more conversations about decisions that were being made.

While most of this was very interesting, the workload and overall stress level of Walid's daily life had increased by quite a bit. Mafulla had noticed that and had arranged the camel ride as a way of giving his friend a needed break away from the details of governance and all the royal paperwork.

Not that much time had passed since the violent attack on the palace, but it had been a period of great change in many ways. Both Walid and Mafulla seemed to have gotten taller and put on even more muscle weight as a result of intensified workouts with Masoon. They still had every bit as much fun with each other, as time allowed, but there was also a new seriousness of purpose in the backs of their minds. The trauma of the attack and the deaths of some good people they knew had educated them both at a new level as to what it meant to live at the center of a major country's government. They now had a clearer sense than ever about the many dangers of the world and how deeply misguided people could do so much harm. They also understood in a new way the need for good people to work hard and even fight when necessary for what they know is right.

In addition to all these philosophical insights, Walid had realized just recently that every time he saw Kissa, she looked more beautiful and mature than ever before. He didn't know it, but Mafulla had been thinking the same thing about both Hasina and Kissa. The recent events had made a big difference for them as well. They were working hard with Hoda with a new focus and a deeper sense of the importance of their Phi training, beyond anything they had ever felt before the recent events. In the challenging circumstances they had lived through, they had come to appreciate on a new level the vital importance of the ancient secret society in which they were included, and the way that the skills of Phi could make a decisive difference in the course of kingdom events, as well as in their personal lives. They had both come to realize that Hoda and Layla were working hard to prepare them for new and expanded responsibilities.

Legend had it that the society of remarkable individuals known to its members as "Phi" had been around since before the time of the first pharaohs. It was reputed, at least among insiders, to have helped raise the great Egyptian kings of the past to prominence, and also to have played a role in the cultural accomplishments of Greece and Rome, in the ancient world. Phi, as they were collectively referred to, were connected to something deep and immensely powerful through the openness of their minds and hearts, and their spirits. They were bound together in a community of friendship and support for the purpose of encouraging each other's development, as well as doing great good together in the world. Kissa's mother Hoda, and Hasina's mother Layla were both Phi, as their mothers also had been. So, Kissa and Hasina had sensed the true importance of Phi ever since they were first told about it and learned that they were now among its members. But after the brutal attack on the palace, they had an even stronger appreciation of its meaning and purpose.

They also, of course, in a sense were still girls, the way Walid and Mafulla were still boys, and they continued to have just as much fun as ever in their daily activities. But there was an extra measure of awareness and appreciation deep in their souls as well, and it was steering them into the future in a new way. Life is serious, but it's not meant to be somber, and so they lived days of joking and laughing and enjoying themselves, while at the same time realizing more completely their potentially vital roles in the bigger scheme of things.

Mafulla had no clue, but today was when Kissa and Hasina were going to meet Hasina's mom, Layla, out at the royal stables for their first serious horseback riding lessons. Layla considered this still to be an important ability for any Phi to have and, as an expert level rider herself, was taking on this aspect of their Phi training. She was going to teach the girls to ride well, and also to use various weapons while on horseback and moving. As a prominently active community leader in the capital city, she was often busy during the week with volunteer work for various organizations serving both the city and the kingdom. But at least one day a week would most often be free, and she had been looking forward to starting these lessons with the girls on this particular morning.

Walid finished his reading, got up, splashed some cold water on his face, and walked down the hall to Mafulla's room to get him for a quick breakfast. "Ok, let's go, Camel Joe," Walid said, pushing in on the already open door.

"Good! Oh, I like that—Camel Joe: a nice, authentically Egyptian nickname, especially the Joe part, which, I'm sure, must date back to at least the building of the pyramids. But just a minute before we leave. There's a second part to your early birthday present."

"Really?"

"Yeah. Give me a moment—however long exactly that might be—and I'll get the additional item." Mafulla got up off his bed where he had been reading a book about American movies, walked over to his big dresser, and pulled out the top drawer. Taking something in his hand, he said, "Close your eyes."

Walid laughed and replied in a voice of amicable caution, "Ok, maybe, but first you have to promise that nothing's going to bite me or surprise me or humiliate me, or gross me out, and there's no real danger of even a trivial kind that lurks in your hands."

"Ha! Do I see a study of the law in your future? That's an impressive list of conditions. I promise you that it will be a good surprise, not a shocking or unpleasant one, and nothing will jump out at you or touch your body in any way without your prior visual perception and enthusiastic agreement. There's absolutely no threat of any kind involved, however trivial, and this is not a practical joke of any sort whatsoever. I just want to be able to approach you more closely with the gift unseen until I tell you to open your eyes."

"Oh, Ok, then, that's fine." Walid closed his eyes.

"Total trust between friends is so nice," Mafulla said.

"Yeah, I cherish it deeply," Walid replied.

Not even three seconds later, Mafulla had stepped closer to Walid and said, "Ok! Open your eyes! Tada!"

Walid did what he was told and was shocked at what he saw. He just said, "What?"

"What do you mean, 'What'? Hollywood movie star sunglasses for the camel ride!"

Walid just stood with his mouth open for a couple of seconds.

"You look like a hungry camel, my friend." Mafulla reached out toward Walid, offering him the gift. "This pair of sunglasses is for you, Prince of Camels as well as people. I have my own to match, since I'm at least a duke or a satrap or something."

"You're really something, all right! But … Hollywood movie star sunglasses … from Hollywood? From … America?"

"Well, from Atlantic City, to be precise, in New Jersey, The United States of America, within sight of the sparkling blue waves of the ocean, from a man named Sam Foster who sells them at the beach."

"New Jersey?"

"Yeah. But they're exactly what the Hollywood stars are wearing."

"How did you get these?" Walid asked while taking the pair of sunglasses from his friend and turning them over and admiring them.

"I know a guy who knows a guy, and so on. What can I tell you? I have major connections. Come to me with your more exotic needs."

"But, how did you even think of this?"

Mafulla had a huge grin on his face at this point. He said, "I know how much you like the movies, and I do too, and I thought it would be a great birthday present for you to get these for both of us, so we could be the super cool camel jockeys of the desert today."

"This … this is an awesome present!" Walid just continued to stare at the gift in his hands, now with a very big smile on his face as well. "This is just the best!"

"Well, I mean, what do you get a prince? You have everything you want—at least pretty much everything you've thought of. So

I had to be a little creative. But it was no trouble. I'm a giver—an immensely creative and thoughtful giver, which, of course, I say in all appropriate humility. But that, certainly, is a given … from me, as you might imagine, the giver."

"Of course." Walid slipped on his glasses. "So, giver, give me your opinion. How do I look?"

"Amazing! Just amazing! Like a true star of the stage and screen! Come over to the mirror."

"The whole room just got much darker, of course," Walid said as he took his first tentative step wearing his new shades and glanced around.

"Of course," Mafulla replied.

The prince just laughed. "I hadn't anticipated this aspect of it all, for some reason."

"Yeah, I know what you mean," Mafulla agreed. "That's simply the side effect of movie cool, my man—the dark side. But not only did the room get darker, you also got darker and more mysterious at the same time, while everything else in the room instantly seemed to center itself around you in a new way. Now, go, look at yourself."

Walid walked over to the mirror that Mafulla was pointing at, and then just stood there for a few seconds and considered himself admiringly.

Mafulla commented: "That's what I'm talking about! Ladies, watch out! The autograph line starts outside. Please be patient. All his fans will be accommodated."

Walid turned back toward his friend to say something and Mafulla now had his pair of sunglasses on as well. Walid laughed, "Ha! Well, there you go! Two stars of the silver screen!"

Mafulla said, "Let's sport these shades down to breakfast—just because we can."

"Yeah, let's do it."

Walid turned from the mirror after one more glance, and then stopped for a second to gaze again at Mafulla's new look. This time, with a completely straight face, Walid did a double eyebrow jump, and that cracked up his friend, big-time. The prince then walked out the door, followed close behind by his sidekick, or co-star, and by the time they were halfway to the breakfast room, they were walking beside each other, owning the hallway in proper movie icon style.

Just that second, the head royal butler, Kular, came out of his office carrying a tray at a brisk clip toward the breakfast room from the other direction. But then, suddenly, he peered down the hall and stopped in his tracks with a look of complete surprise and after a pause said, “What? What’s this? Who are these handsome leading men of the cinema? Am I in the middle of a movie? Where are the lights and the cameras? Where’s the director?”

The boys both started laughing and Mafulla replied, “The real question, my friend, is: Where are the leading ladies?” That cracked everyone up.

“Well,” Kular replied, “unless I’m completely misinformed about the ways of the world, all the ladies should be flocking to you two any time now. If you need someone to handle the crowds, take care of your publicity, and of course oversee your soon-to-be-busy Hollywood schedules, I may know someone.”

“Thanks, old friend. We could indeed need serious management soon, and of course the publicist of whom you speak.” Mafulla looked over at Walid and added, “We’d better start carrying around pens for all these autographs we’ll be asked to give, and of course, bottles of the finest ink, and perhaps a few blotters.”

Walid, looking pensive, said, “Yeah, you’re likely right about that. It pays to be prepared.”

Mafulla then stroked his chin and concluded, “This is all a bit more complicated than I had expected, but … such is the price of fame.”

Kular laughed again and said, “Ok, what’s really going on?”

“An early birthday present from Mafulla,” Walid explained, and wiggled the glasses on his face with a finger.

“Very nice,” Kular smiled and nodded, looking impressed.

“I got him a ride on a camel later this morning, and these little sun cheaters—as they’re called in The USA—are for staying cool as

I ride and glide astride my camel, Clyde, which is what I've chosen to call my own devotedly domesticated desert dromedary, whoever he may be."

"Clyde," Walid said.

"Yes, indeed. Clyde the Ride," Mafulla replied and looked back over at Kular, adding, "And, of course, the shades are mostly for the prince of cool here, thanks to his upcoming birthday."

"Truly a novel, creative, and thoughtful choice of gifts," Kular replied, as he motioned to the door of the breakfast room, which he then moved toward and opened for the boys. "I wish my responsibilities would allow me to go saddle up alongside you two and get some of the reflected glamor I'm sure you'll display and distribute to all who observe you today."

"Yeah, but we probably couldn't keep up with you," Walid said. "I mean, since the effects of the stone seem to be pretty much ongoing and nonstop."

"True," Mafulla said. "You'd likely leave us in your dust."

"The stone's astonishing benefits, I have to say, are as strong as ever. I'm very blessed by the continuing results of what cured the worst thing that ever happened to me," Kular said.

"It's like what Masoon always calls a turnaround," Mafulla observed. "The worst things can sometimes, oddly, give rise to the best things. We live in a very strange world."

"Yes," Kular agreed, "and often most wonderful, if we just know how to view it and make our way through it."

The butler placed the tray he was carrying on a side table, and uncovered some great looking, savory scones. "Stars deserve star quality breakfast delights," he said. "So, please, help yourselves."

Mafulla laughed. "We will!"

"And have fun riding today," Kular said as he walked back toward the door. "There's an old saying in Hollywood show business that I've heard about: 'Break a leg!' But I think, maybe, I won't use that one today to wish you luck."

"Ha!" Walid laughed, and said. "Thanks!"

"Yeah, double thanks from a man hoping to avoid any such

woe," Mafulla added. And then, before Kular got completely out of the room, the boy responsible for all the merriment commented, "I do wish we could snag an extra camel for you to ride today, and even bring it back to the palace for your ongoing use, but I'd hate to be known as a camel thief."

"No! You must never go to prison on my behalf," Kular laughed and stopped in the doorway. And then he grew serious, saying, "Of course, as you both may have heard, there do seem to be some people out and about these days who have no fear of the potential prison time they face, and are stealing animals all around town."

"No, I hadn't heard anything about it," Walid responded.

"Neither have I," Mafulla said. "What's being stolen?"

"Camels, horses, donkeys, and even family pets—cats and dogs," Kular said. "It's really become a scandal. No one knows who's doing this or why. But the newspaper hasn't reported on it much. And that's largely, I think, because so many of the disappearances, or thefts, as I firmly believe, have been one or two animals at a time, nothing big. But people are now talking about lots of these incidents, at least in my neighborhood, at home. I hear it all the time. Almost everyone knows someone who's been affected by this odd new crime wave."

Mafulla looked concerned. He said, "Hmm. I hope we're not going to be riding on any hot camels today."

"No, this morning, they should be cool like their movie star riders," Kular joked. "But watch out this afternoon, it should be a scorcher and the animals will surely heat up along with the air. Remember to observe the law of the desert and give yourselves and the camels a mid-afternoon break."

"You're a wise man, Kular. We'll be careful," Walid assured him. "And we'll give you a full report after it all."

"Good! Have plenty of fun and be safe. Now, it's back to work for those of us who aren't celebrities in dark glasses," Kular said with a smile, and ducked out, closing the door behind him.

As Walid and Mafulla took up plates and began to load them with some of their favorite breakfast foods, Mafulla said, "That's strange about so many animals disappearing and likely being stolen."

"Yeah," Walid agreed. "But I guess anything of value that can be carried or led away is going to get taken at some point by people with greed in their hearts, people who have no love or respect for others."

Mafulla nodded and said, "It's so weird. It's almost like I've been assuming that with Ari and Idi Falma and the al-Khoum brothers and so many of the other old bad guys gone, we'd have this golden age without crime in the city and the kingdom. And yet, so soon after all that happened, then this is going on."

"I know what you mean," Walid replied. "But whenever there's a vacancy in the criminal world, it seems like there's always somebody around who's ready to take the job."

"Yeah, I suppose you're right. It's world history. The bad guys are vanquished and then there's a new crop to take their place. Too bad those people won't just find a normal job instead, and take care of their families, or do something positive with their time. I guess I've always sort of assumed, wrongly, that there's something like a limited supply of bad guys at any given time."

"I suppose I've always thought that, too."

"But it seems like there's never a true shortage. I wonder who we're dealing with now?" Mafulla mused.

"No way of knowing until they're caught, I guess," Walid said as he moved over to his usual place and sat down to eat.

"Man, I just hope that Shib …" Mafulla stopped suddenly, mid-sentence and mid-word, and mumbled, "Never mind."

"What? Never mind what?"

"Nothing, nothing of importance. Eat your breakfast and let's go ride," Mafulla replied as he stuffed his mouth with bread and cheese.

"No, no, no, you never stop mid-sentence and mid-word when you're about to tell me something. I want to know what you were going to say," Walid insisted.

Mafulla just made a face that looked like a human equivalent of the statement, "I don't want to do this."

But Walid was not deterred. He simply said, "By royal decree, it's hereby declared that you will either finish your sentence, or explain to me what you were going to say and why you suddenly chose instead not to say it. And you will do so now, or forfeit the right to any of the food remaining on your plate, among many other potentially worse unpleasant consequences."

Mafulla let out a deep breath. He said, "Jeez. That's severe. I'm too hungry. I cave. I was just going to say that, man, I hope Shibby and her … new puppies won't get stolen by these guys."

"What new puppies?" Walid asked in a voice of complete surprise.

"Yeah, see, that's the issue. Let me explain. I saw Hasina yesterday, and she said that Kissa just told her the news that her dog Shibby is going to have puppies and Kissa wanted to be the one to tell you. And I just started to blurt out the secret without thinking. And now you've made me tell it, by royal decree—whatever that is—and under threat of denying me needed nutrition, which actually, now that I think about it, means that maybe I won't get in as much trouble because, admit it, Hasina probably wouldn't like having to come to the palace jail to see me, a very hungry and super-skinny violator of a royal decree. So, by using that little ploy, you may have gotten not only the information you wanted, but also gotten me out of the hot water that would have otherwise resulted from a spillage of the secret in question. So, thank you, I guess?"

"I see," said Walid. "I'm glad it's all worked out so well for both of us."

"I'm sure Kissa was planning to tell you soon," Mafulla quickly assured his friend.

"Yeah, well, you'll remember that I had things the king needed me to do after class yesterday," Walid said. "I didn't get to talk to her after school. This helping-the-king-to-rule stuff is seriously messing up my social life."

"You'll see her soon," Mafulla replied to make Walid feel better. "But I meant what I said, or at first almost said, and now have actually said, about Shibby. Everybody knows that she's the most beautiful dog in town. She's famous. And if people are stealing pets, she's got to be on somebody's dream shopping list."

"Yeah, you're right. We'd better warn Kissa and make sure she protects Shibby and the new puppies. Maybe after we get back today we can get a message to her."

"Good idea. But for now, if you're well nourished, let's go for a ride … before someone steals our camels."

Walid laughed and said, "Ok, let's go." And so, putting their plates on a side table, they walked out the door at just the perfect time.

2

Camels and Horses

It took less than ten minutes for the boys to pick up everything they needed and get over to the garage where all the palace cars were kept. On their way out, Walid had popped into Kular's office and left him a note for the king, telling him where they were going, what they'd be doing, and approximately when they'd be back. Unknown to the prince, the king was already in on all of this, and had set up the car ride to the stables, thanks to Walid's conspiratorial best friend.

Darwishi, the king's head driver, was sitting in his office reading the morning paper when the kings of cool walked in. "Hi, Darwishi," Mafulla said in greeting.

"Good morning, Dar," Walid echoed, close behind his friend.

Darwishi looked up from the paper and practically jumped up from his chair. "Prince! Mafulla! I … think that's you! I've been expecting you. But, oh, my! Look at these dark glasses you have on! They're so dashing! Mysterious! Enigmatic! I suddenly feel like I'm in the middle of an American detective movie. Come in! Come in!"

Walid laughed and said, "Enigmatic—I love that. You apparently have Mafulla's affection for words."

"Yes! Definitely!"

"He gave me these glasses as part of an early birthday present and, as you can see, got himself some as well.

"I do indeed see."

"So, you like them?"

"Very much! I even have a strange urge to ask you both for an autograph, and perhaps go find a camera so that someone can take our picture together—for my wife, of course, not for me. I like to stay outside the mix of all those people craving a contact with celebrity, however small. But not that you're at all small! You're huge, of course, surely massive—even much bigger than that: gigantic!"

Both boys laughed. Mafulla looked at Walid and said, "See? I told you. The mere appearance of fame is bound to bring it our way. In this world, how you look is the key to many things."

"Yes, but how you are is the key to many more."

"Absolutely—which makes it a good thing, then, that we are … totally fantastic," Mafulla said with the customary and now even expected facial punctuation.

Darwishi picked up some keys off the desk and with a big smile asked, "Are you two men of high fashion, status, and mystery ready for me to run you across town now to the stables?"

"Yes, that will be excellent, my dear sir," Mafulla answered, playing the part. "We're all ready. We both need to have a long session of practice riding, in preparation, of course, for our next big film role. I think it should be *Drama in the Desert*."

"Oh! Very good! Very good! *Drama in the Desert*, indeed! You both have the most wonderful imaginations … an important quality for any top actor, I would venture." Darwishi laughed again and said, "Well, your studio limousine awaits. And it's best to leave before the crowds of adoring fans come to realize your whereabouts. Otherwise, it's difficult to get through them all. So, then, shall we be off?"

"Yes!" Mafulla replied with a grin, and Walid nodded. Darwishi led the way across the open garage area to one of the larger cars, and as they approached it, the figure of another man came into view. He was sitting on a small chair next to the car, reading a book.

"My man, Paki!" Mafulla called out.

"Paki! What are you doing here?" Walid also said in a voice of pleasant surprise.

"Hi Prince! Or at least, that's who I think you are behind those devilishly dark glasses!" Paki laughed, and said, "I signed up for the excursion today as your personal security, compliments of the king. Mafulla got me word that you'd be coming about now. But, Ok, I have to admit it took me an extra split second to recognize the two of you with your super cool shades on. I've never actually seen anyone in person wearing these, only in magazines and the movies, and once on the cover of a French newspaper."

"Exactly!" exclaimed Mafulla. "It's all part of my early birthday present to the prince here, along with the camel ride today."

"I heartily approve," Paki said. "The glasses look great on both of you, and will be helpful in the bright sun. Unless, of course, they … spook the camels," he added.

"Spook the camels?" Mafulla had not thought of this, at all.

"Well, perhaps," Paki said.

Darwishi added, "It happens."

"What?"

Paki explained, "The thing is, I'd wager that your designated dromedaries have never seen such a sight. They don't actually have the occasion to watch movies or read magazines. So, to them, you may just seem to be scary humanoids with the large dark eyes of camel eaters."

"Oh, no."

"If I were you, I'd approach them slowly and with a soothing voice, and perhaps before putting on the glasses. They're not likely to be impressed with the new look, but rather kick first and ask questions later."

"Oops. Once again bitten in the backside by the notorious Law of Unintended Consequences," Mafulla said.

"What's this law you mention?" Darwishi asked.

"Oh, the Law of Unintended Consequences says that for many actions that are intended to have specific results, there will also be consequences that are unintended and unexpected."

"I see."

"It's like when we sometimes do something to bring about a good thing, and something bad happens instead as an unintended consequence of what we've done for quite other reasons."

"Oh, I think this law, as you call it, is insightful."

"I do, too," Mafulla agreed. "It typically applies when we haven't thought through a situation well enough and so have an insufficient understanding of how our actions will alter it. We hope for the best, and get something else instead."

"Yes. I've seen it happen often."

"But I had no idea that it might apply to the two parts of my gift in a problematic way."

"The animals may be fine with the new look you're sporting," Paki quickly added. "Or, they might not even notice. And if they do seem displeased, just tell them that we might be able to get some dark glasses in their size as well, if they'll be on their best behavior. You know how camels always prefer to be cool amid all the heat, and here we're talking about the very coolest of all the new fashions."

"Yes," Mafulla agreed. "They do tend to be quite stubbornly stylish, all decked out in their camel hair coats in even the hottest weather. So they could indeed enjoy the promise of whatever might provide an extra measure of cool."

Paki laughed, and added, "I'm just saying that I think you should be extra careful when you first approach them this morning, and then we'll see how it goes."

"Good advice," Walid replied. "Thanks. You're a full service security guy, for sure."

"I do my best."

"And now," the prince suggested, "if you two camel comedians are ready, let's head out to that fashion hot spot that we like to call the stables."

"All ready," Paki said with a smile as he got up from his chair and opened the car door for Walid and Mafulla. The boys piled into the back seat, and Paki joined Darwishi in the front.

Within less than twenty minutes or so, they were pulling up to the impressive cluster of buildings and barns that sat some distance off the road at the edge of town. Once the car had stopped and they began to get out, Walid thought to ask, "Dar, how do we get word to you and let you know when we're ready to go back home?"

"Oh, I plan to stay here," he explained. "I have work to do here today, interviewing a few new job applicants for the stables and going over some paperwork and supplies. I'll be around and will be able to take you back to the palace whenever you want to go, especially after the first couple of hours, but really at any time. I'll be using the office up front in the main building over to the right, the closest one."

"Very nice," Walid said. "Thanks for making it so easy."

"My pleasure. I was due to put in some time here soon, anyway."

Mafulla looked around and saw four or five men working near the largest stable building and said, "Darwishi, I need to find that guy who helped me set all this up. Could you point him out to me? His name is Mahmood."

"Mahmood?" Walid laughed. "I know Mahmood! He came with us across the desert. Is he in charge of the stable here?"

"Yeah. He's the guy who got us the camels," Mafulla said.

"He's the Royal Director of Stables," Darwishi explained.

"Oh, that's good. That's very good! Mahmood is a great guy," Walid said, looking over his sunglasses and all around the area. Just then a man walked out of the main building with some papers in his hand. "Wait, there he is! Excuse me for a second." Walid walked briskly toward the building off to the right where the man was now standing near the door and he called out, "Mahmood!"

"Prince Walid!" The man broke into a huge smile and waved. "Welcome to the Royal Stables! It's so good to see you again!"

Walid walked up quickly to his old friend and Mahmood bowed, but as soon as he straightened up again, the prince gave him a big hug. "It's good to see you, too!" he said. "It's been far too long! I miss our days together crossing the desert. Well, not the heat, but all the good talk and fun we had."

"I do, too. That was one of my favorite trips ever," the director exclaimed. "And it ended with such unexpected excitement!"

"Yes, it did!" Walid replied.

At that moment, as he saw a second young man approaching, Mahmood said, "Wait! This must be the famous Mafulla Adi!" He reached out to shake his hand, and Mafulla reciprocated.

"Yeah, but I didn't know about the famous part," Mafulla said with a grin. "I'm the guy who contacted you about the camel ride."

"Yes. Of course."

"I really appreciate your help."

"It's my great pleasure."

"Today's the day, and we're ready for a super nice time."

"Good! I'm honored to have the two of you at my stables this morning."

"Thanks again for getting us the camels and for setting all this up."

"Oh, it was my treat. As soon as I heard that it would be an early birthday present for the prince, I got very excited about it. I think I've found you two of the best camels around, and I've charted out a good riding course for you—actually a couple of options, depending on how long you'd like to be out. I've even made a map. Let me go get it for you."

"Great," Mafulla said. "We're ready and eager."

"I'll be right back," Mahmood assured them with another smile and, slightly bowing from the waist toward Walid and then toward Mafulla, he turned and walked rapidly through a nearby door.

The prince looked over at this friend and said, "This is going to be really good. There's no one better with animals than Mahmood. That's his gift. And I'm sure he'll have a great day planned for us. I'm jazzed."

Mafulla said, "Me, too. And notice: he's a man with his mind on business. He's the first person today who hasn't commented on our new look."

"Well, maybe that's just because everybody else sees us on a daily basis and they know the sunglasses are new and different. I haven't seen Mahmood since the day we arrived in the capital, except way across the room at a dinner once. He may think this is the way we normally look, out in the sun."

"True," Mafulla replied and then, looking over his friend's shoulder, he observed, "Hey, another car's coming down the road. And isn't it one of the king's older sedans?"

Walid turned, gazed down the road, and said, "Yeah, that's one of the cars. I wonder who's in it?"

The older but still elegant vehicle kept approaching in a cloud of dust and then pulled up to a spot not far from where the boys were standing. The driver got out, bowed quickly toward the prince and Mafulla, now standing maybe thirty or forty feet away, and walked around to open the front passenger door, from which a lady slowly emerged. It was Layla, Hasina's mother. Then, he opened the back passenger door and Hasina got out, followed by Kissa.

"No way!" Walid said. The girls waved at him with big smiles and he waved back, as did Mafulla. The prince turned to his friend and said, "Is this part of the surprise, too?"

"No, no, not at all," Mafulla answered. "I mean, yes, it's sure a surprise and great, and I'd love to take credit for it, but I didn't plan this part. I have no idea what they're doing here. Let's go find out." And at that, both boys started walking toward the car. Layla waved with a big smile for them but then walked off right away toward the office building, in conversation with the driver.

"Wooo Hooo!" shouted Hasina, with her right hand over her heart. "Hollywood's leading men, right here in Egypt!"

"Look at you!" Kissa exclaimed as the boys came ambling up toward them. "What's up with the new look?"

"You like it?" Walid asked them both.

"Of course!" Kissa said. "Very handsome and mysterious, and like some extra famous person, which I guess you sort of are, any way."

"Mafulla got us these American sunglasses to wear out here today."

"Did you guys come out to watch us?" Kissa asked.

"We didn't know you were going to be here. But we're always prepared to watch you. In fact, we can't help it. I'm already looking closely. Do anything you like. We'll be your very best audience."

"Silly! But then, what are you two doing out here at the edge of town?"

Mafulla jumped in and said, "I procured for my good friend, as an early birthday present, both the sunglasses and a ride on a couple of camels that are being kept in the stable for us. We just got here a few minutes ago to go on our ride."

"Oh," Hasina and Kissa both said.

Mafulla continued, "So, what brought the two of you out here? Was it my personal magnetism operating at a subliminal level?"

Kissa looked very serious and said to Hasina, "Could that be it?"

"No. I don't think so. Not this time, for once."

"But surely," Mafulla protested.

"It was horseback riding," Hasina said. "Sorry."

"I'm crestfallen."

"Well then, the law of the stables applies," Kissa responded.

"What's that?"

"Whenever you fall, get back up."

"Ok. So I'll dust off my crest and self image and rise again."

"That's the spirit."

Hasina explained, "We're really here to do some special training that mom's going to be helping us with at least once or twice a month, and maybe to start, nearly every week."

"Oh. That sounds good."

"Today, we'll just ride in the practice ring, but next time, we may hit the trails."

"Are you going to be doing all kinds of riding—you know, walking, trotting, and whatever it's called when you're going really fast?" Walid asked.

"Yes."

"Very nice."

Kissa then added, "We're planning to do all that, and shooting from the horse, and lots of other stuff—really special stuff." She carefully emphasized the word 'special' and raised her eyebrows.

"Oh, Oh, I see," Walid said. "Good, very good. I specially love the special stuff."

"Yeah, Layla's the super expert on all this, so my mom gets some time off," Kissa explained.

"We haven't done any horseback training, yet," Walid said. "In fact, Masoon hasn't even mentioned it."

"I suspect it'll happen in its own proper time. What are you guys doing with him now?" Kissa asked, moving a bit closer to Walid so that their conversation could not at this point be overheard by anyone who might walk by.

"Some pretty strange and wild stuff."

"Really? How strange?"

"Well," Walid nearly whispered, "recently, some totally intense practice, catching … arrows and swords with our bare hands."

"You're kidding."

"No, not at all, but I wish I was." Walid laughed. "What you think would be just totally impossible ends up being possible, but you have to be trained extensively by a true master, or you're likely to get really badly hurt. I mean: it takes a lot of mental preparation for something like that, and the most total concentration you can imagine."

"I bet."

"We started with tossed arrows and fake swords."

"Good."

"I just hope we don't have to learn how to catch bullets."

"Ha."

"I'd rather just dodge them well—a talent you're known for, I should add."

"Yeah, thanks. But you guys, too, I know. And dodging's better than catching, with bullets, I mean. It's not like, if you catch it, you can use it again. And I think it would probably hurt."

"True," Walid agreed.

Kissa said, "The arrows don't get shot right at you, do they?"

"No, no. They're shot near us, meant to go right by us, and we're supposed to reach out and catch them by the shaft as they pass."

"Still, it sounds really dangerous!"

"Yeah, it is, but Masoon's doing the shooting and we're super careful and would never do it or even try it without him there, watching over every detail." Then he said, "We've also been learning how to do that Hoda thing that you and Hasina do when you use your thoughts to get into a bad guy's head and give him the headache of a lifetime."

"Oh, good. That's come in handy several times, as you know. And Layla's really good at it, too. I still don't have a clue exactly how it works, but it really does."

"It's hard," Walid said.

"Yeah, at first, but you'll get the hang of it. It just takes a lot of practice."

"Apparently. Otherwise, I end up being the one with the aching head."

"I know what you mean."

At that point, Layla's conversation ended with their driver, who then entered the office, and she walked back over to where they were all standing around. As she approached, she officially greeted the boys. "Walid, Mafulla, a good morning to you both!" Then, turning to the girls, she said, "I'm sorry to break up your time with some of our favorite fellows, but we've got to keep on schedule. We need to get our horses now and take them to the ring. And there's no time to lose, so please excuse us, gentlemen, and ladies follow me, if you would."

"Ok, Mom," Hasina responded and began to walk behind her mother.

"Have a great session!" Walid said.

"Yeah. Work hard. Have fun," Mafulla added.

Then, looking back at the boys, Layla said, "You know, I'd be remiss not to say that I like the new look for you both—draped as you are today in mystery and intrigue."

"Thank you, dear lady," Mafulla replied in a mannered, courtly tone.

The girls said goodbye quickly as they walked on with Layla toward the stables. Mafulla looked at Walid. "Well, that was an unexpected treat."

"Yeah, for sure," Walid replied and looked around, adding, "I wonder where Mahmood got off to?" But just then, the Director reemerged from the door to his office, carrying what looked like a handmade map.

"Sorry for the slight delay," he said. "There was a matter that came to my attention, and I had to deal with it on the spot. We're just very busy today, as is often true."

"Not a problem at all," Walid replied. "I didn't realize you guys were so active out here."

"Yes. So many members of the government ride, or want to learn how to ride. We have a constant stream of visitors with needs coming through the door. Then, there's the occasional big gift to us, like you two coming out to saddle up!"

"You're kind to say that," Walid replied.

Mahmood just smiled and then showed them the map, explaining the two possible routes he had charted, and saying something about each. Then he took them to see the two camels they'd be riding. They walked the entire length of the largest stable, passing where Layla and the girls were preparing their horses, and continued on down to the very end rows of animals. And, there they were, the two very special camels that had been waiting for them, one slightly larger than the other.

"Wait. No way! Is that … Cammo, my old desert friend?" Walid said aloud, staring in happy recognition at the larger of the two. On hearing his voice, the animal stirred and looked around.

"Yes, yes, indeed! The larger animal here is the one you rode across the desert last year," Mahmood said with a big smile. "He's been in the stables since then. I reserved him for you today, as my special contribution to Mr. Mafulla's gift."

"Wow! This is amazing," Walid said. "Good old Cammo, the camouflaged camel of the burning sands, the calm and brave companion who sheltered and saved me in a bad storm, and then brought me all the way to town."

"Yes! It's a happy reunion! He clearly recognizes you as well," Mahmood said. "Even with your new dark glasses."

"Oh, I forgot to take them off."

"Apparently, it's not a problem. He knows you anyway."

"And the slightly smaller guy is mine?" Mafulla asked, pulling off his glasses instantly.

"Indeed. He's also a good camel for riding—even-tempered, docile, and always quite responsive to his rider," Mahmood explained.

"And ... also, brave and stouthearted?" Mafulla said, expectantly.

"Yes, quite brave and stouthearted," Mahmood laughed. "We like to think of him as a highly courageous camel. Just don't cough or sneeze too loudly while you're on his back."

Mafulla laughed loudly and said, "Very funny."

"And, unfortunately, loud laughter could also set him off, and send him fleeing for his life, and for yours as a matter of fact," Mahmood added, appearing very serious. Then he nearly whispered, to a surprised looking Mafulla, "Just kidding."

"Oh! You got me with that one."

"Mafoolery," Mahmood explained.

"How did you know about that?"

"Oh, your exploits are known far and wide, both the courageous and the comical. Your wit preceded you here today."

"I was wondering where it had gone," Walid said and made Mahmood laugh.

Mafulla looked over and said, "Very clever, but don't miss the main point here, my friend. I'm always trying to tell you. I'm quite a famous personage in my own right these days, in case you still don't realize that. Reflected grandeur doesn't just go in one single direction, my friend."

"Yeah," Walid said and laughed. "Good thing I have these shades to help me see past the exceptionally bright reflection of—what was it? Oh yes. The grandeur that sparkles off you today."

Mahmood chuckled again and said, "Ok then, men of grandeur, wit, and reflections, it's time to get in the saddle, if you're ready."

"We're ready," Mafulla answered, and the boys followed Mahmood as he entered farther into the stall where the camels were standing. After some calm and friendly talk with the animals and a bit of patting them on their sides, Mahmood got the saddles on them and explained to the boys how to do it, as he worked. Then, he took the leads on both camels and tugged down gently, to signal them to kneel for their riders to get on. They did as commanded, and Walid first climbed onto Cammo, showing Mafulla how to do it. Then the younger boy carefully and slowly approached his camel and, following Walid's movements from moments earlier, he was successfully able to get up into his saddle as well. Moments later, on Mahmood's gentle command, both camels rose from their knees, causing Mafulla to go "Ok, then!" The stable director opened their stall door all the way and led them gently through it, out the closest door, and into the open air. With a few final instructions, he placed the map into Walid's hands, and said, "Happy riding today."

"Where's Paki?" Walid was looking around for his older friend.

"Oh, there he is," Mahmood replied, pointing toward the far edge of the stable where the palace guard was already on another camel and coming in their direction. When Paki got even with them, Walid and Mafulla both noticed a rifle strapped to the saddle on the right side of the animal.

"Armament?" Mafulla inquired.

"Always prepared," Paki explained. He patted a travel bag on the back of the saddle and continued, "I have here in my bags, this one, and the one on the other side, several things: food, water, some emergency supplies, snake antidote, and three revolvers with enough ammunition for a small battle—or maybe a medium-sized one." He smiled.

"You pack like my mom—except for the guns and ammo part," Mafulla joked. "Although, once she hears about that possibility, we may need even more suitcases."

"Just standard protection for Hollywood's finest," Paki commented.

At that, both boys chuckled and Walid said, "Ok, then, by the look of the map, this is the direction." He pointed west. "So if we're all ready, here we go." And with that, he touched the sides of Cammo with his heels and led the way forward, initially to the soundtrack of Mafulla saying, in a soothing tone and almost constantly, the words 'Good camel. Good camel,' over and over.

The day was already warming rapidly. The trail, as it led from the stable grounds, passed through mostly level terrain punctuated by dry brush and bushes, with an occasional tree or small cluster of trees for the first couple of miles, and then the landscape grew a bit more desert-like. The boys rode side-by-side and talked. Paki stayed just a little behind them, but not so far away that he couldn't participate in the conversations now and then.

Walid felt good being on his favorite camel again. He had forgotten how much he liked it. Mafulla, by contrast, was at first a little unsure of his balance and a bit wary of what was going to happen next. As a result, he kept vigilant about not falling off the saddle, even while they were talking—or perhaps especially when they were talking. Walid could tell his friend was nervous, not only because of all the "Good camel" comments, but also by how many jokes he was making.

This was Mafulla's first camel ride since he turned seven years old and a very small dromedary had been brought in for his birthday party. And in that instance, his dad had held onto either boy or beast all around the backyard. But he was starting to get the feel for riding this new full size animal and, by the second mile or maybe the third, he was beginning to be a little more comfortable and was even starting to enjoy it all.

"This is great!" Mafulla said. "Just us guys and the desert sand!"

"Well, we're not actually in the real desert," Walid explained.

"Yeah, true, but sand is sand and with a little imagination, we're in the middle of vast and desolate expanses of it, surrounded by nature's most austere bounty."

Walid laughed. "Nature's most austere bounty? Only you could come up with such an expression. But, you know what? You're actually right. I never thought about it like that."

"It helps to view your surroundings with the eye of a poet."

"And the heart of a warrior?" Walid added.

"Of course, always!" Mafulla replied, and he turned back to look at Paki, now quite close behind them, and grinned—with suitable eyebrow punctuation. But then, of course, he also quickly muttered, "Good camel. Good camel." They rode in silence for a few seconds and then Mafulla asked his best friend, "So, you're enjoying the ride?"

"Definitely," Walid answered. "It's completely delightful—a part of nature's less austere bounty that I've been missing. We should do this more often."

"I agree completely. Good camel."

The girls were back at the stables, going around the large riding ring out behind the main building on their horses-for-the-day. Of course, they had to give them each special, personal names. Hasina's was Sheeba, and Kissa's—also named by Hasina—was Queenie. Both Kissa and Hasina had ridden before, but mostly on ponies when they were younger. Layla was getting them comfortable with the larger horses and they were now sitting high in their saddles, walking their animals slowly around the ring while their teacher gave them background information and instructions on how to slow down or speed up the horses, how to turn them, how to stop, and how to dismount. They tried each of these things a few times and did so successfully, although not quite perfectly, from the very first attempt.

They were both quick learners and naturally felt at ease with their mounts. In the car on the way over, Layla had explained the use of their minds in meeting the animals and keeping them calm, reminding them about the power of their thoughts and feelings for helping to create a pleasant experience. They were both now using the techniques she had suggested and their efforts were apparently having the desired effects. Sensitive animals, Layla had explained, can discern basic human intentions, within limits. Even less than fully sensitive animal spirits can be molded and guided by powerful thoughts. Hasina recalled the picnic on the palace grounds where deadly poisonous snakes and spiders had threatened them and they had both used their minds to try to neutralize the threat, despite having no idea how that could work.

Kissa happened to notice, as they rounded a curve in the training circle, that there were three military men at the stable talking with Mahmood. They drew not only her attention, but also her curiosity and even a quick inner wave of concern, which she dismissed when Layla said something to her about her horse. She was talking the girls through keeping the horses calm and controlled in situations of duress, such as coming across a snake prepared to strike or hearing gunfire close by. Kissa completely forgot the men until a few minutes later when she saw them ride off on three of the other horses from the stable. Again, she was struck with a strange feeling as she watched them go down the trail, away from the stable area. But she couldn't get quite clear on what the feeling was.

An hour later, when the ladies all took a break and walked over to the building closest to them to get some water, Kissa noticed Mahmood standing a short distance away, looking in on some animal. She excused herself for a minute and walked over in his direction.

"Mahmood. Hi. I'm sorry to interrupt you but I have a question," Kissa said, as Hasina and Layla continued on to find the water.

"Not a problem, Miss El-Bay. I don't consider any question from you to be an interruption. What can I do for you?"

"I noticed three soldiers here a few minutes ago."

"Yes."

"Can you tell me what they were doing?"

"Certainly. They had orders from Masoon Afah to come here for a long practice ride on three of the horses."

"Oh. Directly from Masoon and not from their immediate supervisor or officer?"

"Yes—straight from Masoon himself."

"Hmm. May I ask how Masoon conveyed his orders?"

"They had a note from him that they showed me. Why? Do you think something's wrong?"

"No, not necessarily. I'm just curious."

"Oh."

"Was the note hand written in Masoon's big cursive strokes?"

"No, it was typed, but hand signed by him."

"Interesting." Kissa had never known Masoon to have anything typed. He loved to slash out notes in his distinctive and very large lettered handwriting. But maybe he had become more of a normal, official administrator at this point. And it wasn't like Kissa had seen lots of communications from him, anyway. She thought for a moment and then asked, "Was his signature big or small?"

"A moderate size, basically appropriate for the page, I'd say."

"How long will these men be riding today?"

"They said they needed to take the horses out for at least three or four hours."

"Did they carry with them supplies sufficient for that length of time at this point in the day?"

"I didn't notice, I must admit. But, now that you ask, I actually don't recall seeing any knapsacks or bags in their possession when they arrived. There were small bags on the horses, as there always are, but the bags were not filled with any food or water, to my knowledge, at least not by any of our stable hands."

"Also interesting. How did the men arrive today?"

"A truck dropped them off and left."

"I see."

Mahmood now looked a little worried. "Are you sure you don't have any particular concerns about these men?"

"Well, not really—not anything specific," Kissa replied. "I was just wondering about them. I get curious about things now and then, and I don't even know why."

"Curiosity is the sign of a good mind."

"Thanks. That's nice of you to say."

"It's something I've seen time and again throughout the years."

Kissa smiled and said, "I certainly appreciate your time to

answer my questions. And, just one more: Do military men come by often for long training rides on the horses?"

"No, not to my knowledge. This must be a special situation."

Just then, Layla called Kissa back to their horses and she thanked Mahmood again for his time. The Director of the Royal Stables was right. This would turn out to be a special situation. But he had no idea how special it was, and what it would eventually lead them all to discover.

3

Dromedary Drama

Paki had just made a joke, venturing his own version of Mafoolery, and both the boys were laughing loudly at what he had said. As the laughter died down, they all suddenly heard a voice some distance behind them shout out, "Clear the way up ahead! Soldiers of the kingdom coming through!"

The path they were on was just wide enough for two camels to walk comfortably side by side. There were, at this point, earthen berms and bushes on both sides of the trail, and on the right, beyond the bushes and down a fairly steep bank, there was a small shallow stream, a culvert of sorts, that connected to the Nile. Paki twisted around on his camel to see who was speaking. He glimpsed military uniforms and said, "Walid, move your camel ahead of Mafulla's and stay to the right, then pull up and stop, both of you."

Paki turned his own camel across the path and brought him to a halt, and then slightly rotated his body and the animal enough to face the three slowly approaching horseback riders. "Greetings to you! What's your brigade and your mission today?"

"We have no time for talk! Just move aside!" The man in the lead position barked out his words in an agitated and even slightly angry tone of voice. "Clear the path or pay a price you can't afford!"

At this point, both Walid and Mafulla had turned their camels around and were facing the horsemen from behind Paki. Each of them had a feeling of something almost like an electric jolt course through their bodies, a sensation that alerted them to the likelihood of imminent trouble. This man's tone of voice was not at all normal or appropriate to the situation. Walid spoke softly the words "Triple Double," just loudly enough for his friend to hear them, and then simply the name "Hoda." Mafulla nodded his head that he understood, even though Walid was not looking his way.

Paki kept his own voice calm and friendly. "I'm just asking for your unit and your purpose today on this path," he said.

"It's no business of yours. Out of the way!" the man said gruffly and motioned with one hand, a sweeping gesture to the side.

Paki answered the horseman, still calmly, "It's indeed my business, and I should point out that this is no way for a uniformed soldier of the realm to approach innocent citizens of the kingdom that you're sworn to defend. Who's your commander?"

"You're wasting my time. Get out of our way, now!"

"No. I'm sorry. I want you to dismount immediately, all three of you. I'm Paki Alexander, Palace Guard, Gold Unit." Paki pointed to the small patch on his chest.

The stranger replied, "I don't care who you are. I'm the man in charge here, telling you to move for the last time!" He stared at Paki for two seconds, and then with no further warning, he pulled out a revolver and had it pointed right at Paki. It was not military issue.

"You've just committed a crime greater than you realize, and you're now on the verge of an act of treason," Paki said with a firm but still calm tone of voice.

"Who do you think … Ow!" The man shouted out in pain, and his free hand flew up to his forehead, mid-sentence, while the gun dropped out of his other hand to the ground. Within seconds, and after two more shouts of pain and a huge spasm, he actually fell off his horse and was now on his knees in the sand, groaning in apparent agony.

Paki grabbed his own rifle, jumped from his camel, and quickly stepped forward to kick the man's gun farther away from him, as he bellowed helplessly yet again. At the same moment, all three horses made loud noises of agitation and fear, and the other two animals suddenly rose up on their hind legs and dropped their own riders to the path. By the time this had happened, Paki was covering all three men with his rifle, and Walid had pulled one of the other guns from Paki's saddlebag, which he had also raised and now held on them from his camelback position.

"Lie down! All of you! Face down!" Paki shouted. The two men in the back, behind the lead rider, began to roll over to face the ground. Walid slid off his camel and ran around to where the leader's pistol had been kicked down the path. He picked it up quickly and stepped back, aiming his own revolver once again directly at that man, who was not immediately complying.

"You heard the officer! Get down, flat on your face," Walid said. The man looked up and just glared at him, unmoving and staying on his knees. Then he spat loudly on the ground right in front of the prince.

"Ow!" He shouted out once more in pain with a terrible expression on his face, as he dropped his head down again and put both his hands to his forehead and yelled out in a voice of confusion and distress, "What's this? What is it? What's happening to me?"

"Unless you want your head to explode right here, and for us to have to shovel your brains off the ground, you'll lie flat as we've instructed." Walid spoke in the same firm voice Paki had used, despite the fact that his heartbeat was booming in his head. He added: "Consider what you're feeling right now to be a warning shot. The next blow to your head may be fatal."

The man, still grimacing terribly, slowly began to lower himself into a prone position. "How are you doing this?"

"It's none of your business," Walid said, echoing the man's own words with a feeling of great satisfaction. "But this will just get much worse unless you cooperate fully. You've managed to attack the wrong people. It could be your last big mistake."

"Don't kill me. It's not worth dying for."

"Hands behind your backs!" Paki said. Mafulla by then also

had in his possession a gun he had pulled from Paki's bag, and he had it tucked into his belt as he slid unsteadily down the side of his now-kneeling camel and walked over to the lead horse to rummage through its saddle bag. Pulling out a modest length of rope, he began to tie up the leader, or at least the surly spokesman, for this group. The man irrationally made a sudden move of resistance and Mafulla jumped into what's called a sleeper hold and, within four seconds, the man was now unconscious, face down on the ground. Paki had been checking the other two horse's saddlebags while Walid held his gun on the men. He found an extra set of reins that he cut in half and used to tie up the hands of the remaining two men, who wisely offered no resistance.

Paki put his foot on one of them and pushed him over onto his back and tied hands. "Who are you and what are you doing here?"

"Say nothing!" the other conscious man urged, with his head turned to look at them. Paki walked over to him and pushed him over as well, with the sun now in his face.

"Did you get a good look at the two young men here who are wearing dark glasses?" Paki stared at one of the men, then at the other. "I hope you did, because they're individuals of great importance. And here's another question: Did you wonder, when I identified myself, why a member of the palace guard is riding with these two? Maybe not: it's not clear that you're thinking at all today."

"What are you talking about?"

"You just attacked the Prince of Egypt and his best friend, as well as a member of their guard, which is why you're on the ground right now under restraint. I don't know if you realize the legal consequences of using deadly force to attack or threaten a member of the royal family, but justice will be quick and severe on you both. Your only hope is to cooperate fully with me right now and tell me what I want to know."

"How do we know you're not lying?"

"You'll know very soon, when we get you back to the royal stables and you're taken into custody by men who'll escort you to your proper punishment. This will be the worst day of your life, and perhaps even the last, unless you tell me what I want to know. Who are you and what are you doing here? This is your last chance. I swear it."

There was silence for five or six seconds, then the first man whom Paki had turned over spoke. "We're just men who do jobs for hire, and we were sent to steal these horses."

"Shut up!" The other man growled.

"You shut up!" His associate replied, "I'm not letting you lead me to my own execution for what little I'm getting paid. You can be an idiot, and a dead one, but I'm not following you into such stupid folly."

He turned his face back toward Paki and said, "We were hired by a man whose name we don't know. He's paying us to steal these three horses and take them to a truck that's waiting for us down the path a bit, probably a mile or so from where we are now. He's likely already there. All we know is that we're to deliver the horses to him and that he's to take us into town and drop us off near where I live."

"Why are these horses being stolen?"

"No one told us," the man said.

"Who's to pay you?"

"The man in the truck, on delivery."

Paki thought for a second and said, "We need your uniforms. I'll stand you up one at a time and take off your restraints, and you'll undress quickly, dropping your uniforms to the side. Then you'll lie back down. You'll have three guns on you while you do this, and we'll shoot you if you try anything. Shooting you here would be a lot less trouble than taking you back."

"He speaks the truth," Walid said.

Paki then turned to the uncooperative man and said, "You first. I'll untie you and you'll get to your feet when I tell you to. If you move before that, you'll die on the sand, under this hot sun, right now. We're all expert marksmen. We don't miss."

Walid and Mafulla held their guns on the man. Paki untied his hands and stepped back a few feet. "Now, stand and strip down." The man did as he was told. "Throw your clothes over here and lie back down on your stomach, with your hands again behind you."

The man cooperated quietly and when he was down again said, "What are you going to do?"

"It delights me to echo what I've heard today a couple of times already and say that it's none of your business. But we'll leave you here for a short time and one or two of us may return for you when we've delivered your horses and apprehended the driver. Your cooperation may indeed buy you a modicum of mercy." As Paki spoke, Mafulla moved around to retie the man's hands.

"Now, you," Paki said to the other man, the one who had answered his questions. "I'll untie your hands and when I say so, you'll stand and take off the uniform. I appreciate your reasonableness." The man cooperated and did what he was told, and was again tied up.

Paki then looked at the lead adversary, the one who had pulled the gun on him, who had by now regained consciousness and was experiencing the worst ongoing headache of his life. "Now you. I'll untie you, and you'll take off your uniform and hand it to me. And remember, you're the one who pulled the gun, so you're in the most trouble of all. I'd advise your complete cooperation." Paki turned to Walid and said, "I'd like to have the man's gun, please." Now he looked back at him, still face down on the ground and said, "I can assure you that if you try anything, you'll be shot and killed instantly with your own gun, which, as you know, is the ultimate humiliation for any man in battle. And we'll make sure that everyone knows the method of your demise. So if I were you, I'd comply completely with my instructions. I'll untie you, then step back, and let you know when you may stand and take off your uniform."

Walid handed Paki the man's gun, and then Paki did exactly as he said he would do, untying the man and then stepping back to tell him to stand up. The formerly tough guy now surprised everyone and did just as he was told. Apparently, he too had calculated the cost of resistance and decided it was far too high, in the circumstances.

The men had all been retied, one after the other, but now their feet as well as their hands were fully secured so that they couldn't stand up or attempt an escape. Then, in addition to their wrists and ankles, their hands themselves were also tied in an intricate way, so that no one could roll over to anyone else and use his fingers to undo a knot.

Paki then took some of the water they had brought for themselves and gave it to the three horses. They put a stake in the ground that they had carried with them and tethered their three camels to it so they would lie down and rest until they could be retrieved a bit later.

Paki, Walid, and Mafulla then sized up the three uniforms, all of which were clearly too big. The plan was for Paki first to put on whichever one would be the least ill fitting for him, since he would ride out in front and be visible to the truck driver before the boys. And then Walid and Mafulla should put on whatever they could and try to disguise the fit, but this was all a bit of a challenge, since all three thieves were tall and two of them were heavy. Still, the three Phi got the uniforms on, and the larger ones, worn by Paki and Walid, were tucked and tied as well as possible to hide the size difference, at least for someone seeing them from a distance, which they hoped might be all that was needed. It wasn't a fashion show. They just had to look enough like the original thieves, to a quick and casual glance from a distance.

Paki instructed the boys to take the white cloth napkins they had brought for their luncheon use, wet them, and drape them over their heads as men in the mid-day heat would often do for the sake of sun protection and cooling, when out in the open. But in this instance, it would be simply to disguise their identities more as they rode up closer to the waiting truck. And at the last minute, Paki remembered to say, "The sunglasses! Take them off!" The boys immediately did so, and put them down in deep pockets for safekeeping.

With all that being done, the three of them left the thieves in the sand and trotted their horses forward. Mafulla, of course, was now even more outside his comfort zone, and could be heard saying, softly, "Good horse; Good horse; Good horse." Within a surprisingly short time of going farther down the path, they saw a sole truck up ahead of them, parked on a road that was near the path at that point.

Back at the stables, Layla stopped her horse and motioned for the girls to do likewise. "Something's wrong," she said. "Something has happened or is about to happen."

"I … just got that same feeling, mom," Hasina said.

"Me too, but without having any idea what it is or why I'm feeling it," Kissa commented. "What do you think's going on?"

"I don't know, but our plans have just changed. Let me quickly get some water for us, and a couple of the wranglers, and we'll go find out what's happening. I have a feeling we should take the path away from the stables that the boys took with their camels. They may need our assistance, somehow."

Layla rode over to the nearby stable, dismounted, and went in to talk to Mahmood. The girls followed on their horses but waited outside. Within two or three minutes, Layla was back with a couple of bags containing water to put on two of the horses. Then, less than half a minute later, two men emerged from the stables on horseback and there were rifles strapped to their saddles. The ladies led the way, and the wranglers followed in support.

Paki could at that point just make out the silhouette of a man in the driver's side of the truck up ahead. He shouted a hello and waved, as if in recognition and signaling, and at that moment, although they were still too far away to hear it, the truck's motor started up loudly. Paki turned in the saddle to give some last minute instructions to the boys, but just then Mafulla said, "It's pulling away!"

When he turned back toward where the truck was, Paki could also now see it actually speeding away. He quickly thought about giving chase, but realized that before he got to the road, he would have to jump the berm and some thick brush and that this would slow him down considerably, and just enough that he wouldn't likely be able to catch up. In the circumstances, all he could do was stare at the escaping vehicle and pay close attention, in an effort to remember every detail about it.

The driver had instantly noticed the handkerchiefs draped across their heads, and he knew that the men he dropped off earlier were carrying no such things with them. That made him look more closely at the uniforms, and he could tell even from a distance that they were now badly fitting in a way that fully alerted him to the ruse that was in play. He was aware of the importance of not being captured on this rare daylight mission, and so he had started the truck and driven away as fast as he possibly could, leaving no evidence behind but the inevitable set of blurry, sandy tire tracks. He knew that the men he was abandoning, if still alive, had no real information about the operation and so would be of no danger to it under interrogation. Horses could be gotten some other way, and at a later time.

The three horses stood still. "I can't believe it!" Mafulla said. "We were so close! And there goes the man who could answer our questions. So much for Phi superiority and success in all things! Good horse."

"Yeah, it's too bad," Paki replied. "I would have liked to find out what was really going on today and who was behind it all. But this is not the end, just an unwanted but not unlikely twist. I'm sure we'll get to the bottom of it all, eventually. We don't give up, and that's an important part of Phi superiority, one crucial key to ultimate Phi success," he said, looking at Mafulla with a smile, who then nodded in understanding.

Walid turned to Paki and said, "Kular told us this morning about the recent stealing of animals all over town. I wonder if these guys are part of some big operation?"

Paki replied, "We don't know what's going on yet. The city police have been in touch with the palace about the thefts Kular mentioned. It's been strange to hear about so many involving animals, and in such a short period of time. But we don't know if it's just a bizarre coincidence or if one or two groups of people might be behind it all. And, of course, we have no idea why it's going on.

The guys today could be part of this bigger picture, or they could just be working for someone who has no connection to any of the other thefts. I hope we can find out soon."

Walid then said, "Me, too. But for now, I guess we'd better get back to our prisoners."

"You're right, Prince. Let's get back and take them to the stables. I'm not convinced they're telling us everything they know."

The three of them turned their horses around and began to ride back down the path to where they had been attacked. It was only five more minutes before they were approaching the site, and as they emerged from a big curve in the path and from behind an odd cluster of heavy bushes and trees beside it, they could suddenly see in the distance some other riders on horseback coming in their direction.

"Riders up ahead," Paki said. "More than three—maybe five. I hope it's not more thieves. Stay vigilant."

Walid and Mafulla both peered forward. It occurred to Mafulla to say, "Hey, let's put on our sunglasses again. They might help us to see better at a distance in such bright light."

"Good idea," Walid said. They both took out their glasses and put them on. Walid stared toward the oncoming riders. "Oh. It looks like ... Layla, Kissa and Hasina. Yeah, it's them up front. I recognize what they're wearing. But there are two other riders behind them."

"They're almost to the place where our prisoners should be blocking the path," Paki pointed out. "I hope the other two riders are friendlies. But be prepared in case they aren't."

Just as they first saw the ladies, Layla spotted them as well. "Hasina, Kissa, I think I see the three soldiers on horseback up ahead, and they're coming this way now. Yes, those are the military uniforms." Then she turned around in her saddle and said to the two men from the stables, now behind her, "Be ready, in case there's a problem." They nodded their understanding and removed their rifles from the straps that held them on the sides of their saddles.

Then she looked back ahead, focusing as well as she could on the still faraway riders. "Wait. Two of them are wearing sunglasses. Could that be ... the boys?"

"Mom, up to the right I can just now see three camels lying down together, up ahead, closer to us, with no riders." Hasina said.

Layla replied, "Those must be the camels the boys were on. I was right. Something's happened." They continued to trot down the path as they talked. "Someone else may be wearing their new glasses."

At almost the same time, Mafulla said to both Walid and Paki, "They were just going to ride the circle today, not the path. Hasina told us. Something's wrong. Something's happened." At these words, all three of them instantly inferred that, with the two additional riders positioned behind the girls, what was going on could possibly be, or involve, a theft and, much worse, a kidnapping.

And as soon as this thought entered their minds, Paki noticed that the two riders in the rear now had rifles in their hands and he said, simply, "Weapons. I see weapons. The back two riders."

He immediately took his own rifle out of the saddle, and the boys pulled their handguns from their belts. And this was seen by one of the two other armed riders approaching them. That man said to his associate, simply, "They have guns."

As they all stared forward, tense in a new way, Mafulla said, softly, "Oh, no."

4

The Cairo Detective Agency

Kular had ducked his head into the door of the king's private sitting room, where the monarch was talking with his good friend and top general, Masoon. He said, "Your Majesty, I'm so sorry to interrupt, but I just received word that there's a young man at the main gate who's asking to see you. He says he's a friend of Prince Walid."

"That's quite all right, Kular." The king looked quickly at his gold Reverso watch and back up at the head butler. "What's his name?"

"Ibrahim Hadad."

"Ibrahim Hadad from Alexandria?"

"Yes, sir. That's what he said to the guard at the gate."

"Oh. He's an important friend to us who's done great things for the kingdom already in his young life. He was with us at the big dinner we had some time after the attack on the palace."

"Oh, I didn't realize."

"Please, instruct the gate to let him in and have him escorted up to see me here."

"Right away, Your Majesty."

King Ali turned to Masoon and said, "I wonder what Ibrahim is doing in Cairo, and here at the gate?"

"I haven't heard anything about his presence here, Majesty. It's a bit of a surprise, but of course a pleasant one. It'll be good to see him again."

"Yes, it will be."

"He's an impressive young man."

"He is. And, of course, the little red book he gave Walid during our trip to Alexandria made a big difference in our ability to deal in the best ways with the recent attack on us."

Masoon nodded. "Yes. I agree. The many secrets it's unlocked in The Book of Phi have been pretty impressive, as well as surprising."

"Indeed. But, as you know, there's that one long section toward the end of The Book of Phi that's still been impossible to crack. The red book at first seemed to give us a key of sorts to that passage as well, but in the end, not like what it had provided for the other coded parts. It turned out to be a key to help me find other keys that I've only now been able to begin to identify. I think we may need something else to unlock all that the long mysterious section contains."

"Yes, it's been a bit of a mystery within a mystery, within a mystery," Masoon replied.

"Like many things around here," the king said and laughed. "And given what we're already finding, I can understand the many layers of concealment. We're going to be brought, it seems, up to the brink of a new vista where we'll be able to see how and why many things in the life of Phi work, and our resultant understanding will go deep down to a new level of insight and, perhaps, even to the depth of a brand new form of wisdom."

Masoon said, "Please do keep me posted as your work continues. I'm eager to hear your results."

"Certainly," the king replied, adding, "And without Ibrahim, none of this would even be possible."

"It was brave and showed great foresight for him to seek out Walid in Alexandria and give him the book that had so long been in his family. And then, when it was stolen, he quickly retrieved it for us, as well. The timing of it all was perfect."

"Yes. He does his family proud, in its entire and exemplary lineage. Did you know, by the way, that he has an uncle here in town now?"

"No, I didn't. Who is he?"

"He was formerly Chief of Police in Alexandria, but retired not long ago. I heard that he might be moving to Cairo, but I didn't know the reason. And then, just a few days ago, someone said they had met him in town. So he's apparently already here."

Masoon replied, "I wish I had known, so that I could have given him a special welcome."

"Well, perhaps it's still appropriate. From what I heard, it didn't sound like he's been here very long. And that may be why Ibrahim is here."

There was a knock on the door. It swung open and Kular said, "Your Majesty, may I present Mr. Ibrahim Hadad?"

"Yes, yes, please bring him in," the king replied with a big smile.

As the young man followed Kular into the room and the head butler motioned him forward while stepping aside, the king stood and said, "It's so good to see you again, Ibrahim! Welcome back to the palace!"

"Thank you, Your Majesty," Ibrahim said and bowed deeply. "I'm sorry to just show up here with no advance notice."

"No, no," the king said, "You're always welcome here. I wish we had been able to find some time to talk when you were last in town, but so much was going on then."

"Masoon, hello to you, as well."

The general had also stood to greet their visitor and he now added his welcome, "We're honored to have you visit us again so soon."

"Thank you so much!" Ibrahim said. "But the honor's all mine!"

The king gestured toward a nearby chair and said, "Please, sit."

"Yes, sir, Your Majesty! Thank you!" Ibrahim said with a big smile and walked over to an available stuffed armchair, royal blue with bold yellow designs and quite beautiful.

"Is this all right?" he asked.

"Perfect," the king replied, as he immediately settled back onto his own plush sofa, while signaling Masoon to once again take the chair that he had been in. The boy then sat down, as well, and Ali said, "What brings you to the capital?"

Ibrahim took a breath and replied, "My uncle Leem recently retired as head of the Alexandria police force, and he had always wanted to live in Cairo, near the center of government and closer to the great pyramids and the sphinx, about which he had heard stories all through his childhood. He moved down here around a month ago and thought a lot about what he would like to do in his retirement. He's not the kind of man just to sit around the house. And in particular, he came to realize that he still wanted to use his talents for investigation, and figuring out difficult situations. So, he thought maybe he'd open a detective agency. But he realized that he didn't know Cairo well, and that this was a real weakness for a detective. I mean, he'd learn the city soon enough, but he decided he might benefit from partnering up for advice with someone who already did know all the neighborhoods and streets and areas. So he contacted an old friend who's lived here quite a long time, a man who also served in law enforcement, and he's helped my uncle open up the Cairo Detective Agency, mostly as an absentee partner and a source of guidance."

"This is marvelous." The king looked very pleased. "It's a great benefit for our city to have such an accomplished and good man doing such work. He'll be of great help to everyone in need who secures his services, I'm sure."

"Thank you. That's kind of you to say."

"As you know, the city police can't be everywhere all the time, and there are matters that are better investigated privately, anyway. This is very good news, indeed. And, so, you're here to visit and celebrate the opening of the new agency?"

"Yes, Your Majesty, and for even more than that. Uncle Leem has asked me to join him as junior investigator!"

"Really? That's wonderful. And you're going to come here to work with him?"

"Yes, sir, Your Majesty. I arrived just last night. My uncle has already offered to put me up with him. But I'd like to give him his own space. I'm hoping to find and rent a small apartment, just big enough for me and Ben—I'm sure you remember our young friend Ben from the streets in Alexandria."

"Yes, certainly. How is the boy?"

"He's been doing very well. It's a total life turnaround. He's now like my little brother."

"Wonderful!"

"My mother's watching him for a few days while I get settled in. She's not been in the best of health, but has gotten much better recently. And yet, the long term care of a boy Ben's age is just a bit too much for her, I think."

"I can imagine. Does she have any help?"

"Yes, sir, Your Majesty. She has a few family members close by to look after her and even help with Ben during the short time she'll be taking care of him over the next few days. Two are even in her apartment building. Plus, I'll be visiting her often once I'm settled in. She's even talked of moving to Cairo herself."

"That's very nice. But you're in town alone for now?"

"I am, for the time being, but Ben's going to come and join me here in a few days. We plan to enter him into a local school and provide for him as normal and happy a life as we can. You know, it'll be nice to get him even farther away from all those bad characters who had exercised such a negative influence over his life back in Alexandria."

"That makes a lot of sense," King Ali said. "I'm sure he'll flourish here. And of course, we'll do everything we can to make him feel welcome."

"That's so kind of you. I think he has the potential to be a good and strong man, and a real asset to the community. We intervened in his life at just the right time, thanks to Prince Walid."

"Walid is wise in many ways," the king said. "I'm glad he saw the potential in Ben and took action about it as he did. We're so affected and influenced by the people we're around, and this is true at a deep level. We can think we're above such influence, but really, no one is. By getting Ben away from the street gangs, Walid showed real love for the boy and a deep concern for his future. Then you matched that love and concern and went the next mile, or began your journey of a thousand miles, by taking him on as your own charge. That showed us a lot about you, as well."

"It's been a joy for me to have him around, and to be able to make a positive difference in his life. I've been able to introduce him to lots of relatives who've all sort of unofficially adopted him as well, and to neighbors who've taken him in as one of their own. He's even met several boys his own age who've now been a benevolent influence in just this short time. I'm sure he'll meet many other friends here."

At this, Masoon spoke up and said, "Do you think it will be hard for him to leave all his new Alexandrian friends at this point, in order to relocate with you and Leem here?"

"We've talked about that. It's actually been a fairly short time since he was on the streets, so his roots aren't yet deep in the new setting back in Alexandria. And his biggest connection by far is with me. So, although he's said he'll miss everyone a lot, he's actually eager to make the move and be near his good personal friend, the prince."

The king smiled. "We'll make sure Walid knows that. And you say that Ben should be arriving in just a few days?"

"Yes, Your Majesty, by train in less than a week."

"Good. That's good. Does your uncle have any work yet for the agency?"

"He does. The day after he opened his office, someone came in with a need to find a relative with whom he had lost contact years ago. Then, two days later, there was a man who wanted him to locate a friend he had known long ago. And the most exciting thing is that an older lady came in a few days ago to engage him to find her two greatly loved pet cats that had somehow disappeared the previous day. She was walking by the agency and saw the new sign and came right in with her problem, and a nice full purse to help us solve it."

"Oh, I see. It's very good that profitable work has found you right away."

"Yes, and I'm sure that this initial work will lead to even more, by referral. Uncle Leem is a very client oriented individual, and treats everyone with kindness. Plus, he's just a very good investigator—the best Alexandria has had during his lifetime."

"I've heard of his fine work there. I hope to meet him sometime soon," the king replied.

Just then, there was another knock on the door and Kular once again appeared. "Your Majesty, the boys are back from their camel ride and would like to see you for a moment."

"Have them come in right now," the king said. And within three seconds, he was clapping his hands and laughing at the sight of Walid and Mafulla walking into the room in their new sunglasses. Masoon also started clapping and laughing, sparked by the king's response.

"Thank you, thank you all very much," Mafulla said, bowing left and right and grinning as he entered. Ibrahim had a big smile on his face as well when he saw his friends with this new Hollywood style look.

The king said, "I'm sure that you've already heard every Hollywood movie joke in the book today. So I won't bore you with repetition. But you do indeed look fabulous with the new dark glasses, or should I say, fantastic, in honor of what are surely all your new fans?"

Walid laughed and said, "Ok, that's a new one." He then added, "I'm impressed as always by the royal wit."

"Mafoolery," said the king.

"Thank you, Your Majesty," Mafulla responded. "As always, I'm honored that my example is adopted by such luminaries as Your Royal Kingliness." As Ali then laughed, Mafulla grinned and took off his shades, and elbowed Walid to do the same.

"You see, of course, that we have a guest."

"Yes indeed," Walid said, and then turning with a warm smile to their visitor, commented, "Ibrahim, I was so surprised when I walked in and saw you sitting here. I hope everything is well."

"Yes, Prince, very well. I was just explaining to His Majesty and the general that I've come to town to join my uncle's new detective agency."

"Oh?"

"Yes! I got here only last night and, after spending the morning and lunchtime with uncle Leem, I wanted to come by as early this afternoon as I could to say hello to the king, if it was possible—and, of course, also you two. And, amazingly, here I sit."

"Good! We're really glad you're here."

"I've come a long way, it seems, since silently stalking you and Mafulla at the Alexandrian docks and in the hotel lobby there."

"Yeah, I'd say so," the prince replied.

"From mystery man to one of our favorites," Mafulla said.

"Thank you, dear sir." Ibrahim did a sort of fun salute to his friends.

The king spoke up again at this point and said, "Walid, if you and Mafulla would like to take Ibrahim down to the informal dining room, I think Kular could lay out some late afternoon snacks for all of you and our friend can bring you up to date on what he's been telling us. Unfortunately, I have a meeting in a few minutes and will need to relocate to my office."

Walid looked at their visitor and said, "Do you have time to stay a bit longer?"

"Are you kidding? Do I have time to enjoy a snack with the Prince of Egypt and his best friend in a private dining room in the Golden Palace? Hmm. Let me think. I am rather busy these days. But sure, I might be able to fit you into my hectic schedule. I'll just rearrange a few things."

"Good," Walid laughed. "We'll go down in just a second, but first, Your Majesty, we have something to report quickly."

"What is it, my boy?"

"Before the report, I want to say: thank you for helping to make today's early birthday gift from Mafulla possible, with the transportation element and the camels and all."

"You're quite welcome," the king replied.

"It was great, great fun."

"Excellent!"

"Then it got really exciting, when some armed men came up on us, riding horses they were stealing from the stables."

"You're certainly kidding."

"No, it's the truth."

"Ok. Tell me what happened."

"Three men wearing genuine looking military uniforms told Mahmood that Masoon had sent them to do a training ride today. And they presented a note from him, typed and signed. Kissa found out all about it and it concerned her."

"Well, I did no such thing. And I don't type," Masoon said. "I know nothing of these men and their note."

"Yeah, that's what Kissa much later suggested to us. But long before we found out about the note and all that, we were on our camels and having a great time. Then, after a fine bit of riding, it turned out that these guys were approaching us from behind and we were in their way on the trail, which is wide enough only for a couple of animals to be side-by-side. So they ordered us to stand aside, then pulled a gun on us, and within less than a minute they were all three on the ground and tied up."

"Good," Masoon said.

"They admitted they were horse thieves, but claimed they were just doing it for hire and didn't know the identity of who had hired them. We found out they were taking the horses to a waiting truck farther down the trail, so we put on their uniforms and attempted the delivery ourselves, but the driver apparently recognized in time that we weren't his guys, and he took off before we could catch him."

"That's too bad," the king commented.

"Yes, it was. We had really hoped to get to the bottom of it all," Walid explained. "But then, on our way back to the guys that we had left tied up and on the trail, we saw five more riders coming toward us in the distance."

"More thieves?" Masoon asked.

"That was our first thought, and then we recognized Layla, Hasina, and Kissa in the front, but there were two men riding behind them."

"They were out at the stables for training today," Masoon commented to the king.

"I see," Ali replied.

Mafulla at this point jumped in and said, "Yeah, we had met them when we first got to the stables, and they said they'd only be riding in the training circle today and not on the path we were going to take, or any other trails, but then, there they were."

"And Paki noticed that the two guys riding behind them had rifles in their hands."

"Oh," the king said.

"So we thought right away that maybe these were more thieves, who could have been caught or compromised by the ladies, and they had pulled guns on them and taken them captive."

"Were you armed at this point?"

"Yes, all of us, from Paki's reserves," Walid said.

Mafulla commented, "And we then saw the two men lift up their guns as we approached them, and we were about to respond and have what likely would have been a very big shootout, with the girls basically caught in the middle. But Paki suddenly recognized one of the guys as a wrangler who works with Mahmood and he stopped us a split second before lots of bad stuff was going to happen. And, I mean, we know the ladies can dodge bullets, at least one at a time, but jeez, we didn't want to be the ones producing half the number that would need to be dodged in a full, all-out rescue gun battle."

"You came that close?" Masoon asked.

"Yeah, we did," Walid answered. "I think the whole situation had worked up our emotions to the point where Mafulla and I couldn't be as calm as we would have had to be in order to listen to our deeper intuitions and feelings."

"And that always causes a problem, as you saw," Masoon said.

"Yeah, big time," Mafulla agreed, as Walid nodded.

"You need a clear heart and mind in such circumstances," the king added. "And clarity can come best from a deep pool of inner calm."

"Yes, sir, we learned a big lesson today," Walid admitted. "It's just a good thing that Paki was a bit more open to the full truth and saw it right before we would have made a huge mistake—I mean, a second before we would have done the absolutely wrong thing. In trying to save our friends in a situation where they didn't need saving, we may have jeopardized them badly. And as soon as we realized the truth, we were relieved and scared and stunned, all at the same time."

"That's why I like it when Paki or Omari or Amon go out with you," the king explained. "They're all a bit farther down the road of inner growth, and you can learn much from them, while they also provide you with the extra security you still need at this stage."

"We sure do benefit, Your Majesty."

"Yeah, we do, and a lot," Mafulla added.

Walid continued, "We're really glad you make the guys available to us. I mean, today, right at the tense focused moment when a lot of shooting was about to break out, Paki waved at them and they waved back. He quickly said to us, 'They're friendlies,' and said it in the nick of time. We all met up where the real thieves were tied tight and still on the ground. We then shared our story and put the bad guys on the camels, and escorted them back to the stables where we called in backup and had them taken to the palace jail."

"Why had the ladies been out there on the trail with the wranglers in the first place?" Masoon asked.

"Oh, yeah, I forgot that part. Layla suddenly had a feeling that something had happened or was about to happen, and so did the girls, and so they got those men to go out with them to see if it was anything they could help with," Walid recounted. "So when Layla first saw us coming and we were wearing the military uniforms, and she had seen three such guys leave earlier, she at first thought we were those guys and were up to something. Then Hasina saw our camels without riders, closer to them, and before she could see the three men tied up on the ground. So they were at first as prepared to think the worst about us as we were about their companions. It was a pretty dicey situation for a few moments."

"I'd say," Masoon agreed. "Well, we're all very glad it eventually turned out the way it did. But did you ever find out why the men were attempting to steal the horses, or for whom?"

"Not yet," Walid replied. "But I'm sure we will, especially now that we have a new detective in town." He looked over at Ibrahim and smiled.

"Well, Ibrahim may be getting ready to deal with a relevant situation right now," the king said, and he stood up, as then did Masoon and Ibrahim. "I'll let him tell you about it and you all can catch up while I go down to my meeting. Thanks for the update on quite an eventful day. We'll work on figuring out what was going on out there at the stables. But, meanwhile, enjoy yourselves. And Walid and Mafulla: I'd like you to come and have dinner with me a touch early tonight. I have something to report to you that I think will be of great interest. Kular will make sure you know what time."

"Yes, Your Majesty, absolutely," Walid said. "Ibrahim, let us show you where we have breakfast every morning."

"Very nice!" Ibrahim said and, turning back to the king, added, "Your Majesty, I just want to thank you again for your always gracious hospitality and for seeing me today with no advance notice."

"It was my pleasure. I look forward to our next meeting. Goodbye for now," the king said, and the boys all left the room.

King Ali had a few more words with Masoon and then he and his general both left as well, and headed down the hallway.

5

An Unexpected Opportunity

Walid and Mafulla thoroughly enjoyed their time with Ibrahim. He explained to them all about the new Cairo Detective Agency and the work they already were getting. When he mentioned the lady whose two cats had disappeared, Mafulla told him what Kular had said about pet and animal thefts in town recently. They ruminated together on the events of the day at the stables and vowed to help each other figure out what was going on. After a good hour of talk, or maybe a little more, Ibrahim's schedule did require him to leave and go meet his uncle for a training session on modern methods of investigation.

The boys walked him out to the main gate and saw him off, promising to be in touch soon. For the next hour, they returned to their rooms, washed up from the day's adventures, and rested a bit with books and their own thoughts. Walid scribbled for a while in his diary. After a bit, Kular came down and informed each of them that dinner was to be held in half an hour, so they put on nicer clothes and Walid went down to Mafulla's room to get him about five minutes before the specified time of their evening meal.

"I wonder what the king wants to talk with us about at dinner," Mafulla said. "I mean, he gets our sage advice on kingly things all the time now, and probably more than he ever even hoped for."

Walid laughed. "Yeah. He said he wanted to tell us something that would be of great interest. But I have no idea what. Let's go find out." The prince led the way, and they walked down to the king's private dining room without their new sunglasses. They had gotten plenty of use and fun out of them already on this day.

"It was good to see Kissa and Hasina earlier," Walid said, a bit out of the blue.

"Yeah, always," Mafulla replied.

"I'm still kind of shook up about what almost happened."

"Yeah, me too, but that 'almost' is the key."

"I'm so glad Paki recognized that guy."

"Yeah, for sure."

"The Hoda thing really worked on the thief with the gun."

"Yeah, it was like we poured it on extra-strength. I didn't realize we could do it that well, yet."

"Neither did I. I wonder if Paki was also doing it."

"Oh. I didn't think of that."

"Maybe that's why it worked so well."

"Yeah. True. And I thought it was all us."

"I did, too, at first. Then it occurred to me that we might have had some help."

"Boy. So maybe we're not yet Hoda-League."

"I could have told you that, anyway."

"True. I do wish I knew how it works."

Walid let out a breath and said, "Me, too. Actually, you know, there are lots of how and why questions that we have to live without answers to, at least for now. And I feel like I have a real need to know that's kind of being thwarted left and right."

"I totally get what you mean," Mafulla replied.

Walid then continued. "I'm still, now and then, having a little trouble living with so much uncertainty. But you know what the king says: Consider the possibility that uncertainty is a gift."

"Yeah," Mafulla said. "I feel the same way. It's like we're being forced to have some sort of faith in all these things and processes that we don't really understand, and sometimes that can just be emotionally tough."

"But at the same time, I can sort of see how it develops something in the soul that's good for us to have," Walid commented.

"Yeah. I agree with that, too," Mafulla said, and sighed.

"Something just hit me," Walid said and stopped in his tracks.

"Well, hit it back," Mafulla replied and also stopped.

"No, crazy man, I mean I just realized something."

"I know, so what is it?"

"I had talked to Kissa earlier when they first arrived at the stables about Phi stuff we were learning and I happened to mention the Hoda mind thing and Kissa said how well it worked, though she really didn't understand it, and that Layla was really good at it, too, just like Hoda."

"Yeah? So?"

"So, how could we have so easily assumed that those guys riding behind the ladies with guns had likely taken them hostage at gunpoint? I mean: the three of them? Kissa, Hasina, and Layla? All of them, helpless victims of two presumably regular guys?"

"Oh."

"Yeah."

"We were idiots."

"Yep. Total idiots. They could have zapped those guys with the Hoda thing so hard that nobody but the girls would have been holding any rifles, and that never even crossed my mind."

"Appearances, my man, can lead to a narrow focus. We were, once again, duped by appearances, super-duped—happy idiots that we sometimes can be. And that is not super-duper at all."

Mafulla said, "You know, it's like what Khalid said in class not long ago about the relationship between a hypothesis and evidence."

"Oh. Yeah."

"You know, that when considering rival interpretations or explanations for what you see, you should treat those the way that scientists view rival hypotheses. He said that, when weighing evidence as to which of two different hypotheses is true, you need to consider all the evidence you can, and not just what's staring you in the face."

"Yeah, we blew that, big time."

"We did."

"I guess our deep concern for our friends, and the emotions that sprang up, just blinded us to what should have been obvious."

"Yeah," Mafulla agreed. "The fact that we had just confronted bad guys made us ready to see the two riders with them as bad guys."

"Despite all the background evidence we have that two guys with guns wouldn't stand a chance against three Phi—and, you know, especially a senior Phi like Layla."

"Yeah, well, even Paki was with us in that confusion for a while."

"True, but he broke through first, and pretty quickly."

"Yeah, he did. And we all should have understood the odds against the superficial 'they're in trouble' belief being the right one. I mean: It wasn't impossible, but really crazy unlikely. We should have been a lot farther away from gunfight mode."

"Yeah. Let's remember to remember what we know."

"Ok, let's. Just remind me of that on a regular basis."

Walid smiled and said, "Will do, Super Phi Memory Man."

They walked the rest of the way down the hall and checked in with Kular and he escorted them into the dining room, showing them to their customary seats and offering them some juice or tea to enjoy while waiting for the king. But just as he took their orders, King Ali came in, and both boys stood quickly.

"Thank you, my friends. Please take your seats," the king said. "And, Kular, you can bring in the food any time."

"Yes, Your Majesty," the butler replied and slipped back out of the room.

Walid decided to waste no time, but to act quickly on his keen curiosity. He said, "Your Majesty, you told us earlier that you have something you want to report to us?"

"Yes, yes, I do," the king said, "and I think you'll find it an intriguing possibility."

"I'm intrigued already," Mafulla said.

"You've gotten my curiosity up even more," Walid added.

"Good. So. Ok, here it is. And, I know you're going to love it."

The king held up an index finger at that point, and then slowly picked up the glass at his place, and took a long drink of water.

"You're messing with us, Your Majesty," Mafulla said.

"Royally," Walid added.

"Yes, I am. I do love a little dash of drama."

"We do, too. But we especially love the dramatic conclusion," Walid said.

"I'm sure. So, in conclusion: Walid, your mother and father have decided to make a trip back to our village to check on the house and the shops they still own there and that are for the moment being managed by a local man."

"I didn't know," Walid said.

"They're considering the possibility of selling all their holdings in the village, in light of their current commitments to the monarchy and to the capital city. But they just want to go back for a visit first and make sure this is the right move at the present."

Walid replied, "They haven't said anything about it to me."

"Well, they've been very busy lately, as you know, and you've been almost as busy on your own things."

"Yeah, I haven't had much time to see them, except to say hi and give them a hug on the run," the prince admitted.

The king went on. "Our overlapping responsibilities have brought us together in quite a few meetings throughout the past two weeks, and when they told me their idea, I let them know right away that I think it's a good one."

"So, they'll be gone for a while?" Walid asked, adding, "I wish I could go too, and see the old village again."

"Well, that's where the story gets interesting, and there's a nice twist," the king replied. "You have a long break coming up, after your birthday—the longest school break of the year, which is three weeks. Your parents have asked me if I think it might be possible for you to accompany them for that duration."

"Really?"

"Yes, and here's where it gets even better. They've suggested that Mafulla might enjoy seeing the place where you grew up, and have proposed asking his parents if you can bring him along—assuming that you're interested, Mafulla."

"Interested? Interested in crossing the desert on a camel just like you two did to get here? You bet I'm interested! I mean, as long as I can have the same camel, maybe, that I rode on today—he was a good camel."

"I heard you tell him that quite a few times," Walid said with a laugh.

"Yeah, Ok, I like to show my appreciation with compliments." Mafulla looked back at the king. "When do we start packing?"

The king also laughed and said, "Wait a second. That's just Part One. Part Two may be of interest as well."

"What's Part Two?" Walid could not resist asking.

"I've made inquiries over the past few days. I have a firm belief that Egyptian Phi should know the kingdom of Egypt well. It's necessary for our greater service, for perspective, and for the knowledge it sometimes takes to be of real help, even to people here in the capital city, many of whom have come from other parts of our land. And this is especially true for Phi who are close to the seat of power—such individuals, in particular, need to know the kingdom as well as they can."

"I see what you're saying. That makes a lot of sense." Walid nodded.

"It turns out that Kissa and Hasina have never seen the western parts of our nation, or our vast desert."

"You're kidding us. You're teasing us," Mafulla said, and then added, "Your Majesty."

"No, I'm as serious as I can be. If you approve, I'll ask their parents if they can go along to the village as well."

"I need to sit down," Mafulla said.

"You are sitting down," Walid replied.

"Well, then I need to lie down."

"I'm sorry. I have to ask that you stay right where you are. It's good to be giddy now and then, and to learn to control your own blood pressure by an inner act of your mind," the king said with a big smile.

"Ok, Ok, stay calm, stay at peace, smooth like a river, floating like a boat." Mafulla's eyes were closed.

"That's pretty original," Walid said, impressed.

"I do whatever it takes," Mafulla replied. "I'm a creative guy."

"Uncle, you're serious—you're really not just kidding around with us," Walid said.

"I'm completely serious. Ideally, your mother and father, you and Mafulla, Kissa and Hasina, perhaps one of their mothers, and a strong Phi contingent, as well as some soldiers, would go on the trip. You'd do a desert crossing the first week, visit the village for a few days, and then come back home."

"This is just unbelievable," Walid said.

"Yeah, it's amazing." Mafulla was still almost speechless.

Kular then walked in with a big platter of food and an assistant butler followed him with some additional beverages.

"Kular," the king said. "I was just telling the boys here that I have a great adventure in mind for them."

"This is wonderful," Kular said. "I think these two live for adventure."

"And good food," Mafulla said.

"Yes, the food Kular brings us," Walid echoed his friend, and the senior butler smiled broadly.

"What's the adventure?"

"A short trip for them with Walid's parents to our home village. And they get to bring along their two favorite young ladies."

"Oh, that sounds ideal," Kular said. Turning to the boys, he added, "And remember the sun glasses. I'd wager no one in the village has seen them before. You'll make an unforgettable impression right from the start. I guarantee you that."

"Great idea," Walid said. "And they'll be nice to have out in the desert sun, which my friend here has never experienced."

"I hear it's hot," Mafulla offered. "But there's plenty of fresh air."

"So I've heard, as well," Kular replied. He always enjoyed the little touches of wit and the jokes he heard when the boys were nearby.

"We'll miss you while we're gone," Walid said.

"Oh, the two of you will be sorely missed!" Kular responded. "This place will be far too quiet without you around. And all the Mafoolery will be up to His Majesty and me. We'll do our best—but still, it won't be the same."

"We'll have to encourage each other to new heights of silliness," the king said to Kular. "We can practice some new jokes while they're gone, and once we have honed our act to a fine polish, they'll be back, and we can try out our material on the real pros."

"Good luck to us, Your Majesty."

"Yes, good luck to us, indeed."

At that, Kular bowed, and said, "Call me if you need anything," and he led the assistant butler back out of the room.

"Your Majesty, you said that we'd have a strong Phi contingent along on the trip," Walid commented. "Do you have anyone already in mind?"

"This may surprise you," the king replied.

"Ok, I'm prepared to be surprised."

"Well, I think we should start with Masoon and Hamid."

"Really?" Mafulla said, mouth suddenly open.

"Yes, and even hungry camels must eat, so don't let my news stop the process here," the king said. "My view is that two and a half or three weeks is far too long to be without your Phi training, and no one can match Masoon for that task. Plus, you're not likely to be bothered by desert bandits if he's along. He's greatly feared by them, as you know, Walid."

"You can spare him from his current duties?" Walid still couldn't believe that they would get the top military man, their personal Phi trainer, and the chief confidant to the king to accompany them.

"We're under no known threats now."

"That's a change."

"Yes. Things on the big scale are calm. It will be a nice trip for him. He loves the village and probably misses it as much as you might. It will be a good excuse for him to visit."

"But Hamid, too?" Walid asked.

"Yes, Hamid may have some business back in the village. He wants to check on the medical practice there, and the physician who's taken over his duties is a man who could purchase your old house, or even the shops. Hamid knows him well, of course, as he trained him."

"With those two, we hardly need any other Phi," Mafulla said.

"Yes, but you know me. I like to be extra careful," the king said. "I've asked Masoon to choose one of the younger Phi to go along. He'll pick one of your friends, Paki, Omari, or Amon. Then, if one of the mothers can also join in, that will make three senior and one intermediate Phi, along with the four young Phi. Eight of you should be more than sufficient, even if you run up against a hundred bandits at one time. You'll also have at least twenty of our most trusted soldiers with you, chosen personally by Masoon, and you'll all be well armed for the trip, and amply supplied."

"Will we go in the guise of merchants on a normal camel train, like before?" Walid asked

"No, this time I think it will be better to go in the guise of a military unit. That way, you won't be even a potential target for thieves wanting money, and it will be assumed that you're heavily armed. That's an extra layer of protection for you."

"So, we'll all be in military uniforms?"

"Yes, even the ladies."

"Ha! This should be good. I hope the uniforms fit a lot better than they did earlier today—Mafulla and I could have actually shared one of those."

That got a laugh from both the king and Mafulla. "Yes," the king said. "They'll be chosen precisely for each of you, and not just handed down from large men who apparently love their food even more than the two of you."

The dinner continued with more conversation about the trip. Mafulla asked a lot of questions about the village and their history there, as well as about the land between Cairo and their ultimate destination. They all laughed a lot and, in the time after dinner, when they had said good evening to the king, the boys sat for a while in Walid's room with continued speculation about the adventure that now lay ahead.

It was Mafulla's idea that they should go the next morning to see his parents and tell them about it, making sure it was Ok with them. He couldn't see any reason they'd object. He'd be learning a lot and be with good friends. He'd also be safe. That was a point that he reminded himself to make prominently, and perhaps many times, when he told his mother. She tended to worry, as mothers do. But she had by this point seen the boys prevail in bad situations often enough that it had built up a little more trust in her heart. Things would be fine. Her boy would be fine. She would just have to remind him to take care of himself and give him lots of advice on how to protect his skin from too much sun, and so on, and everything would be great.

Walid took Kular a note for the king, proposing that the two of them go to the Adi shop first thing in the morning. Then the rest of the evening was spent, as evenings most often were, on schoolwork. They got away with very few hours in formal class sessions because of how much work they did on their own. Class was a place where big ideas were introduced, the work they had done independently was discussed, conversations were held about a lot of interesting things, and, of course, tests were given, to see how they were progressing in the mastery of the material they were studying. Walid worked in his room and Mafulla in his own, but they did visit back and forth a few times to confer over a point or consider some new angle together.

The night was both productive and uneventful, and as the sun rose for the new day, they both awoke rested and ready to begin their preparations for the new journey that now loomed on the horizon.

Mafulla was the first up and he roused Walid for an early breakfast. The prince was still fairly drowsy and felt almost like he was sleep walking down to their breakfast and snack room. Kular had just left the morning's food options out for them, and there was hot black coffee brewed as well. They dug in, and each grabbed a newspaper off the table where Kular piled them every morning.

Walid had *The Kingdom Daily News*. "Hey, listen to this. There's an article on the front page, below the fold, about the recent pet disappearances around town. It's called 'Disappearing Dogs and Other Animals.' Look!" He turned the paper around to Mafulla.

"That's the little girl whose dog we chased and brought back to her," Mafulla said. "At least in the picture, she's holding him, so he must be Ok."

"It quotes her saying, 'I'm so afraid someone will steal my little dog Yippers. I don't know what I'd do without him.' Oh, no. It says here that the picture was taken just one day before the dog quietly disappeared while he was out in their fenced-in back yard."

Mafulla said, "How could anyone take Yippers quietly?"

"Good question." Walid paused for a second and said, "I feel so sorry for the little girl, though."

"Yeah, me too. Somebody's got to put a stop to this. I wonder what's going on?"

"I don't know. It's just too strange. We get rid of almost all the local bad guys, or at least the ones we know about, and there are weeks of peace and almost no crime and then, suddenly, this stuff starts up."

"Who would steal the pet dog of a little girl like this?"

"I don't know."

"It's really terrible."

"Yeah, even if it's Yippers."

"Even if it's Yippers. And, you know, in his case, the act of dognapping does sort of bring with it its own punishment."

"You're right," Walid laughed. "That'll teach the bad guys. Hey, I just thought of something. You know, we should ask your parents if they've heard anything about all these sudden disappearances. They deal with a lot of people and the customers who come into the shop often stop to talk about all sorts of things."

"Yeah, mom and dad are good talkers and listeners. It's incredible sometimes the things they find out just by listening to customers and asking questions."

"Well, let's not forget to ask them about this."

"Duly noted. Maybe this is something The Golden Viper and Windstorm can help solve and stop."

"I was thinking the same thing. I'd hate to leave for a couple of weeks or more, with something like this still going on."

"Well, what else does the paper say about it all? I mean: Is there more to it in the article than just the disappearance of poor little exasperating Yippers?"

"Nothing much. It talks about the frequency of the disappearances and the rumors they've spawned. It doesn't speculate at all about who might be doing it or why. There's just a quote from an unnamed source at the police headquarters who says basically that they're aware of the problem and are currently investigating."

"Oh, Ok. So, there you go. Time for the Viper and the Storm."

Walid just smiled and said, "Well, suppose first we superhero crime fighters at least get ready to go see your parents. I can be presentable and prepared to walk out the door in ten minutes."

"Me, too," Mafulla said. "But let's take the sunglasses, just to see what reaction we get."

Walid laughed and said, "Why not? That's what we do."

"Indeed," Mafulla agreed and gave his double eyebrow jump as an additional silent commentary.

It was early morning on a day of rest, not really a busy time in the marketplace. But it was an opportunity when lots of the merchants went over their inventories and tidied up for the coming days. Some put out new displays. Many figured their profits from the previous week. Most just quietly puttered around, making sure that their establishments, however large or small, were in tiptop shape for the busy shopping days ahead. There would be more people out and about later in the morning. But it was still a quiet time.

The king had left a note with Kular, duly delivered to Walid's room, saying that it was fine this morning for the two of them to go out alone, as long as they were "acutely cognizant" of their surroundings, as the king put it, and tried to make the journey in as peaceful a way as possible. That brought a smile to Walid's face. He knew that the king admired their good deeds outside the palace. But, as always, he wanted them to be careful about whatever they did.

It was Walid's idea to take a little detour this morning on their way to the marketplace, not far out of the way, but a bit off the route they normally followed. He wanted to walk through the neighborhood where the small dog Yippers had disappeared from his backyard. They'd just go down the street where the little girl lived and have a look around, nothing more. It would probably take them an extra ten minutes to get to the Adi store, and that was no big deal at all.

What was a big deal was the tremendous surprise that this little detour would soon bring them.

6

Masked Men

Walid and Mafulla had walked long enough by this point that they were now about three or four blocks from the little girl's house where Yippers had vanished. They were approaching an area where the street they were walking down ran alongside a small city park, a bit of land that had been set aside for the enjoyment of the neighborhood. The park was roughly two blocks long and half that wide. There was a fountain in the middle, and some nice trees and bushes, and even, near the fountain, an extensive area of grass. At some times of the day, on at least several days of the week, the park could be quite busy, with children running around and families having picnics and old men playing checkers or feeding the birds.

But today, so far, there wasn't anyone yet to be seen in the park except one lady and a dog she was walking on a long leash. As soon as Walid noticed the two of them, he took Mafulla's elbow and said in a low voice, "Let's slow down a minute, and watch that lady and her dog," gesturing with his head in the direction where they were to be seen.

"Sure," Mafulla whispered. "What do you feel?"

"Nothing really—except that … maybe we're supposed to stop here for a minute and just watch."

They both veered off the sidewalk and moved over to the corner of a house that was the last on the street before the park started. There didn't seem to be anyone at home. At least, there were no visible signs of an owner or occupant. And yet, the house looked well kept. The boys stood completely still for a minute. And from where they were now, almost completely hidden from the view of anyone in the park by a couple of big shrubs at the corner of the fairly large house they were near, they could see the lady slowly walking her dog along a path in the center of the open area. The two of them would pause in their stroll now and then, and she would give the dog a small treat.

"Very peaceful," Mafulla said.

"Yeah," Walid replied.

"People should be able to enjoy their pets indoors or outside without a threat or a fear that they'll be taken away by somebody."

"Always."

On the street that ran along the opposite side of the park, a car slowly approached from the direction toward which the boys had been walking. There was no other traffic around at the moment.

"Ok, then," Walid said. "Maybe this is the reason we just stopped." Mafulla saw it as well. The car slowed down even more and crept along for a moment and then parked not far from where the lady and her dog now stood. There was still an expanse of grass between them, and some bushes, but the car had stopped along the length of the park at a place precisely opposite to, and aligned with, where the pet and owner were enjoying the quiet of the day. It looked deliberate. "Reversos and masks, just in case," Walid said.

"I agree," Mafulla responded, as he flipped his watchcase over—a simple operation that always amazed him a little bit every time he performed it. Only Reverso watches, made since 1931 by the Swiss firm of LeCoultre, a watchmaker that in later years would be called Jaeger LeCoultre, had this capability. They had been developed originally for polo players who wanted to protect the crystals of often-expensive timepieces while engaged in their sport. It was a feature that came in handy for part-time crime fighters, as well. Ever since the king had given him and Walid these watches, Mafulla had been fascinated with their history and function. After enjoying, as he always did, the faint click the polished steel case made when he repositioned it and locked it in place, he silently slipped a cloth wristband over the soft black strap without even having to look, and then reached into a pocket and pulled out a beige sand mask that he didn't put on quite yet, but just held in readiness. "Ok, I'm ready." He looked over at his friend and then turned back toward the park.

Walid had gone through the same sequence of actions in preparation for anything that might happen and require their response. It was all a matter of trusting his intuitions. They both watched the car carefully, and for the moment, due to their focus, didn't even notice when the lady took the leash off her dog to let it roam around a bit as she sat down on a wooden bench and opened up what looked like a letter, that she began to read. The dog was at first just sniffing near the bench, but then wandered off to some nearby bushes, and within less than half a minute was meandering over toward the far side of the park, following a bird, it seemed. Just then, Mafulla caught sight of the dog and whispered the words "loose dog" to his friend. Walid nodded. It was a Saluki, the kind of dog Kissa owned, elegant and beautiful, and one of the oldest pure breeds in the world. This one had a golden coat and appeared to be young, not a puppy, but not fully mature either.

A door of the car opened on its passenger side, the side closest to the park, and a man got out. Another man followed him, exiting from the back seat. The first one out seemed to have something in his hands. Then it became clear that each of them was carrying something. The first man, a short, wide, heavy individual, threw what he had in his hands, not exactly toward the dog, but more between himself and the dog, over to the side. It was a light toss and the man appeared to be saying something now to the animal, but the boys couldn't hear anything from their distance.

The dog cautiously approached what now lay not far away on the ground. It looked like it must be some sort of food or treat. And then the stout man, the one closest to the dog, lunged at the animal clumsily. The boys later found out that it was a female dog named Lillian, of all things, for Lillian Gish, the star of American silent films earlier in the century. Lillian apparently had no fondness for this man whatsoever—the dog, of course, not the actress; but of her, it would also most certainly be true, as well, though irrelevant to any present circumstances. And when the man jumped toward her, the dog barked and bolted in the opposite direction. Walid put his hand on Mafulla's arm. Their intervention could wait a bit until they saw how this was going to play out. They had too many options at the moment. They could go after the men or the dog, or the car, or two of these possibilities, but not all three, and it was not yet clear exactly what was the preferable course. Watching the scene develop, if only for seconds, they might get a better clue as to the best approach.

Both sand masks went on, as The Golden Viper and Windstorm prepared to rush into action. The lady had just looked up from the letter she had been reading. The sound of the sudden pursuit and the loud bark at its inception had caught her attention. Lillian was running back toward her owner who, now, at that moment cried out, "What in the world is going on?" But a split second before Walid and Mafulla could choose the best course for their own action, two figures came running, full speed, across the park from the opposite direction. One targeted and tackled the large short man as he ran toward the dog and the other flew into his associate, slamming him to the ground.

Walid echoed the lady's words, and whispered, "What in the world is going on?" In less than four seconds, these two additional individuals had appeared, darted across the grass at full speed, and instantly engaged the apparent, would-be dog-nappers, knocking them both to the ground.

"Oh, my goodness! Oh, my goodness!" the lady exclaimed, as she quickly leashed up Lilly, who had run to her, and then walked as rapidly as she could away from the park and the scene of this unexpected melee, glancing back several times as she fled.

"Who are those guys? They're masked like us!" Mafulla whispered to Walid. "Look!"

"I can't believe it! You're right!"

At that moment, the parked car loudly revved its engine and took off, quickly pulling back onto the main street and disappearing down the broad avenue at top speed. The men it had left behind were putting up a fight, but weren't doing very well. Simply stated, they were getting thoroughly pummeled. Before many more seconds had passed, they struggled up onto their feet and fled across the park. They crossed the street at a run and then disappeared between two houses, pursued part of the way by their masked adversaries, who ran after them as far as the street, but then stopped when the men crossed over, and just watched them vanish between the houses on the other side of the broad avenue. Then, in what seemed to be the very next moment, the two masked men took off running again, but now back in the direction from which they had come, toward the far end of the park, disappearing beyond some nearby homes.

Mafulla seemed to be full of some form of nervous energy that he was working hard to contain. "Should we go after those guys?" he asked Walid. "You know, right now?"

"What?"

"Should we follow the masked guys?" he said quickly.

"No, no, I don't think so."

"But, why not?"

"Well, they're not the bad guys, or at least, they broke up something bad that was going to happen, like we would have. They acted like the Viper and the Storm. They even looked a little bit like us. It's so odd."

"And who are they?" Mafulla seemed worried.

"I have no idea. But you know how popular our characters are. They're likely just copycats, trying to be like us."

"What I'm saying is: Shouldn't we find out who they are?"

"Why?"

"What do you mean, why?"

"The problem is that if we confront them about who they are, they'll want to know the same thing about us, too. And I'm not comfortable with that. Plus, let's think about this for a second. They haven't done anything wrong. They got to those guys fast and broke up what sure looked like a crime in process, but they just weren't as careful as we would have been."

"Yeah, they let the car get away."

"Right. The car's the key to crucial information. Those guys stopped the dog thieves this time. We need to stop them for good, and we can't do that unless we know who the criminals are, and why they're doing this. And getting the guy in the car likely would have been crucial for all that."

Mafulla said, "I still can't believe what we just saw. I'm shocked."

"Yeah, it was a pretty big surprise, to say the least. But really, I'm just as surprised that we've never come across such a thing before now."

"But this was a huge, gigantic coincidence."

"Well, maybe, but really, when I think about it, not likely. I suspect that we were somehow supposed to see this. We were here, and they were there, at precisely the same time … for a reason. At least, that's what I think we should suspect here."

"Ok, Ok, you're right. I keep forgetting how everything's connected. So, let's say it's not a coincidence that they were there and we were here at the exact right moment. But then, why do you think we were supposed to see it?"

"I have no idea—no idea at all—zero."

"Oh, well, good, then. At least I know I'm talking to the right guy."

"Very funny."

"I still wish we had followed them."

"To do what? Unmask the guys?"

"Well, maybe or maybe not, literally, but just to find out, really, who they are and why they did what they just did. Plus, I want to know how they were in the right place at exactly the right time to see a crime almost get committed and then stop it."

"Well, it happens to us all the time."

"Yeah, but that's the point. That's us, *us*—Phi sensitive and well trained and sort of almost super-powered us. How can that be happening with two guys we don't even know?"

"Well, like I say, I've heard there are copycats around town, now and then."

"Sure, kids playing at it, maybe, but real guys doing it right, or almost right? And how could they be at the right place at the right time like they were if they're not Phi?"

"Well, it's possible we don't know all the Phi in town."

"Yeah, I guess. But I mean, we should, shouldn't we?"

"The king apparently doesn't think so."

Mafulla sighed loudly. "Oh, Ok, there's that."

"The king's usually right."

"True, true. Even when we don't understand how or why, he's right. But I need to know who the competition is."

"Ha! Competition? What makes these guys our competition? They just saved us the trouble of running across the park and pouncing on the bad guys and getting all sweaty and maybe really dirty before we see your parents. They got the job done for us. Well, most of it."

"Some of it."

"Ok, some of it. But still. They're colleagues, comrades, maybe even compatriots, and not competition."

"Yeah, but what if they're out of control? What if they don't have our good judgment and sense of fair play?"

"You sound like Khalid in class long ago, when the paper first reported on us."

"Ok, good point. Well, maybe then there's something to be said for his worries. When it's us, I trust the masked crime fighters. I happen to know they're great guys with a sound philosophy and ample sensitivity to public needs. When it's somebody else, I'm a little leery."

"Yeah," Walid said, "I know what you mean. And that's the position everybody else is in when it comes to us. So we should understand the concerns that some people might have about the whole thing."

"Another good point. Maybe we should go, before you show me how little I actually know and appreciate about the deeper truths in life."

"That might be a good idea after all," Walid agreed. "And remember, these guys just now didn't replace us. They haven't forced our imminent retirement. They've just augmented our efforts, although we do need to teach them a thing or two about bad guy management and information gathering—some of the big picture stuff."

Mafulla looked thoughtful and said, "We should open a school for masked crime fighting. All advanced students would study bad guy management—as distinct, of course, from bad guy leadership, which we would, most properly, leave to the more advanced bad guys with the talent to get out front and show the way forward."

"Yeah, as distinct from that."

"But, Ok, for now, let's just go see my parents."

"I think that's a good idea, as distinct from all our other ideas."

Mafulla laughed and they both continued on their trek across town. They soon passed by the home of the little girl whose dog Yippers had disappeared, and Mafulla made another remark about how much the thieves must regret this particular choice. They didn't see anything else unusual in the neighborhood, and picked up their pace.

Passing by The Grand Hotel, a place that held many memories for them both, they took a right on another main street and headed now straight for the marketplace and the Adi shop. Mafulla was rehearsing over and over again in his mind what he would tell his mother and dad about the upcoming trip to Walid's home village, hoping that they wouldn't have a problem with it. But at the same time, he kept being nagged by the questions of who the new masked men were and what they were up to. He just couldn't shake his concern. But he basically made peace with the unanswered questions and moved on. That's something we sometimes have to do. We don't always get the answers we want when we want them, and so we often have to just accept what we don't know and refocus our attention. It was a manifestation of Mafulla's newfound maturity and inner power that he was able to do this. But of course, that didn't mean that he would drop the issue altogether, only that it wouldn't continue to bother him all the time.

Within minutes, the Adi Shop was in sight. There had been enough excitement for the morning, and Walid was glad to see their friendly destination. First, he caught sight of Badar Sakat sweeping the sidewalk outside the sandal shop, up the street and across from the Adi store. As they approached, Walid said, "Badar, it seems like that's an endless job that you're often doing."

"Yes, sir, indeed," he said, as he looked up with a smile. "Pave a road in the desert, and you have a cleaning job for life. Build a shop here, and much the same is true. Sand is sand and dust is dust—but it's dirt only if it interferes with our preferential vision of how things ideally should be."

"Wisely said, indeed," Walid replied, adding, "I suppose that many people, without realizing it at all, metaphorically build roads in the desert, and then are surprised at the continuing work that they've given themselves to do."

"You, my friend, are the real philosopher. I just make sandals."

Mafulla chipped in, "And yet you both seek to help others walk better the path of life, with good *souls*."

"Ha! Yes," Walid said, "And the sandal makers, at least, do the job well, by producing such excellent results, I must say."

"Do you both still like the sandals we made for you?"

"Yes!" Mafulla said. "They're the best ever!"

"Most definitely," Walid quickly agreed. "Never have my feet felt so pampered!"

"Thank you. I'll tell my brother and maybe he'll give up his alternative dream of building new pyramids for the modern world."

Walid laughed and said, "Good! I'm glad I can be of assistance. We have enough pyramids as it is, I think."

"Yes, and until we can figure out what to do with the ones we have, I'm not sure we should build any more."

"You're likely right. Tell your brother that the sandals are both practical and wonderful, and are so very much appreciated. Plus, they're becoming actually famous all around town."

"I'll do that. Thanks." Badar never acknowledged Walid or Mafulla's identities or greeted them in public by name. This was important to preserve his cover as part of the king's protective force guarding the Adi family. He was very good at his job, and actually, at both of them, producing a tight ring of security and very nice sandals at the same time.

Shapur Adi was walking out from the back room of his shop with some ornamental vases to put in the front when he caught sight of Badar standing outside his shop talking to someone. Then, as soon as he saw who it was, he put down the vases on the nearest surface and made his way quickly into the street.

"Badar! Chase away this riff raff! Don't encourage them!"

Mafulla turned, saw his dad, and laughed loudly. "We're here to ruin the reputation of the street and keep your property taxes down, as low as possible."

"Well, that would be nice, but we can't have shady people just hanging about and causing trouble. What would the neighbors say?"

"There's always the chance of a purchase," Walid replied.

"Oh, well, then, in that case, it's so good to see you both! Please come into my humble shop."

Shapur did a little bow toward the prince, and motioned toward the door of the store. The boys began to walk in his direction, and he pointed to his son and said, "But I'm still not sure about this rascal."

"I'll watch him like a hawk," Walid promised.

"Ok, then. I suppose he can come in as well, hawk that he may be."

"No, Dad, Walid was the hawk, in his little simile."

"But it's you who may fly around the shop and knock over things with all your flapping about," Shapur said, and then looked over at Walid and remarked to him, about this hawk in their mutual presence, "You must promise not to let him touch things anywhere inside."

"The whole point of the visit was to touch each and every item in the store," Mafulla protested. "Then I could get them cheap and set up my own competing shop and … *hawk* the items to unsuspecting customers."

"Oh. I had not thought of that," Shapur laughed and said. "Which leads to a new idea. We should let the prince do the touching. I can raise the prices. 'You know, this was last touched by the Prince of Egypt'—that sort of thing always sells, for some reason. People like to impress their friends."

"Absolutely," Mafulla agreed, laughing. "That's exactly why I bring Walid here. He's always so impressed with the wit to be found in the shop when we're both here."

"Both, the two of us—or both, the two of you?" Shapur had a funny look on his face.

"Oh! Both boths, or both times two, of course."

Walid said, "This just all reminds me where the wit comes from in the Adi family, and how it must get watered down from one generation to the next."

"Very funny," Mafulla said.

"Sharp, indeed," Shapur said with a big smile.

"Thank you, both. The two of you somehow conspire to inspire me to new levels of humorous observation."

"Any level of humor is fairly new to you, my friend," Mafulla quipped with a grin.

"Ok, enough good Mafoolery," Shapur said, laughing. "What brings my two favorite inmates of the palace to see me this morning?"

"Actually, the king had a great idea for our upcoming long break from school," Mafulla explained. "And we wanted to tell you about it, and see what you think."

"Wait. Let me guess. His Majesty thinks that you should both come to work for me for the three weeks, as interns, not for wages, but for the rich reward of experience!"

"Ha! No."

"Ok. I couldn't resist. But nevertheless, you're here to solicit my advice, an overture that's quite rare for young men of your ages.

I'm truly impressed. So you've already put me in a good mood and prepared me well to offer precisely the opinion or advice that you most likely want to hear—you clever, clever men."

"We're both touched with a bit of psychological genius, I suppose," Mafulla replied. "But not enough, apparently, since you've clearly seen through our otherwise well-constructed ploy."

"It may still work. Flattery could save the day, you know. It often does, as I've learned with your mother."

"Yes, well, that's simply a brilliant observation. You're the single most insightful individual I've ever been around, and it's with the most profound pride that I call myself your son," Mafulla quickly said to his delightfully amused father.

"Oh, please, no more—or you may grievously threaten my modest, yet fragile, sense of humility."

"Ah! Never has self-knowledge of such a keen and exalted sort been found in a man of so many other estimable talents!" Mafulla replied, adding, "For you, humility should be a challenge."

"Ok. I think I'm ready now. I'm as buttered up as warm pita fresh from the fire. What's the idea for the school break?"

"Well, you know I just gave Walid an early birthday present, a ride on a camel and—Oh! We forgot to wear the other part of the present!" Mafulla looked at Walid, and they both turned around, their backs to Shapur, and within four seconds, they whirled back around to face him with their new shades on. Shapur howled with laughter.

"What do you think?" Walid asked.

He said, "That's just the best thing I've seen in a long time. The two of you wearing the sunglasses of Hollywood movie stars! Shamilar! Shamilar! Come see this! Come quickly! Celebrities! We have two famous celebrities in our shop!"

Shapur shouted into the back of the store, and Mafulla's mother came out as quickly as she could, saying, "What in the world is going on out here?" Then, as soon as she saw the boys, she exclaimed, "My boys! Mafulla, Walid! I didn't know you were here! Shapur, why didn't you tell me my boys were here?"

"I just did! Or, well, I called you to come see!"

"But what are these dark glasses you're both wearing? Oh, my goodness! Is something wrong with your eyes? Have you both injured your eyesight? Tell me what's wrong!"

The men all started laughing and Mafulla said, "Only a mother!"

"What?"

"Only a mother would react like that!"

"They're Hollywood movie stars!" Shapur said.

"They're what?"

"They're magic men of the silver screen! Just like in the movies!"

"Be serious!" Shamilar replied. "What's wrong with their eyes?"

"Mom, there's nothing wrong! I promise! For an early birthday present, I gave Walid a ride on his favorite camel and these sunglasses to wear on the ride. They're from America! They're exactly what the famous movie stars wear! And you just don't see them in Egypt. So I got myself a pair, too. We're now living at the highest possible level of cool. Just look at us! Tada!"

"Oh, what a relief! I thought something was badly wrong with your vision," she said with her hand over her heart. "Just the thought of my son and his best friend both losing their ability to see was too much for me to bear. And at the same time! It would be such a tragedy!"

"Geez, mom! Stop worrying! Things are great! There's no problem! Have a little faith and optimism." Mafulla was still smiling and even laughing at the quintessential mother response he had just witnessed. "See? Look into my eyes," he said as he pulled off the sunglasses and leaned in toward his mother.

"Ok, I'm convinced, everything is fine. Your eyes look normal. There are no injuries. But then, if everything is fine, what are you doing here on a day that you're usually busy reading and studying for the school week? Is something else wrong? Tell your mother!"

"No, no, no! Everything's great! I promise! The king just had an idea for something we might do during our long upcoming school break, and we wanted to run it by you guys to see what you think. We just came for your opinion. I'm really excited about the possibility."

"Well, that's very nice. What a good boy you are, at your age still wanting your mother's opinion! So, tell me: What is it, my son?" Shamilar asked as Shapur stood off to the side, letting his wife have this bit of full access to their son, which she enjoyed so much and experienced too seldom these days.

"Well, and this is really good, so don't worry about any of the details, but since we enjoyed riding the camels so much yesterday and everything, the king had this idea. Walid's parents are going to have to make a short trip back to their village to see about selling their house and a business there, and the king thought we might enjoy going along, so that Walid could see the village again, and I could learn about where he grew up, and that whole part of the kingdom I've never visited."

"Oh! But that's very far away, isn't it?"

"Not that far, Mrs. Adi," Walid said. "A few days by camel train."

"Is it across the desert?"

"Yes, it is."

"But, my son, you've never traveled in the desert before."

"Well, that's sort of the point, or at least part of it. I'd learn a lot about our country. I'd experience a lot of new things. And it would all be very educational."

"But would you be safe? The desert can be dangerous."

Walid spoke up again and said, "Yes, ma'am, indeed. The king has provided the most amazing security detail involving top military men and a whole contingent of trusted soldiers. Masoon Afah would be going, and Doctor Hamid, who is a top physician. They have a lot of experience in the desert, safe experience, and can guide us well. Plus, we'd all be going dressed as soldiers, to discourage anyone from thinking they could mess with us in any way."

"My son will be in a military uniform?"

"Yes, as part of our extra security precautions."

"But he wouldn't really be serving in the military?"

"No, not at all. It would just be a disguise to make the trip easier and raise fewer questions in the minds of people who might see us. There are military movements across the sand out there all the time, and no one thinks anything about it. It would just be part of the way the king would provide smooth travel for us and a guarantee of minimal hassle."

"So, you wouldn't be fighting any battles, or doing any sort of dangerous military things?"

"No," Mafulla laughed. "None whatsoever. We're not at war with anybody, in the first place. And, second, I wouldn't actually be in the army. But there would be real soldiers with us to keep us safe. We'd be totally protected in every way."

"Oh."

"It's an educational trip, like the trip to Alexandria not long ago."

"That was followed by an attack on the palace, and our entire family had to be taken to a safe house."

"True, but that attack had nothing to do with the trip. It was just a coincidence," he said and looked over at Walid, since he was now a little reticent to use the word or concept at all. But, for present purposes, it seemed to do the job, since his mother's expression quickly changed.

"Oh. Yes. Ok, you're right. I shouldn't worry so."

"No, mom, you shouldn't."

"But it's part of my job."

"And I've often said that it's a job you do quite well. There's probably no one who does it better."

"Well, thank you, son. I try."

"So, the trip is Ok with you and dad?"

Shapur asked, "How long will you be gone?"

"A few days to get there, a few days there, a few to get back," Walid responded, adding, "Less than three weeks, maybe two and change."

"That's still a long time," Shamilar said.

"It's not so long," Shapur said.

And then, everyone laughed again. "Parents!" Mafulla said. "I certainly appreciate both your opinions. We'll strive to make it as short a trip as we can, while also very educational. We'll encourage the camels to practically scramble across the sand. And I promise we won't dawdle at all, even at meals. I'll also try to sleep really fast. I'll even make my watch tick more quickly."

"You're so silly."

"Honestly. We'd love to get back in time to rest up and just goof off some before classes start back up."

"That makes sense. You need your rest. Are you getting enough rest these days?"

"Yes, mom, plenty. The beds in the palace are really good, and it's quiet at night."

"Good. But if it's ever hard to sleep, you still have your bed at home that you can come and use."

"Yes. Thanks. I'll sure let you know."

"Of course, it's no palace, but it's quiet."

"It's a palace to me, mom, and you're the queen."

"You're so sweet, and not just silly, and smart. You're a good boy. You can go on your trip. Just be careful in every possible way."

"I will."

"And stay away from bandits."

"What bandits?"

"Oh, I've heard about the bandits. Stay away from them."

"Ok, mom, I'm glad you thought of that. Otherwise, I might have been tempted to seek them out, you know, just to hang around and learn some banditry things."

"You see the silliness? All the time, just like your father."

Shapur was standing there muffling a laugh. He pointed at their son and said, "You know, he's always had a hankering to learn a little banditry."

"Not you, too. Stop it."

Mafulla said, "Do you think if I wore a big bandana of bright bands, it might attract some bandits to show me their banditry?"

"Stop this silliness. I'm serious."

Walid said, "We'll all take very good care of Mafulla."

"Ok, all right then, you may go with my blessing, and I'm sure your father's, who probably wishes he could tag along too, just to get in some trouble with you."

"I can't wait to hear all your dramatic tales of wonderful trouble when you return," Shapur said. "That way, I can at least enjoy them all vicariously!" And Shamilar just shook her head.

7

Birthday Preparations

"Kissa! Hasina! The girls are here!" Hoda called out toward the back of the house. Kissa's other classmates, Ara, Cabar, Khata, Bakat, and Kit had just come in the door and, at Hoda's invitation, sat down on the floor of the large front room. As soon as they heard Hoda's announcement, Kissa and Hasina came out from the back room right away. The circle of girls was already buzzing with overlapping conversations and scattered laughter.

"Ladies! Ladies! Thanks for coming!" Kissa said, as she appeared in the room. After receiving scattered greetings in response, she continued. "As you know, our friend prince Walid"—and, at his name, three of the girls at the same time went 'oooooooooo'—and Kissa did a fake clearing of her throat, "Ahem! As I was saying, our favorite prince of the kingdom is going to have his fourteenth birthday in two days and we'll be holding a big surprise party for him tomorrow night."

"Yeah, and as his big birthday surprise present, we should give him what he really wants," Kit said, grinning, and then pointed and added, "You!" And, of course, everyone else laughed, as Kissa made a face and pointed at her classmate.

"Just hush that talk, Miss Kitty Cat. Our friend wanted only a small celebration, and the king agreed. So there will be no formal bands or thousands of attendees. But Walid made one mistake. He didn't specify carefully enough how small a party he had in mind. So I've personally taken the initiative, with the king's permission, to invite you ladies and also the entire boys' class to join us and the king and Walid's family and Mafulla's at the palace for the celebration."

At this, there was scattered applause and a couple of the girls said, "Yaaay." Kissa continued, "The king is going to cater it, of course. So the food will be really good."

"Cake! Let us eat cake!" Bakat said, to laughter.

Kissa went on, "My brothers are going to be making some incredible birthday delights—including cakes of various kinds. But I also thought that, in the meantime, maybe we could get together for a little while this afternoon and make some colorful decorations, drawing on the awesome artistic talents now so amply represented in the room."

"Good idea," Ara said. "We'll wrap you in some bright gift paper and tie you up with a really nice ribbon and a big bow for your beau."

"Ha! But that wouldn't be much of a surprise," Khata said. "He'll see that present coming a mile away."

"He always does," Hasina said.

"Not you, too!" Kissa smiled indulgently and said, "Ok, to reorient our focus properly: Mom has gathered all sorts of supplies, and if we get right down to it, I think we can create lots of festive stuff to put in the palace."

"Where in the palace are we having the party?" Cabar asked.

"The big reception room on the first floor, where we all went after each of the school trips."

"Oh, Ok, that's plenty of space," Cabar said.

"Yeah, but we don't have to fill it, just dress it up playfully. I'm thinking lots of color and maybe pictures or representations of some of Walid's favorite things."

"Ok, then," Khata said, "First we have your photograph blown up to a poster size presentation, and then make lots of copies to plaster all over the room." She was also now joining in the merriment.

"You know what I mean!"

"Ok, just kidding. So, what, other than you, does Walid like?"

Kissa made some suggestions, then Hasina added a couple, and some of the other girls had ideas as well. Within minutes, they had sorted through all the materials available and had gotten down to work, cutting, drawing, pasting, twisting, and putting things together. Hoda was circulating around the room, helping anyone who needed help, answering questions and making suggestions. She was really good at crafty stuff and the girls appreciated her assistance. There were still jokes flying all around the room, but not all of them now at Kissa's expense, and everyone was having a good time together.

Across town, Walid and Mafulla were walking back to the palace from the Adi Shop. At the moment, they were just passing the famous Blue Camel Café, and Walid happened to catch sight of Ibrahim at a table with an older man. "Hey, there's Ibrahim, and I bet that's his uncle. Should we stop in and say hello?"

"Why not?" Mafulla responded. "I'd love to meet the new top gumshoe in town."

"Gumshoe?"

"Movie and magazine lingo for a detective, or investigator—the guy who sneaks around town in soft rubber sole shoes and solves crimes and gets all the dames." At that, Walid had to laugh. Then, Mafulla explained, "You know, like Sam Spade in the *Maltese Falcon*—that book by Dashiell Hammett."

"Well, I don't see any dames with them right now, so we probably won't be interrupting anything too important." Walid smiled and led the way to the front door, and when the proprietor greeted them, he explained that they had a couple of friends at one of the tables and just wanted to stop by briefly to say hello. The man insisted with a smile that Walid still take a menu, in case anything appealed to him, and said, "The hummus is extra good today! And we have special warm pita for it! It's our secret recipe! But in any case, please, enjoy your friends!"

As they walked toward the table, Ibrahim started laughing. He hadn't seen them yet, and was reacting to something the older man had said. Then Walid spoke up. "I'm looking for a guy who can solve a mystery. I wonder where I can find one?"

Ibrahim turned around and stood up quickly and said, "Walid! I didn't see you come in! Mafulla! What are you two doing?"

"We were just out on an errand and saw you sitting here and wanted to say hello," Walid explained. He looked at the older man and introduced himself with a big smile, saying, "Hi, I'm Walid, and this is my friend Mafulla."

"Oh, I'm so sorry," Ibrahim said. "I should have made introductions right away! Please forgive my clumsiness." The older man stood more slowly, with a broad smile, and Ibrahim said in a lower voice, "Prince Walid, may I present to you my uncle, the esteemed former head of the Alexandrian police department, Mr. Leem Hadad? And Uncle Leem, this is His Royal Highness, Prince Walid Shabeezar, and his friend and loyal sidekick, Mafulla Adi."

"It is an honor to meet you both. I've heard so much about you," Leem said, and he did a quick, short bow in Walid's direction. It's not often that I get the chance to run across royalty in The Blue Camel."

"It's a great pleasure, Mr. Hadad," Walid said. "And royalty should get to the Blue Camel more often. I hear the hummus is excellent."

"Please, call me Leem. I like to cultivate informality now that I'm a simple gumshoe. And, yes, the hummus is nice!"

"See, I told you!" Mafulla said to Walid. He looked at Leem and commented, "I was just explaining to my friend here what a gumshoe is, and how much I've wanted to meet a real one, and so this is a treat for me, for sure."

"Give me the time, I'll solve any crime," Leem said with a smile.

"Oh, that's nice. Eat your heart out, Sam Spade. Now that's a detective motto to be proud of."

"Would you like to join us for a few minutes?" Leem asked Walid and then turned to Mafulla. Mafulla then looked at the prince, and gestured toward a chair with an air of expectancy.

"Ok. Thanks for asking. We can sit for a few minutes, and then we have to get back," Walid said. "We were just on a short visit today to see Mafulla's parents at their shop in the marketplace."

"The famous Adi Shop? You're that Adi?"

"Yes, well, the son of," Mafulla said.

"I hear great things about your shop."

"Thanks. We're all very proud of it."

"Sit! Sit with us! It's a double honor."

Mafulla and Walid both pulled out chairs and took their seats, and then so did their hosts. Leem gestured to the waiter and asked for two more cups of tea to be brought over for their guests with a side plate of hummus and warm bread. Walid thanked him for his kindness and then, right off the bat, Mafulla looked at Leem and said, "I have a professional question. It may seem to come from out of the blue, but it's about a strange matter in town."

"Certainly, ask anything," Leem responded. "You already have my curiosity up."

"What do you think about all these disappearances of animals around the city, recently?"

Leem thought for a second and said, "Well, I haven't been in town that long, and I have no idea whether anything remotely like this has happened before."

"Not to my knowledge," Mafulla interjected, "And I've lived here my entire life. And even some older people who've been here a very long time seem to think that it's a completely new problem."

"Well, then, it's definitely a strange situation. I have a client whose two pet cats just suddenly disappeared. They were expensive animals, but more than that, beloved members of the family. And I'm only starting to look into it. Do you gentlemen have any perspectives on these matters that it might help me to know?"

Walid looked at Mafulla and said, "We were riding camels out at the royal stables at the edge of town yesterday and three men dressed as soldiers of the kingdom attempted to steal some horses from the stables."

"Oh, my," Leem responded.

"With a palace guard, we were fortunately able to stop and interrogate them, but the men we questioned had just been hired to take the animals and claimed they didn't know who was behind it. They were going to be paid by the driver of a truck they were to meet, and he sped off before anyone could apprehend him."

"Do you know anything more about the purpose of the attempted theft?" Leem asked them both.

"No, not really," Walid responded. "But today, we happened to see another attempt, this time, to take a beautiful dog. We were walking to Mafulla's family shop in the marketplace and maybe a mile or two away, we caught sight of a lady in a park with her pet Saluki."

"That's a wonderful dog, as a breed, I mean, and so attractive."

"Yes. It had a gorgeous golden fur. And suddenly two men jumped out of a car and tried to nab the dog. But two other gentlemen who were passing by intervened and stopped them, and the criminals ran away, while the car took off without them."

"Really?"

"Yes, they were thwarted by apparently concerned citizens willing to take a chance to stop a crime."

"Were these the now famous Golden Viper and Windstorm?"

Mafulla was taken off guard, and swallowed hard. "I don't think so," Walid replied. "We couldn't see them very well, and weren't close enough to know who they were. It could have been almost anyone, from our point of view, but we really didn't get that good a look."

"Yeah, it was likely a copycat thing, but what do I know?" Mafulla said.

"I wouldn't be surprised. I've heard that the two famous men, the original masked crime fighters, do great good in the city," Leem said. "They're extremely popular here, and even in Alexandria there's admiring talk of them."

"Really? In Alexandria?" Mafulla said.

"Yes, especially among the younger crowd, your age, but all over town you hear people speak of the Viper and the Storm who defeat crime down in Cairo."

"Wow, that's pretty amazing." Mafulla was clearly impressed.

Walid jumped back in and said, "It's good to hear that these active citizens who seem to be genuinely concerned about the safety of their neighbors are getting positive attention in Alexandria. In the palace, we're big fans of anyone who will help the police and assist in stopping criminals from their intended deeds, but without crossing any lines, of course."

"Of course."

Walid continued. "In the second case I was just now mentioning, the one involving a lady and her dog and two men apparently set on taking the animal, there was a third person in the car that had brought them, and as I said, this individual took off when his associates were intercepted and stopped by the other men we saw. Then both the thwarted criminals made their own escapes pretty quickly by foot and got away as well."

"At least their intended action was blocked," Leem commented and scratched his head. After a moment he said, "So, you've both been witness to two incidents of the attempted thefts of animals … in how long a period of time?"

"In just two days," Mafulla replied.

"In two completely different parts of town?"

"Yes, and quite a distance apart."

"Then this is apparently a bigger problem than I had imagined," Leem said.

"So it seems," Walid commented.

Leem asked, "But why now? And why is this involving so many animals? You two have lived here for much longer than I. Do you have any views on this at all?"

"I haven't heard any good answers," Walid replied. "In fact, I haven't heard any answer to those questions, yet. The people I've come across who know anything about this just seem puzzled by it all."

"Well then, as I seek to recover my client's lost pets, I'll keep an eye on the bigger picture, as well. This is the sort of mystery that I very much enjoy solving. And it's activity that needs to be stopped."

"I'll also enjoy helping to solve and stop it," Ibrahim said right away as his uncle smiled at him and nodded.

"That's why I thought you'd be perfect for the job," the older man said. "You have a strong motivation for success in whatever you do, a good mind, a good heart, and reliable instincts about people. You're going to make a truly great assistant gumshoe. And maybe Dashiell Hammett, or someone, will have to write about you one day, in a compelling novel."

"Cheers to that," Walid said and lifted his teacup.

"Indeed," Mafulla said, "To Cairo's favorite new gumshoes!"

"Now, I have to try that hummus," Walid said.

The Birthday Decoration Session at the El-Bay home had just broken up. The girls had made lots of great streamers and pictures and other embellishments that were going to turn the occasion of Walid's birthday into a fun and festive party. Many of the decorations were beautiful. Some were funny. A couple of the moms had dropped by to pick up their girls, and they couldn't have been more effusive in their praise of what they saw.

Ara's mother said, "You girls are just so talented! This is going to be quite a party!"

"Three hours of hard work and silliness," Hoda replied. "And the talent level of these girls is, indeed, pretty unusual. I think The Birthday Boy will be suitably wowed."

As the girls left, Kissa said her goodbyes at the door and thanked them all once more for their help. Hasina stayed, as she always did, to help clean up. And after about fifteen minutes of cleaning and straightening, Kissa said, "Mom, Shibby's been pent up in my bedroom for all this time. She really needs to get outside."

Hoda suggested, "Why don't you and Hasina take her for a walk?"

"That's a good idea. I'd like a little fresh air myself. Hassi? Are you up for it?"

"Sure, get the leash and let's take her down the street to that big open area. A very pregnant lady like The Shibs needs some good, easy exercise every day."

Walid had not had the chance to tell Kissa all that he knew about the animal disappearances and apparent thefts around town. He hadn't even brought up the fact, yet, that he had already heard about the doggie pregnancy and expected puppies, thanks to Mafulla. And Kissa would not, of course, know anything about the attempted abduction of a Saluki just like Shibby, except a different color, earlier in the day, and only a few miles away.

So she leashed up Shibby and she and Hasina took the grateful dog out for a late afternoon walk, with no worries at all about being on the lookout for dog thieves. As far as they knew, it was just a normal day for a stroll. Within a couple of minutes, they were down the street and casually meandering along in a fun, animated conversation about their friends and what different girls had said during the day's decorating party. Hasina's mouth suddenly got very dry and her stomach felt weird. She didn't say anything but just got quiet, as she listened to what Kissa was saying about Ara and Ara's mom and how nice they were and how active in the community, and she couldn't believe that Ara could volunteer her time so much and still do so well in school. Neither of them heard the car coming up slowly behind them, an older vehicle that the boys would have recognized right away. But the boys weren't there.

The street was not a busy one. It was part of a generally quiet residential neighborhood. Those who lived here considered their peaceful environment to be a great blessing. They were close to the palace and near enough to various shops. But they didn't have to worry about crowds or traffic. A car would go down the street now and then, and an occasional donkey cart might even rumble by. There would be pedestrians, too, but not many—someone walking home from work, or from a store, or going to visit a friend nearby. But there was never much traffic of any kind on the road. And, at this moment, there was no one else on the street but Kissa, Hasina, Shibby, and now the car that had turned onto the quiet avenue a few blocks behind where they were taking their stroll.

Shibby had already gratefully answered the call of nature and was comfortably sauntering along with her loving owner and their truly mutual friend when the car slowly approached them from behind, barely rolling along now at a walking pace. A man cranked down the passenger side window and leaned slightly toward them.

"Excuse me, Miss. Is that a pure bred Saluki?"

"Yes, she is," Kissa answered in a friendly tone. The car stopped, and so did the girls, almost as a reflex.

"I'm so very sorry to interrupt your walk, but I'm a great lover of dogs, and I volunteer for an organization that finds homes for abandoned or otherwise homeless animals. I come across a lot of dogs in my work, and I have to say that this is the most beautiful animal I've ever seen."

"Oh, you're so kind. Thank you very much. She has a sweet disposition to match." The man talking to them had a pleasant and smiling face, and he seemed genuinely interested in Shibby.

"I was actually trained in veterinary medicine at the university and, by chance, am writing a book on the history of the Saluki breed in Egypt. Would you mind terribly if I hopped out and had a closer look at her facial features? Her eyes and face generally are amazing, and not quite like any other Saluki I've ever seen."

"Sure, that'll be fine. Sit down, Shibby. Good girl." The man opened the car door next to them and got out slowly, still smiling. "Again," he said, "I'm quite sorry to be so intrusive and interrupt your time, but as a doctor of veterinary medicine and a great lover of dogs, I just couldn't pass up this opportunity to look a bit more closely at such a stunning specimen—especially in light of my current research."

"We don't mind at all. We're just out for a little walk. And there's no hurry."

Hasina was getting a strong and strange feeling as the man bent down and looked at Shibby's face more closely. And this confused her, because Kissa was showing no signs of alarm, and she was normally a great judge of character. But maybe her mind was too much on other things, like the birthday. Hasina looked up toward the car. By a quick glance, she could tell that there were two more men sitting in it, one driving and one in the back seat.

"Oh, I just remembered," Hasina then said nervously, "Mom's going to be along any minute now. We'd better get Shibby back to the house."

Kissa was just puzzled for a moment, but before she could

respond, the man said, "Thanks for this closer look. But I have to ask: How much does this wonderful dog weigh?"

"We haven't weighed her recently."

"Would you mind, and would she, do you think, if I carefully picked her up, oh so gently, just to see? I have an almost perfect sense of body weight and can tell you, to the pound. It's all my work with animals. I have a sense now." As he asked, the man was already reaching down to pick her up. "Good dog, Good dog." Shibby began a slight growl low in her throat and seemed to tense her muscles.

Kissa noticed this and said, "I'm sorry. I think it would be best not to, right now. As you may have noticed, I'm sure, she's pregnant, and she's pretty far along. She's actually due quite soon. And she's a little protective of her space right now."

"Oh!" The man stopped right before hefting her up and said, "How wonderful! You'll have a house full of beauties, soon, no doubt." With these words, he reached down and grabbed Shibby's leash, but that very instant, Hasina had done the exact same thing, and as the man looked up quickly, he saw that she was staring into his eyes with a very stern look on her face.

"No," she said with authority, while pulling against the pressure of his tug on the leash. Forgetting his ploy by the suddenness of this reaction, the man actually raised his left hand to slap her hard across the face and take the dog. But before he could even begin his forward motion toward Hasina, Kissa had realized what was happening and had exploded into a kick to his groin that doubled him up. And as he was going down, she had somehow managed to launch another kick, this time to his face. The first one wrenched from him an awful involuntary groan and the second knocked him into the side of the car and down to the ground.

"What are you doing?" Kissa shouted at him. She was so focused on him and on Shibby that she didn't at first notice the other two men jump out of the car from the driver's side door, opposite to them, and come around the car, one in the front, and one in the rear, to take over where their colleague had failed. Shibby started barking loudly and backing up, to the extent that she could.

"Stupid girls! Back off!" The driver shouted, as he actually pulled out a gun, a small revolver that suddenly left his hand as soon as it had appeared, thanks to an unexpected and perfectly placed kick from Hasina. The gun hit the hood of the car with a loud metallic bang and clattered to the ground as the man froze for a moment, stunned at what had just happened. Without a pause, Hasina then reached down and scooped up a stone from the side of the road where she stood, one about the size of a golf ball, though not as spherical. And before the man had a chance to see what was going on, she had thrown it with great strength and absolute precision into his face, smashing the pair of glasses he was wearing and cutting him in the process. Now, with blood dripping into one of his eyes, he bent over and involuntarily shut his eyelids for protection, raising his hands to his face, unable to see anything. He yelled out in pain and shouted, "What have you done to me?" He dropped his face into his hands and caught a faint, blurry glimpse of the hot sticky blood that was now basically blinding him on one side. One more kick from Hasina then crumpled him up and put him fully down, into the dirt, face first.

The other man, coming around the rear of the car, had a British police-style billy club, or truncheon, in his right hand—a piece of wood filled at the core with lead and shaped a bit like a small baseball bat, measuring most a foot long, and an inch and a quarter in diameter. As soon as he got close enough, he swung it viciously at Kissa's head. She ducked his swing and, taking advantage of his momentum, used a combination of moves to get him off balance and force him up against the car, and at that moment, she slammed his hand and wrist through the glass of the back window, breaking both the glass and his wrist—an action that also cut him severely and, of course, forced the club out of his grip. Hasina, meanwhile, had completely knocked out the man with the glasses, and he now lay unconscious on the ground. All the while, Shibby continued barking, but kept at a distance, as if knowing that her first job was to protect her unborn puppies.

As Kissa's opponent desperately removed his hand from the broken window glass, Hasina gave him a roundhouse kick to the stomach that knocked all the wind out of him and collapsed him to the ground as well. Kissa had by then picked up the gun off the road and was holding it on them all. "Bad mistake," she said. "Nobody takes my dog." And, as the first man, the one who had actually grabbed Shibby's leash, started getting up from the ground, she administered one more bone shattering kick to him that turned out his lights for the duration.

"Don't mess with Phi!" Kissa nearly shouted into the face of their one, still conscious, adversary, pointing at him, a man already nearly overcome with the pain in his wrist and hand and stomach. She instantly couldn't believe she had said it, and neither could Hasina.

On hearing the word, that mysteriously powerful word, actually, in one sense, no more than the name of a letter from the Greek alphabet, but known by legend to many in the criminal underworld, the man looked totally shocked and started groaning and saying, "No, no, no, no! Don't kill me! Don't kill me! Please don't kill me. I didn't know!"

"If you ever breathe a word of what you just heard me say, or what just happened, you'll wish you had never been born. I promise you that. Your silence buys your life."

The man had true terror in his eyes as he looked up from the dust in which he now lay, trembling uncontrollably.

"Go get mom," Kissa said to her friend. "I'll shoot anyone who tries to move."

"Are you sure?"

"Yeah, but first, take Shibby's leash and tie up those two guys before they wake back up."

Hasina did as Kissa had asked, and then took off at a medium run back toward Kissa's house, with Shibby right behind her, even without a leash. "Good dog, Shibby."

Within four minutes or so, Hasina was coming back down the street with Hoda. It was not a good day to be a dog thief.

8

Better Late Than Never

There had just been a big laugh around a table at the Blue Camel Café. "We didn't mean to stay this long and interrupt your time together," Walid said with a smile, looking at Leem and Ibrahim. "But it was great to visit for a few minutes and get the chance to meet you, Leem. And the hummus was pretty spectacular! Thank you so much for that, and for the tea. We do have to run, now."

"We're so glad you stopped by," Ibrahim said, as his uncle nodded his agreement.

"It was a great pleasure to meet you, Prince, and you, Mafulla," Leem said. "Please stop by the Cairo Detective Agency at Number Four Luxor Road any time. We're just down the street and around the corner, not far away from here. In fact, The Blue Camel may become our second office."

"We'd love to visit your headquarters," Walid said and stood up, as then did Mafulla, Ibrahim and Leem. They shook hands all around, and Walid said, "Thanks again for the hospitality and the treats."

"You're quite welcome," Leem responded, as Walid turned to leave.

Mafulla said, "Hope to see you guys again soon," and followed his friend out of the café.

"That was fun," Mafulla commented to Walid as soon as they were on the sidewalk. "I like Leem a lot. He seems like a really good guy."

"He sure does," Walid answered. "No surprise there, for the Hadad family. They've had so many prominent family members over the years. I'm really glad that Ibrahim's going to be part of the new agency. He seems excited about it."

"Yeah, he does."

"Hey, look who's coming," Walid said loudly down the sidewalk. "There's far too much riff-raff on this side of town—too many shady characters." He still had Shapur Adi's earlier joking words in his head.

It was Malik and Haji, walking toward the boys and followed close behind by Bafur. "Hey, man!" Malik said, loudly.

"What are you guys up to?"

As they continued to walk up closer, Haji said, "We were just wandering around today, and we met up with Bafur a few minutes ago."

"Yeah, I was in the Sahara," Bafur said.

"The desert?" Mafulla said, joking. "You got back fast!"

"The café, funny man. They've got the best bakery in town, no competition. Walid, the guy who runs it says he knows you."

"Who is it?" Walid asked.

"A guy named Ammon. I didn't get his last name. He said that when I see you I'm supposed to say hi from Ammon."

"Ammon's a great cook! I know him well! He was our main man with a pan on the trip across the desert that brought us here last year! I'll have to go in and say hi to him. I didn't know where he had ended up. No wonder you say the food there is so good!"

"Well," Bafur continued, "I was just having a little afternoon snack and saw these two walking by. I lured them into the shop by promising a couple of bites of utter delight."

"Yeah, he was right about the baked stuff," Malik said. "We sampled a few things and, oh, man—delicate, sweet fruit and nice buttery pastry, a marriage made in heaven."

"I had to order a second time!" Bafur said, raising his hands.

"You didn't have to!" Haji said.

"No! I did!" Bafur said to Walid and Mafulla. "These guys were eating all my stuff! They were ravenous! If I'd known, I would have hidden behind a menu and not called them into the place."

"Ha! Well, I'm glad our friends have been well fed today," Walid said.

"Guess what?" Mafulla said to all of them.

"What?" Haji responded.

"We saw some pretty great Golden Viper and Windstorm type action, earlier today—a little while ago, over near that park not far from the Grand Hotel. You know, the one in the nice neighborhood?"

Malik said, "You did? That's incredible. What was going on?"

"Well, there was this lady walking a dog, and some men came up in a car and tried to steal her pet. And boom, suddenly there were these other guys wearing masks who came out of nowhere and tackled the men and broke up the dog-napping."

"No way!"

"Yeah. And the bad guys ran away. I mean: that seems like classic Viper and Storm stuff."

"Wow, that's pretty awesome. What were you guys doing over there?"

"Just taking one of our walks, actually on the way to my dad's store."

"Did you get a look at the crime fighters, close up?"

"Not close enough. We were actually about a block away when we saw it all happening, and I wanted to go ask for an autograph, but Walid said we should leave them alone."

"You came that close to getting an autograph?"

"Well, we weren't that close, physically. But I could have caught them, afterwards, I think, and asked them. I wish we had taken a camera along with us. Wouldn't it be super cool to have a photograph of the famous masked men?"

"You have a camera?" Haji asked.

"Well, the king has some in the palace, a couple of the really nice smaller Kodak cameras."

"That's very cool," Haji replied.

"Wait. If you guys were walking to the Adi Shop, why were you going through that neighborhood? It's sort of not on the way," Malik asked.

Walid jumped in and said, "We had read about a little girl's dog disappearing, and the newspaper mentioned her neighborhood, and we were out, like Mafulla said, going to his dad's shop to visit a bit, but there was no hurry and we were curious about the girl losing her dog, so we just decided to walk that way. Actually, I don't really know why I wanted to, but I just thought maybe we might see something that would help solve this big mystery about the recent vanishing of pets all over town. It's got to be so distressing for the owners."

"And for the animals," Malik said. "Animals have a lot more sense and intelligence and emotional life than most people give them credit for."

"Yeah. I think you're right," Walid said.

Malik went on, "It must be terrifying for the animals that have been taken from their owners and, let's face it, their families."

"That's a good point," Mafulla said. "I hadn't really thought about it that way before."

"Most people don't," Malik said. "I mean, just think about the philosophers who've believed, on the basis of theory alone, that animals don't have souls or feelings. The famous Descartes was a really bad influence in that way. Set was telling me all about him the other day, you know, a while after Khalid had mentioned him in class."

"Yeah, come to think of it. You're right. I remember Khalid talking about that stuff not long ago. He said that, in order to believe human beings have souls, you don't have to follow Descartes and deny that animals do."

"That's right." Malik nodded.

"We're different from the rest of nature in many ways. We don't have to be different in that way. We can be distinctive in the world and important as human beings without refusing to believe what's completely obvious to anyone who's not blinded by bad theories."

"Absolutely," Malik said.

"And you know, when I thought about it all some more," Walid continued, "I came to a philosophical realization of my own."

"What is it?"

"Well, I don't know for sure, but I tend to think that there's, generally, a lot more mind and soul in the world than we catch sight of. It goes a lot farther out beyond the circle of human beings than we ever might guess. I mean, dogs and cats, sure, and Jabari's monkey Manni, obviously, but I suspect that soul, or at least something like it, can be found even far beyond the normal examples."

"I agree totally. Completely."

"When in doubt," Walid concluded, "we ought to assume some connection with spirit, rather than the opposite."

Malik looked impressed. "Well said, man, and very deep. And remember what else Khalid told us: The great philosophers of the past tended to be really insightful when they were reflecting on practical matters of living, but then, when they got off onto theoretical topics far removed from daily experience and common sense, they often spun out theories that served only to make other philosophers into either disciples or adversaries."

"Yeah, I remember that."

"Khalid said that to count as a great philosopher, you don't have to be right about everything, or even much, you just have to be original and really interesting, interesting enough to get people to notice what you're saying and then either to get excited or mad about it. And that could then spark their own thoughts."

"I didn't realize you were so interested in philosophy," Walid said.

"Well, mainly where it touches on other things I really care about, like animals."

"And people too, sometimes—come on, admit it," Haji said, jokingly.

"Oh. Ok, and people," Malik conceded, with a funny reluctant tone. "I like the practical philosophy stuff about people and animals and life."

"Me, too, man," Walid said, and then added, "I'm really glad we ran into you guys, just for this conversation. I'd been thinking a lot about the recent animal disappearances that are probably almost all thefts, and how strange it is for this to be going on, all of a sudden. And I was feeling really bad about it just from the owners' points of view. But you've brought out a whole new side of the situation that I hadn't seen at all. And this makes me want even more to help do something about it. I mean, all the poor animals and how they must feel—it's really terrible."

"Totally," Malik said. "That's exactly my point."

"Well, the good news is that we just had tea with two guys who are going to help figure out the situation and put a stop to it," Mafulla added.

"Really? Your new friends, the Viper and the Storm?" Haji said.

"Hardee, Har," Mafulla replied.

"I wish," Walid added.

Then Mafulla continued, "Yeah, Tea Time with our good buddies, the Terrific Twosome. No, it was the founder of a new detective agency in town and his assistant."

"Really?"

"Yeah. They have a client whose pets just vanished, and they're going to investigate for her, and also work on the bigger picture of what's going on."

"That's good to hear," Malik said.

"For sure," Bafur offered. "But, who are these detective guys?"

"Remember Ibrahim from Alexandria? The guy we met in a bookstore while we were there?" Walid offered.

"Yeah," Haji said. "He came to the big dinner the king had after the attack on the palace had been put down. I met him. He's a nice guy."

"He's the assistant detective, and his uncle Leem is the head senior investigator. His uncle's just started this new agency."

Haji said, "Is this the Leem Hadad who was Chief of Police for a long time in Alexandria?"

"Yeah, how did you know that?" Walid replied.

"My dad's talked about him now and then and what a great job he always did. That's a pretty famous family, I think."

"For sure, and now two of them have moved to town, and plan to do future famous stuff here," Mafulla said.

"Well, let us know what's going on, if you hear anything," Malik said. "I'd like to be able to help stop this animal kidnapping stuff, and at least I'd love to hear what your friends learn."

"We'll keep you in the loop, man," Walid said. "No problem. Whatever we learn, we'll pass it on."

"Good deal," Haji offered.

"Man, that's an ugly bruise on your arm," Mafulla suddenly said to Haji. "Ouch. What happened?"

"Oh, you know, the rough and tumble of life," Haji replied, looking down at it.

"Yeah, he's covered with bruises and scrapes pretty much most of the time," Malik said. "I may have to become a doctor like my dad just to be able to patch him up on an ongoing basis."

"Hey, man, you get dinged up too," Haji said.

Malik looked at Walid and Mafulla and shrugged and said, "We've been doing some extra workouts recently."

"Oh, yeah?" Walid smiled.

"Yeah. I read a book on the martial arts and then got another one, and we've been trying out some of the stuff described in the books. Some of it's way cool, but learning it, you have to take some pretty big lumps."

"Between football and that, I'm not sure I've had a pain free day in quite a while," Haji said.

"Well, don't kill yourselves," Mafulla said. "We need you guys, and not just limping around like old men."

"Ha! Hey, it's lucky we're not both on crutches already," Haji said with a smile and grimace at once.

"And people wonder what I've got against exercise," Bafur made sure to comment. "I mean: I'm all for moving around and walking and stuff, but what these guys do? It's way too much pain."

"I know what you're talking about, " Mafulla replied.

"Yeah."

"But isn't there an old saying: No pain, no gain?"

"Hey, I've managed to gain plenty without any of the pain," Bafur answered while patting his stomach, and that made them all laugh again.

"Still," Walid said, "A good hard workout is an awesome thing. You sweat, you strain, and the hurt muscles grow."

"Just thinking about it makes me want to take refuge in a nice big warm falafel."

Mafulla and Walid both laughed again at that. "Well, we want you to be healthy, too, my friend," Mafulla said. "But not everyone has to be a super hero Hercules figure."

"Hey, no super heroes here," Malik said. "Just some perpetually sore guys trying to stay fit and ready for anything life might throw our way."

"Try to be careful and don't hurt yourselves the wrong way," Mafulla said, and then made a face, adding, "Jeepers, I sound like my mom."

"Well, it's about time we got that advice from somebody," Haji commented.

"Better late than never," Mafulla concluded.

"Yeah. You're right. Thanks, mom."

"Ha!"

"Well, we've got to go. Good to run into you," Walid said. "See you in class tomorrow."

"Yeah, see you guys," Malik said.

"Take it easy," Haji said.

They parted company for the time being, walking in slightly different directions. Walid and Mafulla were headed back toward the palace. The other boys veered off in the direction of where Bafur lived.

Something had been on Walid's mind since the incident in the park. He said to his friend, "Hey, is it Ok with you if we go by Kissa's house before we go back to the palace?"

"Sure, why?"

"I haven't had a chance to tell her what we know about the animal stuff, I mean, beyond what she saw at the stables yesterday. I want her to be extra careful with Shibby and the new forthcoming … Shibbettes."

"Yeah, you're right," Mafulla said. "I'm fine to go by there on the way back. It's not that far out of the way, we've got time, and it's a deed that needs to be done. But you need to make sure she knows that you had to pull the information out of me—about the puppies, I mean."

"No problem," Walid replied. "I'll make sure she understands that you revealed the secret only under the most severe duress."

"Ok, fine, then. But you don't have to mention that food was involved."

Walid smiled, and then after a second or two, he took a deep breath and said, "You know, that stuff Malik was talking about really got to me. We usually think about how crime affects the victims, but when the victims are not only people but also animals, we can sometimes forget to factor in their feelings, too. I didn't know he was so tuned in to things like that."

"Yeah. I didn't either."

"And it puts an extra perspective on the need to protect Shibby at a time like this."

"It really does."

The boys stepped up the pace a bit in their walk to Kissa's house. On the rest of the way, they had quite a philosophy seminar on animal thoughts, animal feelings, and the issue of animal rights, something that occurred to Walid as an important topic that almost never got talked about. This led to more reflections on the nature of the soul and the mind, and the boys arrived at Kissa's street without even feeling the passage of time, they had been so engrossed in their conversation.

"So, maybe we should ask to speak to Shibby about all this," Mafulla concluded.

"Ha! You're probably right. She's the only one in the family we've never consulted about a pressing philosophical issue, and maybe she holds the key to this one."

"Yeah, but she's probably not talking," Mafulla said. "You know how she is, all regal and calm and aloof but still genuinely loving at the same time—just not much of a chatterbox, if you know what I mean."

"Good point."

"I mean: I've only heard her complain once."

"I'm almost afraid to ask."

"Yeah, she had been having some sort of doggie skin problem and was on a medication and I asked her how it was going, and she just said, '*Rough.*' That's all."

"Ok, first, you're using old material on me. I've heard it. And second, they've been telling that lame joke since the building of the pyramids, if not before."

Mafulla made a gesture with his hands that expressed something like "Oh, well, what can I say?" and he actually replied, "I guess the dogs back then, even long ago and *fur* away, had a hard time, too."

"Ugh."

"Hey, I'd continue in this jocular vein, but instead I'll *paws*, because, otherwise, you'd think of me as too much of a *wag*."

"Oh. Gee."

By that point, they were right in front of Kissa's place. Walid walked up to the door and knocked. Several seconds later, Hoda opened the door and said, "What a surprise! Two of my very favorite young men! Come in, please."

"Thanks, Hoda," Walid said.

"To what do we owe the honor of your visit today?"

"I was just hoping to talk to Kissa for a second."

"She's in the kitchen, having a foot massage and icing her other foot and ankle a bit," Hoda explained.

"Really?"

"Go on back. I have to get something from the other part of the house. I'm sure she won't mind receiving visitors, mid-foot-rub."

"Ok. Thanks." The boys walked into the kitchen area. There sat Kissa with her right foot in some ice water that was in a large pot. And she was rubbing her other foot with both hands.

"Hi," Walid said.

"Oh! What a surprise! Hi to you, sweet thing and prince of the realm," Kissa replied. "And to you, too, Mafulla, man among men. Please excuse me if I don't stand to greet my most welcome visitors."

Mafulla laughed and said, "What's up with your foot?"

"A small overuse injury," Kissa said.

"Too much walking, or running, or dancing around the house?"

"No, just the result of taking down a bunch of criminals with some very nice, well-placed kicks, but I got a little carried away and overdid it a touch."

"What?" Walid exclaimed. "Are you kidding? What happened?"

"Oh, no, I'm serious. But nothing to talk about," Kissa said, playing with her friends a bit. "Just normal girl stuff."

"No. You have to tell us!" Walid said.

"Ok, but it's no big deal."

"So, what happened?" Mafulla added.

"Well, Hassi and I were out for a walk with Shibby and three guys came up in a car and tried to take the Shibs away from me.

"Oh, no!"

"And one of them pulled a gun."

"What?"

"Yeah. And another one had a small club and Hassi and I had to put them out of commission real fast."

"Did you get hurt?"

"No, actually, I just love to ice my feet now and then for fun. It's a great way to stay cool in hot weather. You should try it."

"Ok, I'm sorry. I mean, other than the sore feet, are you Ok? And is Hasina Ok?" As Walid asked this, Mafulla was just standing there with his mouth open, looking shocked.

"Where's Hasina?" Mafulla finally spoke again.

"Hassi's fine. She's home doing homework. She actually took out the guy with the gun."

"What?" Mafulla was truly stunned to hear all this. "What did she do?"

"He pulled the gun on us, and she sort of Windstorm-style-kicked it out of his hand. Bang! It hit the car hood and fell to the ground."

"Really?" Now, Mafulla had a big smile on his face. "I mean, really?"

"Yes, indeedy."

"All right!"

"Then, before I knew what was happening, she'd picked up a good size rock, I mean a nice big one, and threw it into the guy's face like she was going to take his head off."

"Wow."

"It smashed his glasses and he was bleeding and yelling that he couldn't see."

"Really?"

"And he was all bent over at that point and she decided that one good kick deserves another. And the next thing I knew, he was face down in the dirt, unable to move. And she didn't even get a sore foot."

"Nice," Mafulla said.

"What else happened?" Walid asked, still a little off balance about all this.

"Oh, I took out the other two guys."

"The other two?"

"Yeah, hence the sore foot, or I should say feet, but one's a little worse than the other."

Mafulla just said, "Amazing."

And Walid asked, "Were there any more guns?"

"No but one guy tried to take me down with a billy club—you know, those wooden clubs the police sometimes use? This one had a metal rod in it and it would have really hurt."

"He didn't get you?"

Kissa smiled. "Dear, dear, sweet Walid, you should have no worries in that particular department. If I can dodge a bullet now and then, I can deal with some caveman swinging a club at me."

"What happened?"

"Let's just say he didn't last long. And I had already dealt with his friend, a guy who grabbed Shibby's leash and tried to take her away from me after pretending to be a veterinarian and lover of animals."

"Oh man, I came here today to warn you about animal thieves and possible dog-nappers on the loose in town. We actually saw three guys earlier today across town try to steal a lady's golden Saluki."

"You did?"

"Yeah. We were walking over to the marketplace to visit Maful-la's parents at the shop and took a different route—you know how our adventures go—and in this park we saw a lady and her dog and a car pulled up and two guys got out to grab the dog."

"What color car?"

"Dirty dark blue."

"That's the same car."

"Really?"

"Yeah. So, did they get the dog?"

"No, and this is where it gets super strange. We were a block or so away and were about to go all Viper and Storm on the guys as soon as we saw what they were trying to do. But we were waiting to see how it played out and what direction we should take in breaking it up, and then, suddenly, two other guys come running from the opposite direction, wearing masks like we do."

"What?"

"Yeah, two other masked guys, and they tackled the thieves. And the car had a third guy as driver waiting for them to get the dog, and when he saw that, he took off. And the other two guys went running for their lives. And the unknown masked men let them go."

"So they got away."

"Yeah, the masked guys let them get away. But, they stopped the crime. And I was coming to warn you to watch out for Shibby."

"Better late than never, I guess," Kissa said with a smile. "But that's quite a story."

"Yep."

"Who do you think the masked guys were? Obviously, they're Viper and Storm copycats, but who are they, really?"

"We have no clue," Mafulla said. "I wanted to chase them, but Walid got me to cool it."

"Yeah, but enough about us," Walid interjected. "Your stuff just happened, I mean, this afternoon?"

"Yes, indeedy, just a normal afternoon around the El-Bay house. We were a couple of blocks away, Hassi and I, walking Shibby on her leash, heading for that open area where she likes to sniff around, and, you know, commune with nature and play."

"So, how did the guys approach you?"

"They drove up in the dark blue dirty car, the three of them."

"I can't believe it was likely the same guys," Mafulla said.

"Yeah, it's almost got to be the same three you saw earlier. You can go look at the car if you want. It's at the main police station."

"Really?"

"Yeah."

"How'd it get there?" Walid was still interested in hearing more of the story, and so was Mafulla.

"Well, when they pulled up to us, there was no other traffic or anyone else around. One guy rolled down his window and started asking me about Shibby, saying that he was writing a book about Salukis and that she was so beautiful and could he have a closer look at her distinctive features. And he was really polite and I, like an idiot, totally believed him and said 'Ok, fine,' and he got out, and then all the fun began, pretty quickly."

"What happened to the guys after it was all over?"

"Oh, I got their gun and held it on them, and Hassi tied them up while two of them were unconscious."

"I'm really, really proud of you two," Mafulla said, interrupting. "You two are awesome."

"Yeah, me too," Walid said.

"Yes, of course you too," Mafulla said, "You're also totally awesome, which goes without saying. But you don't have to remind us now—remember, we know you're the prince and the Viper."

That made Kissa laugh.

"That's not what I meant, and you know it," Walid protested in mock irritation.

"Just trying to lighten the mood," Mafulla explained.

Walid then looked back at Kissa and said, "So, what happened once they were tied up?"

"Oh, so Hassi came back here and got mom, and they both rejoined me at the scene of the almost-crime, and mom asked the guy who was conscious what they were doing and why they were doing it."

"She did?"

"Yep."

"And what did the guy say?"

"He sort of made another major, major mistake at that point, a big one, and called mom a name and spit at her."

"Oh, man," Mafulla said and grimaced. "Death wish to the max."

"Yeah," Kissa agreed. "So she repeated the question, really slowly. 'Why … Did … You … Do … This?' And he said something just mean and nasty that I won't repeat."

"Ouch," Mafulla said. "Seriously bad judgment."

"She decided at that point to relocate herself onto the guy's left wrist, and let's just say that, very quickly, there was what we can call a break in the case."

Mafulla and Walid both laughed and Walid said, "Really?"

"Yeah, but first, I promise, you have never heard anybody howl like that. I think she did a little twist on it. Then, it looked like she mentally zapped him."

"Yeah?"

"And he sort of screamed like a big baby. And when he could breathe again and speak—which we knew because he started begging for mercy—she politely asked again and he answered all her questions."

"Wow."

"Yeah. Strange. He suddenly seemed eager to answer questions. He actually got pretty talkative. And then we loaded them up in their dirty, stinky smelly car, and dropped them at the police station for further conversation."

"The car was bad on the inside?"

"It was horrible. I don't see how those guys could ride around in it, if they have any sense of smell at all."

"I wonder why?"

"I think they had maybe carried around a lot of scared animals in there recently. Plus, their own personal hygiene wasn't the best."

"Oh. Geez," Mafulla said.

Walid quickly asked: "Well, what did you find out—I mean, from what the guy told you?"

Kissa said, "It's pretty interesting … and really strange."

9

The Real and the Ideal

Class had gone well, as usual. Khalid had brought up the newspaper article about animal disappearances and possible abductions around town, and the boys as a result had gotten into a very lively and fruitful discussion about animals and people, and such things as mind, body, spirit, emotions, and even the nature of intelligence. Khalid was surprised at the direction the discussion took, but it was in part because of the spontaneous conversation that Walid and Mafulla had experienced with Malik and Haji the previous day. The flow of ideas in class, as a result, had been incredibly wide ranging. Everyone had contributed. Walid knew that Malik and Haji would both have interesting things to say, but some comments by Set and Jabari and Bafur really surprised him. This was a very philosophical group.

The most perplexing side discussion, one that sort of became the focal topic after a few minutes, was about the nature and origin of the mind. Khalid was pretty well informed about the classic philosophical discussion of this subject, from at least Plato on. Philosophers could be cited whose opinions were all over the map. There were dualists, who believe that mind is something completely different from matter or any physical stuff, and that the universe contains both these two distinct substances—a dualism.

And there was, of course, also a contrasting philosophical view known as monism, declaring that, deep down, there is only one kind of fundamental stuff in reality.

The monistic view that the boys had likely heard of, Khalid said, was called materialism, the belief that the entire nature of everything is material, or physical, with mind just being an aspect of physical stuff, or else an illusion brought about by the impressive neural activity of the brain. He pointed out that there's also a different and common use of the term 'materialism' or 'materialistic' to refer to a lifestyle or person who values obsessively, or even only, physical things and luxury. But he made it clear that this was not what he was talking about now in reference to the mind and the body. He actually said they were going to be talking about metaphysics, and not shallow people. That's how he put it.

Then, to the surprise of pretty much all the boys, who thought that those were the only options available on this issue, there was also, according to Khalid, a group of monists called idealists, who turned it all around and believed that everything in existence is either a mind or an idea in a mind—a mental thing. These philosophers hold that materiality or physicality is in some sense the illusion. They don't deny that what we call physical things exist—trees and rocks and houses. They deny only that these things have an ultimate reality or form of existence distinct from, and independent of, mind. To them, the world and everything in it is just a play of minds and ideas in minds. It's all just mental. And also, Khalid said, the debate between these three different positions has gone on for a very long time: Dualism, Materialism, and Idealism.

Jabari interrupted at this point to say that, so far as he could tell, Bafur was a different kind of dualist, dividing ultimate reality into two other categories of basic stuff—foodstuff and nonfood stuff, or what's edible, and what's of no matter. And this of course got a laugh. But Bafur protested that his fundamental metaphysical distinction, as he put it, is really between the empty and the full—very much like the difference between the evil and the good, he explained. That also got a laugh, even from Khalid, and with Bafur smiling, they continued on.

Malik said that he thought an idealist was just a person with ideals, or high principles and values that they lived by. Khalid explained that what Malik was referring to was simply another, different use of the word, more common, but not the precise philosophical usage they were discussing. He added that idealism in this common sense was usually opposed to, or juxtaposed with, realism—which also, in common sense lingo, meant sometimes having to compromise your highest ideals in order to get anything good done at all. But, in the strictest philosophical sense, when the nature of mind or the ultimate metaphysical constitution of reality was the focal point of discussion, Khalid explained that idealism was the view that only minds and ideas in minds exist. He also mentioned that, in examining this distinction, they were working in ontology, or the theory of being—of what exists.

Set then asked whether anyone is actually an idealist, in this metaphysical sense of the word. He wanted to know whether it was any more than just a logically possible theoretical position and something that anyone actually believed. He said that he personally knew both dualists and materialists, but wasn't aware of ever having met an idealist. Khalid smiled and nodded and pulled a notebook from the top drawer of his desk. He said he had recently recorded a passage in his idea journal, something that he had come across in a newspaper interview. It was a statement by an eminent British scientist named James Jeans, a very accomplished man who was devoting his life to some of the most profound scientific questions.

Khalid turned to the middle of the notebook, flipped back and forth a page or two, scanning what was there, and then looked up at the boys, and down again at the page, and prepared to read. But first he said, "These are the words of physicist James Jeans, and here we begin the passage." And he then shifted into something almost like a British accent and a formal academic delivery as he read.

"I incline to the idealistic theory that consciousness is fundamental, and that the material universe is derivative from consciousness, not consciousness from the material universe. In general the universe seems to me nearer to a great thought than to a great machine."

Their teacher then looked up from the notebook as he placed it on his desk. "Now, this is an important living scientist who is candidly giving his personal philosophical opinion. He sees the universe as more like a great thought than a great machine. Can he prove what he's saying by a use of the scientific method that he employs throughout his work in physics? No. And he doesn't pretend otherwise. He says here that he 'inclines to' the idealistic theory, and he uses a phrase like 'seems to me,' to signal that he's giving us his best judgment, his refined intuition, you might say—his most careful opinion as a man who has reflected deeply on these issues. But he doesn't present this as a well-established and certified result of normal scientific methods. And he's clearly giving voice to the idealistic point of view. He would, then, be a good example of a philosophical idealist."

Set looked puzzled. He said, "But you can touch a desk or a dog and you can't touch a thought. How can things be made out of thoughts? How can they even result from a thought or a mind that's somehow more 'fundamental,' in the word the scientist used, than they are?" Set was really trying to wrap his mind around this new idea.

"Well, Jeans is not the first ever to suggest such a thing," Khalid explained. "There have been other philosophers through the centuries who have given mind a pride of place in the overall economy of being."

"Can you give another example?" Mafulla asked.

"Sure thing. There was a philosopher in the early eighteenth century, Bishop George Berkeley, and even though his name is pronounced by the Brits as 'Barkly,' it's spelled 'B-e-r-k-e-l-e-y'—and there's a city in America named after him, with a different, Americanized pronunciation of the name, where a great university sits."

"That's confusing enough," Bafur commented.

"Yes," Khalid agreed, and continued. "Anyway, such details aside, Berkeley believed that only two kinds of things ultimately and truly exist: What he called spirits and ideas. Spirits are active beings, or minds, like you and I in our innermost nature, entities that can produce or perceive ideas, or sensations, or various forms of mental content. Spirits exist, and ideas produced or perceived by those spirits exist. Everything else is somehow the result or appearance or consequence of these two things. There is no separate or distinct or independent physical or material world apart from spirits and ideas."

"So, according to this guy," Walid said, "Your desk is either a mind or an idea in a mind."

"Or an array, or set of ideas."

"Well, it's clearly not a mind."

"Clearly," Khalid agreed.

"So your desk is an array of ideas."

"Yes."

"In some mind." Walid added.

"Yes."

"In all our minds?" Mafulla asked.

"Right now, perhaps, yes."

"But how?" Set asked. "Isn't a desk a fine example of an independent physical object, existing in the room regardless of the existence or activity, at the present moment, of any mind or spirit?"

"Well, try to get access to the desk. You can look at it, but as a result of that, you have just mental sensations, in this case, visual ideas or images."

"But you can touch it and feel that it's a hard, solid physical thing."

"Yes. You can go touch it. But then you have only more sensations, in this case, tactile sensations, as of hardness and smoothness, and extension. And again, these sensations are not themselves physical objects but are ideas in your mind. Berkeley thought that all the things we call physical are just like this—ideas in minds."

"He really believed that?"

"Yes. Or at least, we think so, in our minds—as a result of his writings." Khalid smiled, and continued. "Now, you might say, 'Yes, yes, but there is a thing behind all the sensations that causes the sensations and that is the physical object we properly call a desk.' And Berkeley would say, 'How do you know this, since you can access only your own sensations?' His point is simple. We can know, first hand, only our own ideas, or impressions, or sensations and nothing other than those sensations, or perceptions. But the things around us, surely, we can know; therefore, the things around us must be bundles of sensations, ideas only."

"Jeepers." Set expressed the puzzlement everyone was now feeling.

The boys sat, absorbing all this, and Khalid went on. "But here's a question. What do you think happens when we all leave the room and none of us is here to perceive the sensations of the desk? Does the desk cease to exist? Do I turn off the lights, close the door, and metaphysically destroy the furniture, at least for the evening?"

"Wow, did Berkeley think of that?" Jabari was impressed with this.

"Yes."

"Well," Set said, "What did he say?"

"When none of us is around to perceive the ideas constituting the desk, as well as when we are, it is perceived, and thus maintained in existence, by the one infinite mind that is ever-producing and ever-perceiving, the one and only mind that never leaves, and never sleeps."

"God," Malik said.

"Yes, God."

"So, on this view," Walid observed, "God is not just the creator of all, who launched everything into existence a long time ago, but God is the constant, or continuous, creator of all the things that we think of as parts of the physical or material universe—and he does it all with thought."

"Correct."

"Wow," Haji said out loud. "People actually come up with stuff like this?"

"Yes, and then their neighbors call them philosophers, and even sometimes worse names than that." Khalid smiled and some of the boys laughed.

"So are we all just ideas in the mind of God?" Bafur was weighing in, heavily, with this one.

"No way. God doesn't have any bad ideas," Mafulla said with a straight face.

"Hey!" Bafur protested with a pretended indignation.

"I wasn't thinking of you, my good friend. God has plenty of big ideas."

"There you go," Bafur said. "But who were you thinking about, then? Ari Falma?"

"Oh! Well. Wow. That's a challenge. I guess God had a good idea, created a … good person, and the spirit—the person—because of its freedom, turned bad."

Khalid said, "But then according to a person like Berkeley, God isn't thinking about Ari Falma any more, at least not in the same way, and perhaps we shouldn't either."

"But really," Bafur said, "how can we be minds and ideas at the same time?"

"Well," Khalid said, in answer to Bafur, "we're spirits. We're minds. And so we have our own form of existence. We're not dependent in quite the same way as a desk or notebook on the active and creative perception of some other mind. But then, every believer in God who credits the existence of all creation to some form of divine causation will still ascribe our existence as well, in some way, to God. We're not just passive ideas in his mind, on Berkeley's view. We are ourselves created in the image of God. We are indeed minds, beings that are ourselves productive of ideas and perceptive of ideas. But we still somehow depend for our original creation and current continuity, as ongoing souls, on the divine mind. I'm not completely clear on that fine point in Berkeley's views, and I'm really not sure he ever made it thoroughly explicit. I have to admit that it's been many years since I read his work carefully."

"So, for Berkeley, minds exist, really and fully exist." Bafur repeated, to make sure he understood.

"Yes, and they, or we, are fundamentally involved in the existence of other things, though those other things are never wholly dependent on us, except perhaps for the fleeting thoughts that we entertain privately in our own inner, personal mental realm. And even those things, if they're dependent on us, and we're dependent on God, are themselves then also dependent on God and not just us."

"So, do you and Hoda walk around the house talking about this stuff?" Mafulla had to ask.

"No. Not usually. Next question?"

The boys sat quietly for a few seconds, still soaking this all in. It was pretty complicated stuff to get a grip on right away. Then Khalid summed it up, by saying: "Ok. There's been a great debate, raging throughout the centuries, between materialism, dualism, and idealism. No one can prove to all sincere seekers which view is right. But surely, there is a truth, a single fundamental truth, regarding such a question. Nonetheless, as another great philosopher, the very difficult to read Immanuel Kant, said years after Berkeley's work, it's the human condition that we can ask far more questions than we can answer. And yet we carry on, courageously, surrounded by the unknown, the unproved, and even the unsuspected."

"Kant said that?" Set was keen to catch every detail here.

"Yeah, except for that last point, which was sort of my own personal flourish," Khalid replied.

"Wow."

"Yes, wow, indeed."

"We can ask a lot more questions than we can answer."

"Correct."

"Wow," Bafur said. "And here's even something crazier. We can cook a lot more food than we can eat." Several of the boys smiled at this.

Mafulla said, "In your case, that is hard to get my head around."

Walid was convinced that there has to be a true answer to the question of dualism-materialism-idealism, however hard it might be to establish, or prove, philosophically. But he was also willing to entertain the possibility, the one that Khalid had just alluded to, that on this issue, it might just be actually impossible to prove what the truth is—at least, to the complete satisfaction of all interested parties. And maybe, he thought, just maybe there's a reason for that.

This itself was a new idea to most of the boys, the thought that truth and proof could diverge in this way. It had never occurred to many of them that there could ever be a truth that had no proof. But Khalid pointed out that for any proof, you need to start somewhere, with premises or prior beliefs that were themselves accepted for some reason, or on some basis, other than proof, or at least derived from something accepted without proof, or we could never get around to proving anything at all. You have to start somewhere. When they discussed it later, Walid and Mafulla both felt pretty comfortable with the idea, given many of the things that they had talked over with the king at various times. But on every occasion when such topics came up, they still felt a twinge of wonder at the mystery of it all. No matter how certain we feel about our beliefs, there are always things we can't certify or verify with a proof that all reasonable people would agree to as proof indeed.

By the time the school day was over, the whole class was convinced that proof was maybe one of the most overrated things in the world. And yet, at the same time, they also came away with a conviction that reason, in all its various manifestations and workings, is still vital, and absolutely crucial for human life in nearly every context. There was a complexity of issues here that could be hard for a novice to get his head around. But they were clearly talking about some important things, and these were likely things they could indeed make more progress on with dedicated persistence.

And that's true of most things in life. Persistence pays off. Dedicated, committed effort can accomplish things that at first look impossible, and that otherwise would be impossible. Too many people simply give up when they don't get quick results. But questions are always easier than answers, and careful, creative persistence alone will get us the answers we seek.

Maybe the mind, whatever it's made of, is a little bit like a muscle in one sense: The more you use it and exhaust it, the stronger it eventually grows. And then it can accomplish more than you would guess.

"So, I have a question," Mafulla said to Walid as they walked out of class and started down the hallway in the direction of the palace living quarters."

"Ok. But first, I have to warn you that I can't promise answers, not after that discussion just now," Walid said.

"Oh, this one's easy."

"Ok, shoot."

"Who's going to be at the birthday dinner tonight?"

"You mean, mentally *and* physically?"

"Ah. Yes, of course. That's my question, if you don't *mind*."

"Not at all! It's a question whose answer will surely *matter*."

"Nice retort."

"Thank you. But, of course, we still must be in the realm of the most esoteric theoretical philosophy, despite any superficial appearances to the contrary, because I have absolutely no good answer to your question—no proof, no evidence, and no intuition, even."

"Come on."

"Ok, I told Uncle Ali that just a small party with family, including you of course, would be nice. But if you happen to have other plans already, I'll understand. I'm most keenly interested in the attendance of those who haven't yet given me their presents, and need a special occasion for so doing."

"Oh, I see how it is," Mafulla said. "The economy of the birthday party rears its ugly head—the commercial side of age, the main concern of pirates and certain mercenary birthday boys: Loot. Booty. Treasure."

"No, no, no. I just happen to believe that there are people in my family, and my immediate circle, who are by nature and deep disposition great givers, like you. And I love to provide them with the opportunity for the personal satisfaction that freely and generously giving brings with it. It's really nothing more than pure altruism on my part. I'm concerned to allow any appropriate giving to take place on this occasion simply for the self-fulfillment of the givers, you see."

"Oh, yes, I see, for certain. Yes, I do," Mafulla said with a big smile. And then he added, "Well, you can consider me already immensely gratified and utterly fulfilled."

Walid laughed and said, "I do. I do. But don't worry. You're still invited."

"Good, because I'd hate for all the new cologne I just purchased to go to waste."

"You don't have to use it all tonight, you know."

"No, but an appreciable amount is always … appreciated."

"A barely detectable amount might be vastly preferable."

"I haven't heard any complaints from the ladies."

"Because they can't get close enough for you to hear what they say."

"Ha, ha. There's no need for jealously, my friend. You're the prince, and you can afford the benefits of cologne, too."

"I've always made do by simply standing down-wind of you."

"Yes, I know, in terms of wit, wisdom, and that manly aroma that ties it all together."

Walid just shook his head and laughed. And then, as they passed Kular's office, the butler heard them and stuck his head out the door. "Dinner tonight in two hours and fifty-five minutes."

"So exact!" Mafulla said.

"Actually it's two hours and fifty-six and a half minutes, and diminishing by the second, but I rounded down to create more of a sense of urgency, because I don't want you to be late."

Walid laughed and said, "Thanks, Kular! Very funny! We'll be there." Then he turned to Mafulla and said, "Well, assuming it will take us twenty minutes to freshen up and change for the dinner, we have approximately two hours and thirty-five and a half minutes to do something. What do you want to do?"

"Two hours and thirty-five minutes flat, at this point, most likely, but who's counting? I happen to know that Kissa and Hasina are going to be studying in the library this afternoon, or at least for the next hour."

"Really? Why didn't you say anything earlier?"

"Well, first of all, you didn't ask. Second, they won't be there that long. Third, they do have work to do. Fourth, I wanted to bring most of my school stuff back to the room, anyway. And fifth, I knew if I told you before we got back here, you'd want to go straight there, and I need to use the bathroom and then do a little eau de Mafulla aroma refreshment and get rid of these heavy books."

"Can we skip the inevitable, forthcoming reasons six through twelve, or whatever?" Walid asked.

"Yeah, Ok. We can do that for the sake of time management. Let's just take one book, travel light, and go back to see them. I know they both have an assignment and are doing some serious research, but we can hang out and maybe talk for a few minutes, I'm sure. They'll be glad to see the birthday boy. Even though it really isn't until tomorrow, we all start celebrating early around here, as for example, with tonight's dinner."

"Hey, the early bird gets the ..."

"Loot. Booty. Treasure."

"I was going to say, Opportunity to Spread Fulfillment."

"Yeah, that."

"Ok, then. I'll stop in to my room while you do what you do. Come get me when you smell good. But if that never actually happens, I'm going in ten minutes, tops."

"All right, man-with-a-down-to-the-wire-schedule, and a faulty olfactory sense. I'll most likely see you in eight. Check your Reverso."

It ended up being more like twelve minutes, but still within Walid's window of toleration, so when Mafulla stuck his head in the door and said, "Ok! Let's go," the prince was almost asleep, having something like a half-nap, sprawled out on his bed.

"Geez, what's it been, an hour?"

"No, silly: twelve minutes, five seconds. Six. Seven. Eight ..."

"Ok, stop, stop, I get it. Teach a man to count, and he can

become oddly fixated. But then again, maybe I should have just left you here counting, and when I got back, you'd probably still be sounding the time like a human alarm."

"I'm what in advanced watchmaking circles they call a minute repeater."

"No, you're something I'm sure is completely unknown in advanced watchmaking circles—a second repeater."

"Either way, you can rely on me for your precision time-keeping needs."

"Yeah, so let's go. It's time."

"I *second* that," Mafulla responded with a grin, and Walid with a groan.

They walked out the door and briskly down the hall, then down another one, across the palace and straight to the main library. Entering, they saw Set in the far corner and Kissa and Hasina at the first table in the room. "Hey, guys," Walid whispered to the girls. He put down his book on the table, across from Kissa, and said, "Be right back," also in his Best Library Whisper, as Mafulla slid into a chair.

The prince walked back to where Set was bent over a book and said, "Hey, man. What's up?"

"Oh, hi, Walid. I'm just doing some extra reading."

"What's the book?"

Set turned it over so that Walid could see the cover. The prince read the title aloud: "*Three Dialogues Between Hylas and Philonous.* By our new friend, George Berkeley."

"Yeah, it's probably his most popular book," Set replied. "Or that's what I just read in the encyclopedia a few minutes ago. Hylas and Philonous are these two characters. Hylas is a materialist, and Philonous, whose name in Greek means, 'lover of mind' is a metaphysical idealist, representing the author, Berkeley."

"So you really got into this stuff in class today."

"Yeah, big time."

"How's the book?"

"So far, so good. The language is a little eighteenth century, but I basically understand what I'm reading, which is always a good start."

"Cool. Keep me posted if you learn something we didn't cover today in class."

"I will."

"Good. Idealism is wild and interesting stuff."

"For sure. Will do."

"Ok, I'm going to go sit and talk with an ideal young lady right about now."

"Ha. I would too, if I were you."

Walid smiled at that and said, "See you later on." He then walked back to the table where the girls were working and sat down next to Kissa.

He leaned over and whispered, "You know, tomorrow, I become a much older man."

Kissa just smiled and shook her head.

"I've heard that young ladies often find themselves very attracted to older men."

"Stop it!" Kissa whispered. "Almost-much-older Prince of Silliness and Distraction, I have to work."

"Ok, Ok, but seriously, I just wanted to say that I'm still pretty amazed at what you told me about the dog-nappers—you know, what the guy said under questioning by your mom."

"Yeah, I think we need to look into it more and do something about it soon," Kissa whispered back.

"I agree. But what?"

"You're the older and wiser man. You tell me."

"Oh, very clever. You turned that one back on me pretty quickly."

"Well, I may be a mere youth, but I'm sharp."

"No doubt about that."

"I think I'm going to talk to mom about what the guy said, and then maybe we can make a plan."

"Sounds good."

From somewhere else in the large room, beyond a high row of bookshelves, they both suddenly heard the universal library sound of "Shhh!"

10

Something to Remember

Walid opened the door and stopped in his tracks, completely stunned.

All at once, there was a huge burst of laughter and hoots and shouts and applause as all the students saw him and Mafulla standing there in the doorway wearing their new sunglasses, which Mafulla had insisted they put on right outside the door since, as he said, "Your parents haven't seen them yet and they'll get a big kick out of how we look with them. You know how much your dad likes American movies and movie stars." Mafulla actually just wanted to make the big entrance and get exactly the reaction they instantly produced.

Then, as soon as everyone else remembered what they were supposed to do, more than two-dozen voices burst into the song, "Happy Birthday to you, Happy Birthday to you, Happy Birthday dear Walid ... ('Leading man of the silver screen,' someone added, in the pause) Happy Birthday to you!" They all sang with gusto, stretching out the last note and then bursting again into applause and cheers.

Walid laughed and bowed to the room and that created a second wave of acclamation and cheers. "Thank you," he said. "Thank you all very much! What a surprise!"

"Welcome to your party!" Mafulla exclaimed.

"Thank you for this!" Walid said loudly, to basically everyone.

"Thanks for being born!" Somebody in the room responded.

"And for coming all the way here from Hollywood for the occasion," someone else yelled out and got lots of laughs and cheers again.

Walid grinned—half proud, half embarrassed, and still completely surprised. And he said to the room of friendly faces, "I appreciate you all being here! Now, please return to your merriment and I'll mingle and hopefully say hi to everyone." Then, turning to Mafulla, Walid now added, in a quieter voice, "Who are all these people?"

"Funny man!" Mafulla gestured around grandly as he said, "The girls' class did the decorations, with Kissa in charge of art and music; the kitchen cooked the vast array of treats, and the boys carried in all the heavy presents—the main loot." While he was explaining this, Bafur came up to pat Walid on the back, and Ara and Khata moved toward him to personally wish him a great next twelve months.

"Then, this time next year, let's definitely do this again!" Ara said. "I love a good party."

"Great! I just got here. What's been going on?"

"Lots!" Khata said.

Then Ara added, "We had to come early to surprise you, so we've been pretty much eating and drinking the kitchen's best concoctions and having fun nonstop until they told us to be quiet a couple of minutes ago. Now we can be noisy again."

"Good start on that," Walid replied.

Malik at that point walked up and said, "Nice party, boss."

"Thanks, man. I'm glad you could come."

"Me, too. The food's great. Here, have some." He held out a cup to Walid and a small plate. "I brought you some stuff I thought you might like. I knew everybody would want to say hi, and it would probably take you, like, twenty minutes or more to get over to the table with the food. So, this is a start."

"Oh, man, that was nice of you. I appreciate it, big time," Walid said.

Kissa and Hasina had borrowed a palace record player and had on some American jazz that was really nice background music for the festivities. And the big room sure looked festive, too. There were colorful decorations everywhere—the number '14' in various wild fonts, scripts, alphabets and languages, along with drawings of camels, and the desert, and a football, here and there, and there was even a huge, amazing, super realistic painting of Walid's Reverso watch that someone had done, complete with the black strap. There were also posters and streamers and handmade lanterns hung around the room—all items that had been created just for the party. The place looked like they were in the middle of a carnival, and not a formal palace room.

Somebody took hold of Walid's arm from behind and before he knew it, Kissa was giving him a little peck on the back of his left jaw near his ear, the tiniest little quick kiss imaginable, and she almost whispered, "Happy, Happy Birthday."

That produced on his face the biggest smile ever, and he said, "Thanks, K." and gave her the fastest possible little hug. "This is all incredible. I love the music and the decorations. And I just recently heard from a reliable source that you were in charge of both."

"Yep. That's me. I was an eager volunteer organizer and director and I loved doing it. But all the girls helped. We had a pre-party party at my house yesterday just to make the decorations. Everybody worked hard and we had lots of fun together doing it. I really wanted this to be a special occasion for you, something to remember, since it's the first birthday of yours that I've been able to be a part of."

Walid looked surprised. He said, "You're right. I hadn't even thought of that—wow, very nice."

"It's hard to believe that we met for the first time less than a year ago, that day in the marketplace. And you were such a gentleman!"

"I remember that as vividly as if it had just happened a week ago! I was so afraid I'd never see you again! I was all panicked about it until I had a bag thrown over my head and got shoved into a box and had something else a little more immediate to be panicked about."

"I remember the whole crazy story! First, we meet, and then the kidnappers arrive."

"And then Mafulla came into the picture."

"What a day that was!"

"But none of it distracted me from really missing you again a short time later. I mean, when Maffie and I got out of our little prison room at The Kidnapper's Hotel, I started trying to figure out, right away, how I could find you in this huge city with so many people. It seemed impossible and I was worried, but I wasn't going to give up."

Kissa smiled. "You do say the sweetest things!" Hasina walked up just then and Kissa turned to her. "Hassi, I'd like you to meet the single sweetest man having a birthday today at any spot on the surface of the earth."

"Hello, sweetest birthday boy!" Hasina said. "And I don't think you'll be single forever. So don't worry. But I'm pleased to meet you, once again!" Kissa made a funny face and her friend just laughed.

Across the room, there was suddenly a new form of music. The record had finished playing, and something else had started up.

"What's that?" Walid asked.

"Jabari!" Hasina said.

"Doing what?"

"Playing a ukulele!"

"A what?"

"A musical instrument that's like a teeny tiny guitar from the islands of Hawaii in the middle of the Pacific Ocean, and it's called a ukulele."

"Ha! You never know what Jabari's going to show up with! One day a monkey, the next day a ukulele."

Mafulla came back over just in time to hear Walid say that and suggested, "Let's go watch him play!"

The boys led Hasina and Kissa over across the room, closer

to where Jabari was sitting, surrounded by Bafur, Set, Bakat, and Kit. He was strumming chords and singing a typically silly Jabari song that he was probably making up as he went along. He then strummed hard and dramatically to a crescendo finish and everybody laughed and clapped, including the prince. Jabari looked over at him with a huge smile and said, "How do you like my flying flea?"

"Your what?"

"My flying flea! That's what the word 'ukulele' means in Hawaiian!"

"Ha!" Walid and Mafulla both laughed out loud.

Mafulla said, "Well it sounds like we've finally got a really good potential new nickname for you, my friend—The Flying Flea!"

Whereupon, Jabari started strumming and singing:

"Come over here and see
Egypt's Flying Flea!
For musical enlightenment
You can depend on me!
Strum! Strum!"

And, of course, he sang the words, 'Strum! Strum!' as he did his two big concluding strums to this new little spontaneous, extemporaneous song.

Everyone clapped again and laughed. And of course Mafulla had to say, "Oh so witty! A ukulele ditty!" And that made Jabari laugh.

"Yeah, I like to call it 'The Brief Ballad of the Flying Flea.' I think a small bug deserves a short song, but with a big title."

"Indeed." Mafulla turned to Walid and said, "I was hoping you'd have a memorable party, and this is certainly something to remember."

"Yeah, very true," Walid replied.

Right then, and at first out of the corner of his eye, the prince saw on the far side of the room that Mafulla's parents and his little brother and sister had just walked in through another door with his own parents and the king. Even Mafulla's uncle Reela was with them. Walid said to Mafulla, "Hey, family in the back!" and led the way through the crowd of students and other friends to where they were now standing. As he walked across the room, he greeted Paki and Amon and Omari and Masoon and Hamid, who had been hanging back against the wall, not wanting to intrude on the students. Naqid was even there, and so was Darwishi. Walid couldn't believe it. He thanked everyone for coming as he passed, and several of the older attendees patted him on the back or the arm with a personal birthday wish.

Sasha, of course, Mafulla's little sister, ran to the prince and practically jumped up into his arms. He gave her five kisses right away. She had just celebrated her own fifth birthday and loved a party. Sammi, Mafulla's little brother, smiled broadly at Walid and said, "Hi, Prince! Happy Birthday! Sorry we're late! It was mom!"

"Oh, Walid, I'm so sorry we were delayed," Shamilar said, looking happy and flustered at the same time. "I do apologize! We had a couple of mishaps with some of the party clothing and it took longer than we realized to get it all fixed and then make our way here to the palace! But better late than never! So, Happy Birthday, young man!"

"Thank you! And don't worry for a second about the time of your arrival! It's great to have a second wave of birthday guests show up." Walid then greeted Shapur and Reela and hugged his own mom and dad and bowed to the king.

Many birthday greetings and felicitations were spoken among the family group, and several of the late guests set presents down on a table in the back with all the others that were already there. Mafulla hugged everyone and joked about Walid's advanced age. Then he offered to go get anyone some punch and treats, or else to lead the way to the table and "plow through all the competition," as he put it.

They decided they would descend on the food tables together, but the king and Reela hung back to talk some more. Walid noticed that when everyone else walked off, they seemed to get more serious in their conversation. Reela nodded several times, and the king was making some hand gestures. It was all pleasant enough looking, but also, at the same time, what he saw suggested that something important was being discussed, if only for a few moments. Everywhere else, there was laughter and joking and more ukulele entertainment.

The party went on in all its liveliness for another hour, or even an hour and a half. Everyone had such fun, there was so much good food and drink, and the palace probably had never heard as much general, raucous merriment as was echoing down the halls from the party room. The cheer was the loudest yet when the big official birthday cake was brought out with candles blazing, and Walid made a silent wish, during which all the girls looked at Kissa, and then he blew out the fourteen little flames with one huge breath. He then instantly commandeered a knife and like a pastry chef began to slice into the huge confection, laying pieces onto small plates and inviting the guests to help themselves. Everybody grabbed a cake plate immediately and picked up tea or coffee or juice to accompany it. The real palace chefs had outdone themselves on this one. All through the room, people were exclaiming about how excellent it was, how moist and richly flavorful, without being too sweet.

After fifteen minutes or so, there was a loud clinking on a glass and everyone realized it was King Ali getting their attention, which of course they gave him right away. He beamed with a big smile as he said, "Thank you all so much for coming to this informal dinner and party. I hope you stuffed yourselves on the goodies that were brought out from the kitchen, that you enjoyed all the fabulous decorations … and music … and that each of you has had a wonderful time in celebration of our Walid's fourteenth birthday." At this, there was another loud cheer all around the room.

He smiled and nodded and lifted up his hand. And when the noise settled, he went on. "I hate to break up the merriment, but we don't want to keep you out too late, since tomorrow is a work day for some of you and a school day for most of you, and we need to give you plenty of time this evening for either rest or preparation, and in particular, for any school work that needs doing. I would not want to get into trouble with Khalid or Hoda! So, please, grab any last second snack you'd like, and within the next few minutes, allow one of the palace butlers to escort you out. Your presence here has been a marvelous birthday gift to our prince, and a great joy to us all!"

At that, everyone applauded, and there were many utterances of the words, "Thank you." There was a lively buzz all around the room as people began to say their goodbyes, and as Bafur fixed one more heaping plate of food, "to go," as he insisted to everyone who commented on it in a joking way, and "for later," as he said to Mafulla, who in response looked at the plate, and then at his watch with a skeptical face. But even small Jabari grabbed a few extra goodies, as did many others, while at the same time preparing to make their departure for the evening.

The king came over to Walid and with a smile said, "I'd love for you and Mafulla to come visit for a few minutes when everyone's left."

"Yes, Your Majesty, absolutely. Where would you like us to meet you?"

"My sitting room would be nice. I have something interesting to share with you."

"Good! Sounds great. I'll say goodbye to Mafulla's family and mom and dad, and some of the older guests, and then come down as soon as everyone's gone."

"That should work nicely," the king replied. "I'll say my own good-nights to Shapur, Shamilar, and Reela, as well as to the little ones, and then take my leave, right away."

Within another fifteen minutes, Walid and Mafulla were in Kular's office. The butler seemed to be in high spirits, but then, he most often did. He said, "It was a very nice party, Prince Walid! I was in and out a lot during the evening, making sure that all the food and drink was arriving as scheduled. But I did also have a chance to greet some of the guests and hear their gushes of appreciation. Everyone seemed to have a marvelous time."

"Yes, they did, and you sure worked hard to help make it happen!"

"Thank you. It was my honor. I wish I could take credit for the decorations and the music, which were both marvelous!"

"Kissa did a great job, for sure," Walid said. "And Jabari, on his uke!"

"Yes, indeed! I even had to dance around a bit with that special music, but in a low key way, of course."

"I bet you're a great dancer."

"I certainly do enjoy it. Oh, I almost forgot. I should tell you that I've made sure all the presents will be brought shortly to your room."

"That's very considerate. Thanks!"

"It's a great pleasure and a joy to contribute in any small way to your birthday celebration."

"I really appreciate it. I know everyone had fun."

"Yes, I could see that throughout the evening! I did love that ukulele music. I may have to ask your friend Jabari to teach me how it's done."

"I bet you'd be good at it!"

"It would certainly be fun to try! But for now, let me tell the king you're here."

"Sure. Thanks."

He opened the door, said a few words, and looking back at the boys, announced, "His Majesty will see you now. Please, go on in."

As Walid walked in, followed by Mafulla, the king stood up from his sofa and clapped his hands three times, giving the birthday boy one more round of applause, making Walid laugh. Then Ali said, "I think this was a joyous occasion—a time of gladness for all. And that was most appropriate. I am, in particular, extraordinarily glad that you were born on the day you were, in the little village across the kingdom, fourteen years ago, as of tomorrow, at dawn."

Walid smiled and said, "Thank you so much. I couldn't possibly be more glad that I came into the world with an uncle like you waiting for me."

"Sit, boys, sit and let's talk for just a few minutes."

Walid and Mafulla moved over to their favorite chairs, and after the king had sat back down, they made themselves comfortable as well.

"First, congratulations on what a great job you both did to help host the party, one of the best this palace has ever seen, I'm sure."

"Thanks, Your Majesty, for letting it happen here and for coming yourself. I know what a busy time it's been for you recently."

"I wouldn't have missed it for anything."

"I was so surprised! I thought it was just going to be a small gathering of family."

"There was a groundswell of popular sentiment. Everyone wanted to be there," the king replied. "And it was clearly a great time for all. We certainly need a break now and then, and there's nothing quite like a good party to restore the soul in a distinctive way."

"That's for sure," Mafulla responded.

"So, Your Majesty, what other surprises do you have for us this evening?" Walid asked as he adjusted his position in the armchair.

"I wanted to share with you both something that I was able to read for the first time yesterday, rather late in the evening."

"Something in the news?" Walid asked.

"Something about the animal disappearances?" Mafulla offered.

"No, no, nothing about contemporary goings-on in quite that sense; rather, something more philosophical and cosmic—actually, something metaphysical."

"Really?" Walid replied.

"Yes."

"You have my interest, to the max," Walid responded.

"Mine, too," Mafulla said.

"Good. Now, you'll remember that I've been using the deciphering keys in the little red book that Ibrahim gave us in order to read parts of *The Book of Phi* that were written in code—a code that we couldn't otherwise break, without its help."

"Yes," Walid said. "I knew you had been at work on that."

"Already, the keys had allowed us to interpret passages that had not likely been read in many decades, even perhaps in generations. And you know that there were still some passages that even a diligent straightforward application of the keys could not directly decipher."

"I remember hearing you say that," Walid responded.

"Now, I've finally been able to decode and translate a crucial and most fascinating section."

"What's it about?"

"The big picture for everything we already know and for the many remarkable things that we can do, variously among us."

"Wow," Mafulla said. "I'm excited to hear about this."

"Yes. Wow is a good response. I have indeed been wowed by what I've read. I've long had an intuition concerning the world in which we live. And I was able to confirm it, in a way, by what I read last night in The Book of Phi. It's a perspective, I believe, that's of vital importance for us to know and to keep in mind. It assures us that we aren't strangers here in an ultimately alien world, but that we're rather fully at home in our fundamental existence, in the deepest possible sense. And this perspective will also explain, or at least help to account for, our Phi abilities, skills, and experiences that seem to go so far beyond what can be made sense of from a purely physical point of view, or even an expanded commonsense perspective."

"What do you mean, Uncle?"

The king leaned back on his sofa and said, "Let's specify that by the physical cosmos we'll mean the entire array, in all its unimaginable vastness, of the planets, suns, particles, fields, entities, and energies studied by physics, astronomy, and all the physical sciences like biology and chemistry. We can allow that, in addition to our sun, there are trillions of suns, in billions of galaxies, and there are planets and asteroids circling these suns beyond numbering. Plus, there may be even more entities in the vastness of space than we have yet identified. But in addition, let's also even allow something else that's in a distinctive way almost beyond any form of imagining: specifically, that there are possibly even more universes than ours, perhaps as many more as the planets in our universe outnumber the ones in our small solar system, and even beyond that. And against that immense backdrop, here's the metaphysical news. As enormous beyond thought and emotion that this staggering cosmic expanse might be, it stands in a formal relation to what you might call the closest level of nonphysical realities that undergird and overarch it, and this relation can be spelled out in your favorite famous mathematical ratio, the one that's expressed by the numbers 1 to 1.618."

"No way," Mafulla couldn't help but say.

"Yes. And then, there may be even more levels yet, and we have no idea how many, but they are each standing to the next one out in the same ratio of magnitude."

"Phi? The golden ratio?"

"Yes."

"How do you know?"

"We're told in The Book of Phi, in the passage that I was able to read last night for the first time, that the non-material, non-physical plane of existence closest to our own dimension so far exceeds the material, physical plane in extent and density of being that it goes more than half again as much beyond the full expanse of our largest, most enormously vast cosmic home on the physical plane. And then that repeats, on up through further dimensional scales."

"But how can this be?" Walid jumped in with a sense of astonishment.

"*How* is often a hard question. As you know, a *what* often comes before a *how*."

"But. Why is this?"

"Why not?" the king replied. "If we believe that the cosmic array in all its magnitude arises somehow from a spiritual source, and that there's a spiritual domain of some sort closely akin to this source, a domain that has also come to be as a result of the immense creativity of the source, then, why not expect a domain more closely aligned to that source to be greater than the physical realm? Wouldn't that make sense in somewhat the way that a cause in this world can be greater than its effect in the extensiveness and expanse of its being, or its robustness of reality?"

Walid said, "You mean, the way I can be a cause of something and be greater than the thing I cause? Like, I can be a cause of hummus going onto a piece of pita, and I'm greater or more extensive in my being, as an intelligent agent or doer, as a human being, than the small covered piece of pita?"

"Yes. And that was quite a creative analogy."

"Thanks."

Then Mafulla said, "By the spiritual domain, do you mean God?"

"Actually, at this point, I'm not yet even attempting to speak much of the ultimate source itself, of God, a perfect being of infinite depth and expansiveness and responsible for everything else that exists. I'm now referring, instead, to the closest created domain beyond the physical, and to our ultimate home dimension, that of the spiritual, whose inventory would be parsed in terms of souls or spirits, and modes and methods of conscious being and knowledge and action and care—connections and causes that are behind the scenes of the entire physical expanse and are ever interpenetrating it in many ways we can't even begin to imagine. And then, there are, apparently, levels above levels from even this."

"I'm holding on by my intellectual fingernails here," Mafulla responded.

"Yes. It's a big idea. In his great and famous play, *Hamlet*, the profound author William Shakespeare wrote a passage in Act One, Scene Five, where he has the prince of Denmark say to a friend, 'There are more things in heaven and earth, Horatio, than are dreamt of in your philosophy.' What I'm telling you could be understood as one way of spelling out such a vision."

Walid jumped back in. "But how could someone know something so big, deep, extensive, and so far beyond our experience? I mean—this is a huge and very specific claim. How could anyone originally authoring The Book of Phi ever know, in particular, that there is such a layered relationship of being and that the golden ratio describes it?"

"Indeed. That's a legitimate and natural question. But then again, how can we know much that we know of the most fundamental matters, and even of everyday surprising things? Mafulla often knows things in a way that we can't fully explain. So do you, Walid, when you listen carefully to the inner voice. So do I. And you know how often this seems to be true with Hasina and Kissa and Hoda and Layla. You've seen it in Paki. Remember the occasion when he revealed to you that you're Phi, and he showed that he knew exactly what was happening some distance away with Masoon's assault on the kidnappers who had taken Shamilar, Sammi, and Sasha. How did he know that? How could he know that? Well, he's Phi."

"Ok. I get that—sort of. But this is a different kind of thing to claim to know, of a much bigger magnitude. It's a different sort of knowledge."

"And you may worry," the king went on. "How does that work? What's the means? What could be the mode or mechanism or type of conveyance for such knowledge? The answer is simple: We don't know. All we can say is that it's somehow apparently connected with the nature of the reality that stands to our physical world in a relationship delineated across levels by Phi, the golden ratio. That's what The Book of Phi now tells us. How do we know then that we can trust this source on such a grand claim? Well, whatever else it's told us before now that we've been able to act on and check out and possibly confirm has indeed been confirmed, no matter how strange or wild it initially might have seemed. The book has well established an immense degree of credibility and authority beyond our full understanding."

"That's certainly true," Walid said. "But again, this is strange on a totally different scale."

"Yes, but, ultimately, strange is strange. We live amid mysteries."

"I suppose that's true." Walid still looked a bit puzzled, but at the same time, more accepting of this new claim. "So, this means that the famous ratio found all through nature and in human art, the ratio that gives us a sense of beauty and proportion, possibly does so because it reflects what may be the deepest relationships of proportion in all of the created realm, across both physical and spiritual domains?"

"Yes, so it now seems."

"But, what does The Book of Phi want us to do with such an idea, with this sort of wild information?" Mafulla asked.

"That's a good question. It doesn't say, at least not in the same passage. There are still things yet to be deciphered, and I suspect that there's much yet to be revealed."

"Oh, man, that's kind of spooky," Mafulla commented.

"Well, remember that everything already revealed to us has been of tremendous help to us, and has assisted in times of great need."

"That's true," Mafulla conceded. "But still."

"There's nothing to be feared in these claims," the king emphasized. "Awe, however, is appropriate, in the sense of wonder. These are holy things, in the root etymology, or meaning, of the word—set apart from the mundane matters of our daily attention, but somehow undergirding them all and breaking through, now and then in powerful ways."

Walid said, "I guess one thing this does is to remind us that as thinking, spiritual beings, we're at home in a world that ultimately supports us with resources far beyond what we normally would imagine."

"Yes. And that should build your confidence in times of challenge. We have immense resources to draw upon, and that's very good news. But there is, I'm sure, indeed much yet to be revealed, and that's also something to remember. Anything we need will be given to us to have and to know, I believe, when the time for it has fully come."

II

A Class and a Mission

"So, what do you think about that stuff the king told us last night?" Mafulla took a sip of his tea, as he and Walid sat in the breakfast room for their morning meal before school.

"I don't know quite what to think," Walid answered. "I mean—it's pretty strange and sort of … overwhelming."

"Yeah. That's for sure."

"It's a huge Big Picture for life in the world, and it's really wild about the golden ratio, but I haven't yet even started to figure out what its impact on our day-to-day lives and thoughts and feelings should be."

"One thing that hit me as soon as I woke up this morning," Mafulla offered, "is what the king said about there being maybe a lot more resources to draw on than we ever imagined."

"Yeah," Walid said. "But what do you think that really means?"

"It's like, clearly, when I realize that something's happening to somebody I care about, at a distance, I'm tapping into some sort of unusual resource for information. When you and I dodged those sniper bullets outside during the palace attack, we were in touch with some sort of resource for knowledge and action. When we zap somebody Hoda-style, there are resources we're drawing on, or plugging into, or something, beyond our physical bodies."

"Yeah, Ok. That all makes sense."

"And it's all been totally hazy to me up until now, but with what the king told us last night, I've started to feel a bit more confident in the resources available to us, you know, as if I understand a little more about maybe what it is that we're in contact with—a whole different realm from the obvious physical dimension that seems so clearly to define life in the world. And somehow, what we draw on goes beyond the physical, and yet, at the same time, is in another sense intermeshed with the physical—connected and sort of merged together. And we don't usually see that at all. But, as the king often says, things aren't always, or even usually, what they at first seem."

"That's a good way of putting it," Walid conceded. "But I just had a thought."

"What?"

"If there are all these really vast resources that you and I and the king and Masoon and Hoda and all our Phi friends tap into, then could there be a bad guy, or group of bad guys, who also learn how to tap into that?"

"Like Farouk al-Khoum?"

"Well, yeah, like Farouk, except a lot more."

"What do you mean?"

"Remember, Farouk just had a very limited amount of Phi training before he dropped out, and we had no reason to think he worked hard after that cultivating any of his natural Phi abilities. He just focused on making lots of money and piling up worldly power, and that was pretty much a full time job."

"Good point."

"So, what if there are guys like Farouk out there in the world who are not just obsessed with money or regular worldly power, but are extremely focused on developing the deeper power of their minds and the resources that their minds can tap into? And what if they have nothing like what we would consider good intentions at all?"

"There could be such people, I guess," Mafulla replied. "And that would really be scary."

"Yeah."

"I hadn't had that thought at all, until just now."

"Well, remember the two powers, what the king sometimes

calls The Double Power Principle: Anything that has power for good has equal and corresponding power for ill; it's normally up to us how we use it."

Mafulla looked down at his food and said, "So, if there is this huge realm of layers or dimensions of spiritual stuff and resources and, actually, other-worldly power that's available to us for good, it's also, at least in principle, available to people who are up to no good at all."

"Maybe so," Walid said. "At least, that's my concern."

"It's probably worth being concerned about," Mafulla said. "We should ask the king what he thinks."

"Yeah, that's a good idea," Walid replied.

"Well, enough worry about super-powered villains. Let's finish up here and get ready for class," Mafulla said.

"Ok, you're right. Enough worry for now—or, concern, to be more precise."

"Yeah, concern. That's what I meant. But, there's one thing."

"What?"

"It just occurred to me this morning how important it is that we often get a new piece of information or a new insight, or something comes into our lives, just before we're going to need to know it or use it. The king sort of hinted at that last night."

"Ok."

"So, I'm just saying that I hope we're not sometime soon going to come up against some super villains who are super busy plugging into the 1.618 bigger immensity next door, and maybe even beyond that, and doing it really well, for their own violent and nefarious purposes."

Walid sighed. "Good thing to hope. And, I agree, it is a little troubling that things seem to come our way right before something big happens and we need to know whatever it is that we just found out."

"Yeah. So, we should really be on the lookout," Mafulla concluded.

Walid said, "We need at least a minor version of the Triple Double awareness going forward."

"That sounds like good advice—even wise. See what comes with advanced age? You're now an official source of wisdom."

"Ha! Just remember the wisdom of The Triple Double, my friend."

"Yes. Prepare, perceive; anticipate, avoid; concentrate, and control. I'll remember. And, oh, by the way, speaking of remembering, I almost forgot something else important."

"What?"

"Official Happy Birthday today."

"Oh, right, thanks. Probably half the people at the party think my birthday was yesterday just because that's when the party was. But, yeah, I was born in the early morning hours on this date. And when I woke up this morning, I said to myself, 'Year Fourteen—Done and official! Launching Year Fifteen: Let's make it a good one.' Nothing like a little inner birthday cheerleading."

"Why do we call you fourteen when you're actually living in your fifteenth year?"

"I think it's because you're thought to be as old as the highest number of years you've actually succeeded in living through completely. I just completed year fourteen, so I'm fourteen. I'm working on fifteen but I just started it and haven't completed it, yet. So I'm officially just fourteen completed years old."

"Ok. I got it. That makes sense. And, speaking of getting things, you, my friend, got some really nice presents in celebration of those fourteen completed years."

"That's for sure."

"We can use some of them on the trip."

"Yeah, I thought the same thing."

"You know, we need to get our stuff together this week, pretty soon, and maybe we should start after school today."

"You're right. It's hard to believe the trip's coming up so soon. And I'm really excited about it."

"Me too, except I have to admit that sometimes I wonder if I'm going to like the desert."

"I think you will. It's interesting and beautiful in a very strange way."

"Yeah, Ok. Good. I hope you're right. I mean, you probably are. After all, you've actually been there."

"Yep."

Mafulla let out a deep breath and said, "I know this may sound weird, but I'm sort of afraid that way out there in the middle of nowhere, surrounded by vast expanses of nothing, I'm going to feel really small and exposed, and … vulnerable."

"Just remember the 1.618. You're big, you're strong, and you're plugged in. No matter how big the desert seems, you're part of something a lot bigger. Plus, you've got me, and a bunch of fellow Phi, watching your back. And, you know, you are the Windstorm."

"Ok, Amigo. You're right."

"I'm totally right."

"I needed to be reminded. I guess I'm as ready as I can be. We can conquer the sand together. And maybe this is the only reason we needed the new information, to build my confidence for the trip."

"Yeah, maybe so. That would be nice." Walid got up, and took his plate and cup over to the side table where they always left their dishes. And Mafulla followed his lead.

The boys then went back to their rooms and got to some last minute reading they both needed to do for class. For a couple of weeks, they had been studying the Greek and Roman gods, with a little bit of world mythology from other cultures thrown in, as well. Now, they were reading a wild Anglo Saxon epic about an ancient warrior named Beowulf.

Later in the morning, class got off to a good start. Khalid asked Set to give them the basics of the Beowulf story they had read. He looked around the room and answered, "Ok. There was a king who was having trouble. A monster had invaded his big fancy hall for feasting and drinking, where all the top soldiers hung out, and the monster had killed some of his men. And then the monster came back again. And it kept happening. Nobody could stop this powerful creature. There was no one nearly strong enough. But when Beowulf, a great warrior in a country not far away, heard about the problem, he gathered his men and sailed there to help out."

"Why did he do that?"

"I think he just liked doing great things, things nobody else could do."

"Ok. So. What happened?"

"He got there to the other kingdom and to the fancy building they feasted and partied in, and he spent the night with the king's men there in the drinking hall, and the monster showed up again and he fought the thing and it was a huge battle, and Beowulf eventually tore off the monster's arm and, as a result, the fearsome creature died."

"Yes. Then what happened?"

"So, then not long after that, the monster's mother shows up for revenge, and she's even bigger and scarier and Beowulf has to follow her to an underwater cavern or den or something to fight her, and she almost gets him good when a famous sword he's using breaks, but eventually he wins again, like he always has. Then, there's a big celebration and the king of the country is really grateful and Beowulf gets a lot of praise and rewards and treasure and goes home."

"Then, what takes place?"

"Oh. Ok. And then in later years, he becomes a king himself, and at some point down the road, he ventures out to fight a dragon, and now he's a little too old to do it all by himself, but he keeps trying to do exactly that, and he gets killed."

"Good summary," Khalid said. "Why, then, did Beowulf die in the end? Mafulla?"

"Because everyone dies in the end?" Mafulla made a face.

"Well, let's be a little more specific to the story."

"Ok. He had gotten a lot older and I think he wasn't as strong as when he was young, but it was like he couldn't accept that. He couldn't let in that important element of self-knowledge, and so he kept trying to do everything by himself, the old way. And that particular dragon was too big to go up against alone."

"But he was a king then. Didn't he have an army?"

"Yeah, but he treated them like his audience, spectators for his personal accomplishments. It was like he was always saying, 'You guys stand over here and watch this!' It doesn't seem like he ever really trained them to be like him—brave and strong and skilled and persistent."

"Why would he not do that?"

"Maybe habit," Set said. "He had always fought his battles alone and had always won. We all have habits."

Then Walid added, "Maybe he needed to prove something, or, I mean, he felt like he needed to prove something to other people and maybe to himself."

"And so that resulted in what?"

"His untimely death," Bafur answered. "I mean, there was this one guy who at the end rushed in to try to help him, one young guy, who was maybe destined to be the next Beowulf, or something. But he came in too late, and when he tried to get the other soldiers to help out, they were too afraid."

"Because they hadn't been trained," Malik said.

Then Haji said, "Yeah, Beowulf was so great in so many ways, but I think he was too much in his own head, having to prove himself and show his greatness and not looking at what he really should be doing for his friends and his people."

Malik jumped in and said, "Can you imagine what would have happened to the dragon if Beowulf over the years had trained all his soldiers to be more like him? Can you imagine a whole army of guys like Beowulf?"

"Yeah, really," Jabari said. "That would have been awesome."

"But instead," Khalid said, "We see one guy unable to change with the times, always doing things the same way, and either unable or unwilling to teach others to become great themselves and collaborate with him, to partner up with him, for the greater good of them all."

Mafulla thought for a second and said, "His outrageous personal strength was really the cause of his ultimate weakness, and so really sort of responsible for his downfall."

"How so?" Jabari asked.

"Well, he was so great and strong as a young man that he got used to fighting solo and winning, and that blinded him to the need to have partners in combat, and that's what set him up for failure, ultimately."

"Good point," Khalid said. "And you know what's really, really strange in the story?"

The boys just looked at him in anticipation. He paused for a couple more seconds and then said, "Each of the two monsters he fought was so powerful that Beowulf, with all his strength, was barely able to defeat them, one on one. He did it, but just barely. If they had come at him and faced him together, in partnership, and not just one at a time, the outcome might have been really different."

"Oh, man!" Mafulla exclaimed, "So, Beowulf ended up making the same mistake that the monsters had made!"

"Yes, and he could have learned from their example, but he didn't."

"You can end up repeating the same mistakes that you see others make, without even realizing it," Mafulla added.

"Wow, that's something to think about," Malik said.

"Yeah," Walid and Mafulla simultaneously replied.

The discussion went on like this for a bit longer and class, generally, was great. All the boys were engaged in the topics, and that made the time fly, like it always does when you're really absorbed in whatever you're doing. There's nothing worse than being bored and disengaged, and having to wait for time to drag itself over the finish line at a pace slower than anything you could ever possibly have imagined. Yet, too many people fail to realize they can do something about that and avoid the slow and painful experience altogether.

The way to make friends with time, and engage it as your ally, is to be fully alive, maximally engaged, and totally all-out participating in whatever's going on, throwing yourself into your activities with a wholehearted focus and passion. Then, you get outside your own head and you enter the version of eternity that's readily available on earth, at any moment—time seems to move so fast that it actually vanishes, and you're on to the next challenge or enjoyment before you realize what's happening. It's a total rush. And, ironically, you never feel rushed.

By the end of class, the boys were full of new ideas and insights. And they wanted to keep talking. But the first order of business was going to be kicking a ball around outside for a few minutes, a new one that Set had brought to school with him. And after enjoying that for a while, Walid and Mafulla both caught sight of Kissa and Hasina walking by. They broke off from the game and went to talk to the girls for five or ten minutes. And then, as they walked back toward the residential area, they reviewed some of the Beowulf insights.

"I guess that's why the king always seems to want to involve groups of Phi in most missions, even if he or Masoon could single-handedly get the job done," Mafulla said.

"Yeah, and even allowing us to do our crime fighter stuff," Walid said in a lower voice, "he's helping to prepare us for the bigger stuff we might have to face in the future."

"Can you imagine if Beowulf's guys had gotten the training that Masoon's giving us?" Mafulla said, "Boom! No dragon."

"Yeah, for sure," Walid agreed.

"Or, at least, a dragon with a really massive headache so bad he'd have to lie down and bother no one any more."

Walid laughed. "Yeah."

"Hey, don't we need to buy some new water canteens for the trip?"

"Yeah. Maybe so."

"I've seen the standard military ones, and there are some others I've heard about that are supposed to be much better. I don't want to cut off our Beowulf insights, but for some reason that just hit me. Canteens."

"Well, good," Walid replied. "We'll need two individual canteens each. And I agree. I don't like the normal army ones, either."

"Where do we get the good ones?" Mafulla asked.

"The king told me that I could use a shop about eight or ten blocks away from the palace, toward the marketplace, and they would charge anything we needed to the palace account. It's sort of a big general store that has most travel needs," he said. "I bet they have those canteens. I might even have heard somebody say so."

"Good. You want to go there this afternoon and get started?"

"Yeah, why not?"

Just up ahead, they saw Naqid coming down the staircase that they were about to take to get upstairs to the residential area.

"Naqid! What's new?" Walid said in greeting.

"Too much, Prince Walid! Too much!"

"Why? What's going on?"

"Well, for one thing, we're following up on several leads that developed when the local police questioned the men who attacked Kissa and Hasina in the attempted dog theft."

"Really?"

"Yes, it seems that the local network of people involved in all this is broader than we had imagined."

"That's interesting. Is there any progress yet?"

"Nothing really to report, but we're on it. We were going to leave this rash of animal disappearances to the police, as you might guess, since there was nothing going on associated with them that seemed to impinge at all on the palace, but then there was the attempt to steal palace horses, and when those men attacked Kissa and Hasina, things definitely changed and we got fully focused on it."

"I'm glad you're involved, Naqid."

"Thanks, Your Highness. Also, I'm working on some assignments for the top soldiers and palace guards to accompany you on the trip across the kingdom that's coming up. In consultation with Masoon, we're putting together a crack security team."

"That's good."

"What are you up to this afternoon?"

"Shopping for a few supplies for the trip, a couple of things that the king isn't already supplying us."

"That should be fun."

"I hope so! Well, we'll let you get back to what you were doing. Thanks for the chat," Walid said.

Naqid bowed and said, "Always a pleasure!" and bid them a good day.

Within ten minutes they had dumped their books, gotten a quick snack from Kular, and were headed back down the stairs toward the side door of the palace. Walid was going to lead the way, using the directions the king had provided. He knew he had seen the store before, but he still needed a reminder of exactly where it was.

They left the side palace gate and were barely five minutes away when, about a block and a half ahead of them, they could see that a man and woman had just come out of a large building whose sign said, "First Bank," and were making their way down its outer steps and onto the sidewalk. While he and Mafulla were talking, Walid happen to notice the couple then turned left off the main thoroughfare and onto a side street, a smaller shopping street that soon became a residential avenue. The man and woman were both laughing at something the man had said, and even their gait indicated a sense of happiness. They stopped for a moment so that he could show her something in a big envelope he was carrying. Walid smiled in response, without realizing it—in a sense, participating at a distance in their apparent joy.

But something suddenly changed. "Trouble," he said, feeling an instant reversal of emotions.

"What?" Mafulla asked.

"Up ahead, the man and woman—they just came out of that bank and are happy about something, but look at those two men heading toward them. They seem a little rough."

"Yeah, I see. You're right. Reversos?"

"Yeah."

Both boys flipped their watchcases over with that distinctive Reverso click. And they pulled out the wristbands they always carried for covering the watches, whenever needed, and put them on, as always, without looking, as they continued to walk forward and track the unfolding drama.

"We're magnets for trouble," Mafulla said, as they now picked up their pace.

Walid responded, "Trouble is the magnet for us. I bet the man got money from the bank for something the two of them want and these guys have been watching for someone they thought would make an easy target."

"Sand masks," Mafulla reminded the prince.

"Oh, yeah." They both quickly pulled out their masks and put them on, drawing closer to what was about to happen.

"Triple Double."

Now the two sketchy men came up to the couple, within five feet of them. At a distance still, Walid could barely hear one of them say, "Give me your envelope, right now!"

The lady shrieked and the other bad guy said, "Shut up! Shut up or die!"

The man holding the envelope said, "No! This is what we're going to use to get married and start our new life!"

One of the thugs said, "Not now you won't. Give it to us, or else you'll have no life!"

Walid and Mafulla, pretending not to notice all this, were continuing to walk along the main road until they got to the intersection. And at that exact moment, they both broke into a full, all-out run toward the thieves. One of them heard the running and turned just in time to see Walid a half second before he leaped into a flying tackle, which took the man down to the ground and knocked the wind out of him. The other man had a knife out, and so as he ran up, Mafulla did one of his well-practiced kicks to take it out of the guy's grip. The kick did its job, but the man was still standing and Mafulla was off balance, so the guy surprisingly did his own instant retaliatory kick into Mafulla's back. Walid was on the ground wrestling with the first man and punching him near various vulnerable spots, but not yet landing the crucial blow to end the fight.

"Stop now or we shoot!" Another voice came booming out over the grunts and groans of the action underway. A warning shot was fired and everyone froze. Walid looked up to see two other men, just as scruffy as the ones they had jumped, holding guns pointed at him and Mafulla. The boys didn't move for a second more and the criminals they had attacked took that moment to break free, retreating to a defensive position beside their now apparent comrades. "Eyes to the ground, all of you!" The voice yelled out. "You two love birds, on your knees! Put the envelope on the ground beside you! Eyes down!"

"No, please," the innocent man, the one holding the money, said. "Don't harm my fiancée or take our money! Leave us alone, I beg you!" The young woman began quietly to cry.

"No talking! On your knees now! We should shoot you all, right here."

The man barking out orders suddenly yelled, "Ow! What's this?" and then groaned in pain. "Oh! My head!" Walid glanced up and saw him grabbing at his forehead with his free, left hand. But the man's gun was still pointed at him and the other man's revolver was still aimed directly at Mafulla. Their next move was not obvious, except to continue to use their minds to pour on the pain, and then try it with the other guy.

The gunman they had not yet targeted said, in a voice of great concern, "What is it? What's wrong, Hassan?"

"Don't say my name, idiot! Are you going to give them my address, too? Ow! What's happening to my head? Oh!"

"What? What's going on?" the other asked, almost pleading with confusion.

"I don't know, just … just shoot the ones who attacked us and take the … OW! Oh! Oh!" At this point the man who was being given the full Hoda treatment—as the boys liked to call is—fell slowly to his knees. His three partners were all standing there looking at him in a state of sudden shock and confusion. One moved toward him to try to offer help with whatever was happening. The others were frozen in place, uncomprehending.

Suddenly, loud yells of a different sort echoed off the building behind the Viper and the Storm, who were still looking down at that point and trying to decide what action to take next. The immediate sounds of bodies colliding and grunts and then yells confused them completely, and they looked up just in time to see two other men now taking the second gunman to the ground, face first. At that, both the boys leaped up and launched a full attack into the original two thieves.

Walid and Mafulla were both like machines, relentlessly pummeling the big men with fists and feet. The criminals tried to fight back, but it was to no avail. The Golden Viper broke one man's jaw, then his left arm. He bent the man over in pain and, as this adversary was going down, slammed his knee into his face and came down hard with both fists on the back of his head. Something cracked loudly and the overwhelmed criminal fell into the dirt without any further efforts at resistance.

The other man had tried to choke Windstorm, and that was a big mistake. Within two seconds, he was on his back and Stormie was stomping his upper stomach and solar plexus, ridding him of air and rendering his body and mind so totally full of pain he couldn't think or move any more at all, except to roll back and forth, groaning.

With their original opponents down, they now looked quickly over at the others, the new men who had produced the guns. To their total surprise, those guys were both face down at this point and being tied up, their revolvers now five or six feet away in the sand. The two individuals who had taken them to the ground were also wearing sand masks. "Ok," one of them said, "This guy's tight."

"Mine, too," the other replied.

They looked like the masked men from the park. Walid said, "Wait. Who are you guys?"

One of them turned around and, in a voice of total shock, said, "What?"

"Who are you guys?"

"Walid? Is that you?" Then he faced the Viper's partner and after a second's pause, said, "Mafulla?"

12

A League of Their Own

There was a moment of shocked silence all around, as the questions "Walid? Is that you?" and "Mafulla?" hung precariously, and shockingly, almost ominously, in the air.

"Who's … asking? Walid replied with great concern. His heart started pounding. His mind went from totally blank to racing a thousand miles a second. He was trying to decide what the best way might be to handle this situation, as it had now developed. Should he tell the truth, and give away his secret identity to someone he may not know, but who just helped him out of a tight spot and knows, or at least recognizes, him, or somehow, his voice? Or does he stick with the crime fighter identity and refuse to answer the personal question? But this guy can't be a stranger—he recognized Mafulla as well. These two, they're both about the same height and weight as me, he noted quickly. And there was a very familiar sound to the voice asking the question, a familiarity that might have been much more obvious without the cloud of uncertainty and action and adrenaline and sheer mind-blowing surprise that framed the situation.

The young man and woman who were the targets of the attempted robbery had gotten up and run down the street with their cash at the first sight that the robbers had lost their guns and were subdued. So this suddenly unexpected conversation was not taking place in front of them. And the other mysterious masked man noticed just then that one criminal had regained consciousness, so he stooped over and quickly changed that fact, so they could talk without anyone else hearing. Walid thought again to himself that these were the guys who had stopped the animal abduction the other day. They had intervened here at a crucial time for the Viper and the Storm, who had not been prepared for the extra two criminals to appear, and with guns.

The masked man asking the question suddenly broke into an unseen smile and then laughed. "Malik," he said, and then added, "and Haji. Secret crime fighters at your service."

"No way!" Mafulla had been standing silent until now. "No way!" he repeated.

"Yeah," the other masked man said. "It's us—your good friends, Malik and Haji. But what are you guys doing wearing masks and taking on armed robbers in groups?"

"Malik? Haji? Unbelievable! We should ask you two the exact same thing!" Walid was stunned and could hardly think.

"Ha! Well, those are our civilian names, the names you know us by. We've got secret identity names as well."

"Why?"

"Well, you know, we've been really inspired by The Golden Viper and Windstorm, and I guess you guys have, as well—I mean, by the looks of what you were doing."

"Wait, there come some people," Walid said. "The gun shot attracted attention. We should leave these guys tied up and get out of here as fast as we can—to preserve your secret and ours."

"Agreed," Malik said, and they all walked quickly around the back of the bank building to the other side, taking off their masks at this point—Malik and Haji first, then Walid and Mafulla, so that, when they reemerged onto the main street, they wouldn't be seen in their small bit of secret crime fighting gear. The wristbands were also slid off silently as they walked.

"I can't believe this," Haji then said.

"Neither can I," Mafulla echoed.

Walid now spoke to their friends as they continued down the street. "Well, first of all, thank you for the needed help just now. We like to think we can get out of any situation, but that was a little more difficult than we had planned for. And, second, where in the world did you guys learn how to attack armed men and take them down like that?"

"Surprise sure helped," Haji said. "While they were focused on you, we came out of nowhere as soon as we saw what was going on. But the real answer is our dads. We've both been learning self defense and military stuff from our dads since we were little."

"Yeah, it's incredible what they've taught us over the years," Malik added. "And it comes in handy now and then, for sure."

"Amazing. Ok, guys, if you don't mind, let's go down this next side street so that we can stop and talk without causing any unwanted attention anywhere near the crime scene."

"Good idea," Haji replied, and all four of them walked a short distance more and turned onto another residential street. There, they were able to stop and stand and talk about this unusual situation that had just developed, and with no one else around.

"How did you happen to be here?" Walid asked.

"Oh, we were going over to some general store to get some stuff for the trip," Malik said.

"Wow, us too," Walid replied.

"So, what are your crime fighter names?" Mafulla suddenly asked. "I mean: You said you have crime fighter names, right?"

"Yeah, of course, like the Viper and the Storm, but listen, you have to promise you won't laugh," Malik said.

"Ok. We promise," both Walid and Mafulla responded.

"I'm The Wild Camel and Haji is The Silver Sabre."

Walid smiled and nodded. "Good names. Original. And sure to inspire fear, at least in Haji's case, and Malik, in yours, maybe paralyzing giggles—which could also be useful."

"Ha!" Mafulla laughed loudly and then held his hand over his mouth.

"Very funny." Fortunately, Malik smiled. "Hey, you might get kicked or bitten by a wild enough camel. They can attack viciously! And they keep on going! They never get tired!"

"True," Mafulla said.

"So," Malik responded, "What are yours?"

"Ours?" Walid said.

"Your crime fighter names—you do have crime fighter names, I hope. Otherwise, the criminals you stop might try to get back at you later, or worse, get revenge on your families or friends. That's the reason for the masks, too, and of course, because our heroes, the Viper and the Storm, use masks, as well as cover names. So, what are your cover names?"

"I'm not sure you'd believe us," Walid replied.

"Sure we would! Why not?" Haji said. "You just believed us!"

"Well, there's a lot to believe," Mafulla explained. "A whole lot."

"What do you mean? You guys are being mysterious, even for guys who sneak around in masks."

"Ok, first, we promise not to reveal your crime fighter names to anyone without your permission," Walid reassured them.

"Good." Haji replied. "I mean, I sort of assumed that, but good."

"So we want both you guys to do the same, and promise the same thing," he said.

"Ok, not a problem," Malik responded.

"No matter what," Walid emphasized.

"Sure, no matter what," Malik echoed.

"Same here," Haji said. "Even though this is a lot of caution among friends with made up names."

"Yeah, but there's a reason," Walid explained.

Malik and Haji had the exact same idea at precisely the same time. Walid certainly had to be extra careful about all this because of his distinctive and exalted position in the kingdom. He was, after all, the Prince of Egypt, and could never let word get out that he also patrolled the streets in his spare time stopping petty crime, wearing a mask and using a crazy made-up name like the famous Viper and Storm. Those great crime fighters had, of course, inspired everyone, but especially young men wanting to make a difference, and a few guys from the palace school weren't likely the only well-intentioned copycat imitators out around town trying to spread the good work that the originals had started.

"I understand," Malik said.

"You do?" Walid replied.

"Yeah, sure, I mean, you're the prince and everything and you can't let word get out that you're doing this crime fighter thing like me and Haji, who are just, you know, normal guys, private citizens trying to do whatever kind of good we can."

"Yes, you're right, and, well, there's also a bit more to it," Walid began. "First, you have to understand that less than a dozen people know about me and Mafulla, and we can't let that number grow much at all, for several reasons."

"Wow, that's already a lot," Haji said, surprised. "Why do so many people know about you guys doing this?"

"It's a little complicated, but we had to let certain people know. The king guessed it one day and advised us to share this sense of mission that we have with our parents."

"With your parents?" Malik said. "Oh, man. Did they totally flip out?"

"No, no, I sure thought they would," Mafulla said. "But we approached the subject carefully and reassured them about how cautious we're being, I mean, other than our stupid mistakes today, from which you bailed us out. And it took them a little while, but they came to accept it. We just want to do something good, like you guys."

"And they understood that?"

"Yeah."

"Wow. That's very nice. You guys have great parents."

"Yeah, we're really lucky, and it's nice of you to say that."

Haji said, "Thanks. But so, now, with all due caution and promises and commitments made, and we do swear to honor our promises to you about this—What are your crime fighter names? I'm just too curious. I bet they're good ones. You guys are pretty creative."

"Oh, they're good ones, all right," Mafulla replied. "And it won't hurt our feelings a bit if you guys don't believe us at all," he added.

"Why wouldn't we believe you? We know you. You're good guys, and honest, and we don't think for a second that you'd lie about something like this—I mean, not to us, not now," Malik responded.

"Ok, good," Walid said, and took a deep breath. "So here's the story. We started doing this not with any plan, but just because some bad guys had set up shop in the Adi store in the marketplace, pretending to be working for the king. And one day we realized who they really were, and it developed fast that Mafulla's family was in danger. And we had to help break the situation up, and the crooks got taken to jail, and then later, we thought about how it would be nice to have secret identity cover names, for just the reason that you guys said, in case anything remotely like that ever happened again—which we really didn't intend at all. So we came up with names, mostly just for fun, and never thinking we'd actually have to use them, ever."

"Ok," Haji said.

"I wanted to call myself The Desert Viper," Walid revealed, "but Mafulla talked me out of it."

"Yeah, that would have been too much like The Golden Viper, too close, far too copycat."

"Well, this was before any publicity about The Golden Viper, and actually before anyone had even heard the name The Golden Viper."

"Really?" Malik voiced the surprise that both he and Haji felt at this little revelation. "You mean you were coming up with that exact crime fighting name even before the famous crime fighters, The Golden Viper and Windstorm, hit the newspapers?"

"Yeah, well before that," Mafulla answered.

"Wow, you guys were ahead of the times, for sure," Haji said, clearly impressed.

"That, we were," Mafulla agreed. And he added, "but I'll let Walid continue at this point."

"Ok," Walid said. "So, Mafulla talked me out of The Desert Viper, because, he said, I wasn't in the desert, I was in the city, and that would probably be where we would do any good deeds that might require secret identities. So, he said I shouldn't have a name tied to the desert. But I liked the Viper part a lot, because I had seen one in the desert and knew how scary and dangerous they are. And Mafulla thought that because of where I live, in the palace, that maybe my name should be The Golden Viper—you know, for The Golden Palace—and not The Desert Viper."

"Ha! Now that is a crazy, amazing coincidence! Mafulla, you actually came up with the real, famous crime fighter's cover name—the exact name—before any of the publicity about the Viper and the Storm hit the papers and the radio?" Malik was amazed.

"Yeah, I did."

"That's really, really wild!"

"Yeah, it's pretty wild," Walid said in apparent agreement. "But what comes next is even wilder—to the point that you might find it very hard to believe, I promise."

"Try us," Haji said.

"Ok, so, Mafulla wanted a scary name for himself, and I had told him about a bad, scary storm that had blown up in the desert while I was traveling here, initially, and how intense and unbelievable it was, and he said he wanted a name that would conjure up all those fears and that feeling, and so he said, why not Windstorm?"

"You're kidding us, now, right?" Malik said.

"Yeah, you're joking with us," Haji agreed and looked at Malik.

"See? I told you that you wouldn't believe us!" Walid answered. "And no, I'm not kidding."

"Ok. Look. It's a little too hard to believe that you guys came up with both the famous crime fighter names before you ever heard anything about them in the news, unless you're totally psychic or something." Malik continued. "And I happen to know that you sometimes get things wrong on tests just like everybody else. You can't be some spooky knower of all things," he added. "So, come on, quit messing with us. What really happened? What are the real names?"

"I promise and solemnly swear to you both that I'm telling you the absolute truth," Walid said. "I'm not messing with you. You guys are our friends. We admire you guys. We're not going to kid you or lie to you and lead you on to believe something false and stupid. You know me better than that."

"Ok, Ok," Malik said. "But you have to admit … this is so crazy that it's almost sort of supernatural."

"Yeah, well, just wait," Mafulla said, with a very strange look.

"What do you mean?"

"He turned to Walid. "Go on."

"Ok. So, for a long time, we just joked about our names—not as much as you could joke about 'The Wild Camel,' but still," Walid said.

"Hey," Malik replied. "It's a good name."

"You did make us promise not to laugh, so you know what I mean."

"Ok." Malik sort of puffed out some air.

"But I do like it," Walid said. "Anyway, one day we were in the marketplace and I saw a lady get attacked by a guy trying to steal her purse, and I ran out of the store I was in and chased the guy. And I didn't realize it at first, but Mafulla was right behind me. And together, we caught the guy and tackled him and got the bag back. And the king had asked us to wear sand masks on that day, because it was windy and he wanted us to have a little anonymity when we were out and about, so that people wouldn't recognize me as the prince and I wouldn't be a target for people who don't like the king."

"Ok. That makes sense."

"And so we gave the lady her bag and she asked who we are and we just sort of spontaneously said, The Golden Viper and Windstorm."

"No!" Haji said, looking totally shocked and skeptical at the same time. "No way!" He looked over at Malik with his mouth hanging open and then back at Walid.

"Yeah, that's what happened, and the lady apparently told a

bunch of people about it, and *The Kingdom Daily News* wrote about it. And we were shocked. And the king saw the article and knew we were in the marketplace that day and, like I said, he had given us the sand masks to wear, and he guessed it was us. And he was right."

"No way!" Now it was Malik who was voicing his shock. He felt almost dizzy with confusion.

Haji had recovered just enough at this point to say, "So, wait, the next day, when we talked about the masked crime fighters in class … that was *you guys* we were talking about?"

"Yeah," Mafulla said. "Our ears burned the whole session. It was super strange. But everybody said really interesting things and we learned a lot from the discussion."

"I hate to go back to this now, but come on, really—surely you're kidding with us and this is all a big joke," Haji said again, as serious as he could be. "I mean: I can believe the names—maybe the guys who became the Viper and the Storm somehow heard them after you made them up—like maybe they overheard you talking on the street or in a café or something and they decided to use the same names. Or it's a huge, gigantic, ridiculous coincidence. I can even maybe buy that, too. But, you're not really also claiming to have done the first thing that the Viper and the Storm were reported as doing—wrongly, I guess, if what you're saying is true, and that you did it instead of them, but using their same exact names? That's just way, way too crazy! There's no way we can believe that!"

"No. We're truly not kidding now. We did do that thing in the marketplace, and we said our names were The Golden Viper and Windstorm, and that's what the paper reported."

"But then, when did the real Golden Viper and Windstorm get into the act and start doing all the other stuff?" Haji still could not fully process what he was hearing, and neither could Malik, who at this point was just listening and trying to put together the pieces of the puzzle.

Walid took a deep breath. "Well, and this is the hard part, but what we're saying is that there were and are no other crime fighters with the secret identity names The Golden Viper and Windstorm."

"What?"

"What do you mean?"

"Everything that's been reported about them that was true has been about what Mafulla and I have done around town—the two of us."

"Wait. Whoa. No, no, no."

"Yep."

"You're saying that you guys are the real Viper and Storm?" Haji was now in a thick fog, and trying to fight his way out.

"Yeah, I'm afraid so. I'm the one and only Golden Viper, and Mafulla is the one and only Windstorm."

"No."

"Yeah. Almost every time we left the palace, for a while, things would happen and we would be in the right place at the right time and we'd intervene and stop whatever was going on. And the newspaper wrote up some of the stuff, and other stuff started rumors, and there you are. It was all just us—your friends—the two of us."

"You guys."

"Yeah."

"But. But, where did you learn how to do the things you did?" Haji was still speaking for both of them, since, as confused as he was, Malik was feeling even more off kilter right now and was still silently just trying to soak in what he was hearing.

"Your dad has been giving us intensive sessions for a long time, in self defense and military stuff and fighting techniques."

"My dad?"

"Yeah. Thanks to the king."

"What do you mean?"

"It all started because the king wanted me to be able to protect myself whenever I might be threatened without a security detail around, and since Mafulla is usually with me, and no chain is stronger than its weakest link, Masoon had to train both of us."

"So … that's why you were able to do what you did on the train, on the class trip to Giza?"

"Yeah."

"And during the attack on the palace?"

"That, too. The training really, really helped."

Mafulla jumped in. "We couldn't have done most of it, otherwise."

"So … you're saying that you, our friend Walid, are the famous Golden Viper, and that you, Mafulla are the equally famous, one and only Windstorm?" Malik this time asked the core question, even though his mouth was so dry he could hardly speak at all.

"Yeah, but we never did anything to be famous," Mafulla said, "Walid already had that sort of wrapped up with the prince thing, as if it was important at all, in the first place. But, yeah, we're the guys who started the whole thing, without ever trying to. We just stepped in a few times when somebody needed help and this huge myth and legend grew up, out of control, without our assistance or encouragement at all."

Malik actually had to sit down at this point. He said, "So it's you guys who inspired us to do what we're doing?"

"Well, at least the myth and legend that were spawned without our encouragement—so, yeah, I mean, I guess so." Walid was trying to be careful of his friends' feelings in how he stated everything at this point. He quickly added, "And I know I can speak for Mafulla as well as myself here and say that we're really glad you guys were inspired by the various reports of the stuff we did. We were hoping to get other people to take action against crime as well, and you guys have. And that's really good. We saw you break up that attempted animal kidnapping a few days ago."

"What?"

"We saw you in the park save a lady's dog, and we were really super glad—we didn't know who you were at that point, of course. And we almost jumped into action to do it ourselves, but we saw you guys get to the scene first and deal with it well."

"You saw that?" Malik said.

"Yeah, good, fast work. That lady has her dog now because of you."

"But … we've been collecting newspaper clippings and articles and stuff about The Golden Viper and Windstorm all this time … and it was all about you guys?" Haji was still trying to make sure he had his head around this completely surprising news.

"Yeah. Yeah. I'm afraid so. And the radio show, and the cartoons, and everything else—all of it got started because we were just trying to do some good for a few people who needed help."

"And the big scandal about all the bad guys getting murdered in that warehouse across town where Set and Jabari were rescued … the newspaper was falsely accusing you two guys of mass murder?"

"Yeah," Mafulla said. "It was bad. And when we found out the police were after us—that sort of got us worried. And the paper was working so hard to get everybody to hate us and there we were, totally innocent of the trumped up charges and just trying to make a little positive difference in the world, but we couldn't tell the paper what the full truth was, so it was a little dicey for a while."

"Man! You sure did a good job of keeping the secret!" Haji exclaimed.

"We had to," Walid explained, "for the safety of other people, as well as for our own freedom to do other things in basic civilian mode, and not have bad guys breathing down our backs all the time and everywhere."

"This is just all so hard to put together," Malik said.

"I can imagine," Walid replied.

"But … I guess I believe you, as crazy as it all sounds. I mean, this is you, and we know you, and Ok, I accept what you're telling us. But, gee whiz."

"Me, too," Haji said. "But that just shows how much I think of you two, because, by itself, this is all just way too hard to believe."

"I knew it would hit you like that," Walid said. "But your dads have known from early on. The king pressed us to bring them in on the secret, for our own good."

"Really?"

"Yeah, and so they can confirm everything I've just told you. And, of course, if you'll grant us a small exclusion clause in our promise about the names and the identity of you guys, I should really tell the king, now that we told you, and also what the circumstances were under which I revealed the big secret, so that he'll understand. I hope you're Ok with that. I'm sure he'll think it's fine, since he knows you both, as long as the news doesn't go any farther at all."

"Oh, wow, really? Are you sure?"

"Yeah. I think it's important. And everything's going to be fine."

"Ok, then. No worries," Malik said. "We're cool with what you need to do, and the story on our part will still be a well-kept secret."

"Yeah. No worries," Haji repeated. And then he said, "After all, even if we tried to tell anyone else, who would believe us, for even a second? I mean—Mafulla Adi, the Famous Crime Fighter, Windstorm?"

"Ha! Very funny," Mafulla replied. "But, hey, I'm not the small, fragile yet wily beanpole I was when I first met Walid."

"That may be true, but I'd have to say that you still might not strike many people as mythological legendary superhero material," Haji said and laughed.

"Ok, Ok," Mafulla responded, "I'm no Beowulf. Yet. But give me time. And lots of goat cheese." At that, everybody laughed.

Haji said, "I don't know if there are enough goats, in the world."

To that, Mafulla replied, "Oh, I see how it is. So, in addition to your crime fighter name, you maybe should get a stage name too, since you're such a comedian, and that's a context in which you'll really need to keep your true identity secret, or else people will be egging your house on a regular basis. In fact, I think I can get my hands on a few spare eggs right now." He looked around.

And they all laughed again at that.

"I'm still a little bit stunned by all this," Malik said. "Or a lot."

"Yeah, we know, it's pretty stunning," Mafulla agreed. "And, thanks for believing us."

"Yeah. I would say 'no problem' but it was a big one; so, just, yeah. Yeah."

"Wait. I just had an idea," Walid said. "What if we had something like a League of Crime Fighters, masked men who would join forces and help each other when needed, like today?"

"That's a good idea," Malik said. "Who would be in it?"

"Just us, I guess," Walid said. "Unless we discover that there's somebody else doing this stuff, and somebody we could equally trust. But for now, we'd be the whole membership."

"The League of Crime Fighters," Haji said.

"International," Mafulla added, with his usual panache, and a grin.

"Ha!" Haji responded.

"The L.C.F.I." Malik thought to himself that he liked this a lot.

"All for One, One for All!" Mafulla said.

"Whatever that means," Walid commented.

"It means …"

"Yeah, I really know," Walid said, "I promise."

"Oh, Ok. I never know when you're kidding. Most people, when they're kidding, you know it, because … it's … funny. But the way you do it, it always catches me off guard."

"Uh, huh," Walid replied. "And I think I've heard your little slogan somewhere before."

"*The Three Musketeers*," Malik said.

"But there are four of us," Haji worried.

"There were four of them, too," Mafulla quickly explained.

"Wait. You're saying that there were four people in *The Three Musketeers*?" Haji was confused again.

"Yeah, just like us—sort of."

"As long as we're in the mode of believing crazy and hard to believe things today," Malik said.

"No, really," Mafulla replied. "In the book by Alexander Dumas, there were the original three musketeers, just three—Athos, Porthos, and Aramis—but in the story, they were joined by a guy named D'Artagnan and together they became the four friends or the four companions, but *The Three Musketeers* probably makes a better title. And yet, the book is about all four of them. All for one and one for all, as D'Artagnan himself, Mr. Number

Four first stated in giving them, as a group, their motto and now us, ours."

"How do you know all that?" Haji said.

"He surprises me like this all the time," Walid explained.

"I've never read the book, so I don't know what a musketeer is," Malik said.

"Oh! It's a guard for the royal household in France two or three centuries ago, a guy who sometimes carried a musket, or muzzle loading rifle." Mafulla was the professor today, for sure.

"How you manage to have just about any esoteric fact ready to hand always amazes me. Where did you learn all this stuff?" Walid looked over at Mafulla with a funny expression on his face.

Mafulla sighed. "I had far too much time on my hands before becoming The Windstorm. And anyway, I like to be a well-educated man of the world, up on scintillating details from science and literature. I may be slightly smaller in body compared to you three, but I carry with me a very large body of knowledge, so keep that in mind."

"Duly noted," Walid said.

"So what's The League going to do?" Malik said.

"Good deeds," Mafulla replied.

"More specifically?" Malik pressed, and all four of them thought silently for a few seconds.

"Maybe we let each other know about patrols, now and then, or when we're going to be out and about." Mafulla said.

"Oh, Ok, that makes sense. That's at least a place to start." Malik nodded his head in agreement.

"Yeah," Haji said. "We could be your backup."

"Yeah, our backup. Or we could be yours."

"Ah! Oh! Yes! I have an idea for a first big joint work-sharing venture!" Walid said.

"What?" Mafulla asked.

He paused for a moment as the other three looked at him, and then added, "Ok, this is really good."

13

The Adventure Begins

The big day for Walid's trip back home with his parents and Mafulla and other friends had finally come. There was a sense of adventure enveloping the palace, almost like a light, bright morning fog. Walid's friends were going to experience something new and very different. But he was, too. And he couldn't even guess at the outset how unexpected and genuinely astonishing the results of the trip might be.

Whenever you've been away from a place that had long been home, there will be a new tone to your experience of it, if you happen to return. You won't feel exactly as you once felt. You won't see as you once saw. You're different. And your perceptions will mirror that fact. Any experience of something new is tinged with a certain kind of magic. In a case of returning home after an extended absence, there will be a mental and emotional distance, initially, and a sense of the new mixed with familiarity, and a newness that's almost akin to what you might experience on a first visit to a place you'd never seen.

Walid's comfort was now in and around the palace. And this was also true for Mafulla. Anything that took them far away from this and into a different environment was going to awaken them in new ways. That's what travel, at its best, always does. It sharpens our senses and our minds. It awakens aspects of our drowsy souls. But the boys had no idea how abruptly they were going to awaken on this trip. They didn't even know that they had been, in any way, even partially asleep in their daily mindset and throughout their ordinary sensibilities.

In fact, if they had been asked about this, they would likely have said, and quite sincerely, that they were both more perceptive and attentive in their daily experience than ever before. Part of their Phi training had to do with this issue. And they were learning well. So they might have been right to think their daily perceptions were keener than ever. But there were still plenty of levels for awakening possible for each of them. The trip would open their eyes in several new and unexpected ways—if they could live long enough for that to happen.

The last school session before the long break had been a good one for both classes. Some students were staying home during the vacation. Others were going off to see relatives in other cities, some in Egypt, a few elsewhere. Bafur was getting to travel all the way to Paris with his dad for a big food convention, featuring gourmet products and world-famous chefs. Needless to say, he was excited. A week in advance, he had said that his stomach was churning already in avid anticipation. Ara was going with her family to London for a visit. Kit was off to Spain. Everyone seemed excited about the long break. And that, of course, appears to be simply a particular instance of a universal truth: No matter how much students like their classes or their teachers or their school, they typically like breaks and long vacations even more because of the freedom these times bring.

The king had made sure that everyone and everything was prepared for the big trip to Walid's home village, known locally and on the map as "Dromeda." Its name came from its well bred local dromedaries and its proximity to the main caravan route across the desert to Cairo, where those particular camels could often be seen doing their customary work. Walid happened to overhear Mafulla mispronounce the name, as "DRA-mada," with the accent or emphasis on the first syllable, and he quietly took him aside to explain that it was locally pronounced, "Dra-MEE-da" with the accent on the middle syllable, even though the spelling would itself allow for many different pronunciations, like "DRA-meeda," or "DRO-meeda," or variations with the short 'e' sound, or even where the 'e' is pronounced a bit like a short 'a' normally would be. At the end of the discourse, Mafulla exhaled loudly with a whistle and replied that he was glad to be friends with such an obvious master of word form, inflection, and village pronunciation. There had surely not been such a wizard of words, or pharaoh of phonics, since the famous Phoenicians, he declared. And, of course, this, as usual, made Walid laugh.

Kissa and Hasina were coming! So was Layla. Masoon and Hamid were in charge of security, which of course consisted mainly of them. But Omari and Layla and twenty-two of the kingdom's top soldiers were also backing them up. Plus, Masoon had personally chosen the military men who were going on the journey. Hoda had wanted to come as well but, as it turned out, she had to stay behind during the break to handle some extended family matters.

The funny thing about the king's plan, at least from the point of view of the students, was that they had all been issued standard military uniforms for the trip, which were surprisingly comfortable. They were the distinctive desert uniforms, made of a thin but durable material that was particularly light and loose and breathable. Despite the primary utility of the clothing, Layla still looked like a fashion model wearing it, and the same was true of her daughter and Kissa, but that fact really surprised no one.

Walid had even walked up to Kissa and said, "The way you ladies look in these uniforms, all the women of Egypt will soon be signing up for the army, or at least shopping in military surplus stores!"

She smiled and just said, "Silly."

But he added, "And I bet the top magazines will shortly have on their covers photographs of beautiful models in desert field garb."

"You're very kind, soldier boy, and I should say that you look pretty impressive yourself," Kissa replied, with a coquettish tone of voice and turn of her head.

Mafulla walked up and said, "I look fierce, right? I mean, really."

Kissa laughed and said, "You have indeed the most frightfully fearsome aura in those clothes, Mr. Mafulla. At one glance of you, I'm sure that any enemies of the state would flee instantly."

"Yeah, and at one sniff of him, everyone else would," Walid joked.

"Hey!"

"But we tolerate the fierceness and the cologne—or I should say, 'of the cologne'—because we know he would never intentionally harm us, his friends, even in our delicate olfactory capacities."

"Of course not. I'm your protector in all things," Mafulla said.

Walid looked at Kissa and remarked, "I think he actually holds back while splashing on his favorite weapon when he knows we'll be near."

"I agree," Kissa said and laughed, adding, "I'm sure we're warmly cocooned in the innermost parts of his affections every bit as much as in the aromatic field of his tonics."

"Ha!" Mafulla replied, "As long as by 'we' you two mean not only yourselves, the rapier wits in my immediate proximity, but also, of course, the lovely Hasina."

"Always!" Kissa said.

"Of course!" Walid replied.

"Here the dear girl is, in person, and in uniform." Kissa laughed, and she said to Hasina, who was right then walking over to them, "I was just admiring how good you look in military couture, and how fierce Mafulla appears—or at least, that was his word for it."

Hasina laughed hard and said, "Mafulla, you are exceedingly dapper, dear sir."

"But dangerous, too, right?"

She laughed again and said, "Yes, not only dapper, but of course ready for action and terribly, terribly dangerous."

"Not just to others, but often … to himself," Walid interjected with a serious expression, and made everyone laugh once again.

The plan was this. They would all start the trip in military convoy trucks, and then at a small crossroads army post a full day's ride outside of town, everyone would transfer to camels that had been gathered there for them. Leaving Cairo, they would use at first a paved highway, and then a well-maintained dirt road that, for a distance, skirted the northern edge of the desert area they would finally cross by camel train caravan, the old way.

You couldn't actually pave a good road through the desert. Or, maybe it would be more accurate to say that you could try, but you couldn't get the substructure you needed to keep it secure and level. And, even if you got around this problem, the road would always be covered up with deep sand and would have to be cleared over and over, after which the winds would then cover it once more. It would be an effort sufficiently parallel in its own way to the famous Myth of Sisyphus, who in Greek mythology had to spend his life rolling a rock up to the top of a hill, from which it would just roll back down again. And he would then be forced to repeat the task, over and over, literally forever. Clearing sand off a paved road in the desert would have been even more continuous a task.

Because of this, there had come to be a common proverb, "Never pave a road in the desert," and an accompanying expression, 'building a road in the desert,' for utterly futile enterprises. If, for example, you tried to teach an erratic, totally inconsistent man how to perform some job consistently well, someone would likely tell you that you were "building a road in the desert." In other words, you shouldn't even try.

But the road they planned to use at first was a new one that had been constructed just beyond the worst of the blowing sand. And it would cut at least three days off their trip in each direction. That would give them more time to spend in the village itself. Everyone would still have the full camel caravan experience and would even be able to visit one of the oases along the standard route, the one where the king long ago had begun sharing deeper wisdom with his nephew, Walid. But they would not have to endure all the drawn-out difficulties of a full desert passage.

Walid's parents, Rumi and Bhati, were busy loading some last minute supplies onto one of the trucks. Or, to put it more precisely, they were carefully supervising the loading of those supplies. King Ali also had plenty of people working on the preparation and pack-up to make sure that nothing was forgotten, or put in an awkward place.

Everyone was now eager to get into the troop transport trucks and be underway. The small army base where the king had positioned all the camels had been built at a point where the road they would initially travel took a sharp turn to the north and away from the desert. In preparation for the desert segment, His Majesty had also made sure that they would have, along with the camels, two strong and fast horses, in case messengers ever had to be dispatched from a remote location. They would make the desert passage, overall, in a caravan of nearly the size that had initially brought the king and Walid to town.

The prince and Mafulla walked over to the king, who had just finished talking with Masoon. Walid said, "Your Majesty, thank you again for making all this possible. I think we're going to have a great trip."

"Yeah, thanks a million, Your Majesty," Mafulla added.

"You're quite welcome, my boys. I think it will be a wonderful and engaging experience for all of you. We'll certainly miss you here in the palace. But such is life. Sometimes, we have to go away for a while in order to come back richer and wiser."

"Richer and wiser sounds good," Mafulla said.

"Do I see a red convertible in your future?" Walid asked, teasingly.

"Possibly, yes! But only if it would be the wise choice, of course."

The king chuckled and said, "I think Masoon's ready for departure. I want you boys in the third truck from the front. You can go over there momentarily. It's our time to say our goodbye, for now. Have a great trip! And I'll eagerly look forward to your safe return."

"Thanks, Uncle! Bye for now!"

"Yeah, thanks, Your Majesty! See you soon!"

Walid and Mafulla walked over to the truck the king had indicated and learned, to their great pleasure, that Kissa and Hasina would be joining them, along with Layla and Hamid. Rumi and Bhati were in the second truck, with Omari and several soldiers who happened to be well known to them. The first truck held Masoon and a small group of their top sharpshooters. In a fourth truck would be, to Walid's initial surprise, a couple of other men who had made the crossing with him and his uncle the previous year—Baldoor Farsid, and Dubin Shabar, each of whom had some business to attend to in the village and who thought it would be much more pleasant to travel there and back with the group. They were both good friends to the king and had served him well in vital capacities since the revolution, so he heartily approved of their joining the group, and made the arrangements for them to be included. A few soldiers accompanied the two of them, as well. The fifth and final truck contained the last of the military detail and, along with truck four, most of their collective supplies.

Baldoor and Dubin had both served in the army many years earlier, and ever since they had arrived and seen each other near the trucks, they had been joking about their uniforms and all the medals and rank indications that were now missing, for some strange reason.

"That's a nice look on you, old friend," Dubin had said, when he first walked up and saw Baldoor in his desert clothes.

"Yes, thank you—and on you, too, young friend, but I tell you, I want to know where my Distinguished Achievement Ribbon is!" Baldoor gestured toward his chest and kept poking a finger at this and that spot, as he spoke. "What happened to my Marksmanship Pin, and the Civilian Service Award, and the Meritorious Battle Insignia, and quite a few other indications of my ample accomplishments while on active duty? They've vanished! You could hardly see the cloth on my chest for all the awards I had hanging on me in the old days!"

Dubin nodded and said, "Oh, I'm sure the old uniform you once wore so handsomely would not even come close to fitting these days, my friend, and when they chose this new, much more ample size for you, where there is clearly now plenty of room for all your ribbons and awards, my guess is that the kingdom's official Humility Police intervened and decided to keep the medals off this uniform."

"Why would they ever do such a thing?"

"Oh, I imagine, because it would be better for your soul and for the rest of us, if so many trophies of adornment were left behind for the duration of the trip. But don't worry, old pal—if necessary, I'll gladly testify to your superior and distinguished service record, whenever anyone, man or camel, might ask."

"They would never believe you!" Baldoor replied. "It's just too far fetched that any one man would acquire so many recognitions and tokens of merit during a normal stint of service."

"Well, unlike you," Dubin said, "I'm glad to be free of the burden of my own awards. The sum total just weighed me down badly. They were far too heavy for me to carry all of them on my uniform here at my current age. The weight would not be good for my knees. In fact, it's a very good thing I got out of the military when I did."

"Why is that?"

"Oh, they had completely run out of room on my uniform for the continuous stream of awards I was winning. They were going to have to start hanging medals and ribbons on my trousers as well. And I'm sure they would have made it down to my boots, eventually."

"Oh?"

"Yes! I must admit that I seem to have astonished the generals so much that soon they were going to have to make up brand new medals, just to mark my unanticipated and unparalleled brave accomplishments. I'm sure I saved them a lot of trouble and expense by retiring to private life." And, at that, Baldoor laughed loudly.

It went on like this for several minutes, and the two of them had each other laughing again and again and patting one another on the back, with jabs and boasts and jokes as they waited to get onto their assigned truck. Walid had overheard some of this silliness, and he smiled to remember what they had been like on the previous trip across the desert—always good to have around, inevitably joking, and reliably in good moods. They would be great companions for this journey, as well.

On Masoon's signal, everyone got into the trucks. He then double-checked that everything was ready, and the convoy began to make its way toward El-Wadi, where their first destination, the small military outpost, was located. The first few hours of the trip were uneventful and fun, as people introduced themselves to any passengers on their trucks that they might not previously have known, and those who were already among friends shared their excitement and thoughts about the days to come. The chatter of nervous anticipation quickly became the conversations of good companions.

Kissa, Hasina, and Mafulla each peppered Walid with questions about his early years in the village, what growing up there was like, and how he imagined it might have changed since he left and so much of the local population had then relocated to the capital city. Walid loved all the questions and tried to give everyone a complete history, as the king had told it to him, about how his grandmother had fled into exile and ended up in the village, how village life was then, and the various ways it developed over the years. He talked about the general store, the bookstore where he had worked, and the many people in town he knew. He told them about watching caravans pass by and talking, even as a small child, to some of the travelers when they stopped and visited in the village to get supplies, or just to rest. He also asked Hamid various questions along the way, and the doctor entertained them with many background facts that Walid had never heard about people and places around the village.

The prince said he didn't know how the place might have changed since he left, but he was prepared for some pretty big differences. Even though it had just been about a year, so many people had come from the village and its general area to help the king take power, and then to serve in the new administration of the kingdom. It was certain to be quite a different place in many ways. Rumi and Hamid had made sure that there would still be good medical care in the community, and the general store had been turned over to a new manager who seemed like he would do an excellent job. Walid explained that, while it was not a city by any stretch of the imagination, it wasn't just a one camel town either. There were a number of businesses like a leather goods shop and a hardware store and a place for pottery and a small grocery that he hoped would still be open and doing well when they returned.

They didn't stop and camp for the mid-day sun as they would have had to if they were on camels. Inside the trucks, there was as much shade from the sun as they would have had in tents, and so they could continue to make progress through this hottest part of the day. They did have to stop for refueling at another small army facility that was almost half the distance they would be driving in total. And that was a good chance for everyone to get out and stretch their legs and enjoy some fresh air. The local soldiers, who knew they were coming, had also prepared a nice mid-day meal for them all. So it was a considerable break, very refreshing, and one that they all had needed.

They also had a signal. If anyone on any of the trucks felt an urgent call of nature and had to respond, they could alert the driver of their truck and he would blow his horn. Then, all the trucks would pull over and anyone else who might feel such a need could perform that most necessary basic function as well. It was a system that worked well. No one stopped the convoy without good reason, and they were able to drive for fairly long stretches of time and make a lot of progress toward their destination. So, when anyone did cause a horn to be sounded, a wave of relief typically spread throughout the trucks. And at most stops, there were many people who took advantage of the opportunity. Separate privacy areas for men and women were quickly set up, and each was put in place in less than a couple of minutes. Then, everyone who might need to use the opportunity took a turn, and when they all got back on board, a soldier in the lead truck checked to make sure that there was no one left outside the vehicles. Finally, on his signal, they started off again.

This was the rhythm of the day.

As the sun eventually arched farther across the sky and began its slow downward slide, everyone was feeling a bit tired. Some chose to nap, others to read quietly. By the earliest onset of dusk, they drew close to El-Wadi. Their timing could not have been better. A good dinner was awaiting them, and they could spend this last night in a level of comfort resembling real beds, inside the camp's barracks. Then, they would leave on camels before first light.

The soldiers had built a large campfire outside for their guests to enjoy during dinner. The flames rose high and crackled and popped as everyone loaded their plates with the prepared food and took them, with good drinks, to a spot in the sand where they could enjoy the stars spread out above them, as well as their small distant cousin on the sand burning bright and warm, the blazing fire in front of them. The desert at night cools quickly, and even though they were just on the edge of that great expanse, they felt the heat of the day drain away and the crisp cool of the evening begin to set in around them.

Walid and Mafulla were, of course, sitting with Kissa and Hasina, enjoying the fire and the stars. Omari came up with his food and said, "I don't want to be an interruption, but would you four mind if I sat down with you for a while?"

"No, please join us," Kissa said.

"Yes, here, right beside me," Hasina added.

Walid and Mafulla were both glad he had approached them.

"So, Omari, what do you think of the trip so far?" Walid asked.

"Excellent. It's been a smooth day of travel, I'd say. And it's good to see this outpost again. I was stationed here once for six months, some time ago."

"You were?" Mafulla was surprised. "I didn't realize you had served in the army."

"Yes, it was a good experience, despite the nature of the monarchy at the time."

"That's right, it was the time of the previous regime, I guess." Walid commented as he ate.

"Yes, that's correct. I joined up to be of service to the good people of the kingdom, and because I wanted to develop military skills and a close acquaintance with all the military equipment."

Then he lowered his voice and added, "I had already been given very advanced special training from a member of the community we enjoy, and wanted to be sure that I'd be prepared in every way for whatever kind of service I might be called on to perform."

"That was smart," Walid commented. "Mafulla and I sometimes wish we were old enough for a stint in the military."

"Well, for you, it will be different," Omari said. "You have access to anything you want to learn, and anything you want to master, from the palace. You've already been through more action than most active duty military in the kingdom's history. If I could, I would put some medals and badges on your uniforms," he added with a laugh.

"Oh, no!" Walid said. "That would drive Baldoor and Dubin crazy!"

Omari laughed, but Mafulla, Kissa, and Hasina just looked puzzled.

Walid explained to the ladies, "Before we got on the trucks this morning, I heard the two of them carrying on about where all their medals had gone and why their uniforms were unadorned with ribbons and meritorious badges. They were pretty funny."

"Yes, those two can be hilarious," Omari agreed. "If you listen to them long enough, you'd think they fought in a battle every day during their time of service, and singlehandedly won each of them!"

"Yeah, I guess we really didn't need all the extra security, with them along," Walid joked.

"Well, the problem is, we don't have any medals to award in our little unit, so it might be harder to motivate them into action than you think," Omari said with a smile, and everyone laughed.

And, at that moment, as they laughed, the big fire in front of them, which had just been blazing brightly, crackling and popping with energy, suddenly went out completely. It vanished in an instant. It just disappeared. It was the strangest thing anyone there had ever seen. It went from a three-foot or four-foot high roaring blaze to nothing, like someone had flipped off a switch.

Immediately, there were many voices around the fire, or the previous place of the fire, exclaiming things like, "Whoa! What was that?" and "What just happened?" "Did you see that?" Masoon and Hamid stood up, and then so did Omari. Everyone then grew quiet. Walid began to stand as well, noticing that the more senior Phi were all looking about in every direction. There was no wind, no breeze, and nothing else that could be perceived anywhere around them that could have made the fire just vanish as it had.

The camels, even though they were all some distance away, resting in a fenced-in area, could at that same moment be heard to stir and complain loudly. There is no sound quite like that of an agitated camel. It's almost like a huge walrus gargling. And then multiply that by over thirty animals, and you can imagine the cacophony of sound. But not even ten seconds later, as suddenly as the fire had been somehow extinguished, it burst back to life fully, every bit as bright and hot and big as it had been the very instant before the bizarre occurrence that they had all just witnessed.

The re-ignition of the fire was just as startling to everyone and every bit as weird and scary as its initial disappearance that had blanketed everyone in pitch-black darkness, despite a low remaining glow of coals and wood below where the fire had been dancing wildly a moment before. It had taken a few seconds for everybody's eyes to adjust to the night without any lights other than those twinkling still from above, and then, when the camp's fire burst once more into the air, as if from an invisible torch, everyone was nearly blinded by its flare of sudden brightness. In fact, this event was probably a lot more alarming than the oddity they had just witnessed moments before. It evoked a big gasp from the group, including the soldiers of the army base, whose commander immediately rushed up to Masoon.

"Has anything like this ever happened here before," Masoon asked quickly, wasting no time.

"No, sir! Nothing! I can assure you!" The commander responded with a look of concern that Masoon could see in the renewed firelight.

"What kind of wood are you using?"

"The same as always!"

"Who stacked the wood for the fire?"

"I did it myself. I supervised four of the men, four good men, in bringing out the wood and preparing the fire. It was all done the same way as we always do it."

"What then could it be?" Masoon asked him.

"I … don't … know," the man said, and shivered, despite the blast of heat that had returned to the place where they now stood. "I've never seen anything like this in my life."

14

Forces at Play

"Something's coming. Someone's coming. I can feel it." The small man had popped his head into the doorway in a state of high agitation.

"Perhaps."

"No, definitely."

"I can assure you, I know what you know, but also a good bit more."

"Well, then," the would-be messenger hesitated and said, "what can you tell me?"

"Only that I've addressed the situation. That's all you need to know for now."

"But."

"No. Nothing more. Good night, Hadrat."

"As you wish, sir, as you wish. Good night." The man took a deep breath, bowed silently, and left the doorframe empty once more, as he stepped away and then paused.

The man he had come to alert now looked out the window with a flash of intensity in his eyes and said, aloud, but merely for his own ears, "We shall see. We shall see."

Outside, Hadrat walked slowly back to the barns and stables for a last look around before he retired for the day. They were miles from the nearby older village, and off quite a distance from the nearest good road. They had all the isolation that the man in charge had needed and sought. There was no one around to hear the many sounds that came from their compound, especially during the day. The owner of the property was not well known in the area, by his own careful design. In fact, he was hardly known at all. He kept to himself. And no one had a clue what he was doing or where all his money had come from. In addition to a large compound of specially designed buildings surrounded by vast open land, he had many men working for him, and guards keeping other people off the property and far away from his focused work. The guards told any inquirers that the property was an agricultural research facility, on the rare occasions when they were asked. But they would never say much more than that.

The entire complex had been built by a great number of men brought in from elsewhere who lived on the property during construction. It had been started only about ten months earlier, and completed within less than ninety days, total. Even the workers themselves thought of it as a miracle of modern fabrication. They were far enough away from other people not to attract too much unwanted attention during the entirety of the project, or since it was finished. When the main phase of construction was over, the vast majority of men hired for that part of the project left and went back to their towns of residence, mostly in other countries. They were all bound contractually, and under dire threats, not to speak of the work they had done, or of the place where they had done it. They had been told that the men who had found them once, to hire them, could always find them again, to kill them, if they told anyone about the project. It was all as top secret as an advanced military installation might be.

Suddenly, Hadrat heard a loud noise in the night—the sound of wagon wheels, and more. He turned down his lantern and peered into the dark. Within five seconds, he could see the faint outline of a horse drawn wagon coming toward him. He stepped away from the barn to see it better. "Who's there?" he shouted.

The wagon rolled forward and came to a stop. "I'm sorry, Hadrat, but we had to make this delivery tonight. We were delayed along the road and there's no safe place for us to spend the night outside the compound, not with our current cargo."

"I understand," Hadrat said to the driver. "Take everything into the big building. There's a man there who'll help you unload. And, of course, you may spend the night as you have before with the workers down the path over here."

"Thank you, my friend. It's been a difficult day."

He didn't say anything, but the manager could not help but think, "More difficulty may be coming our way, regardless of what's said." He momentarily looked up into the sky for any more omens that might present themselves, but then remembered the man in front of him.

He said to the driver, "I'm just glad you made it. Explanations for anything that goes wrong, or that goes in a way different from our schedule, just do not work around here, as you know. So we keep our peace. And we manage. Please plan on having your breakfast with the men in the morning and then you can be off. The less you say about the trip here, the better."

"Very good. But first, a word if you wouldn't mind."

"What is it?" Hadrat stepped closer to the front of the wagon, as the driver leaned over.

"I had to stop near the town for water."

"Yes?"

"And there was some talk."

"I know all about it. I was in to buy some things earlier."

"Then, you heard?"

"Yes. It's being dealt with."

"Good. I just wanted to be sure you were informed."

"Thank you. I appreciate your concern. I've been assured we have it well in hand."

"That's a relief," the driver said and straightened back up in his seat.

"There's no cause for worry."

"Ok."

"Good night to you." Hadrat waved his lantern in the direction the driver needed to go, and the man jerked his reins for the horses to move forward toward the building that had been mentioned. The manager then happened to notice, as they passed him, that both the horses pulling this wagon were completely black, and not the usual white and sandy ones that most often brought cargo onto the property. He thought to ask, but let it go.

Across the kingdom and upstairs in the palace, Kular stuck his head around the door and said, "Your Majesty, I'm so sorry to disturb you, but there's a telephone call for you in the office."

"Thank you, Kular. I was just finishing up. Who is it?" The king asked, with a look of curiosity on his face.

"Reela Adi," Kular replied. "He's calling from the embassy in Algiers."

"Oh. Good. I'll come right down and get it. Please precede me and let him know I'm on the way."

"Certainly, Your Majesty." The head butler walked quickly down the hall, as he was accustomed to do, with a spring in his step and at the pace of a much younger man. The king, meanwhile, gathered up some papers that were on the table in front of him and, glancing over the last one he picked up, reread three or four sentences and then put the bundle of reports into a satchel that was sitting next to the table. He paused for a few moments more, stroking his short beard in thought, as he often did when contemplating something of great importance, and then made his way out the door toward his office.

When Ali walked into the office, Kular was listening to the telephone and taking notes. "Yes, yes, I can do that. Certainly. Ok. What was that? Yes. Got it. Oh! Here's the king now! It was nice speaking with you, Mr. Adi. I'll take care of everything." Kular quickly handed the phone over to King Ali. "Your Majesty."

"Thank you, Kular."

"Certainly, sir, you're most welcome," Kular said with a bow as he left the room. The king watched him go for a second, remembered something he wanted to ask Reela, and then turned to the phone.

"Hello, Reela. How's your time with our friends?" The king smiled by natural reflex and nodded his head. "Good, good." He moved toward his chair a foot or two away and sat down. "He did? That's indeed very funny. You tell him I feel the same way. Uh, huh. What have you been able to learn?" His look became serious for ten or fifteen seconds and then he said, "Oh, well, that is interesting, indeed. I see. Yes. You mean there and in Tripoli as well? Hmm. I had no idea. And … did I just hear you right? You say, possibly also in Tunisia? That's important to know. Ask the ambassador, if you would. Yes, he has a way to find out. And get back to me with that, if you can, as soon as you know. Yes. Thanks. I look forward to it. Thank you for calling. Surely. Goodbye."

Ali put down the telephone and sat for a few seconds in thought. He picked up the phone again and dialed an internal number. "Naqid, could you get a message to Masoon, please, before they leave El-Wadi in the morning? And also ask Hoda if she can spare an hour tomorrow to come by the office. Yes. Anytime. Ok, here's the message for Masoon."

Not far from the palace, Khalid walked into the front room of their home where Hoda was sitting at a desk, writing. He yawned and said, "Come to bed. We'll be getting up early in the morning."

"Yes, you're right. I got lost in thought and all the records I was reading through. I didn't realize how long I've been sitting here."

"Your aunt's estate is a bit complicated, so I'm sure there's a lot to get lost in. And for her illness to have come on so suddenly, I know it's been difficult for you to go over all these things in so short a time."

"It has. Ana has been true to her name throughout her life. She has shined like a sun for all of her extended family and friends. But so many of her close family have gone on before her and, at her age, I know it's difficult to take care of any of these arrangements when you're so sick. So, I feel honored to be of help."

"I'm sorry Kissa couldn't be here to lend a hand, but I'm sure the trip will be an important one for her. It's quite an adventure."

"Yes. I had a strange feeling moments ago that her adventure is beginning in earnest right now."

"What do you mean?"

"Actually I have no clear idea what I mean, and I have no worries about her, but it's interesting that you mentioned adventure. I think that could be what's coming up for our Kissa—a big adventure." As she spoke the word 'adventure,' Shibby came into the room and sat looking at her.

"Shibby, what are you doing?" Khalid asked in jest. "Did you hear Kissa's name?"

At the same moment across town, Ibrahim Hadad came out of the back bedroom where he had been reading and preparing for sleep. He walked slowly into his uncle's front room where the older man was also sitting with a book and said, "I just had a very strange feeling."

Several blocks away, Hamid's son Malik turned over in his bed and relit a small lantern that was sitting on a table next to him. He opened a bottle of black ink, picked up a pen, dipped it in, closed the bottle, opened his journal, and wrote: "I just had a very strange feeling."

Kissa and Hasina's classmate Khata sat on the edge of her bed, staring at the wall in front of her and shaking her left leg, bouncing it actually, toes on the floor and heel jumping up and down in a nervous tic. Her mother stuck her head into the room and said, "Khata, what in the world are you doing?"

"What? Oh, mom, nothing."

"You're staring into space and bouncing your leg."

"Oh, yeah, I guess I am."

"What's wrong?"

"Nothing."

"No, those are signs that something's wrong. Tell me."

"I … I don't really know, mom. I just … I just had a very strange feeling. That's all."

"About what?"

"Not really about anything. It was just … strange."

"Oh well. You should go to sleep, you know."

"No school tomorrow."

"True. But it's still good not to get too far off schedule during the vacation."

"Yeah, mom, I know—but come on, one night."

"Ok, all right. But let me know if there's anything you want to talk about."

"I will. Right now, I think I just want to read some." Khata took a deep breath.

"That sounds good. Call me if you need me. I'll be up a little longer, as well."

At El-Wadi, Hamid had just sent the soldiers of their security detail to go out in pairs to surround the open area in which they had all been sitting and enjoying their dinner and talk before the sudden strange incident with the fire. The camp commander had also called out some men to join in searching the area around them for anything unusual. Hamid then walked up to Masoon. "We should talk," he said to his friend.

"Yes. Ask Baldoor and Dubin to supervise the security detail and check on the men, pair by pair. That will give them something to do and they'll do it well. I'll ask Rumi and Bhati to stand and speak with the commander, in case anything else comes up. Then let's sit and talk with Layla and Omari and our younger colleagues for a few minutes." Hamid nodded and went off to grab Baldoor and Dubin. They were both near the food table.

"Hamid, what in the world just happened?" Baldoor asked.

"We're not sure. The fire went out, instantly, and then came back, just as suddenly."

"Yes, so it seemed. But: How?" Dubin now asked. "How can such a thing happen?"

"We have no idea, but to make sure we're all safe, we've just put the security detail around the perimeter in pairs. Soldiers from the base will be doing a search to see if there's anyone or anything in the area that should concern us. We need the two of you to supervise our soldiers, to go from pair to pair, checking on them and asking if they've seen or heard anything. You have the right backgrounds for this. Circulate for the next half hour or so, if you would. Make sure there's nothing in our proximity that would pose a threat."

"Good idea," Baldoor said, and Dubin agreed.

Hamid pointed to a couple of nearby soldiers and said, "Begin with them, starting now. Spend a few minutes with each pair. Tell them you've been asked to play a support and supervisory role for the time being, and ask them if they need any help. Then, inquire as to whether they saw or heard anything unusual right before the fire went out, or after it came back. In addition, see if they've noticed anything unusual, or out of the ordinary, since then."

"Will do," Dubin replied, and the two of them walked off.

Hamid went back over to Masoon, who was now talking with Omari and Layla. She broke away and motioned for the girls and boys to join them. They all sat, now alone, a bit farther from the fire than they had been earlier, so that the popping and crackling noises would not inhibit a conversation in suitably low voices.

"What do you all make of the strange events we just witnessed?" Masoon began by asking.

"It's very concerning," Omari quickly replied.

"Yes, it is," Layla agreed and went on: "There's an ancient mystical tradition, one of which I've read. And in this tradition, it's explicitly said that an interrupted fire—and that's how it's been stated—an interrupted fire is a bad omen. I never quite knew what that meant until just now. We definitely had a fire that was interrupted."

"I've heard of this," Masoon replied. "It certainly startled everyone, and I think it gave many people a physical shiver unrelated to the temporary loss of heat, which was quickly restored, of course. It was after the restoration, in fact, that many felt a shiver of unease."

"It's a common enough psychological response to the uncanny and unknown," Hamid said. He then looked at Layla and asked, "Why is the interrupted fire, as you call it, considered a bad sign?"

She answered, "Fire is one of the four elements, of course, and each element has its own integrity or wholeness. Earth is what it is, through changes and reconfigurations. Air has a continuity of its own, also through alterations. Water maintains its hidden identity even as it radically changes forms. And Fire—well, it endures in the stars, and in a smaller way on earth. This endurance shows in the fact that there's a certain natural history to any fire that's set anywhere in this world. It begins, flames up, and burns, and if it's supported by a limited amount of ordinary materials, such as wood or grass and oxygen, it eventually starts to wane, flickering down and finally out into the embers that are its proper end, and from which, of course, a new fire can be set, if it's desired, and sometimes, even if it's not. Fire, like the other elements, has its own integrity and continuity, and it endures, at least through the normal cycle of a natural process. An interruption such as we just saw shows that there's something unnatural intervening, and this is a sign that physical or spiritual forces are in play, powerful forces that can overrule even one of the four elements, and that should not be confronted or resisted without all due understanding and caution."

"So, it's a sign and a warning?" Masoon said.

"Yes."

"What do you think it's signaling or warning us about?"

Layla sat in silence for five or ten seconds, as all other eyes were on her. She took a deep breath. "Someone doesn't want us to make this journey."

"Oh, man," Mafulla said. "Oh, Geez."

"What?" Hasina asked.

Mafulla explained, "Something like this could be connected with a worry I've had."

"What do you mean?"

He looked over at Walid, who nodded. "Well, the king just spoke to me and Walid about a recently interpreted passage in The Book of Phi, one that talks about the spiritual resources or spiritual power that's available within the created world—the range of resources that make Phi power … possible. And he talked about how extensive these resources are, beyond what we can even imagine."

"Really?" Kissa said. "So what made you worry? That should have been reassuring, right?"

"Yeah, it is on one level very reassuring. We have huge resources to draw on for what we want and need to accomplish. But then, I started to wonder: What if there's somebody out there, a bad guy, a guy with no moral compass, and no concern or compassion for others, and he has a mind that's somehow open to these resources, and he then cultivates himself as rigorously as we do, like real, advanced Phi training, and he gains access to more and more of these resources. Can you imagine what a threat a person like that could be?"

"Like Farouk al-Khoum?" Hasina said.

"Well, in a superficial sense, but worse—far, far worse," Mafulla replied. "And that's the worry."

"What do you mean?"

"Remember, Farouk was spotted as Phi when he was in his teens and given a little bit of training, but he left Phi. He had the raw abilities, but so far as we know, he never sought to develop those abilities in a deep and powerful way. He may not have known that was even possible. I mean, he thought so highly of himself, it seems, that he would not have imagined that he was just at the beginning of a huge journey that he needed to take to really develop himself."

"So, Farouk was just a novice, really," Hamid said in agreement. "He had powers, but they still lay mostly dormant. He used what he knew he had, and he used all that expertly, but indeed we have no reason to think he spent any time whatsoever developing his gifts after he left his official training."

Mafulla said, "So, take a guy like that, and maybe even a lot more gifted—much more—and imagine him developing his access to these huge resources of the mind and spirit for decades, working hard, digging deep, and growing ever stronger. My worry was, if Farouk was so hard to deal with, what if we ever had to take on a Super Farouk, who was maybe ten times or a hundred times stronger? What would that be like?"

"That is a scary thought," Hasina conceded. She looked at her mom and over at Masoon and Hamid and asked, "Have you guys ever worried about anything like that?"

Masoon and Hamid looked at each other briefly. Layla made eye contact with each of them as well, and then she spoke up and said, "There's always been a legendary version of that worry. I heard the story originally from Hoda's mother."

"What did she tell you? What was the story?"

"She first told me the legend of the monster. That's all that the individual of the story was called: the monster. In the story, the way it's been passed down, apparently for a great many generations, the monster started out as a distinctive boy, a young man who was different, gifted, and set apart in his childhood abilities. He was made fun of, shunned, and criticized by other children, and even their parents, for being so different. Thoughtless people bullied him, people who had no idea who he really was and what he was, or soon would be, capable of doing. He became resentful and angry and grew full of hatred toward these others, and vowed revenge one day on them all. The desire for vengeance and to prove himself better than all the others burned in his heart and began to consume him."

"Wow. Scary," Hasina nearly whispered.

"But as he grew older, this boy one day came to realize that the fire of anger inside him would eventually burn him down and hollow him out, leaving nothing more than the charred shell of a man behind, unless he tamed it. So he set out to control and calm this fire within. He studied meditation. He was told by teachers to embrace compassion. But he had no compassion for anyone; so he simulated it for himself, seeking to bathe himself in care and concern and compassion, but misunderstanding what that would really take. Nevertheless, through various mental disciplines, he began to calm his emotions. His meditations started having an effect, and there came a day when the destructive fire seemed to go out. The hot hatred was not burning him. His desire for revenge was now more of an abstract motivation, an intellectual thing driving him, rather than a raw emotion, and yet still a deep need, but not the roaring hot fire that it had been."

"So, what happened?" Mafulla asked in a low voice.

"He studied and worked, and read and sought guidance, but

never from the right people, from our point of view—yet often helpful people, from his own distorted perspective. He read ancient texts. He found forgotten manuscripts and studied and experimented. He discovered ways of augmenting his personal power, not just developing it, but adding to it from other sources. He fed his need to grow in power. And he became a monster seeking to impose his debased will on the world and crush anyone who stood in his way."

"Jeepers."

"Then, one day, the fire returned, the fire that would have destroyed him before he had accumulated all his new inner strength. But with his systematically acquired monstrous energies, skills, and powers, he could use that fire now without being quickly cremated himself, inwardly and outwardly, and he could focus its flames to destroy others, to burn to the ground and incinerate anything he didn't approve or want."

"That's pretty scary," Mafulla said. "Especially the part about the fire going out in the monster and then coming back, like what we saw tonight."

"Yes, it is concerning. And that's why the tale had to be told to you now. But also, by the way, there is a legend about the legend."

Kissa now spoke up and said, "What's that?"

"The secondary legend has it that the Sphinx, the great and mysterious Sphinx of Giza, was built precisely to ward off—to keep away—such a monster, if he ever were to appear, outside of legend and myth, and in the real world. The Sphinx was crafted with a powerful intent that should such a figure arise, it could not be in the very positive, deeply spiritual area of Giza. So the Sphinx is always on the lookout. It's forever on guard. The legend even further states that the sand around the statue is itself imbued with a power that the monster can't resist or overcome. And, to my knowledge, there's never been such a thing, or person, to arise in that part of Egypt and, I'm sure, there's no such thing there now. But we're headed toward a part of the kingdom that's about as far away from Giza as it's possible to get, and yet still be within the embrace of our ancient domain."

"Oh, man. I had never heard that about the Sphinx," Mafulla said. "There are so many mysteries about it, and this is a new one to me. But, Layla, how did the original legend end?"

"Oh, yes. It ended with a warning that there would be only one way to resist and defeat this monster, should he ever actually walk the earth in the time of anyone who hears the tale."

"What was that way?" Mafulla could barely speak; he was so inwardly tense and engrossed in what was being said.

"That was not explained as a part of the legend," Layla reported. "I suppose it will be up to his opponents to discover the way."

After a few seconds of silence, Masoon said, "That's a very good representation of the legend as I've heard it."

"Yes, you've told it extremely well," Hamid added.

"Why haven't we heard any of this before?" Walid spoke up and asked, to the adults generally.

Masoon explained, "This legend … is not often told. There's a superstition about it. Some people seem to have believed, for a very long time, that if it's told, then something bad will very soon happen to the one who spoke of it."

"What?" Hasina said.

"And in addition, it's not deemed to be an appropriate topic of discussion for young Phi."

"Deemed by whom?" Walid protested, but in a mode of keen curiosity.

"By the senior Phi who've heard the legend and understand how it has affected them, deep down. This has been the judgment of wise people in more generations than we can name."

"Oh, Ok," Walid replied.

"It's a mercy to share certain things only when the time is right," Hamid added. "And that's a general truth in life."

"Well, I guess we're still very young Phi," Walid said.

"Yes and no," Layla said. "You're very young in physical years, but no longer too young, in a spiritual sense," she explained.

"Mom, how do you know that?" Hasina asked.

"Because I'm senior Phi, and I know all four of you well." Layla paused for a moment and said, "I've seen you do what you've done,

I'm deeply aware of what you're capable of doing, and just now, I suddenly knew, with a certainty in the moment, that the time was right for the legend to be spoken to you."

"But what about the rumored danger from telling the story?" Kissa asked what all the young Phi were thinking.

"I'll take my chances," Layla said and then smiled.

At that very moment, something in the fire popped almost as loudly as a gunshot and instantly all eyes turned toward it again, as Masoon and Hamid reflexively stood, prepared for whatever might come next.

15

A New Phase

Walid slept fairly well, but woke up early and couldn't get back to sleep. It took Kissa and Hasina a long time to fall asleep, but once they did nod off, their slumber was solid and refreshing. Mafulla had a more fitful night, tossing and turning. He dreamed of a monster, not even remotely human, and of its rampage through a town.

The senior Phi had made peace with the situation—the events regarding the fire and the eerie connection with the ancient legend that Layla had spoken of with such care—and they had all slept soundly. They seemed to share the king's perspective that worry and anxiety help nothing and fix nothing. They were certainly concerned about what had happened. It had put them on a new level of alert. But as the younger Phi were more fully starting to grasp, senior Phi always had a form of something like alertness going on inside them, yet without any stress, strain, or emotional negativity involved. They were constantly paying attention to things around them. They were confident in their abilities to deal with surprises and have trained themselves to perceive their circumstances well, connecting everything up with anything else that might illumine any small bit of their experience. Because of this, they could free themselves from anything like a feeling of anxiety over the unknown. They somehow managed to live in the broad rich present moment, while also welcoming the future yet to come.

In all walks of life, a master knows what a novice can't even imagine. But every master began as a novice.

The early breakfast they all enjoyed was a good and hearty one, prepared again by the soldiers of the outpost. There were, of course, several jokes made about keeping the fire going this time, since it was actually cooking their food, unlike the ornamental blaze that had put on such an unexpected performance the previous evening for the astonishment, and now entertainment, of everyone—as if it had been just part of the festivities planned for these esteemed visitors from Cairo.

"It didn't surprise me so much after all," Baldoor had said, over the coffee. "It was a bit like my marriage. After a while, the fire seemed to go out, and I worried. But then I came into some money, a large inheritance, and the flames returned to my bride immediately. She once more ardently burned for her sweet Baldoor!" At that, several of the men laughed loudly and Kissa scowled, looking over at Hasina, and then at Walid, who was smiling at all the laughter, but for only a second or two, until he saw Kissa's look.

She lowered her head close to Hasina and said, "Men! Listen to how they speak of their loved ones! It's simply not right, even in jest."

"Not all men joke in that way," Hasina reminded her.

She sighed and said, "You're right, not all men." And she looked over again at Walid.

"And even some who do it mean no harm, like these, I'd venture," Hasina reminded her. "Some men, or boys, not to name any names, just like to joke around, and it's really all nothing more than a little game—often masking and diverting attention from genuine concerns that are unsettling for them to address head on. And at other times, its just foolishness for the pure sake of foolishness."

"I suppose you're right, Hassi. You're so sensible. I think I'm just a little on edge from everything that happened last night, and all that was spoken about."

"Yeah, me too," Hasina acknowledged. "I imagine we all are, at least those of us who sat and talked together after the strange event. We understand the potential significance of the really odd disruption we saw."

"It's still possible that the whole thing has a perfectly natural and reasonable explanation, and we simply don't know yet what it is," Kissa pointed out.

"Yes, absolutely." Hasina said this just to be reassuring, because in her heart, she felt there was something more than that going on.

Kissa herself then seemed to sense the emptiness of her own words and said, "I mean, I sure hope so."

Hasina added, "I'm going to be more on alert, though, than I would have been if it hadn't happened. But I do hope it was just a strange event that means nothing."

"Me too. That's a wise approach. Hope for the best, prepare for the worst, and be at peace either way."

"Actually, here's what I think," Baldoor continued on in a fairly loud voice, speaking to several of the men sitting around. "I take the interruption of the fire last night to be a good omen. The sun will cease its normal assault on the desert during the time of our sojourn, and then regain its fire once we're safely back." He lifted his cup.

"Here, here!" one of the other men said.

"I'll drink to that!" Dubin said, holding up his mug.

"You'll drink to anything!" Baldoor joked.

"Hey! It's strong coffee!" Dubin retorted.

"Good!" Baldoor replied. "May it make you strong as well so that, possibly, you can keep up with me today, old friend, or at least come close! I'd hate to leave you too far behind in the desert."

"Ha! You'd better speak to your camel about that, after you apologize to him for the unduly heavy load he'll be bearing today."

"I already had a few words with yours!"

"Oh?"

"The poor thing. He begged me to interrupt your breakfast and prevent you from having seconds, or else to please trade you my beast for him!"

Dubin laughed, as did several of the other men. He responded, "Yes! Every camel wants a rider who's no smarter than he is, so that they'll have more in common and can communicate well." That of course created more laughter. Hasina turned to Kissa and said, "See? It's just their silliness. They intend no harm."

"They can be funny," Kissa admitted. "Ok, you're right. I feel better about them already."

Walid and Mafulla were over at the drink table, talking with Hamid and Masoon about the order of the caravan riders for the morning. Masoon had asked the boys to ride near the girls and to stay roughly in the middle of the line of camels. That way, they would be equally secure from the front and the back of the caravan. Masoon pulled out a map and, with the help of a nearby lamp, showed Walid their intended route for the day, roughly where they'd camp for the night, and what the rest of the trip would involve. They anticipated two days to the oasis, a day there, and three days to go the rest of the way to the village after that. They would stay in the village for probably no more than four days, then return five days across the sand and a full day truck ride back to Cairo. They'd be home several days before the end of the long vacation and could rest before school started again.

Masoon then went over how they would carry the weapons and ammunition they had with them for the trip. "It's ironic," he said, "how some of the heaviest and most burdensome items to carry are precisely the things we hope not to use at all during the trip, unlike the food and water and other supplies we take with us."

"Well, I suppose your reputation makes it possible for us to carry a bit less than we would otherwise have to take," Walid said.

"You might be surprised," Masoon replied. "Since I've been in the capital serving as your uncle's top general, some careless individuals seem to have assumed that I must have grown soft, spending my days, as one of them recently said to me, "fighting papers and pens on the battlefield of a desk."

"Really?" Walid responded, surprised to hear this.

"Yes. One drunken man with big muscles and a small brain

said exactly that to me in front of his intoxicated friends not too many days ago, at a café in town."

"Amazing," Walid said.

"Then he threw his glass at my head."

"No way. What happened?"

"He missed of course, and was doubled over in pain on the floor before I even got to him," Masoon laughed. "I showed him some mercy, the door, and the unfounded nature of his assumptions."

Walid laughed. "Man, people can be so stupid."

"Yes, and both they and we can suffer from their lack."

"I guess that's right."

"Sometimes I feel like it's raining idiots—and I'm just glad I brought my umbrella."

That really tickled Walid and made him laugh again.

A new phase in the trip now awaited them all. Right before the first faint light of day began to dawn, everyone had been given twenty minutes to be packed and at their camels and ready to leave. The security detail, augmented by soldiers from El-Wadi, helped any of the novice riders get their gear and belongings on the camels and then mount their animals. Mafulla was thrilled to have his friend Clyde, straight from the Royal Stables, and Walid had Cammo as his companion of conveyance. And then, of course, for the first hour out of the fort, Mafulla could be heard praising his slightly smaller animal with the words "Good camel. Good camel."

Walid turned around and remarked to his friend, "That's got to be the most highly praised dromedary in kingdom history."

Kissa added, "I was about to say the same thing."

"A well placed investment, I can assure you, my friends," Mafulla replied with a big smile. Kissa was riding alongside Walid, and Hasina was next to Mafulla, who was acting all calm and in control on the outside, but as usual, the amount of joking around he was doing showed his true feelings. At one point, he had Layla and Omari right behind him laughing so hard it looked like they were going to fall off their saddles.

Walid only overheard him say, "So, after that, no camel was ever allowed in my parents' store again—even if they had money on them and were clearly paying customers." Walid looked over at Kissa and grinned. They had missed the story, but couldn't fail to hear the laughter it had evoked.

Kissa said, "I wonder if he'll run out of Mafoolery before we get as far as the oasis.

"I think it's a bottomless well, to judge from the past year," Walid said.

The morning travel was completely uneventful and thoroughly pleasant. The sun did seem to be more moderate than Walid remembered from his previous trip across the sand. Perhaps Baldoor was right, and the interrupted flames of the previous night had presented a favorable omen for their travel. But as soon as he thought this, he found it hard to accept the optimistic interpretation, and that troubled him, at least a little.

It was just a quiet morning at Number Four, Luxor Road in Cairo. And then there was a knock at the door, a welcome sound for any business owner hoping for a new client. "Come in!"

A thin man opened the door slowly and took one step hesitantly over the threshold. He blinked his eyes. "Hello?"

"Welcome to the Cairo Detective Agency!" Those were the words of robust greeting he heard as the man at a desk inside the room stood up and smiled.

"Thank you," the visitor replied and took off his hat. "Are you the person I should speak with about some possible new business?"

"Yes. I'm the chief detective, Leem Hadad, at your service."

"How do you do?" The man nodded his head. "I'm Mansur Baram Arobi."

"I'm very well, thank you. And it's a pleasure to meet you, Mr. Arobi."

"Please call me Mansur, if you would. I don't stand on formality."

"I'd be glad to, Mansur. And I'd be honored if you'll call me Leem."

"Indeed, Leem, thank you."

"Please, have a seat." Leem gestured toward a dark wooden

chair across the desk from where he now stood, facing the door. Mansur pulled the simple armless client chair back a bit and sat down, as Leem also returned to his regular perch.

"You have a convenient location."

"Yes. Thank you. We just opened the office recently. I had a long career in Alexandria and have always wanted to live here in the capital city."

"It's nice here."

"Yes, it is. The locals have been very welcoming. One of them became, in a sense, my startup partner in this enterprise, a man who has lived here all his life. He made many introductions and helped me find this office."

"I see."

"The gentleman also taught me all about the city and its history. Now we're up and running on our own, but the initial local contact made it a lot easier for us to get established."

"I would imagine," Mansur said, nodding his head.

"But of course, not all our work is local. We investigate without borders. Wherever your problem is, or wherever it leads us, we go."

"That's good to hear. And it may apply to my own case."

Leem nodded. "Excellent. What then can I do for you, Mansur?"

"I need to discover some information."

"Let me get out a pad of paper and take notes as we speak, if you wouldn't mind."

"No, not at all."

"Now, what's your problem I can help solve? What sort of information can I track down for you?"

"There's a man. I think he's from Egypt. He may be from here in Cairo. I suspect so, but don't know. I need to learn his identity."

"Well, what can you tell me to start my thinking?"

"First, I suppose I should ask the fee for your services."

"Oh, yes. Forgive me for just jumping right in. We're so eager to solve our clients' problems that we always want to get to work right away. Our fees are simple. We ask for a retainer up front, before we officially begin the investigation. The flat fee is fifty dollars for a thoroughly local pursuit, one hundred for an investigation that may go beyond the city limits, and one-fifty for anything that may likely go beyond national borders. Then there's a five-dollar per diem for each investigator who works on the case. You can cap the number of days a month or the number of men—typically one or two men work on any given investigation, but not always together each day. Then, we also bill for our normal expenses—travel, food on the road, anything like that—nothing out of the ordinary, I can assure you, and we keep good records on everything. You're then, of course, free to examine the records at any time."

"This seems reasonable."

"Good. Should we proceed?"

"Yes. I believe we should."

"You were about to give me some background on the man you're seeking to identify, or on the circumstances in which he came to your attention, and perhaps the reason for your interest. Anything will help."

"Indeed. Well, there's a man—the man whose identity I'm here seeking—who has been making … certain inquiries in a number of national capitals of late, within our region of the world."

"Which capitals, may I ask?"

"Tunis, Algiers, and Tripoli."

"So, capital cities in North Africa."

"Yes."

"During what period of time has this been taking place?"

"In just the past couple of weeks, possibly a bit longer."

"Good, that's good. So the trail will still be warm, so to speak."

"Yes, it should be."

"Ok, then, what has the man been inquiring about, and to whom has he been addressing these inquiries?"

"He's apparently been visiting various government officials in these capital cities, and also some individuals who are thought to have been a part of the clandestine services in those countries, at least in previous years, and perhaps some of them currently."

"I see."

"He's also made some form of contact with the chief of police in each of these cities as well."

"Interesting. And you haven't been able to learn his identity from any of these individuals themselves?"

"No. There are some delicacies involved in asking directly, or even indirectly, through sources closely placed to these individuals. At least, neither I nor any of my associates can be the ones asking the questions."

"I see."

"I need a third party, such as yourself, to gather this information, a party far removed geographically from the people this man has been visiting, and someone not previously connected to me."

"Yes. I see. It seems that we're dealing with a delicate issue."

"Yes."

"And the man whose identity you're seeking, when he visits these individuals in Tripoli and Algiers and Tunis and makes inquiries, may I ask what it is that's the subject of his inquiries?"

Mansur looked around the office for a few seconds and then replied, "He's asking some questions about recent criminal activity in these cities, whether there have been crimes of a certain sort."

"May I ask of what sort?"

Mansur took a deep breath and expelled it. "Must we speak of this at all?"

"I can assure you that it will help immensely to narrow down our investigation, and for making sure that we ask the right people the right questions, and especially if we need to proceed carefully or indirectly, even diplomatically. Also, let me reassure you that everything you say to me is taken in strict professional confidence. It will not leave this room, except confidentially, in the heads and hearts of the detectives who seek only to serve you."

"That's good. I understand. The man is asking about certain disappearances in those cities, about what he apparently thinks could be … abductions."

"Kidnappings?"

"Of a sort."

"Of what sort?"

"Involving animals."

"Disappearances or abductions involving animals?"

"Yes. He's apparently seeking to learn if such events have been happening in those cities, and if so, how many, and involving what sorts of animals, and under what circumstances."

"Ok, I see. And may I also ask the nature of your own interest in his inquiries?"

"I'm sorry. What's the relevance of this?"

"Simply to fill out the picture in as many ways as we can, to assist in the investigation. It may allow me to frame my inquiries in the right manner, or suggest the best ways I might move forward. The more light I have, the more quickly I can succeed."

"All right. I understand. I'm at liberty to say that I'm employed by an individual whose legitimate and fully legal interests may be threatened by this man and by the ways in which he's making his inquiries."

"I'm not sure I understand."

"Ah, but at the present, I'm afraid that this is … as it must be."

"I beg your pardon?"

The man smiled in a fairly weak way and said, "I must seem like such a mystery man. But I don't intend to be, as you can tell by my giving you my own name right away when we just met. My employer is involved in some highly complex endeavors, big projects that may have substantial payoffs for great benefit, but right now he has concerns regarding this man who's asking about various animal disappearances in these capital cities. I'm sorry, but to explain the nature of the concerns would involve my embroiling you in some immense complexities and legalities, and we would first have to investigate you, and then have you sign reams of non-disclosure agreements, to prevent any unwanted competition for my employer, and there's simply no time now for such delays."

"I see."

"But I can assure you that everything is on the up and up on our end. We may even be able to be of help to this man with his questions. It's just that the way he's going about his own investigation is leading him, we think, down some false paths that, unfortunately, will be mutually inconvenient and quite embarrassing—both to him and to us—unless he's soon enlightened about some relevant truths, and redirected onto a more promising path for his searches."

"Yes," Leem replied in a friendly and continuing business-like tone. "Well, I appreciate your desire not to burden me with undue and unnecessary complexities, especially of the legal sort. Our work is much easier without all that binding us and complicating things."

"I was hoping you'd see it that way," Mansur responded, and then added, "Have I given you enough to go on?"

"I think we have enough to start us off. But do you have any physical description of this gentleman that you can provide for us?"

"No, I'm afraid he's something of an enigma himself. No one that I've spoken to has seen him in person, or is willing to admit to it."

"How did you hear of his activities?"

"We have associates in many places."

"You do?"

"Yes, and they pay attention to what's going on in their communities. Word of unusual activities, especially activities that may impinge in one way or another on our endeavors, tends to make its way into the right ears for me to hear about it in no more than a short period of time."

"I see. I see. Good. Well, I do indeed think I have enough to get me started. And a name is all you want?"

"Well a name and an address would be ideal, or some way of contacting the individual and speaking with him."

"That sounds reasonable."

"How long do you think this might take?"

"It's hard to say," Leem answered, "But if we get on it today or tomorrow, we might be able to wrap it up and provide you with what you need within a week, or maybe two weeks at the most."

"That would be very nice. Spare no expense. And use as many men and days up front as you need. We're prepared to pay what you charge, and if you can provide us with the information we're requesting within two weeks, I think my boss will also want to extend to you a nice bonus to express his thanks for a job well done."

"That would be very nice of him."

"Here's my card and a telephone number through which I can normally be reached. It's local. Please don't hesitate to be in contact with any concerns that might stand in your way. We need the information soon."

"I fully understand and can assure you of a quick and intense investigation."

"Thank you."

"It's my pleasure."

Mansur then stood to shake hands with Leem, who also stood again. The new client then put on his hat and said, "I bid you a good day," as he turned toward the door.

"And a good day to you, as well."

"Oh, and you'll have the retainer later today by messenger, probably within a couple of hours—the one-fifty, because of the international locales involved."

"Good, very nice, thank you again."

The door closed and Leem sat back down, looking over his notes and saying aloud, but nearly under his breath, "I'm intrigued. This is a new sort of request, for sure, very mysterious and unexpected." He turned toward a doorway off to the side behind him that opened into a short internal hallway and called out, "Ibrahim! Can you come in here for a moment?"

The young man got up from his chair and walked quickly into his uncle's front office. "What is it, Uncle Leem?"

"We just got a new case."

"Very nice."

"It's a strange one."

"Really?"

"Sit. I need to fill you in quickly and ask your opinion."

16

A Strange Feeling

The caravan had stopped for the heat of the day, as is the custom and need of travelers in the desert. Tents were pitched and naps were enjoyed by those whose excitement didn't prevent sleep altogether. Walid and Mafulla, despite being drowsy from the temperature, even inside the tent, had talked quietly for nearly two hours. They speculated more about the fire experience the night before, ruminated a bit on Layla's troubling story, and reflected on these first few hours of camel travel that had launched them into the most highly anticipated part of the journey, at least for Mafulla.

"When did you and the king first start talking about life and wisdom and the power of the mind on your trip across the desert last year? I think you told me once, but I'm not sure I remember exactly what you said."

"It was at the oasis closest to my home village—the one we'll be able to visit," Walid answered. "When we had a couple of days there to rest and just read and talk, that's when Uncle Ali began to share so many philosophical ideas and life lessons with me."

"Had you ever talked about these things before?"

"Occasionally, in small bits, but never in such a focused way and on so many important topics."

"Was it this hot?"

"It was much hotter."

"Really?"

"Yeah, that was a month of pretty high temperatures, with a few exceptions. Some days were like this, but others could be totally brutal."

"How did you philosophize about life when you were burning up?"

"Actually, it often made me forget the heat. I got so wrapped up in what Uncle Ali was saying, I was totally distracted and was able to ignore, at least during our talks, the oppressiveness of the heat."

Mafulla lay on his blanket silently for a few seconds, and then said, "Your uncle is sort of like my personal hero."

"Yeah, mine, too," Walid replied.

"He gives us so much time and attention, no matter how busy he is. We're really lucky," Mafulla added.

"Very true."

"I sort of miss everybody already who didn't come on the trip," Mafulla suddenly revealed.

"Oh, yeah? Me, too, actually."

"Especially the other guys."

"Yeah, I would have loved to see Jabari and his monkey in the desert on a camel."

"Ha! I hadn't even thought of that," Mafulla responded. He was quiet for a few seconds and then said, "You know, Malik and Haji are good men."

"Yeah, they are," Walid agreed, and added, "I'm glad about the new surprise they gave us, and the League that's resulted from it."

Mafulla laughed. "I thought I was going to swallow my teeth when they recognized us and started asking us questions."

"I can't recall a surprise bigger than that in a very long time," Walid said and also chuckled. "I didn't know my mind could race and freeze at the same time. It was like we were about to fall off a cliff of some kind, but then look at where it all ended up."

"Yeah, with good stuff and now, more support."

"Appearances and realities, my friend."

"Yeah, appearances and realities. What scared me at first, ended up being really good."

"I wish they could have come," Walid added, "but I'm glad they're on the job while we're gone."

"As long as nothing super big happens until we get back. They're still pretty much novice crime fighters."

"Hey, they saved us."

"True. But we would have found a way."

"Yeah, I guess we always do. But they were the way on that day, and I'm really glad."

"Me, too. And I have a strange feeling they're going to play a big role in something else soon."

"Yeah, I know what you mean. I sort of have that feeling, too."

The conversation went on like this for a bit longer, as the boys touched on such topics as Kular's remarkable continuing fitness, their current Phi lessons, the girls, of course, and the odd animal stuff that was going on in the city. But eventually, the heat and their tiredness began to overwhelm the sheer nervous energy they had brought into the tent and to their spontaneous, wide-ranging discussion.

At this point, their comments gradually grew shorter and farther apart and quieter and, at one long pause, Walid was the first to fall asleep. Mafulla could hear his regular breathing, and stared at the side of the tent nearest him until this barely audible sound put him under as well. He sank into the sweet repose of unconsciousness, and then, after a time, he dreamed of a boat and a man in the boat on a river. The boat was bright blue. It was floating rapidly forward, and as it moved along with the current, it grew larger and larger until it was almost as wide as the channel between the banks directing it. And that was it. When Mafulla woke up, he remembered the dream, but didn't speak of it. It wasn't troubling or alarming in any way, just strange like dreams can be. And it didn't seem revelatory of anything they might face here in the desert, so he just let it go and it faded, as dreams tend to do, until he would have had great difficulty recalling it at all.

The boys slept for roughly two hours of undisturbed rest before hearing the call to eat quickly, break camp, and get back underway. Voices outside helped them to wake up and clear their heads from their naps. Mafulla yawned really big, and then so did Walid. They got their stuff together and went out of the tent to see what was going on. The soldiers were already passing around some food and drink. Everyone had a cup of water, the best drink in the desert heat, and a light lunch. Then, their simple tents were quickly disassembled, repacked, and loaded once more onto the camels that, as always, bore these necessary burdens without agitation, regret, or complaint.

Walid watched the animals for a few moments as they received their heavy bags and stood, unmoved, ready for the next phase of the trip. He pondered their calm reliability, and the thought crossed his mind that there's a lot we can learn from our animal neighbors if we'll just watch, pay attention, and contemplate what we see.

Before they left town for the trip, Walid had asked Malik and Haji if they would go visit with Ibrahim toward the beginning of the vacation. He wanted them to get to know each other better. He wasn't sure why, but he felt strongly about it. He had told Ibrahim earlier that these two were good friends who could be counted on for almost anything and that they had done many brave things to help the kingdom, but that they didn't know anything about Walid or Mafulla's Phi status, so this was the one and only subject that shouldn't be a topic of conversation with them. Ibrahim understood completely and said that he was eager to know them better.

When Malik and Haji were on their way to say hello, and in fact were now just across the street from the building that housed the Cairo Detective Agency, they happened to see Mansur Arobi leave the front door, descend the short flight of steps, glance about, and then walk briskly down the sidewalk, away from them. Haji looked at Malik and said, "I've got a strange feeling about that guy."

"Really? I guess I do, too, but I wasn't going to say anything about it."

"Something's wrong. He's up to something."

"Should … we follow him for a bit?"

"Yeah, I think so, but carefully. We can't let him notice." The boys stayed on their side of the street, allowed the man to get a couple of blocks down from them, and then began slowly to walk in his direction. It was a major street and there was quite a bit of traffic going both ways, by car, cart, and foot, so their movements would not easily stand out, or call attention to themselves. Arobi kept up his pace for several more blocks, and then turned right onto a side street.

At this point, the boys jogged to catch up, so that they could keep track of his location before he disappeared into a building, or down another street. But when they arrived at the cross street he had taken and looked down in the right direction, he was nowhere to be seen. Calculating the time since he made the turn and the pace he had been walking, Malik concluded that he could have gotten no farther than two blocks down from them. But in those two blocks were two more side streets intersecting with this one. So Haji jogged ahead to look both ways down the first street, and Malik ran on to do the same at the second intersection down from them.

Malik made it to his spot and quickly looked both ways, but saw nothing in either direction. He then looked up and saw Haji shaking his head no as well. Malik then gestured broadly to all the buildings in this two-block segment and indicated by hand signals that he would cross the street and work the other side, from where they had started, to across from where Haji was now. For his part, Haji understood that, at the same time, he was to go door-to-door on his whole side, and window-to-window, working his way back.

There were law offices, a small insurance establishment, a tailor shop, a sandal and shoe repair place, a ladies' store, some other professional offices, and a doctor's office. But what Malik noticed right away was that Haji had passed by a small café with only indoor seating. It was called "the Falafel Stop." He made a beeline for the door and, opening it, saw Mansur right away in the back left corner, just that very moment sitting down at a booth with another man, who already had coffee or tea in front of him—but that was a fact not immediately seen. Arobi's back was to the door, and so he had not seen Malik come in. As the proprietor then approached the boy, he made a universal signal with his index finger signifying "just a moment" and popped his head back outside the door, signaling Haji, who saw him and came walking at a quick stride in his direction.

"I was hoping my friend could join me for a bite, and I wanted to make sure first that you had a table for the two of us," Malik explained to the café owner, who now stood nearby with small menus in his hands.

"Yes, certainly. I'm happy to have you," the man said. "We do have several customers in right now, but there's always plenty of room for hungry young men."

"Could we be seated near the back?" Malik asked, just as Haji came through the door.

Haji smiled and said, "If they have room for us, let's get a bite to eat."

"Yes, we do! Please follow me, if you would," the proprietor replied and guided them past several tables of diners and coffee or tea drinkers, whose conversations created a bit of a buzz in the relatively small space.

"I see a booth I like already, the next to last one on the left side, if that would be all right," Malik specified.

"That will be fine," the man responded. The boys sat, as their host motioned toward their seats, and the man put his menus in front of them.

Haji at that point nearly whispered, as if his voice was a little hoarse, "We'll study your offerings for a few minutes before ordering, but first could we have two cups of your best tea, and a few cookies?" The proprietor nodded, assuming the tea was needed to sooth a sore throat.

"I'll bring lemon and honey," he said.

"Very nice," Haji replied, and the man walked back toward the kitchen area.

Malik could tell that, the moment they were seated, the man in the next booth they had been following had lowered his voice considerably. But the boys could still make out some of what he was saying. As they sat quietly, looking as if they were studying the menus they were holding, they heard the words, "Yes, I think he'll get us the name and location. I agree. The man has to be stopped. The whole thing could come unraveled. No one else knows that the animals are coming from so many places. Yes. We'll keep our distance. No. No one will even suspect. The detective has no idea what he's helping us to accomplish." Then, something else was said, too softly to hear, and both men laughed in a muted way. The man opposite Mansur, as a result, coughed loudly, twice.

For the most part, Malik and Haji could hear only Mansur's words. The other man's mumbled responses were almost entirely indecipherable in the context of the relatively noisy café. The only words of this second individual that they could hear clearly were the last ones he spoke, as he got up to leave. They were: "Just make sure it happens within two weeks. No excuses. We have to stop him ... permanently. And then, cover the trail." At that, he walked by the boys without even glancing at them, and went out the front door.

Haji had the best look at him—medium height, not thin, but not particularly fat either, maybe slightly stocky, and he had a full gray beard, not particularly long or flowing down from his face, but bushy and thick. They didn't know it, but if The Wild Camel and The Silver Sabre had just approached a certain situation in a neighborhood park a bit differently in the very recent past, they might have seen at that time, and today would have been able to recognize, the driver of the car that got away while they were intercepting and thwarting two of his associates. He had eluded them in the park and driven off before they could catch a glimpse of him. He would nonetheless have ended up in the Cairo Central Jail and been unable to have a meeting in the Falafel Stop on this day if he had not, on that previous occasion, had an appointment he needed to keep after the incident involving the lady and her dog. Because of that, he had traded his driving duties with another colleague across town, shortly after he had pulled away from the park and found his men and driven back to where they were all staying. That's the only reason he had not been among the men apprehended later that day by Hoda. In fact, if any of several things had gone even slightly differently, Malik and Haji would not now have this thread to follow that had just been presented to them. Of course, it would have seemed even better at this point if they had seen the man earlier and recognized him now, filling in the picture more fully. But we don't often get everything we might have wished in such situations. And yet, we sometimes get just what we need.

"We have to see Ibrahim," Malik whispered to Haji, right before the proprietor returned with their tea and cookies, put them down, and took out his note pad.

"What else will you have today, boys?"

"I'm so sorry," Malik said, "I just realized that we have to meet a friend minutes from now and can't yet indulge in the meal we had hoped."

"Oh, my," the man said. "What a shame."

"Yes, but we'll make up for it. Please, let us pay you for our tea and thank you for it. And then we'll plan to return for our big meal, perhaps tomorrow, or the next day."

"I understand," the man said, adding, "that will be fine. It will be good to see you again and share with you the bounty of our kitchen."

The boys paid the man, left a little something extra, sipped their tea quickly, and made their way out the door.

"Wait. Shouldn't we follow the strange guy a little more, or at least one of us?" Haji asked, as soon as they were out the door. "I mean: We don't know where he lives or who he is, or how to track what he's up to. And what about the guy who just left?"

"I don't know if we need to."

"Why not?

"I'm thinking that Ibrahim probably can get contact information for the guy who came out of their building. It sounded like the man must have hired his uncle to do some job, and they surely have a way of contacting him. And then, if we need to, we can track the other guy, too, most likely through the same means, since they seem to be working together."

"True. I didn't think of that."

"Let's get back to the agency as fast as we can. Ibrahim needs to know what we heard."

"Good idea."

They jogged all the way back. Walking up the steps that they had watched the stranger come down earlier, they opened the outer door and entered a hallway. The first door on the left had a sign painted on it in white: "The Cairo Detective Agency." Malik knocked.

"Oh, this could be a busy day," Leem thought to himself. And then he said, somewhat loudly, "Come in!"

Malik walked in first, then Haji. They both looked a bit surprised, as if they had expected to see Ibrahim as soon as they walked through the door.

"Hello, boys. What can I do for you today?"

"Are you Mr. Hadad?" Haji asked.

"Yes, I am."

"We know your nephew Ibrahim and were coming by to visit him earlier. Prince Walid suggested that we might enjoy getting to know him better during our school vacation that's going on now."

"You're friends of the prince?"

"Yes, I'm Haji and this is Malik. You may know one of our fathers. My dad, Masoon Afah is the king's top general. Malik's dad is Hamid, the head military doctor."

"Oh! Yes! Indeed! Your fathers are quite famous for their good work in support of the kingdom! I'm so pleased to meet the two of you."

"Thank you," Malik said. "And we've heard great things about you and your good work as well. You've honored your illustrious family for decades in your own service to the kingdom."

Leem smiled and said, "I thank you for your kind words. Ibrahim is in his office. I can get him for you."

Haji said, "Good. We've just seen and heard something that you both may be quite interested in knowing."

"Oh? Well, then, let me fetch my good nephew immediately." Leem walked back to the open rear door and called down the short hallway, "Ibrahim! You have visitors who have just arrived, two of Walid's friends."

Within seconds, the young man was entering the room with a smile. "Malik! Haji! Good to see you!"

"You remember us!" Malik said, with a big smile.

"Certainly! Walid regaled me with your exploits after the big palace dinner a while back. Your discoveries and actions were crucial in the protection of the monarchy."

"It was our privilege to be of help," Malik said.

"Please, everyone, sit," Leem said, adding, "Ibrahim, you might want to bring in your chair."

"Oh, yes. Certainly. I'll get it."

Then, turning to their visitors, Leem made another quick request. "My boys, there's this chair at the desk, for one of you, and another, over there, in the corner. Pull that one up, too, if you don't mind, so that you can both sit near the desk and we can talk."

Haji grabbed the chair in the corner and put it into place next to the other one that was already facing the desk. The boys then both took their seats as Ibrahim came back in, sliding his chair into the room. Within seconds, they were all comfortably seated.

"Ibrahim, your friends have told me that there's something they need to pass on to us, some information they just discovered and that we might find interesting."

"Really?"

"Yes," Malik said, and Haji nodded.

Then Leem said, "Please, tell us what's happened."

Haji looked over at Malik, and in response, Malik recounted the entire story, from their intention to stop by and say hello, their witnessing the man leaving earlier, the fact that they both had a strange feeling about him, and then, most of the other details as to what happened when they followed the man from the front door and down the street. At this point, Haji interrupted his friend and, looking at Leem, said, "Please, Mr. Hadad, we don't want you to think that we'll make a habit of following your clients when they leave your office!"

At that, Leem and Ibrahim both laughed. "I'm relieved!" Leem said, joking. "That could otherwise be bad for business. We'd have to put a rather unusual warning on our door: 'We Investigate Our Clients. You Will Be Followed When You Leave.' It might scare away most of our business!" At that, everyone laughed.

"Yes, Uncle, I think most people would leave as soon as they read the sign!" Ibrahim got another laugh from them all with that.

"So, to get back to the story," Malik said, "we noticed a small café on the street where our man had disappeared. I went inside, and there he was, just taking a seat in the back, at a booth with another man, a bushy bearded man. I got Haji and we entered to have tea, asking for the booth next to theirs. When we sat, we heard some of their conversation. And, again, I'm very sorry for this. We don't make it a habit to poke our noses into other people's business, but we both had a very strong feeling about this man. It was an unusual situation."

"Don't worry," Leem assured them. "I don't think there's anything wrong with what you did, under the circumstances. Now, tell me: What did you overhear that you think will be of interest to us?"

Malik went on, "Well, we couldn't hear much from the other man. He was speaking too softly. But we heard our guy say stuff, and I have a good memory, so this is pretty much word-for-word from his side of the conversation. He said: 'Yes, I think he'll get us the name and location. I agree. The man has to be stopped. The whole thing could come unraveled. No one else knows that the animals are coming from so many places. Yes. We'll keep our distance. No. No one will even suspect. The detective has no idea what he's helping us to accomplish.' Then, one of them said something else and they both sort of laughed and the other guy coughed a couple of times."

Leem looked very serious, as Malik went on. "But then, this other man, the one with the full beard, after saying some things we couldn't hear, stood up and right before he left said softly, but still loudly enough for us to hear, the words: 'Just make sure it happens within two weeks. No excuses. We have to stop him … permanently. And then cover the trail.' That's what he said and then he walked away."

Leem was slowly nodding his head. "I knew there was something wrong, even perhaps badly wrong, and this fills in the picture a bit."

"Could we ask you for more of the picture that we don't have?" Haji said.

"Yeah, that would help a lot," Malik added.

"Well, ordinarily, we have a strict rule not to discuss a client's business with anyone else. But I also have a strange feeling, a strong sense, that this man is a criminal and not a legitimate client. He wants to use us to gather the information he needs, and then he plans to cover the trail, which means, most likely, getting rid of us so that no one outside his organization can possibly connect him with what he intends to do, and that sounds like … eliminating the individual whose identity he has asked us to find."

"Oh, my," Ibrahim said. "This is terrible."

"Yes, I agree. I'd hate to lose a potential future client."

Ibrahim had to laugh and shake his head at that.

Leem continued, "But I'd hate even more for him to lose me."

Ibrahim replied, "So, Uncle, what should we do?"

"I think we should share with these two young men what we were told by our visitor earlier, what we were asked to do, and the constraints that existed on the information I was trying to get. Then, we take all this to the king—after we take the promised advance payment, of course."

"The king?" Ibrahim was surprised.

"The individual we've been asked to find has been visiting national capitals and speaking with former and current intelligence officers, it seems, in addition to chiefs of police. I can follow up with the chiefs myself, but I suspect that no one from Cairo could have gone to such nearby capital cities with the proper access without being a friend or associate of the king or even, perhaps, representing him on this mission. And this man's life is in danger. So the king should know, right away."

"I agree," Malik said, and Haji was nodding his head.

"But first, I'll tell you what happened during the stranger's visit here, what I asked, and what he answered. I took notes. My memory isn't what it once was, but between neurons and notebooks, I'm fairly reliable."

"Neurons?" Haji said. "What are those?"

"Oh, nerve cells in the brain," Leem explained. "I recently read of their discovery by a research scientist in Spain, a brilliant man named Santiago Ramón y Cajal. Neurons are apparently cells that form the basis for memory, and support our thoughts."

"I see," Haji said. "So, the brain is made of these nerve cells?"

"Yes, and some of mine still work, so let's see what I can recall and share with you about our visitor." Leem then launched into the whole story and when he was finished, said, "I'm telling you boys this because you're so close to the prince and the king, and we may need your help, moving forward, since our man in question has no way of connecting you with us."

"If there's anything we can do, we'll be glad to be of help," Haji said. And it was good that he had this attitude, one that he shared with Malik, because at the moment, they had no idea the full extent of what they'd be called to do, and the danger that would be involved. In the mix, they might actually have a chance, after all, to meet the man who drove the blue car away from the site of the attempted pet abduction, and it would turn out to be very fortunate that they didn't ever come face to face with him that day in the park, as they should have, had they done everything properly.

Sometimes what looks like a failure can oddly be the one doorway that exists to lead us to what we truly need, and this is a wonderfully ironic feature of the way things work in our world.

17

Danger in the Desert

The day of travel was now over. Walid, Mafulla, Kissa, and Hasina were variously sitting or lying down in the sand outside Walid and Mafulla's tent, just a few feet away from the slightly larger one that was shared by Walid's parents, who were his new next door neighbors, Rumi and Bhati. The four students were already much more physically sore from the ride than the three friends of the prince ever would have imagined being at the end of their first day on camels. Walid had basically forgotten his own first experience of this until someone mentioned it. And they could hardly believe it when he said, "You think you're sore now? Just wait until tomorrow!"

That evoked major groans and loud protests of "You've got to be kidding!" and "Don't even think such a thing!"

Walid laughed and said, "Unfortunately, I know what I'm talking about. I'm speaking from intimate personal knowledge here. Your first full day on a camel is something your body is going to feel for several days. But the worst, the very worst, will be tomorrow, all day long."

"Why didn't you warn us?" Mafulla said, articulating what all three of them were thinking.

"Do you think I wanted to go on this trip without you guys?"

They all groaned again. Hasina said, "Don't make me throw something at you or, or … I don't know: bury you in the sand!"

"If you could, you'd be a lot less sore than me. I can hardly move," Mafulla said to her. "And what really gets me," he continued, "is that right now, Clyde probably feels fine, and he was lugging me around all day. I was sitting. I'm worn out and in lots of pain … from sitting. It makes no sense at all."

"That's for sure," Hasina said.

"Yeah, I guess we're all a bunch of wimps," Walid laughed, and then added, jokingly, "but especially … you guys."

"Speak for yourself, Prince of Wimps," Kissa retorted and laughed. "I think I'm being very brave about it. You haven't heard me say a word of complaint."

"Well, that's true," Walid had to admit. "But I did see you sit down more carefully than at any other time since I've known you. And yet, I will have to admit that, by suffering in silence, you've demonstrated your superiority to me in this regard and so, I bow to you."

"You're not supposed to bow to any human being," Kissa reminded him.

"I'll make an exception with you."

Hasina looked at Mafulla and said, "Now, that's what I like to hear."

"Wait! I'll bow, too, in recognition of your intrinsic superiority, as well!" Mafulla was looking straight at his special friend, then he glanced quickly at the other two and then back at her, saying, "I mean, when I'm no longer so sore I can't move, I'll bow—I promise, I'll bow!"

"Too late," she responded. "You heard him say it first and just copied him when I pressured you. So, it doesn't count."

"No, no. I can assure you, I'll make it count! I'll both bow and scrape! No prince is allowed to scrape, and there are no exceptions possible. I'm sure of that. It's somewhere in the laws. But I'm allowed! And I'll bow and scrape! In fact, I'm doing it already, verbally, as you can tell! Plus, I beg your humble forgiveness and forbearance!"

"Ha! You're supposed to be the one who's humble, not me."

"What?" Mafulla looked confused.

Hasina explained, "You said you beg my humble forgiveness, but you should have said that you humbly beg my forgiveness."

"Whatever you say! I humbly beg it! I beg you! I would get on my knees if my knees still worked," Mafulla joked, and they all had to laugh.

"Now, that's bowing and scraping of the most elevated and truly impressive sort," Walid commented.

Kissa added, "Yes, it could even represent the pinnacle, or perhaps, more appropriately, the nadir, of bowing and scraping," and Hasina laughed.

Walid then sighed theatrically and commented, "I'm quite humble already, but apparently still not enough." He looked at his best friend and continued, "I've just now been beat out once more, and this time in depth and displays of humility, of all things, by my favorite Duke or Earl, or Satrap, or whatever in the world you are, and long may be."

Mafulla then replied, in a playfully haughty tone, "In light of the talents I've just displayed, Your Royal Highness, I would think that something like 'His Non-Royal Lowness' might be the most apt form of address, henceforth, for my distinctive personage."

"Well, then, Your Non-Royal Lowness, when do we eat?" Hasina asked, in a mock-serious tone of continued merriment.

"Ha! I don't know, but I beg your humble … wait … I humbly beg your patience, once more, while I will gladly and expeditiously seek to retrieve that information for you." He turned to Walid and, raising high his eyebrows, said, "Your Highness: May I ask what might be the answer to the lovely lady's question?"

"Yes, most certainly, you may," Walid deadpanned and then smiled silently.

"Well …"

"A deep subject," Walid remarked.

"Oh! Humor of the most ancient sort!" Mafulla exclaimed.

"You recognize it?"

"Yes! It's a joke that has long stood the test of time, and must stand no longer! So, will someone please push it over, at this moment, once and for all?"

"And, presumably, knock it far down the … well?" Walid added.

"Yes! Throw the world's oldest, driest joke to the bottom of the deepest well where it will become sufficiently waterlogged that it will never again rise to the surface and see the light of day!"

Hasina looked at Kissa and said, "Meanwhile, my question goes without an answer, as His Lowness and His Highness make bad jokes about a bad joke—a situation which, my growing hunger informs me, is no joke at all."

"Ok, Ok," Walid said. "I think the soldiers should have something ready for us in less than half an hour. That's the impression I got when I saw Masoon earlier, right before we pitched camp."

"Thanks, man," Mafulla said, wiping fake sweat from his brow.

"I'm so glad the king sent two soldiers who can cook," Kissa said. "I'm hungry, too."

"Yeah, these guys are pretty famous, at least in the army, for what they can put together. They were both trained at some culinary school. I overheard one of them joke, poetically, 'I devote my life, to fork and knife!' and the other said, right back, 'Perhaps quite soon, you'll get to the spoon.' Very clever."

"Oh, my, utensil humor! They're almost as good as us," Mafulla commented. "We need to watch this competition closely." Then he added, "I just hope my poor, sore body can lift a fork and knife. But if not, Hasina, will you feed me? Pretty please?"

"Gladly," she said. "That will give me the opportunity to decide exactly what you eat, and how much."

"Oh. Yikes. Forget Plan B, then," Mafulla replied. "We'll stick with Plan A." Then he looked down and said, "Fingers! Hands! Arms! By the waning power vested in me, I command you to function properly, and to eat heartily and freely this evening!"

"And what do they say?" Hasina asked.

"My fingers declare that they have it … nailed—no bones about it."

"Ugh," Hasina and Kissa said at once.

"Wait. It's a … joint effort."

"Stop," Hasina said, wagging her own finger at him.

"No, no, I can feel their agreement and utter commitment to our mutual good," Mafulla explained. "I'm now at peace. Bring on the grease."

The groan and laugh that this evoked was suddenly interrupted by the loud nearby sounds of Bam! Bam! Bam! Bam! Bam! Bam! Bam! Bam! Altogether, there were eight rifle shots, rapidly delivered, and overlapping, as if from two or more guns, from not far away, and in the direction of where they would all be going in a few minutes to eat. Walid, Mafulla, Kissa, and Hasina all instinctively jumped up and began to move toward the sound of the gunfire, as an effect of their training. Masoon, Hamid, and Omari were running to the same area from different directions. Omari and Masoon both had guns with them as they ran. Other members of the security detail were also rapidly converging on the spot, armed and ready.

Walid and Mafulla got to the scene right after Masoon, and no more than two seconds before the girls, and they heard one of two soldiers standing there quickly explain. "I'm so sorry, Masoon, for the sudden disruption and the shock it must have caused everyone! There were five large vipers together! Five deadly poisonous vipers here in the sand! We were patrolling the area and happened to see them in the last vestiges of the day's light. They were moving toward where we are all going to eat! And they were fast! We had to act quickly."

"I understand. You did the right thing," Masoon replied. "I would have done the same. We can't have such snakes in our midst, of all things. Please gather your colleagues who are not preparing our meal, and do a thorough perimeter search with lights, immediately. Cover as wide an area as you can, perhaps as much as thirty to forty yards out, in your sweep. Make sure that we've not inadvertently set up camp near a source of such threats. We'll also have each tent checked."

"Yes, sir," one of the soldiers responded. "Right away," the other replied, as they moved to organize their fellows, many of whom had just arrived at the spot, fully armed and ready for action.

Hamid had also come up in time to hear the explanation. "Strange," he turned and said to Masoon.

"These snakes are mainly nocturnal creatures, and so, this is their time to venture forth."

"But five, and all together, and right here?"

"Yes, that is a bit odd."

"Have you ever seen five together in the desert?"

"No, I have to admit that, with all my travels, I never have."

"Maybe I'm overly cautious, but I think we should keep this fresh in our minds and be alert to any further anomalies we may come across, tonight or tomorrow. Remember the fire."

"I agree, my friend."

"Something tells me this is no random occurrence."

After the excitement died down a bit, they all heard the dinner bell ring and began to make their way toward where the food was going to be served, not far at all from the place of the shooting.

"Has anyone seen mom?" Hasina asked her friends, generally.

"No, not since we arrived and pitched our tents," Mafulla answered right away.

"She would usually be among the first responders to the gunshots we heard," Hasina pointed out, as she glanced around.

"You're right," Kissa replied.

"Let's go to our tent," Hasina said, and she began to walk quickly in that direction.

"Good idea," Kissa said and motioned for the boys to follow them.

As they approached the tent from a distance, they didn't see Layla anywhere around it. But as they drew closer, they noticed that her gun lay in the sand in front of the closed door-flap to the tent. It was not like Layla to put a firearm directly onto the sand like that, or to leave one unattended. And the gun looked more like it had been dropped, and not placed gently onto the ground.

"Mom!" Hasina said in a loud voice, looking around outside the tent.

"Layla!" Kissa yelled out as well. But there was no answer.

In Cairo, at the palace, Kular leaned through the doorframe of the king's dining room and said, "Your Majesty, I'm sorry to interrupt your dinner, but you have visitors who have asked to see you and have said that the matter of their concern is urgent."

"Who are the visitors?" the king asked.

"Mr. Leem Hadad, Ibrahim Hadad, and with them are our good friends, Malik and Haji."

"Oh. Well, this is a bit of a surprise. But I'm almost finished anyway. Please take them into my sitting room, and I can meet them there momentarily."

"Yes, Your Majesty." Kular bowed and left to do as he had been asked.

The king then took a few more bites of his dinner, sipped his drink, and rose from his chair. He walked over to the inner door and made his way into the private sitting room from its side entrance. His guests were already seated on chairs and a sofa and, on his appearance, all stood quickly. The phrase, "Your Majesty," was repeated by every one of them.

"It's good to see you all," the king said. And then he added, "Ibrahim, is this your uncle?"

"Yes, Your Majesty. Please allow me to present to you Mr. Leem Hadad."

Leem bowed and Ali said, "It's a great pleasure to meet you after hearing about your wonderful work in Alexandria in service to the kingdom all these years."

"Thank you, Your Majesty."

"My nephew, the prince, has told me how much he recently enjoyed making your acquaintance, and Ibrahim has filled us in on your new venture here in town. I couldn't possibly be more pleased to have you in our fair city and doing the fine work here that you've chosen."

"You're most gracious, Majesty. And it's the work that brings us here to see you this evening."

"Oh. I see. Well, please sit, all of you, and tell me your concern."

"We're so sorry to interrupt you at dinnertime," Leem said.

"No, think nothing of it," the king replied. "I was just finished anyway, and I always enjoy visitors."

"We do come about a fairly urgent matter," Leem further explained.

The king nodded and said, "Feel free to tell me anything."

"We knew you'd want to hear this soon, Your Majesty," Malik added.

"I appreciate your coming to see me with any information of importance."

Leem thanked the king, looked over at Ibrahim, and began the narrative about his caller earlier that day, the potential client who had introduced himself as Mansur Arobi. Leem told the king all that had been said between them, how evasive the man had been in many ways, and how, even as they spoke, he had a strange feeling about him that something was not right, or at least not how it was being represented to him. He then turned the story over to Malik and Haji, who told the king about going to visit Ibrahim, seeing Mansur as he was leaving, and having both felt very strange about him, to the point that they decided to follow him from a distance. They recounted the café sighting and what they did, along with what they heard. They again repeated it all verbatim as they had heard it, and described both the men who had been together in the corner booth.

Leem then finished out the story with his sense that this was a criminal who was seeking information for the purpose of murder, and that he then intended to multiply his victims by visiting the detective agency once again and cleaning up loose ends.

The king sat silently, carefully listening during all this and, when Leem and the boys were finished with their account, he said, "This is all most interesting, and I'm quite glad that you came over right away to bring it to my attention. Leem, do you know why or how this man, this Arobi, as he called himself, chose you in particular for the investigative job?"

"No, Your Majesty, he didn't say."

The king nodded and said, "Well, what I'm about to tell you should not go beyond us in this room." He took a moment and looked at each face, and they all nodded their agreement. Then he continued.

"The man you've been asked to track down and identify is a good friend that I've sent to these capitals on a fact finding mission. It's none other than Reela Adi, Mafulla's uncle, well known to you, Malik, and you, Haji." Turning to Leem and Ibrahim, he said, "I don't know whether either of you has met him, yet, but he's a wonderful man who served our kingdom for years as a top intelligence officer. He has many contacts abroad, and is assisting us still, at my request, from time to time. And this is such a time."

"May we ask what he's investigating for you, Your Majesty?" Leem inquired.

"Yes. I've been increasingly troubled, of late, by all the animal disappearances and abductions in our city. I've had a strange feeling about it all, and wanted to see whether it was a more widespread phenomenon in our region generally, or was simply local in nature. Reela has reported recently that it's also been going on in all three of the other capital cities he's visited. This is what I had suspected might be the case, but without knowing why. There are forces in motion, things going on, that are troubling in a deep sense. Without being able to explain how I have this inkling, I've nonetheless felt that there's something big afoot that might threaten the kingdom in a new way. And I think it may be connected with this new crime wave. I sent Reela to investigate one aspect of the situation for me, just to learn more about the scale, and perhaps the nature, of what's going on."

"This is all very interesting, Your Majesty." Leem looked thoughtful.

"Yes, it is," the king replied. "So the man you're supposed to identify is our very own Reela. He's the one who'll be targeted for elimination, if your would-be-client has anything to say about it. But let me ask you this: Do you have any contact information for this Mansur Arobi?"

"Yes, Your Majesty," Leem answered. "He left me his business card with a local telephone number on it. There's no address, just the phone number."

"We can trace the number and learn the address," the king said. "In light of what Malik and Haji saw and heard, along with some of the remarks that this Mansur made to you, Leem, we have a most solid indication that there are several people involved in this, along with Arobi, just in our area. If they are, indeed, a part of what Reela is looking into, the network of their organization extends through at least four countries. We need to locate each and every one of the men who are here, but without their knowing or suspecting in any way that they're being identified and tracked."

"We can certainly help with that," Leem said.

At that moment, Kular knocked on the door and put his head in, saying, "I'm most sorry, Your Majesty, but Hoda El-Bay is here to see you and says that it's a matter of the utmost immediate urgency."

"Please send her in right away."

Within two seconds, Hoda was walking through the door. The men all stood, including the king.

She nodded at the others and spoke right away, directly to the king. "Your Majesty, there's something wrong. A good friend of ours is facing something quite serious. Where's Layla right now?"

"They should be done with their first day in the desert, and should be in camp, by this point in the evening," the king replied. They're a full day's ride from El-Wadi.

"She needs our help with an urgent matter."

"She has Masoon, Hamid, Omari, and others, as you know."

"They can't help her now, not in the way she needs, and to the extent that she may need. May I talk with you alone for a moment?" She looked at the others and said, "I'm so sorry. I'll speak to the king only for a very few minutes, and then excuse myself. If this were not a most pressing matter, I wouldn't have interrupted your meeting."

"That's not a problem at all," Leem said. "Gentlemen," he addressed Ibrahim, Malik, and Haji. "We should wander off back into Kular's office for a bit, and allow the king some time." He turned back and said, "Your Majesty. Madame El-Bay." And with that, he led them all out of the room.

"Thank you, Leem," the king said. As the door shut, he turned back to Hoda and asked, "What's going on?"

"It's bad." Hoda took a deep breath and let it out. Then she did her best to find the right words to convey what she needed to say. The king sat down immediately.

A great distance away, the small ferret-like man reappeared in the master's doorway with a feeling of great agitation and said, "Sir, I want to be of help."

"Your help is not needed now."

"But I can tell something's wrong. Surely, I can be of assistance. A late delivery was just made and I'm now completely free for the evening and want to be of help. I'll do anything."

"This is far beyond your knowledge and competence, and is already well underway," the older man said.

"Should I at least gather some of the others?"

"Not now. It won't be necessary."

"But, are you sure it's safe for you to do whatever you're doing, or to face whatever you're facing, alone?"

The only answer to this was silence. And then, after maybe a ten second pause, the older man replied in a calm, firm voice, "Don't ever say such a thing to me again."

"What to you mean?"

"Don't ever underestimate me again or it will be the last mistake you ever make on this earth. If I didn't know of your loyalty and affection for me, and your unbreakable commitment to what we're doing, those would have been your last words. I do appreciate your concern, but leave me this moment and let me get on with it."

"Yes, sir! I didn't mean anything, but are you sure that ..."

"Silence! You're dismissed!"

The man disappeared from the doorway even more rapidly than he had appeared. His cheeks flushed with shame and humiliation, mixed with awe and fear. As he walked quickly through the night air, he could tell that something was moving, coming, approaching, and that the plans of decades were about to be tested.

The battle might be sooner than he or the master had thought. It would certainly be harder. There was danger in the desert, not so far away on this very night—even the stars seemed to testify to that—and it was coming like a windstorm, right for them.

18

The Start of Battle

"Mom!" Hasina had cupped her hands to project her voice into the dark beyond the tent. Then, something turned her around and she quickly raised the tent flap and bent down to look inside. As her eyes adjusted to the deeper darkness in there, she thought she saw, and then, with a jolt of fright, knew she was seeing, her mother sitting toward the back, in a meditative pose, the famous Lotus Position, and with what looked like … a full size viper right beside her leg.

There was an instant second jolt of adrenalin injected into her system. Her skin crawled and her insides seemed to tighten up as a wave of fear coursed through her. "Mom?" Hasina spoke in a lower voice. Then she turned a little and faced just enough away to direct her voice outside the tent. "Guys. Come quickly!"

Mere seconds later, Masoon and Hamid got to her and put their heads into the tent door, and Masoon said, gently, "We're here."

"Mom … is not responding and … there's a big viper beside her, on her right, our left."

Masoon moved quietly around Hasina and then she felt a hand, Mafulla's hand, on her arm, gently pulling her back from where she crouched, just inside the tent door.

"The viper's been cut in two," Masoon said, softly, as he bent over it and lit a match for illumination. "There's a knife here beside it in the sand, as well."

"Was she bitten?" Hamid asked.

"I don't know. I can't tell yet," Masoon answered, in a near whisper, as Layla sat there, completely still, eyes closed and totally unresponsive to anything that was going on around her. The general was also motionless for a moment and looked closely, but couldn't tell whether his friend was breathing. He turned back to Hamid and said, "Come, look."

Masoon then pulled a candle from his pocket and lit it and held it close to Layla's leg, then her sandaled feet, then up to her hands and arms. Hasina had backed up a bit, due to Mafulla's small tug on her arm, and she now had Kissa's arm around her as she kneeled at the outer edge of the door, staring into the tent and praying for her mother's life.

Walid was the farthest from the door, and he felt something deep and strange. A shudder went through him, then a reassurance of some sort that someone was with him and bringing a huge benevolent power into his mind and heart in that moment. He knew, in the next instant, that it was the king. It was as if the king's spirit was guiding his spirit to find Layla's and help her. Walid at first squatted down, and then sat in the sand where he was, six feet from Layla's tent flap. His eyes closed without any conscious intent on his part. He was going somewhere.

It was a desert setting, but another place, with no one visibly around, only a large dune in front of him and a feeling that led him to begin to walk up the side of the dune. It was now suddenly mid-day and hot, and as he got up higher on the dune, he could begin to see the sky beyond it, and it was dark—the deepest, darkest black he had ever seen in nature, and yet it had almost greenish blue aspects to it, and it was somehow full of … malice and anger and power. And yet, he continued to climb toward the top of the dune and as he arrived at the uppermost ridge, he could see Layla down below, sitting in her lotus position, motionless. In that instant, he knew what she was doing. She was holding back the oncoming storm, stopping it in its tracks, resisting its forward movement, all by herself. Her focused power had matched the force behind the storm and had locked it in a stalemate.

Walid could tell that it was his job, with the king and Hoda back in Cairo beside the king, to break this deadlock and help Layla push the storm back, calm it down, and dissipate it. He spontaneously called her name. "Layla!" He shouted, "Layla, we're here!" He felt something behind him like a wave of cosmic energy beyond anything he had ever experienced, and he knew that he was to add the power of his own mind to the flow of this current. And he did, with all the concentration he had, banishing any other thoughts or distractions or feelings, and pushing an intense pure focus of energy through Layla and beyond her, into the storm. For a long, large, capacious moment in which time did not seem to pass, the energy flowed and rushed and then, in the next real moment, a tick of the clock that vaulted him out of the fullness of what he had just experienced and launched him back into the onward movement of time, he could see the storm begin to recede. It moved away, at first slowly, and then faster. The sky grew clear and bright blue where it had been black. And even the dark blackness of the storm, farther away where it now was, began to break up and fade and grow lighter.

At the bottom of the dune, Walid could see that Layla's arms moved and her hands came down into the sand on either side of her. He saw her stretch, and then stand and turn and look up at him, and wave and smile. And at that moment, he was back in front of her tent with eyes open and he could hear Hamid say, "She's alive and breathing. She seems to be in a trance. No snake bite put her into this position."

In the next moment, Layla's eyes opened, and her head moved, side-to-side, and her hands came down into the sand on either side of her. She saw Masoon and Hamid and the candle, and beyond them, her daughter, Hasina. And then, without any further movement, she spoke. "It's gone."

"What's gone, Layla?" Masoon asked gently.

"The storm."

"Was there a storm?"

"Yes, coming at us fast and with a dangerous power."

"Were you attacked by the snake that was beside you?"

"The snakes were just messengers."

"Were you bitten?"

"No."

"What was the message of the snakes?"

"That if we go any farther through the desert toward our final destination, there will be a storm, a massive blast and a mighty concussive wind that will kill us all, quicker than a viper."

"Do you believe the message?"

"I believe its intent and authenticity, but we have defeated the storm, at least, for now."

"Who?"

"The king, and Hoda, and Walid and I."

"When?"

"Just now—in our souls."

"Are you Ok?"

"We're fine. But I'm tired."

Hamid said, "Are you sure your body was not harmed at all?"

"Yes, I'm sure. Help me up, please."

Masoon and Hamid helped Layla stand, bent over as she had to be in the tent, and they guided her out the door, and she breathed deeply. Hasina threw her arms around her. "Mom! I was so scared!"

Layla smiled and hugged her and said, simply, "We're Phi, my love. Fear nothing."

Mafulla let out a breath that it sounded like he had been holding for practically the entire time. Then he suddenly noticed Walid a few feet behind him, sitting in the sand.

Layla looked at the prince and said, "Thank you, Walid."

"Thank you, Layla. And I thank Hoda and the king."

Layla said, "I thank them both, as well. Remind me to hug them when we return."

"Ok, then me."

"I can hug you now."

"No," Walid smiled, "I meant for you to remind me to hug them too, after you do."

"Oh! Ok. But you still need a big hug of appreciation and solidarity," she said and walked toward him, and he stood slowly and they grabbed each other in a strong, hard, embrace.

"We did it together," she said to him.

"We did."

Kissa spoke and said, "You guys! This is all so mysterious! What did you do? What just happened?"

"Yeah," Hasina added. "What in the world happened?"

Masoon interrupted and said, "Let me get some food brought over here for all of us, and snag Omari, and then we can hear the entire story together."

"Yes," Layla said. "That'll be good."

In the royal sitting room, Hoda opened her eyes and turned to the king, who was quietly looking straight ahead, and said, "Oh, my. That was intense. I had no idea of the full force we were up against. Thank you, Your Majesty."

"I thank you, Hoda, and I can be sure that Layla does, as well—and Walid."

"Yes, I noticed Walid with us, in front of us. He was on the dune and saw Layla sitting below and holding back the storm. But, she had been pushed to the limit."

"We joined her at an opportune moment, when the time was fully right," the king said. No more than four or five minutes had passed since the king's other visitors had gone outside to wait for more time with him. The king then rose, and of course, so did Hoda.

"There's more to come," Hoda said.

"Yes, I know," the king replied. "But everyone's safe now, thanks to your intervention."

"I felt the trouble coming an hour ago," Hoda said. "I felt something last night, but an hour ago, I was alerted to the imminent danger and came straight to the palace, as quickly as I could."

"I'm glad you did. I've been too busy with other things. I needed your alertness. I wasn't given the knowledge on my own. If I had been, I might have faced it alone. But it was intended for us to join together in this way, and with the prince. I could feel it, the rightness of it. And I thank you deeply for it."

"I'm humbled by your gratitude. It's my joy to have been involved."

"I know. And, now, you can go home. Have Kular provide you with an escort, a palace guard."

"Are you sure, Your Majesty?"

"Yes. Ask Kular to see whether Paki or Amon might be available. In the aftermath of what we just experienced, I'd like you to walk with another Phi, if it's possible."

"I do feel a bit worn out by what we just experienced."

"Yes. I'm sure." The king showed Hoda to the door and, after she left, he invited his earlier visitors to come back into the room for a few more minutes.

"Is everyone all right?" Leem asked.

"Yes, thank you for asking," the king said. "I'm so sorry that I couldn't take the time to ask whether you knew Hoda, the teacher of the girls in the palace school and the wife of the man who instructs Malik and Haji, along with the other boys their age who are in our school. She's also one of our closest aids here in the palace, and had news of a serious need that, fortunately, I was able to help deal with and solve. So, all is well."

Malik and Haji were each a bit perplexed by what the king had just said. He helped deal with a serious need without leaving the room? And he hadn't sent any messages out of the room—unless Hoda was carrying a message with her. And there was no sign of that. They couldn't see a telephone or a radio nearby, either. So, how exactly did Ali deal with whatever the problem was? It was a bit confusing. And, in addition, they both wanted to ask whether their friends were all completely safe, but they were reluctant to do anything that could seem even remotely like they were questioning the king, or his best judgment. They knew that he was even more concerned about everyone's safety than they were, and they were very concerned, after hearing Hoda's words. But they both realized that the king knew things they didn't know, and in addition, his current calmness of spirit silently communicated itself to them with a deep reassurance they could feel. And that alone, within no more than half a minute, set aside any anxiety they had been experiencing.

"Now, please sit again. And let's get back to the issue we were discussing," the king said. "We have to approach all this carefully."

Ali took his seat and the others also sat where they had been before. Ibrahim spoke first. "Will you just have Mansur Arobi found and arrested, as the first order of business, Your Majesty?"

"Ah, that would cut us off from a potential wealth of information that could be important."

"He might talk in jail, under interrogation."

"True, and then he could, potentially, tell us everything he knows. But it's possible that there's much more to be known than even he's aware of. By arresting him, we'd be taking out of play the one man we know of who can connect us up with any others whose actions are involved in all this. And they may be individuals with access to information that goes beyond his own awareness and understanding."

"So," Leem said, "right now, Your Majesty, it seems that the wise path is to follow him, to see where he leads us."

"Yes, that's my opinion," the king concluded.

"And we have just two weeks, or else I don't get an extra bonus from his boss," Leem said, with a serious face, and the king laughed.

"Mansur seems to know, at least at one level, what's going on with the animal abductions in Cairo and these other three capital cities. So, he must have contacts involved in all these crimes, or who at least know the people committing them. He's also working for someone, the individual who, he said, would provide the bonus. This is, presumably, a man who's orchestrating all the abductions. I have a feeling that even he may not be at the top of the food chain in these matters. But he could represent a level that we need to get to in order to stop these crimes, and position ourselves for the next leap forward in learning, ultimately, what purpose this crime wave is serving."

Both Leem and Ibrahim were nodding their heads in agreement. "Now, let me think for a moment," the king added, "and decide how we should divide up our responsibilities in order to bring this stage of our search to a successful conclusion." Everyone sat quietly for a few moments while the king pondered the possibilities. He then began to make suggestions to each of them, involving Malik and Haji as equal partners in all this and reminding them that, since they were on break from school, they would have the time to perform some important jobs for him.

"I can get a message to Reela right away, and have him return to town," the king said. "I can also provide him with extra security for the trip, starting immediately, to make sure he gets back safely. And that will buy us more time, in case we need it."

Out in the desert, Layla had just finished her tale of everything that had happened, from the moment during meditation when she heard nearby gunshots, to the instant she opened her eyes and saw Masoon and Hamid, and then Hasina and the others. Whatever force had put a viper into her tent had not anticipated the extent of her powers to respond, both to that threat, and to the larger one.

Masoon said, "That's quite an unexpected and dramatic story. We're clearly up against something quite strange and serious—what exactly, I have no idea, but someone does not want us to return home, and is willing to do us great harm in mysterious ways in order to communicate that message."

"What should we do?" Kissa asked.

"Continue on," Masoon said.

"Are you sure?"

"Yes." He turned and said, "Layla, you've told us that this storm has been defeated and dissipated."

"Yes, whether it was a literal or metaphorical storm—whatever was most immediately coming at us has been turned back. We're safe from that. But, for all I know, there may be another attempt of some sort. This could have been an effort to effect our destruction, or it may have been mainly a warning. But there was great power involved, and much more than would have been needed for just a warning, or so it seems to me."

Hamid then spoke up. "These efforts to keep us away give us even more reason than we already had, and I would say, by some magnitude, to go on, and even to get to the village as soon as we can. Whoever doesn't want us to arrive at our destination is trying to keep us away for a reason, and it must be an important one, in order for the person or people resisting us to take on either what they perceive as a military caravan, or what they may know to be a group from the palace, or even a contingent of Phi—whatever they think they're dealing with here."

"Good points," Walid said. "It would be helpful to know more about this adversary we may face. Does anyone have a suggestion about how such information could be sought?"

At that question, all of them sat quietly for a few moments, thinking hard. "Ok, we've got power being exercised far beyond what seems naturally available," Masoon said. "First the fire, then the appearance of deadly vipers, and finally this storm of some sort that Layla and our friends faced and defeated, whatever exactly it was."

"It was huge spiritual energy, but not being used for good, whatever else it might have been," Layla said.

"So, there's someone out there, an individual or a group, capable of drawing on lots of deep spiritual energy, and intent on using it for harm. What does that tell us?" Masoon asked.

Mafulla answered, "Someone like Phi, but without any moral commitment to the good of others. This is what I've recently been worried about—someone who's been trained, or has learned, in whatever way, about how to draw on the full power of the mind and the realm of the spirit, but without the good side of Phi … someone who's far beyond what Farouk al-Khoum was, and may be as advanced as any real Phi, like a senior Phi, and yet completely without the guidance of anything good. It's somebody with no moral compass, and a serious agenda that's unknown to us."

"Someone like the monster in the legend," Walid concluded aloud, and they all looked around at each other.

Masoon speculated. "Maybe we should indeed suppose the worst, a monstrous version of Phi—a person, or even worse yet, a group of individuals, who've spent years and decades striving to develop themselves, physically, mentally, and spiritually, but for no good purpose, just the selfish satisfaction of their own boundless desires, despite what that might mean for others."

Hamid immediately replied, "If it's a group, it would be inherently unstable."

"What do you mean?" Walid asked.

"We saw this in the case of the Falma brothers and also the al-Khoum brothers. Only goodness can dependably unite comrades. Aristotle understood it well. Utterly selfish individuals can come together only as mutual manipulators, but even then, only so long as they see the alliance as in their personal interest—and this is always, in the end, self-destructive. But if, however, by contrast, we could be dealing with basically a lone, dangerous individual, even if backed up with followers, he'd have to be immensely powerful in order to go up against senior Phi. And even then, he'd have serious instabilities in his inner self. An amoral monster lacks certain inner and outer harmonies that are required for resilient and sustainable strength."

"Ok, that helps," Mafulla said with a touch of relief in his voice.

"If he's the equal of a single Phi, a senior Phi, and is truly advanced, then he likely knows of Phi," Omari said.

"That's reasonable to suppose," Masoon remarked.

"It's also possible that he's not yet at the peak of his powers," Mafulla pointed out. "He was perhaps temporarily defeated just now by Layla and Walid, and Hoda and the king. But suppose that simply spurs him on to a frantic development of his power, so that this can never happen again."

"Senior Phi represent and have access to immense power, and to the ultimate power. But, still, it's a sobering thought," Hamid replied.

"I come from a long line of sober thinkers … and worriers," Mafulla explained, and Walid had to smile a bit.

Hamid smiled and said, "No worries are allowed around here."

Masoon wanted to make even more progress in their understanding together this threat. And so he next wondered aloud, "Why would this individual or group of people have such a strong desire that we not go to the village?"

"He must have assets there that he wants to protect. Or he could actually be there, or near there," Walid said. "And … he could look like an ordinary person."

"What do you mean?" Mafulla asked.

"Well, we look like ordinary people. At least, I mean, the guys." Walid glanced toward Kissa. "But I suppose you, Masoon, do look a little too scary to be an ordinary person, but my point still mainly stands. There's always an exception, or two, or five, to generalizations like this one. But you get my point."

Mafulla then helpfully summed up his friend's concern by saying, "Yeah, so, we either look for an ordinary guy, or a female beauty of indescribable splendor, or a really scary character."

"I say we search for an ordinary looking guy," Walid said. "The rare, spectacular lady we won't have to search hard to find. And the scary character will probably come and find us."

"I'm guessing a hermit, or a near-hermit," Masoon opined. "Or, at least a basic loner—somebody with those tendencies."

"Why?" Hasina asked.

"He couldn't live among normal people and be developing himself to this extent, and with malice. Someone would have noticed, and we would have heard about it, I'm guessing. And he's probably not the easiest person to be around, to put it mildly."

"Yeah. A phrase like, 'my best friend, the monster' doesn't quite have the ring of plausibility," Mafulla offered.

"If it's one person, he has immense power, indeed," Layla said. "So, someone would likely have become suspicious about him at some point and told others."

"At least, now we've thought through what we currently have to go on in our effort to identify this person," Hamid concluded.

"Yes. It's good to get our heads around it, to the extent that we can," Layla agreed.

Hamid then added, "It may still be hard to find him, unless … he does indeed find us first."

Walid mused, "Well, I guess, in a sense he has. He sure knows exactly where we are, given the fire disturbance and poison snake placement, and we don't know precisely where he is."

"Good point," Mafulla said.

19

The Oasis

Despite some ongoing concerns and inner reflections experienced by each of the Phi about what they had discussed the night before, the next day of travel was, in all other ways, thoroughly pleasant. Mafulla was a source of nonstop merriment, which Walid immensely enjoyed—but at the same time, he knew that this was his friend's way of dealing with anxiety and nerves. Kissa and Hasina had learned this about Mafulla, too, and laughed a lot at his jokes, in part to help distract him from whatever was bothering him, but mostly just because he was especially funny throughout the day.

Baldoor and Dubin were also at it again, as usual, ribbing each other and laughing and making the most of the travel day. Walid overheard several exchanges, like when Dubin said to Omari, who was riding alongside him, and yet spoke loudly enough for anyone else nearby to hear: "Omari, I'm sure you would not be surprised to hear that my good friend Baldoor was the one person who was glad to see the brood of vipers last night—he started immediately looking around for a frying pan, and already had in mind a sauce we could stew them in. As you can imagine, by the looks of him, he'll eat anything!"

Baldoor, of course, instantly replied, "No, no, no. I draw the line on even trying to cook or eat anything that I would have to go by Dubin to get to—I'm determined to avoid a fight at any time during this trip. The man is like a hungry dog guarding a bone whenever he sees anything remotely edible, however scary it might look to the rest of us! If the snakes had not been shot, they would certainly have fled as soon as they saw his face, and his well-used knife and fork!"

"Oh, I'm the big eater here, am I?" Dubin replied. "I think your very uniform testifies against you! Just ask the poor buttons that are holding on for dear life as we speak. If you even sneeze, you'll litter the desert sand with them, and they'll tell the true tale, my good friend."

And, of course, that's just a snippet of what was going on all during the day's travel. There was always some topic for competitive humor and discussion between these two. They were a real comedy act, and the soldiers along for security especially seemed to enjoy them, since their jocularity touched so often on military topics and wild stories about their own times of service.

The stop for a mid-day rest went smoothly. There were no surprising events, no threats or dangers suddenly manifest at their impromptu camp, and everyone was able to relax and nap without undue wariness. A guard, of course, was always posted, and was changed half way through the rest period, so that the soldiers also could cool down and nap, and there was a rotation as to who would stand guard under the hottest sun each day. That way, everyone got some needed relief and relaxation throughout their time on the sand.

After a light lunch, a long stretch of afternoon travel brought them within sight of the palm-lined oasis that had meant so much to Walid, and that he had often told the others about. They first caught sight of it right before dusk, and they arrived within its welcoming environs before the full darkness of night could catch up with them. Another large caravan was encamped on the north side, so they set up on the southern edge where they had ridden in.

Before the deepest dark of night could altogether cover up the charms of the place, Walid took his best friends on a quick tour. Omari joined them as well. They were amazed at all the trees to be found right here in the middle of nothing but sand in every direction. And there was a pool of water in the midst of it all, with smooth surrounding rocks to sit on. And there were small dwellings built around the pool, but at a distance, so that visitors could enjoy the water without being too close to the houses and feeling like they were intruding in the lives of those who made this their home, as well as their place of business.

The relatively permanent population of the oasis was slight, but filled with people who had the right skills to be of help to long distance travellers, most normally arriving by camel. There were food vendors, people who could repair shoes or sandals and torn clothing, a man who could shoe the occasional horse, as well as perform other blacksmith duties, and even one individual who had been trained in veterinary medicine. There was a general store containing tools and a small selection of clothing for men or women, along with a few things for younger children. Other items were also for sale, like water containers, compasses, saddles, and saddlebags—in short, pretty much everything that might need to be purchased or replaced by people traveling on camel or horseback over long distances. There were even guns and boxes of ammunition for sale in the back.

Some of the shops were still open, and lamps and lanterns burned brightly from inside them. A few men were sitting outside the small general store, not far from the pool, having tea and coffee and various other beverages that they had purchased there, as they talked about the events of the day. Walid didn't recognize most of the people he saw, who were probably from the other caravan that had stopped here before their own arrival. But he did spot a few of the regulars he had met on his last visit.

"Hamish! Hamish! Over here! It's Walid from last year!"

A boy probably nine or ten years old stopped in his tracks and turned around. "Walid? Walid from Dromeda?"

"Yes!"

Hamish smiled and walked over to where Walid and his friends were standing near the pool of water.

"You remember me?" Hamish asked.

"Of course I do!" Walid replied. "We weren't here for very long last year, but we stopped long enough. I had fun playing ball with you and talking about life here in the oasis."

"I remember. But tell me, is it true what I've heard people say?"

"What's that?"

"You're the prince of the kingdom? I heard this weeks after you left and I just couldn't believe it!"

Walid smiled but then put his right index finger to his lips. He said, in a lower voice, "Yes, it's true, but please keep it to yourself, if you can, while we're here."

"Why is that? Is it a secret?"

"We're traveling quietly to my hometown, my village, for a visit, and should be back here within a week. And after that, you can tell anyone you like. For now, I simply want to keep a low profile, and so, I'm just your old friend, Walid."

"Ok, I'll do what you say. It's important for me to stay quiet about it?"

"Very important. National security is at stake."

"Is that why you're in a military uniform?"

"Yes."

"Are you in the army?"

"I'm in uniform only for this trip. But we have many true soldiers with the caravan. The oasis is under our protection while we're here."

"Are we in danger?"

"No, you're safer than you've ever been before."

"Good," Hamish said, and looked at the others. "Are you Walid's friends?"

"Yes," Mafulla said.

"Oh, I'm so sorry!" Walid said quickly. "I should have introduced you."

"Hamish, this is Mafulla, and this is Kissa, and Hasina, and our older friend Omari. They're all traveling with me."

"Good to meet you all," Hamish said.

"Nice to meet you, too" Kissa said, as they all then variously spoke words of greeting to the boy.

"But Walid, can I at least tell my brother?"

"How old is he?"

"Eight."

"Can he be trusted to keep a secret, locked up within him?"

"Yes. With secrets, he can be as silent as a grain of sand—or as mute and mysterious as the Sphinx!"

"Ha! Ok. If you're sure, but only if you're sure. Secrecy is very important to us. To others, we're just the members of a normal military caravan on patrol in the desert, Ok?"

"Whatever you say, ordinary soldier Walid, my very good friend!"

"Now, I have an important question for you."

"Sure, ask anything and I'll tell you … unless it's a secret!" Hamish was a clever boy and playful, and this is part of what Walid had liked about him from their first meeting.

"There was a lady here on my last visit, an older lady who called me over to her while we were playing ball one day and told me things about myself that it was surprising for her to know. And the things she said turned out to be true in ways I didn't even realize at the time."

"Yes, I know her," Hamish said.

"Was she from another caravan that was passing through here at the time?"

"No, she lives here in the oasis."

"She does?"

"Yes, she helps her husband run the general store, right over there. The lights are still on. She may be there now."

"I'd like to see her."

"Do you want me to go and check?"

"Yes, Hamish, if you would, and if she's there, whisper to her that a young man who passed through last year is here again, and that she told me things about a golden future. And I'd like to speak with her."

"Sure! I can do that. Wait here!" Hamish immediately ran off toward the store, weaved his way around the men sitting out front, and then disappeared through the door.

"Would you guys mind, if the lady comes out, and I'd like to speak with her alone for just a minute?"

"Sure, no problem," Omari said and added, "Hey, let's dip our hot and tired feet into the pool. We can sit right over there on the low rocks and give Walid as long as he needs."

"Good idea," Mafulla said.

Kissa looked at Walid. "You're sure?"

"Yeah, for just a minute. I'll give you a full report. I don't want to spook the lady. She has a special knowledge of things, and even things in the future."

"Ok, good plan. But I have a special concern."

"What is it?"

"I'd love to know if Shibby is going to have boy puppies, or girls, or a mix of the two—and whether everyone's going to be Ok."

Walid laughed. "I'll try to remember to ask."

"You will?

"Yeah, sure."

"Ok. Thanks." Kissa smiled big and followed the others over to the rocks next to the pool.

Walid stood there in the cool of the evening for only about a minute and then he could see Hamish come out of the shop with the lady right behind him. They headed straight over to where he was waiting for them.

"Hello there, young man!" the lady said. "Hamish tells me that you remember me."

"Yes, I do, very well," Walid said. "When I was here last year for a brief visit, you told me some things about myself, and even things I didn't know. And you were right."

"Well, I have a gift," the lady replied. "And I love sharing it with others, when I can."

"Hamish," Walid said, "Would you go over to my friends and tell them a little bit about the oasis and what you do here? I'll join you in just a minute. I know they're eager to get your perspective on life here."

"Sure, Walid. I'll go visit with them. You talk." Hamish walked over toward the others, and Walid turned to the lady with a smile.

He said, "I wanted to thank you for calling me over to you and saying the nice things you said to me on that day last year."

The lady replied, "It was my pleasure. I remember well. It was something I felt I should do. I was hoping it didn't seem too strange to you, and that you wouldn't think I was some crazy old woman."

Walid said, "Not at all! It was a bit mysterious to me at the time, but your words stayed with me, and I remembered them. You pretty much predicted the nice things that would happen to me soon after that, in at least a symbolic way."

"I often see symbols, or colors, and sometimes even full pictures of the future. Occasionally, now and then, moving pictures appear to me and I even hear voices and get feelings about things to come."

"How do you do that?"

"Oh, I have no idea," the lady laughed. "But it's sometimes helpful to people. I'm glad I can provide some form of assistance to others, in addition to selling them things they need from my store. Of course, there are times when the news I have to share doesn't seem good, but in the long run, the great gardener provides some form of good to sprout from every seed and every soil, if it's tended properly."

Walid nodded his head in agreement and said, "I wanted to see you mostly just to thank you for sharing with me, but also because I may have a current need."

"Oh?"

"I'm traveling to my home village, Dromeda, to visit for a few days and then return to Cairo."

"Yes."

"There's someone who apparently doesn't want me to complete the trip, and who's been sending powerful signals of his displeasure."

"Yes."

"I need to ask you. I trust you completely. I need to ask you what you see about all this."

"Are you sure, my son, that you want to open the normally locked door of the future and perhaps also discover more clearly the deep secrets of the present?"

"Yes. I'm sure."

"I don't ordinarily look into such things by request."

"I understand."

"I typically see the otherwise unseen only when it comes to me itself, with its own initiative," she explained.

"That's fine. I completely understand if it's not something you can turn on or off. But I wanted you to know that if you see anything, or hear, or sense anything about all this, it would help me greatly for you to tell me, whether it seems good or bad. I'll have peace with it."

"That's good. That's a fine expression of who I feel that you are."

"And this is sort of embarrassing, but there's one more thing."

"What is that?"

"My good friend's dog is going to have puppies, and she'd love to know if they will be male or female."

"Ha, ha, ha," the lady laughed loudly at this, and quickly said, "Two males, two females, all healthy, including the mother."

"Really?"

"Yes."

"That was quick."

"Yes. It was instant. I saw it as soon as you asked. It will be a good birth, and it will happen in about three weeks, or a little more."

"What about my problem?"

"That's not as clear."

"I wonder why?"

"There's a veil. That's the best way I can say what I sense. It's as if there is someone or something that doesn't want these things to be known and, I suspect, is exercising power to prevent any such revelation. There's an interference, a murkiness."

"Can you get around the interference? Can you lift the veil?"

The lady thought for a few seconds and said, "Perhaps. Perhaps I can. You're a special boy. I can feel it all around you. You have goodness and love in your heart. That's a powerful force—the most powerful force there is."

"Can you use that force to pull back the curtain that hangs over this aspect of the present and the future?"

"This is what I'm thinking. Come back to me later. How long will you be here?"

"Only tomorrow, then we leave."

"Tomorrow. I'll seek to have your answers tomorrow. For the meantime, have a good rest here at the oasis. You should sleep well. I can see that far into your future."

"Good, and thank you! I so appreciate your help with my questions."

"Tell your friend not to worry about the dogs. It will all be well. Everyone will be happy, and frolicking around, not long from now."

"Ok, good! Thanks again. I hope we can talk soon."

"Yes. Soon." The lady smiled and turned and walked back to the general store. She spoke to one of the men out front and he got up and disappeared through the trees. She turned and looked back at Walid, and then went into the store and closed the door.

The prince walked over to where his friends all had their feet in the water. "Sorry that took so long."

"No problem, we're just now feeling completely relaxed," Mafulla said, "No worries."

"Where's Hamish?"

"Oh. He had to go somewhere. He said to tell you he'd see you later."

"Oh. Ok."

"This water feels great on my feet."

"Mine, too," Kissa said.

"Yeah," Hasina said. "You should take off your sandals and do this right away.

Kissa added, "And give us a full report on the lady."

Walid did exactly that. He took off his sandals, sat next to the pool, and put his feet in the water along with the others. He then began to tell them all about the lady and their brief and enigmatic previous meeting a year ago on his way across the desert for the first time. He told them what she had said, and how it had stayed with him. He then recounted the conversation that had just taken place, beginning with the good news. "Kissa, I asked her your question."

Kissa laughed in surprise and said, "You did?"

Hasina said, "What question?"

"I told Walid I'd like to know about Shibs and the puppies."

"Oh."

"Yeah, and she said right away, instantly, that Shibby will have four puppies—two male and two female, in about three weeks or a little more. She said everyone is going to be healthy and happy."

"She said that?"

"As soon as I asked, it was like BOOM, she had the answer, and with complete confidence. She said they'd be frolicking soon."

"Oh, wow! That's good news!"

"Yeah, I may have to talk to you about one of those puppies for the palace, or maybe two."

"Ha! Well, we'll see about that."

"Come on! Kular needs a companion. So do Mafulla and I. And, with two, they'd also have each other. Just think about it."

"Ok, maybe. But mom and dad may have already promised the puppies to relatives."

"Oh. Well, keep us in mind, if not."

"Definitely. But did you find out anything else from the lady?"

"Oh, yeah. I told her that someone or some force was apparently trying to keep us from getting back to my home village, and I asked her if she could tell me anything about it."

"You did?" Mafulla said.

"Yeah, and she said that it's veiled, or murky, or something, and she couldn't clearly see anything right away. She said she thought maybe somebody was trying to keep her from seeing or knowing what was going on, but she might be able to get around that."

"How?" Hasina asked.

"Well, this is a little embarrassing."

"Spill it," Mafulla said. "You're among friends here."

"Yes. Good friends. The best," Hasina added.

"Ok. She said that she could tell that I have goodness and love in me, and that this is a powerful force, really the most powerful of all, and that maybe she can use it to pull back the curtain that's otherwise been closed around these events."

"Goodness and love," Hasina said and looked at Kissa while nodding her head. "That's a nice combination."

Kissa just smiled, and said, "Yes, it is," and Walid looked down at his sandals.

Omari now asked, "When is she going to tell you whether she's had success in her efforts?"

"Tomorrow, hopefully. I told her we're leaving early the morning after tomorrow."

"Good. She sounds like a lady with a real gift, an unusual and important one. There are such people in the world, and we should respect and honor them."

"Yeah, she seems really kind," Walid remarked.

Omari then looked past Walid and squinted into the darkness, and in a low voice suddenly said, "There are several men … and they're coming toward us now. I … see what look like weapons."

20

New Developments

Things were busy in Cairo. The king had given Malik and Haji a job to do and some money to spend on meals and incidentals. Their task was to visit the Falafel Stop for a series of lunches and to linger as long as they could, to see if either of the mystery men appeared there again or even passed by. If one of them showed up, it might be a clue that they were living or working somewhere in the immediate neighborhood. Even when the king was able to get an address to go with the telephone number on Arobi's card, through official channels, that would still be no guarantee that either of these men could ever actually be found at that particular location. Such an address would certainly be a piece of the puzzle, but other pieces would also be needed. A sighting of one of the men again in this particular neighborhood could be an important lead. If the boys did see one of the suspects, they were to follow him, if they could, from a safe distance, and report back whatever they learned.

Ibrahim's first job was to ring the number on Mansur's card to see whether he might answer personally, or someone else would take the call. In case a third party picked up, he was to say that he needed to ask Mr. Arobi a few more crucial questions, if he could get back in touch as soon as possible. On the other hand, if Mansur himself answered, Ibrahim had some prepared questions to ask him, but the task had been mainly to see whether the telephone number was a direct indication of where Arobi could be found. The king had Naqid quietly initiating a search to discover the location of the phone.

Leem's job was a bit more complex. He was to call the chiefs of police in Tripoli, Algiers, and Tunis and convey to them the importance of keeping secret their recent visitor's identity, no matter who might appear to ask about it, and regardless of what anyone might say in their pursuit of his name. The senior detective's next job was to ask the chiefs about any leads they might have concerning the animal abductions they had reported to their visitor. Leem was to explain that he was helping various officials in Egypt coordinate their own efforts to stop the thefts. And he was to intimate to them that these odd events might go far beyond their apparent nature and be part of a large scheme that could cause immense trouble for the countries involved, out of all proportion to the precise laws now clearly being violated. He was then to convey back to the king whatever he was told as a result of these calls. Fortunately, because of all his years of service as the chief of police in Alexandria, he knew two of these men personally, to differing degrees, and was confident that he could count on their help, candor, and confidentiality. Even with the chief he had never met, he had some social connections. So he expected some measure of success from the calls he would make.

Leem had been allowed to come in and use a palace phone for these calls. On the first morning of the very first day of his investigation, he struck gold. He had been on the phone with the chief of police in Tunis no more than fifteen minutes when the man revealed something of great importance. He reported that, in a recently attempted animal abduction within his city limits, local police had intervened and chased the suspects quite a distance. Although, on this particular occasion, the criminals had unfortunately eluded capture, one of them dropped two pieces of paper in the scramble to get away. One ragged scrap had on it an address that was not Tunisian, so far as they could tell. And the other was apparently a personal or business card, but had on it no name of a person or business, only a phone number, and it was not a Tunisian exchange.

Leem asked if the chief could provide him with the number on the card. He replied that, normally, he didn't keep evidence of any kind in his own office, but that this rash of animal disappearances and abductions had been so strange and unparalleled in their history that he had held on to the card, among some other things, intending to investigate it all a bit more himself. Leem could hear him opening a desk drawer and then another one, and rummaging around. The chief then said aloud, "Yes, yes, here it is. I have the card right here." And then he read out the telephone number, which was precisely the same as what was printed on the card that Mansur Arobi had given to Leem. A connection was proved. Leem then thanked the chief and said he'd get back to him when he had more information to share. And he immediately made some notes before he needed to go down the hall to tell the king.

Ibrahim had just called the same number, moments earlier. What he heard was a male voice answering with the words, "Hello? Wasa Import and Export."

Ibrahim said, "I'm calling for Mr. Mansur Arobi, please."

The man who answered paused and replied, "I'm sorry. He's not in right now. May I take a message?"

"Yes," Ibrahim said. "He asked me to do something for him the other day and I have just a couple of quick questions for him. His answers will be crucial for my success in providing what he needs. Please let him know that I have to speak with him briefly, if he could be in contact as soon as that might be possible."

"Does he know how to contact you?"

"Yes, tell him that Leem Hadad's assistant called. He'll know."

"Will do."

"Thanks." Ibrahim hung up and contemplated what he had just learned. Wasa Import and Export—that was a name he'd now have to track down. Surely, someone would know where a company like this was located. He'd make some discreet inquiries right away, and then get back to his uncle Leem.

First, he dialed the operator. There were four rings.

"Operator. May I help you?" The voice came through bright and clear.

"Hello. Do you have a number for the government department of commerce?"

"Yes. Shall I connect you?"

"Thank you, that would be nice." Ibrahim waited. A few seconds later, he heard a ring, and then a second, and then a third.

"Department of commerce," a business-like voice said.

"Yes, I have a question about import and export companies."

"Just a moment and I'll connect you with the relevant department."

Ibrahim waited again. Several seconds elapsed, then many more. Finally, he heard the common ring once, a second time, a third, a fourth, a fifth, and four more times. He was about to give up when a tired sounding voice said, "Yes? Import and Export."

"Oh, hello. I'm calling to attempt to find the address of a company named Wasa Import and Export."

"Ok," the man said, and sighed aloud. "I'll look that up for you."

Ibrahim waited. Actually, he waited so long that if he hadn't heard voices in the background, he would have thought he had been cut off. One day, he mused, they should invent a way to play music while you wait, so at least you'd have something to listen to aside from distant voices, or more often, nothing at all. He thought to himself that he'd like to be hearing a little American jazz about now—something fun and bouncy. He actually started humming and snapping his fingers to the beat he imagined as he continued to wait.

There was a loud shuffling, and it sounded like someone had picked up the phone and then dropped it.

"Hello?" the original voice said. "Are you there?"

"Yes, I'm still here—older and wiser, but here."

The man on the other end of the line ignored his comment and said, "I've looked everywhere and we have absolutely no record of a Wasa Import and Export business, spelled 'W-a-s-a,' and even with other possible spellings. All importers and exporters are required by law to register with us. Are you sure of the name?"

"I thought I was, but I'll double check and call back."

"Ok. Call again if you must. Good luck."

"Thanks." Ibrahim hung up and stared at the telephone in front of him. His first thought was: If there's no Wasa Import and Export, then why did someone answer the phone with that name?" His second thought, close behind the first was: It must be a fake business or an illegal one with a phony name, not registered with the government and operating outside the regulatory system. Why then would they answer the phone with an unregistered name, the name of an illegal business? This is too bold. It could get them into deep trouble. Oh. Wait. The card and the number must be given only to people who are in some sense on the inside of their activities and would never check with the authorities or report them. This thought made Ibrahim nervous. "Ah," he said to himself, but in an audible whisper. "They have no clue who we are. They gave their card to the wrong guys."

Ibrahim had been using a telephone in a law office down the hallway in the same building as the agency. He and his uncle did not have their own phone yet. It was too expensive and required a lot of paperwork and a long waiting period. The lawyer was a good man and had been very welcoming to them when they moved into the building. He had even offered to field important incoming calls for them and have his receptionist bring messages down the hall. Then, Leem in turn would offer the attorney his detective expertise when needed—within reason, of course. It was a good and friendly arrangement. Ibrahim now thanked the receptionist for use of the phone and quickly left to walk to the palace where he knew his uncle was making his own long distance calls at the same time.

The front gate had Ibrahim's name on a special visitor list, and so he was escorted quickly into the building and to the communications room. He met Bancom out front, asked for his uncle, and was escorted to the place where Leem was sitting and pondering what he had discovered, just moments earlier. Bancom left them to be alone with their work.

"Uncle Leem," Ibrahim said.

"Ibrahim!" Leem looked up from the desk. "What brings you to me so soon?"

"I've already learned something important."

"What have you discovered?"

"I called the number on the card. A man answered with the words, 'Wasa Import and Export.' I asked for our man, and he said Mansur wasn't there but that he'd take a message. I left the one we had planned. And then I called the department of commerce to find where the Wasa offices are located, but the man there checked for a long time and then said there's no such company registered with them. And all import and export companies are legally required to register. So it's a fake name, or an illegal company."

"I'm not surprised at all."

"Is the king still having the number itself traced to a location?"

"Yes, some time this morning."

"Good. So, what should I do now?"

"I'd say go back to the office and wait to be contacted by Arobi."

"But, shouldn't you be there?"

"No, not right away. I have to see the king momentarily. I'll be back to the office soon. If Arobi comes in or somehow contacts you before I can get there, you know what to ask. Or you can merely apologize that I had to be out on some business, but will return soon. You could ask him if he might come back, or if there is a suitable place we could meet. Can you do that?"

"Yes, sir. But do you think it could be dangerous?"

"Not at all. We haven't given him what he wants yet. He needs us."

"Oh, yes, that's true. I'll get right back."

"Ok, good. You go now, and I'll join you soon."

"But what if I see him and he asks whether we're yet making any progress?"

"Just tell him yes, that we're making unexpected progress and should be getting back to him soon."

"Good. Ok, Uncle. I'll do that."

"I'll see you soon," Leem said. Ibrahim nodded and smiled, said a quick goodbye, and made his way back to the main gate and out onto the street, where he headed straight for the office.

Malik and Haji, meanwhile, were just ambling over toward the Falafel Stop. It was still a bit early for lunch, but they were especially eager to be helpful and thought that they might wander around the larger neighborhood first for a little while before they went to the café, just in case they saw anything that might be of interest or relevant in any way to the investigation.

On the walk, they had a discussion about whether this particular mission counted as an official Wild Camel and Silver Sabre activity or not. Malik thought it did. Haji had his worries. "But we're not masked," Haji said. This was his first statement of concern.

"Yeah, but it's still us and we're fighting crime, and our true identities are not at all clear to those who will come in contact with us."

"Good point. But our faces are clear to all. They could still recognize us on the street later, or in another context."

"Yes, but to avoid that, we'd definitely have to put on the masks, and that act itself would prevent the main activity we're supposed to be doing."

"What do you mean?"

"We can't show up for breakfast in a public café, sitting indoors, and wearing masks. First, you can't eat or drink with a mask over your mouth. And second, people would think we were there to rob the place."

"Good point again, times two," Haji said, adding, "But, if the proprietor thought we were robbers, he might give us our food free, just to keep us from sticking him up."

"Very funny," Malik responded. "And likely, we'd get a place to stay for free as well, in the city jail, until someone showed up to explain that we were guilty only of serious stupidity."

Haji laughed and said, "Another good point." Then he walked for a few seconds in silence and said, "I wonder if The Golden Viper and Windstorm—I mean, Walid and Mafulla—ever think of themselves as doing official crime fighter stuff, Viper and Storm stuff, if they aren't masked."

"I bet they do."

"Why do you say that?"

"Well, remember the class trip to Giza and what they did on the train?"

"Sure! How could I forget it?"

"They were pretty amazing, the way they played off the monkey's antics and took down those armed robbers. That was classic Viper and Storm stuff, for sure, but there were no masks involved."

"Good point."

"You're saying that a lot, do you realize this?"

"Um, yeah, sort of."

"It sounds like you're basically agreeing with me," Malik said, adding, "despite any misgivings you might have had."

"Oh, all right, I agree. We're the Wild Camel and the Silver Sabre, masks or not, as long as we're fighting crime, but it just feels different."

"Feelings aren't always the best guides to truth. Remember what Amon says."

"Yeah, feelings aren't always the best guides—except for when they are."

"You're right. And of course he says that, too. We just have to know how to tell the difference. So let me ask you this: Was your feeling that this isn't really Camel and Sabre stuff a deep feeling, a deliverance of instinct or intuition in the bottom of your heart?"

"No, no, I don't think so, not really. It was more sort of a simple superficial thing about not wearing a mask."

"Well then, case closed."

"Ok, Ok," Haji said and added, "Camel Man."

"Thank you for being so reasonable, Sabre Man."

"You're welcome."

"Ok, we're here," Malik said as they crossed a main street. "Let's just walk around a bit and look closely at everything we pass."

"You got it," Haji replied.

"Camel concentration," Malik added.

"Sabre sight," Haji responded. These were apparently common slogans they had used in their crime fighting exploits of the past. And the little phrases helped the boys to focus all their attention on any detail in the environment that might be telling. Actually, they were going to be using at least part of Masoon's famous Triple Double for dealing with trouble: Prepare, Perceive; Anticipate, Avoid; Concentrate, Control—with the whole toolkit in the backs of their minds, in case any form of real trouble did in fact present itself on this bright, sunny day.

Then, out of the blue, Haji said, "I hope Walid and Mafulla and the girls are Ok."

"Why do you say that? I mean, I do too, of course, but why did you think that thought just this moment and say it?"

"I don't know. There's just something I feel, and it's not the superficial sort of feeling." Haji was then pretty much at a loss for words.

"They've got our dads with them and Omari and Layla and lots of top soldiers," Malik reminded his friend. "And they're just crossing the desert for a trip to Walid's village. It's not like they're in some battle or something, right?"

"Yeah, maybe so."

But as soon as Malik had used the word 'battle,' he felt something strange in the back of his mind and, actually, in his chest and throat, if that makes any sense, and he remembered Hoda's urgent visit to the king and he said, "I really do hope they're all Ok, too. Let's just do our jobs right now, the way they would if they were here. We should focus on what we're doing."

"Ok, you're right. I need to focus."

"Wait," Malik suddenly said in a low voice and grabbed Haji's arm. "Stop and get behind this bush, quickly."

At the oasis pool in the desert, Omari sprang to his feet with a deliberate smile on his face. There were now clearly guns, but none actually pointed at them yet, as the armed men continued to approach, and Omari always hoped to avoid a confrontation of any sort, if it wasn't necessary. The entire group around the pool now began to focus their minds and mental energy on the men coming their way, not with the Hoda intensity of attack, but with positive thoughts and friendly feelings, in so far as they could marshal this in the face of armed strangers in an unfamiliar location at night.

"Good evening to you, my friends," Omari said, and held up his hand in greeting. "I couldn't help but see you coming this way." The men suddenly stopped. Omari saw one of them move slightly the arm and hand in which he held a weapon. He kept the smile on his face, but prepared himself instantly for the worst. One thought came into his mind, and he sought to project it like a beacon blasting across the sand from where he stood, through the darkness, and to their encampment, mere minutes away by foot. The thought was simple and directed by Omari, and you might even say, given wings and momentum as it was inwardly uttered. It was one word. "Masoon."

"Are you the group with the golden boy?" One of the men spoke in a rough, deep voice.

"What?" Omari didn't immediately make the connection with what he had just heard.

"Yes," Walid said and stood up. He patted his chest and said, "I'm the boy."

"We've been sent … for you," the man said.

"Wait," Omari replied.

"Why?" Walid said at about the same time.

"The lady of the pool has sent us."

"For what purpose?" Omari asked.

"We're to watch you and your friends while you're at the oasis. We'll be your personal guardians. You'll be our special guests, under our careful protection."

Omari, Walid, Mafulla, Kissa, and Hasina instantly felt their hearts flutter and a wave of relief course through their bodies, in an almost electrifying way. Each took a deep breath, the first that any of them had taken for the several seconds during which they had been primed for any challenge imaginable, including an immediate threat of death.

"That's very kind of you," Walid said.

"It's our pleasure," the man said.

"You're so gracious to come and tell us this and to provide your skills in our behalf," Omari then replied. "But we do have plenty of security with us, armed soldiers of the kingdom, and even officers."

"Yes, but the oasis is a different place, and it occupies a space that's distinctive in the kingdom," the man who had been speaking said, as he walked up closer and offered a hand of greeting to Omari. "We have a feel for things around here, good and bad, and can perhaps anticipate challenges that would not register immediately in the consciousness of anyone who had not lived here for a time."

"I think I understand what you're saying," Omari replied. "We'd be deeply grateful for your additional security. We're camped just over there at the south edge of the oasis," he pointed and explained.

"We know," the man responded.

At that instant, Masoon and Hamid appeared from around a thick growth of palms and bushes, striding forward to where the two groups were in conversation. Two of the strangers shouted out, "Masoon! Hamid!" And the spokesman for the group said, "We didn't know that you're part of this group! Greetings, old friend!"

"Bamur! Shaz! It's good to see you!" Masoon replied with a big smile.

"It's good to see you as well!" There were some quick embraces and back-slaps along with handshakes, and the man continued, "We were just telling your friends here that we've been asked to serve as additional security for your caravan while you're here as our visitors."

"That's nice of you," Masoon responded. "Who made this request, if I may ask? Was it the lady?"

"Yes. The lady of the pool," Bamur said.

"Madame Golan is her married name," Shaz added, speaking for a moment mainly to Walid and Omari. "But we address her as 'my lady' and refer to her as 'the lady of the pool' since she lives and works right over there," he said, pointing at the still lighted shop. "And magical things tend to happen around the pool whenever she's out here. She's a very special person."

"Yes. I've shopped with her and her husband many times, as I was crossing the desert," Masoon said. "And I've had some great conversations with them both."

"I've had the same good fortune," Hamid added.

Then Masoon said, "I've heard some things about her personal distinctiveness, but have never pried into these matters, out of respect. But I do understand that she has an unusual gift and will share it on occasion when she's convinced that doing so will promote the cause of goodness in the world."

"Yes, you understand well," Bamur replied. "And even though it might seem silly to suggest that a group of which you are a part would ever require additional security, I bow to the wishes of the lady and gladly offer our extra eyes and ears, if that's acceptable to you."

"Thank you for your kindness. I'll gladly yield to her insights and wishes, as well," Masoon said. "You prove yourselves in every way to be the gracious and benevolent hosts that your reputation has long announced."

"We appreciate your generous words, as well, Masoon. May we position ourselves in a rotation around your camp tonight and for as long as you're here?" Shaz asked.

"Yes, indeed. We plan to be here for two nights, on our way to visit our old village."

"We're glad to have you for as long as you can stay."

"We intend to return again in several days, possibly then for one more night on our way back to Cairo."

"Good. We'll be honored to provide the same service when you come back," Bamur said.

"This is very nice," Masoon replied. "Perhaps you and I will have more time to talk, and you, Shaz, as well. Hamid and I relish the occasions when we've had the opportunity to sit with you in the past."

"These are all members of your group?" Bamur asked, gesturing toward Omari and the others.

"Yes, my close associate, Omari, and Walid here, and his best friend Mafulla, and their very close friends Kissa, here, and Hasina, here."

All five of the men who had been sent bowed in greeting and muttered various phrases of welcome.

"It is nice to meet you all," Walid said.

"Yes, it is," Mafulla added.

Then Walid said, "I hope to get to know you better while we're here, all of you." The others all nodded their pleasure at his words.

Shaz said, "Some of you seem young for military service, and it's quite unusual to see young ladies in uniform this way."

Walid said, "Oh, that's just a disguise for our trip, to help keep the bandits away."

Shaz smiled and said, "I see. It's a good idea. It will help with any who haven't heard that Masoon is with the group."

"Indeed," Masoon then said. "And perhaps this would be a good time to introduce you all to our internal security team, who will also be posted in shifts through the night. Please follow us to the camp now if it's convenient, and I'll personally make the introductions."

"Yes. That will be fine. Shaz replied.

"Good to see all of you," Bamur said to Omari and the students.

"Yes, nice to meet you," Shaz added. Omari bowed.

"Thanks, again. Thanks very much," Walid said, again serving as the main impromptu spokesman for his group.

As Masoon and Hamid led the group of oasis men away toward their camp, Walid and his friends stayed right where they were and watched them go.

"I thought my goose was cooked," Mafulla said.

"Yeah, me, too," Hasina echoed the sentiment.

"We have to teach those guys to smile more, especially when they're walking up on strangers, armed, at night, and to do them a good deed. They looked a little bit like an execution squad," Walid said.

"You got that right," Omari replied. And then he laughed and added, "What a relief!"

"Yeah," Kissa said. "And all because of … the golden boy!"

"Stop," Walid said, smiling.

And at that, all the rest of them, except for Omari, bent over and scooped up double handfuls of water, instantly following Kissa's lead, and vigorously splashed the golden boy, pretty thoroughly. But Omari joined them fully in the resulting laughter.

21

What Happens Next

Juan Osvaldo Santiago had been born in Spain, of Moorish descent. His middle name meant "divine power," because his parents, who had thought they couldn't have children, considered his conception and birth a miracle. But then it was odd that, as a child, he was made to feel more like a curse than a blessing. His mother had a strong, unpredictable, fiery temperament and was almost impossible to please. His father stayed out of the house as much as he could, to avoid the storms of emotion always erupting in his wife. The young boy grew up in an oppressive atmosphere of emotional tyranny and under a nearly constant barrage of criticism. His mother needed him to have all the success that she thought she had missed in life. His triumphs would then be hers. But he constantly disappointed her, because of her desperately and unreasonably high expectations.

He had gifts, talents, and personal abilities that were uncommon among children his age. He was different. He asked questions about everything. His early drawings and writings showed the sparks of a most creative personality. But rather than being encouraged and praised, he was scolded by his mother and his natural interests were dismissed. She had her own ideas about what he should be and do.

In school, he felt estranged from most of the children. He was not rough and crude like so many of the other boys. And he ended up being taunted and teased for the things he liked to do. As a result of all the hostility and rejection that he felt every day, he gradually changed inside. His father seemed to understand him, but from a distance. The older man left him alone to fight his battles, basically abandoning the needy child when he was most desperate for support.

Juan began to simmer in resentment of others and their treatment of him. And this resentment began to transform gradually into something even worse, and vastly more ugly—a true hatred for what he considered the superficial, empty-headed kids in his neighborhood and school who showed such ongoing contempt for him. He had to demote them all in his heart and mind to a level where he could say to himself that their stupid opinions didn't matter to him, or at all. But still, one day, he vowed, he would get even with them. He would show them. He would crush them as they were trying to crush him. He would become great and leave them behind and they would be desperately sorry they had treated him so badly.

Juan made it through school and onto a university path. He was far more advanced than others his age. Instead of socializing with his peers, he was always studying and developing his body as well as his mind. He was badly beaten one day in a robbery and vowed never to allow that to happen again. He began to study all the pugilistic arts of boxing and wrestling. He worked his body vigorously and intensely every day. He then began to hear of other martial arts from around the world, and he launched a lifelong quest to learn and master whatever techniques he could from each of them. He had no fear, and an immense tolerance for pain. He would often say to his instructors, "A man on a mission feels no pain, only progress."

In the most agonizing times he experienced while seeking to build his strength, he would say to himself, "This is the feeling of success." When his arms or legs screamed for him to stop, he would think, "This is the feeling of success." When an advanced instructor would bruise him or even accidentally break one of his bones, which happened more than once, he would say, "This is the feeling of success." He learned to feed on adversity. He focused. He persevered. He never quit. The fire in his heart would not allow it.

Then he gradually became aware that the fire inside him was burning a bit too brightly—that he was in danger of being consumed by its awful intensity that was growing quickly out of control. So, he sought and found teachers of meditation to help him gain some measure of control over his thoughts, attitudes, and emotions. Many of these teachers preached compassion for all beings. And he listened. But he found that he felt no compassion for anyone except himself. So he sought to feel it more completely for himself. And yet, he didn't really understand the true nature of compassion. His distorted love for himself made him punish himself so that he could harden into an unbeatable foe capable of punishing and eliminating anyone who had the reckless audacity to stand in his way.

He eventually found that he could draw on resources beyond those of his own mind and body, and then did whatever it took to seek out the few and rare teachers who could help him to increase his ability for this. He soon discovered that most mystics who believed in and accessed something beyond the normal powers of this world were thoroughly moral individuals, concerned about goodness and love. He learned to repeat their words, but couldn't fool them into thinking he would be a proper student. So, he sought for anyone who could break through to the spiritual realm without what he considered the heavy baggage and needless constraints of mere ethical concerns.

Juan's father was a wealthy man, but he had hidden most of the money from his wife and their son until she died under mysterious circumstances. And then he gave his son a huge bequest, as if to make up for his absences throughout the years when Juan had needed him the most. A large bank account in Madrid, and an even larger one in Geneva, Switzerland, allowed him to travel and hire teachers, and pursue his life's ambition of power and personal dominance. He didn't seek the worldly power of business or politics. His quest was instead for something more personal, and at the same time, wildly more ambitious. His intent was dominance over an alternate kingdom of the mind and the will—one that would position him to overwhelm any natural power, any physical or commercial or political force that might ever be so bold as to block his path forward.

His searches took him to the most desolate and remote part of northern Sweden and to a very strange man named Asmund Borgström, whose given name in old Norse meant "divine protection," but whose personal course through life had mixed little with the truly divine. In his forlorn region of the northern country, Borgström was feared and often thought of as a practitioner of what were sometimes called "the dark arts." Juan went to study with him for months, and stayed for nearly ten years, starting when he was in his late twenties.

There is a period after that when not much is known of his activities or travels. He's rumored to have sailed to South America, in order to visit certain legendary figures in Peru and Argentina, and then his search took him up through Central America and Mexico. There are some who claim he studied with two old Native American spiritualists, but this is disputed. He also was said to have lived for a time in northern Siberia, and for a period after that in the most remote area of Tierra del Fuego, at the southern tip of South America, long after his original sojourn on that continent.

At one point, a book was being written about his life, but the author disappeared and the partial manuscript that was known to exist could not be found until many years later. Santiago had moved around a lot during his adult life, and all of the travel was in quest of his goal. And then, he made a discovery that could take his powers to a new level entirely, if he was right in everything he had come to believe. In order to follow through on what would be his most distinctive life adventure and power experiment, something not tried by anyone else, he had moved to a remote area of Egypt, because of the kingdom's special history with the extraordinary. He had long wanted to live near the pyramids, but could never get there, for one reason or another. So he settled in an area with a great deal of land and privacy on the western side of the country, where he would create his own distinctive and extraordinary mysteries, near a village called Dromeda.

He hired building contractors from far away and a crew from another nation to come in and build a compound where he could pursue his grand experiment. And when he arrived, he came with disciples, ardent followers, and a staff, along with a well-trained militia as his personal security detail—as if he needed the protection of their guns and knives and swords. With all the power he had accrued over the decades, he was, in effect, an army of one. But he preferred never to intervene in ordinary unpleasantness unless necessity dictated it or a perverse form of pleasure suggested it. He liked to keep himself pure, by his own standards, and his powers pristine and uninvolved in mundane challenges that could be solved by ordinary means. According to the legend surrounding his many secrets, he had occasionally killed men whenever he had needed to, or wanted to, and once in large numbers, and always without any experience of hesitation, regret, or the least hint of remorse.

His inner fire had now returned, in a more controlled way, and he was on a mission like never before. He was not about to allow a young prince with possible powers of his own to come close enough to his secret place to have even a remote chance of interfering with his furtive activities and his current, quite clandestine quest. He was prepared to unleash terrible power on any person, or army, or even nation that might try to stand in his way. He was utterly determined that nothing would ever stop him, Juan Santiago—nothing on earth, and nothing beyond the earth.

Only one man was ever allowed into his private dwelling on the large compound surrounded by vast stretches of undeveloped land, a follower and servant named Hadrat Anami. This man had himself developed some impressive powers, despite his diminutive physical stature or, perhaps, because of it. But in comparison to Santiago, he was merely a surprisingly strong man with eerie abilities and an above normal intellect. However, his personality had become completely enslaved to the wishes of the individual he now called "Master." And his awe and reverence for the man were surpassed only by the fear that had resided and grown in his heart since he had witnessed this severe master do what even he considered monstrous things to several individuals who had made the fatal mistake of disappointing him or, worse, resisting his expressed will.

Hadrat Anami had enough sensitivity to the world beyond this manifest universe to know that something was coming. Someone was coming. And even though the master said there was no cause for concern and that he had everything under control, Anami felt something about the forces that could be arrayed against them, something of their magnitude that Santiago's ego would not allow him to perceive. And yet, Santiago had never been wrong before in any of his predictions or determinations or attempts to defeat whatever resistance had threatened his plans. He had made himself into a force that apparently could not be overcome. He might yield in one thing, in order to surprise and conquer in a more important way. But, in the end, he always seemed to prevail.

On the street near their destination in Cairo, Malik held onto Haji's arm and nearly pushed him into a tight space between two large bushes next to them, bordering the building they were standing beside. "What is it?" Haji whispered.

"Arobi's friend, the heavily bearded man," Malik answered. I just saw him come out of the Falafel Stop and look around and then turn right, to walk in the same the direction we're going. I wanted to make sure he didn't see us. Just stay here for a few seconds and I think it'll be safe for us to follow him. We need to see where he's going."

"Put on your sand mask," Haji suddenly said.

"What?"

"It's windy. Sand is blowing in the air. I've seen maybe a dozen people wearing sand masks today while we've been walking to get here. Put yours on and I will too, in case this guy turns and sees us.

At least, that way, he won't likely recognize us as the two who were in the booth behind him last time."

"Did he even look at us then?"

"Not that I could tell, at least when he left, but maybe when we arrived. We just need to be careful, and there's no reason right now not to put the masks on."

"Good point."

"Now, you sound like me," Haji said and smiled, right before the mask went over his own face.

"Ok, it was a great idea. Now let's go," Malik said.

In the palace, not far away, Bancom came over to Leem and said, "The king would like to see you for a moment. We just got word."

"When?" Leem asked.

"Now."

"Ok, I was just going to go up there anyway and try to see him with some information he'll need."

"I know he has a lot of meetings today," Bancom replied, "so if you hurry up there as quickly as you can, you can probably get in to see him right away."

"Thanks, Bancom."

"My pleasure."

Leem left the communications room, which was actually one large room attached to two others. He walked upstairs and found his way to Kular's reception office, where he ducked his head in. "Hi Kular."

"Hello, Mr. Hadad. I think the king wants to see you."

"Good. May I go in?"

"Certainly. Allow me to announce your arrival." Kular stuck his head around the door and informed the king, and then said to Leem, "Please, go right in."

Leem entered the king's sitting room and bowed. "Come in," the king said. "I have news for you. But first, do you have any for me?"

"Yes, Your Majesty. The chiefs of police have been very helpful. They've assured me that Reela's identity is secure. And they've provided more information about the animal abductions and disappearances in their cities. One piece of news is crucial and surprising."

"What's that?"

"The chief in Tunis told me about a recently attempted abduction that was seen and stopped by his men. They pursued the criminals but couldn't apprehend them. However, in the chase, a couple of pieces of paper fell from one man's pocket. There was a scrap with an address, and a personal or business card with just a phone number."

"A phone number?" the king said.

"Yes, and it's the same as the one on the card Arobi gave me."

"This is, indeed, interesting."

"Ibrahim called the number this morning before he knew any of this. And a man answered, saying, 'Wasa Import and Export'—but when Ibrahim then called the commerce department to check on their address, he was told that there's no such firm on record in Egypt."

"So it's either a fake name, or a criminal operation, or likely both," the king concluded.

"Precisely. Ibrahim first asked to speak with our man, and was told he wasn't in."

"As I suspected," the king said.

"Yes. Then he explained to the guy who answered the mystery number that he's been asked to do something by Mr. Arobi, but that he has a couple of questions he needs to pose to him, if they can meet somewhere soon. Ibrahim is back at the office by now, and I'll be returning shortly to see whether we can find out more about our dangerous would-be client."

"Well, this is good to hear," the king replied. "I've also just received some crucial information about that number. We have an address where that telephone is located, and we've already rented an office across the street from it, with a view of its front door. Within an hour, we should have a team of two men there to engage in surveillance around the clock to see who comes or goes through that door. And we've also made sure that there's no other entrance."

"How did you do that?" Leem asked.

"A street repair worker, actually one of our men in the right uniform, walked around the building to check for a side door or a back entry. There are two windows, but high up from the ground."

"Good. Out of curiosity, could you share the address, Your Majesty?"

"Yes, but please don't go near it any time soon, or allow Ibrahim to do so. We don't want anything to alert these men in any way that we're on to them."

"Absolutely, Your Majesty." The king shared the address with Leem, and he wrote it into a small notebook that he always carried with him. Then he said, "Thank you, Sire."

The king said, "You're quite welcome." And then added, "You know, Leem, I do appreciate your bringing the initial information to me so quickly about this Arobi fellow."

"It was my pleasure, as well as my duty, Your Majesty."

"You're giving Ibrahim a good example of how to work effectively in your business, and you're showing him that no work is more important than doing the right thing."

"Thank you. I'm most honored by your gracious remarks. I truly believe that only ethical businesses can flourish over the long run," Leem said. "And when I'm teaching Ibrahim how to work as a private detective of the highest sort, I'm planting seeds into very good soil. He's already a man of high character, as you know, even at his relatively young age."

"I can tell," King Ali said. "And I want you both to know that by bringing me the information you have, and the new details that you continue to convey, you're most likely helping to solve a vastly greater crime than meets the eye."

"Yes, I'm already getting that impression. But I have no idea what all is going on."

"I firmly believe that the animal abductions, the primary concern of Mansur Arobi, are a small part of a much larger scheme that's playing out in our kingdom and across our region of the world. I have only hints and intuitions to go on at this point—nothing clear—but I trust the guidance they're giving me. And if I'm right, then you and Ibrahim will be helping to stop something that's not only illegal and unethical, but perhaps truly monstrous as well."

"Oh, my."

"I'll certainly explain more as my own clarity about it grows."

"I do appreciate your trust."

"As I, your trustworthiness. But for now, know that what you're doing may be of national, and even broader, importance."

"It's gratifying to be able to make a contribution, Your Majesty. I do appreciate your sharing such thoughts with me at this juncture, early along as we are. We'll work our hardest to solve any piece of the puzzle that's presented to us. And we'll strive to find more of the pieces to assemble into a picture of the larger events playing out on the grander scale that's presently beyond our purview."

"I know you will, Leem. That's why it's such a great blessing to all of us that you're here with us now, and engaged in the line of work for which you're so perfectly suited."

"I'm humbled by your kindness, and will strive in all things to make sure you're glad that you've said such things to me."

"I have no doubt," the king concluded and rose from his seat.

Leem instantly rose as well and bowed. He said, "I'll be off now and report back to you the next development that happens."

"Good! Kular will show you out. May your work bear fruit in many ways."

Leem thanked the king again for his time and turned and left the room. He spoke with Kular briefly, and then followed him down the hall and onto the staircase that took him to the main front entrance of the palace.

Far across the desert from Cairo, the day at the oasis had gone smoothly. Everyone had an opportunity to go to the pool, soak their feet, and relax, and many members of the caravan also had a chance to visit the shops of this restful grove. Walid's parents sat and talked with him and Kissa for quite a while in the morning, and they enjoyed their time together immensely. Then Bhati and Kissa made the rounds of the shops, while Rumi and Walid visited only the general store to look at a few things they had thought about picking up before the last leg of the trip.

The lady of the pool was nowhere to be seen throughout the morning and into the afternoon. But Walid made nothing of this, since she had only assured him that they would talk before he left the oasis. He and Rumi and Omari met some of the men in the other caravan that was stopping for a rest, and Rumi was actually able to be helpful to a member of that caravan who had sustained an injury.

Masoon and Hamid disappeared during part of the day to do their exercises, as they always did while traveling together. And they later returned to the encampment energized and ready to hang out with the other soldiers, telling stories and jokes and answering questions about many legendary exploits of the past that had featured either of them. Masoon even demonstrated with Hamid a few unusual defensive and offensive moves that the other men had never seen, and he let several of the men try their luck at doing them. But, of course, they made sure that no one was hurt in attempting such things, knowing that the security mission for all the soldiers must come first and not be compromised by a needless injury.

It was the middle of the afternoon and still well before the heat of the sun would even began to fade, when Walid had contact again with the lady of the pool. He was sitting at this point in the shade of a tree, on a nice long flat stone beside Mafulla, their feet cooling in the water. There was a bit of breeze, of a sort that often graced visitors to this special place. The lady approached from behind them and surprised them when she said, "Young man."

Walid turned, saw who it was, and stood immediately, saying, "Yes ma'am, I was hoping to come across you today."

She smiled and looked into his eyes deeply. "It's good to see you again." Her own eyes sparkled with an unusual depth and energy.

Walid commented, "We've had a very nice day here at the oasis. We're much more rested and ready for the remainder of our trip."

"Good," she replied. "That's why we're here."

"I wanted to ask whether you have any fresh insight about the challenge we may face as we travel toward my home village."

"Yes, I have a few insights," she said.

"Can you share them? I need very much to know what I should do to face whatever awaits me."

She looked at him with great kindness and said, simply, "Should I speak in front of your friend?"

"Yes. You can speak freely."

She nodded and responded, "Good. Then I have a simple message. You will do what you were born to do." And she smiled.

Walid said, "But."

She continued, "You're on a mission, a journey that will introduce you in new ways to your destiny. You'll continue to be given what you need for what's to happen. So don't ever despair or fear the future. Never lose hope or give up. Things are rarely what they seem. Those who are with you have been provided for you, and you for them. Nothing that will happen is an accident. Nothing will be random. There will be no unintended happening, and no mere coincidence. At one level, at the base of nature and the natural world, so it may seem, as our science will soon discover—and the appearance may long be impenetrable. At another level, though, and the one that impinges on our small but distinctively human lives, what you'll experience will be guided, in some way or another. So embrace the challenges and the revelations. They are meant ultimately for your good and the good of many." The lady then just looked at him.

"I thank you for these words. But if I may say so, with all respect and great gratitude, they seem a bit general and mysterious."

"Yes."

"I would love to ask you a very specific question."

"You may."

"What will happen in the village when we get there?"

"What is to be will then be."

"But."

"And you will always have a choice, at every step, then and later, even when it seems you do not, as will your good friend here. Use your power of choice wisely in all things, both of you." She looked from Walid's eyes to Mafulla's and repeated, "Both of you."

Mafulla nodded his head slowly, understanding her words on one level, but wondering about them on another. And Walid said,

"Can you see any details of what's to come when we arrive in the village?"

She took a deep breath and let it out. "I can see some things. I can see enough to know what I can and should say, and I can hear enough to know what I cannot and should not say. Some mysteries are necessities. Some fogs are needed, for an hour or a day, or even a season. Sometimes, uncertainty is the element in which we are meant to proceed. There is a reason. There is often a reason, even if we have no clue as to what it might be."

"Is this the most you can say?"

"It is the most."

"You're sure?"

"Yes. You have all that you need."

"Can you give me your blessing for what lies ahead?"

"Why do you ask?"

"I know it will help."

"Yes. You're right. And I do bless you as you go forward." She reached out her right hand and spread her fingers wide, pointing her palm toward Walid but not touching him or even coming close to him. She spoke several words in a language he didn't know or understand, and in a strange tone, both softly and quickly, with her eyes closed. And then she opened her eyes wide and said, "May you and your friends be richly blessed as you move on deeply into the adventures that now await you. May a firm faith and a resilient hope be with you and in you at all times. May you persist with courage and prevail through any difficulties you're called upon to face. And may you then be able somehow to share the story of your journey with future generations. Great blessings will go with you and be on you, enduring blessings to you and your friends and all who learn of you, my golden young man of the kingdom. We are blessed to have you with us for this short time, Prince Walid."

And with those words, she smiled again, and turned, and slowly walked away.

22

Pieces of the Puzzle

Haji and Malik had on their sand masks and were following the heavily bearded man, staying a couple of blocks behind him. He turned left onto an intersecting street and they ran to catch up so that they could see if he entered a building. But as they rounded the corner, he was nowhere in sight. By Malik's estimation, he had gone into a building in the first block. The two of them went down one side of the street, intending to go just as far as the next cross street and then to turn, dash over, and walk back down the other side, glancing in each building, window, or door. It was one of those streets with residential apartments on one side, the far side, and various small businesses on the other—a bakery and a coffee shop, an insurance office, and a cleaner, a dentist, and another shop of some sort.

They went down, turned, and came back to where they had started. "No sign of him," Haji said.

"He has to be somewhere on this block," Malik insisted. "He could live here or have an office here. Or he could just be doing business or going to an appointment in one of these places."

"Let's wait down here," Haji said, pointing to the tea and coffee shop with a few outdoor tables. "That way, if he reappears soon, we can keep following him."

"Good idea," Malik replied. They removed their masks, walked over to the shop, took a table with a good view of the block, and ordered tea. Malik said, "If we see our guy, we'll duck our heads down, like we're looking at something on the table, so he won't recognize us. Then, when it's safe, we'll stay behind him, masked again."

"Ok, good thinking."

"I have a feeling about this—that we're not wasting our time."

"Me, too."

Within ten minutes, they saw the man emerge from a building on the other side of the street and begin walking away from them. Malik put down payment for their tea and they began once more to follow him. The pursuit went on for nearly a mile and they ended up at the edge of the university. As they crossed onto the campus, they watched him enter one of the buildings. Jogging to catch up, they saw next to the door he had entered a sign: "Department of Philosophy and Religion."

"This is strange," Haji said, as he and Malik climbed the outer stairs the man had just used. They opened the large door and entered a hallway that apparently connected various classrooms. But there were also internal stairs, and they could hear footsteps above them. Quietly following and going up those stairs, they were careful to keep back and out of sight, now again without their masks, since they were indoors. On the second floor landing, Malik walked through to another hallway just as he saw a door closing halfway down. He had caught a glimpse of it the split second before it shut.

"Seventh door, left side," he whispered to Haji. They walked slowly down the hall, being as quiet as they could.

There was a black sign on the door, whose white letters said, "Dr. Hashman Arib." Haji put his ear to the door and looked at Malik and shook his head no, to communicate that he was hearing nothing from inside. Then he motioned for the two of them to get out of there, the same way they had come. They glided quickly back down the hall, practically flew down the stairs, but again, doing their best not to make any loud sounds, and when they emerged onto the sidewalk outside, Haji let out a big breath and said, "This is so bizarre. The bad guy's a professor?"

Malik replied, "We have to go report this."

"You're right," Haji said. And they began to walk as briskly as they could back to the office of the Cairo Detective Agency.

About five hours later, they were in the palace with Leem and Ibrahim, waiting for the king to return to his private sitting room where, a short time earlier, they had revealed the new information. Kular had brought them snacks to enjoy until the king could rejoin them. At that moment, he entered and they all rose from their places.

"Thank you," he said. "Please sit. I'll share what I've just learned." The king eased back down into his favorite chair. "The pieces of the puzzle are beginning to come together."

"Hashman Arib is indeed Associate Professor of Egyptian Religious History at the university, specializing in the role of animals in ancient belief and ritual."

"Oh," Leem said. "That's interesting."

"The building where the telephone is located that Ibrahim called and heard the words, 'Wasa Import and Export' is an office not far from the university that's used by Mansur Arobi. We've now seen him entering and leaving the building multiple times. The business name, we've come to believe, is indeed a fake, although it's only partially misleading. They do no importing at all and no legal exporting, but they do engage, we think, in a great deal of smuggling."

The king continued, "When Arobi leaves the building, he goes many different places, but we've seen him once drive to the outskirts of town in an older model car. His destination was a compound of three large buildings. The main structure has a sign over the door that says, 'Cairo Veterinary Clinic and Hospital.' I've learned that the place has been known for a long time as a legitimate business where, historically, animals, mostly working and farm animals, have been cared for medically. But there's a strong possibility that the clinic, or at least part of it, is now being used for the criminal activities we're investigating."

Leem spoke up and said, "Your Majesty, it makes sense that, when these men steal animals, they need a place to keep them before they do whatever they do with them, or send them somewhere else."

"You're right."

"Do you suppose the animals are kept in one or more of the buildings associated with the clinic, which would provide excellent cover for these activities, and then smuggled out, thanks to the Wasa people?"

"Those are my thoughts exactly, Leem."

"What's the role of the professor?"

"I would guess he might have been brought on initially as a consultant, since his specialty is animals in religious contexts."

Ibrahim looked puzzled. "But what could be the connection with religion? I don't get what's going on at all."

"Well," the king replied, "whenever anyone steals something, they obviously do so for a reason—typically, either to sell it or to use it. These local people are coordinating a wider ring of thefts, it would seem, and so they're either going to be selling or using these animals. But the animals don't fit into one easy category—like camels, or horses, or donkeys, or oxen—a type of animal would have a simple and obvious use. I suspect then that these men are merely providing the animals to someone else. But something tells me that they're not free agents selling to the highest bidder. I suspect they're employed by someone wanting the animals for a peculiar use."

"What would the use be?" Ibrahim continued in his perplexity.

"I know this will sound exceedingly strange, but the involvement of the professor seems to confirm my own suspicions." The king reached down to the table and picked up a cup of tea that he had been sipping all long, and took a larger drink. He set it back down and said, "My feeling is that there's someone receiving all these animals, in their wide variety, who then seeks to use them for religious or philosophical purposes."

"You mean, animal sacrifice?" Leem asked, with a look of surprise, shading into disgust.

"Actually, and fortunately, no, although that would be the first guess to be made. I suspect that something even much more keenly interesting is going on."

"What in the world could it be, then?" Leem could not help himself from asking.

"Well, as you know, there's a long history of association in world mythology between gods and animals. And in our own kingdom, in ancient times, the various gods were often depicted with certain features reflecting humans, and others resembling some animal. Along with a mostly human body, overall, the sun god Ra has often been represented with the head of a falcon, Sekmet with that of a lion, and Anubis with a jackal's head. Even the head of a cat was included in traditional representations of the goddess Bast, or Bastet, as she was often called. It's also well known how the great Sphinx turns that around, and has a human head with the body of a lion."

The others sat, rapt, listening to the king's words. "I had never really thought about it, but that's right, Your Majesty. Leem looked especially interested in the topic. And the king continued.

"My best intuition here is that there is someone who wants to explore, and possibly exploit for his own purposes, whatever relationship there might be between animals, at least certain animals, and the divine—or more broadly, the realm of the spiritual. He's collecting animals far and wide to see if some of them can connect him more fully with powers beyond those of this world."

"Really?" Leem was surprised at the idea. He added, "In even hearing this, I feel as if I've already entered another world beyond the one we think of as normal."

"The normal is highly overrated," the king said and laughed. "Or perhaps, it's more accurate to say that what's normal is more complex and mysterious than we normally would even begin to understand or, for that matter, remotely suspect."

Leem replied, "You're right, I'm sure. So, you think we're up against someone who's stealing animals to see if they can somehow connect him with divine powers or spiritual resources beyond what would ordinarily be available to human beings." He was clearly fighting to overcome his initial perplexity, in light of the puzzle pieces that he saw might fit together if this supposition were right.

"Yes, that's what I think," King Ali said. "I admit it's very strange, and I could be wrong, but I wouldn't bet against this theory."

"So, even if we apprehend and stop these local thieves, we'd still not have cut off the head of the snake, so to speak," Ibrahim said.

"You're correct," the king replied. He then added, "But I think their apprehension would still do great good, if only for the time being. And it's a step along the way that we must take. Even alone, it would prevent or postpone much anguish being felt by animal owners, and most likely by the animals themselves, as this rash of abductions otherwise continues, day after day."

"That's for sure," Malik said, speaking up rather boldly.

Haji glanced all around and explained, "Your Majesty, Malik's been talking to me and some of the other students lately about animal intelligence and animal emotions, and it makes a lot of sense. They feel more than we imagine. They suffer more than we want to realize. And they have psychological needs just like we do—maybe not all the needs we have, but important ones, still."

The king was nodding as Haji spoke. The young man then continued: "In fact, an important source of motivation for us, and something that made us want to really help in this investigation, is our empathy for the animals involved. We want to stop the trauma on both sides that arises just from the abduction and separation. But also, Your Majesty, if this theory you suggest is right, then who knows what's being done to these poor creatures to test their powers and their connections with the divine, or the spiritual, as you say? We could only guess and dread the answers."

"Precisely. And then, we need to add in the fact that there must be a compelling reason the mystery figure behind all this is doing it, and that any quest for an unusual accumulation of power inevitably has political implications. Plus, we have to stir in that with the fact that he's using criminal methods. And with all this considered, we have at least the beginnings for a portrait of a dangerous, power-hungry man who may pose more of a threat to the rest of us than we can at present imagine."

"What should be done with everything we now know?" Leem asked.

"I'll issue an order to round up all the known suspects, from the Wasa Smugglers, Unincorporated, to Mansur Arobi, to Hashman Arib, and, ultimately, the owners and staff of the veterinary clinic—although I may want a little surveillance there first, to see more of what's going on. We have three men already in custody who've been involved in this, as you know. And despite their bluster and general intransigence up until now, they've made some remarks under questioning, and otherwise, that lead me to think our theory is true."

"Do you suppose the mastermind is nearby?" Ibrahim asked.

"No. Actually, I don't. Proximity to a major city would be too dangerous for him, I'd suppose. I have some reason to suspect that he's in our kingdom, but not close to us here in the capital. I'd imagine he's well hidden, far from here. But I have a feeling we may locate him soon."

"Would it be inappropriate, Your Majesty, to ask your reason for thinking this?" Leem said. He added, "I'm just trying to get my head around the entire situation, to make sure I am not missing anything that might be relevant to our concerns."

"It's fine for you to ask, Leem. You're a man I'd trust with my life. I'll certainly trust you with information that you request."

"You honor me, Majesty."

"You've done much to honor us all," the king replied. "In answer to your question, though: As you all know, Walid and his parents are journeying back to their home village in the western part of the kingdom in the company of some of their friends and many good men who are providing security for their travels. In the very recent past, since they left, someone has been trying to discourage them in their venture, sending signs and warnings that they should turn back."

"Oh."

"And some of these warnings are so strange that they indicate their origination in a very unusual person, or group of people. That's all that I'm utterly free at this point to say. But someone is trying hard to discourage or prevent our caravan from reaching its destination of Dromeda, the place where many of us in the palace lived before coming here to restore the rightful monarchy."

"I see," Leem commented.

"This could be completely unrelated to our animal puzzle," the king acknowledged, "but I personally don't think it's a mere coincidence that these two things independently baffle us right now. They're parts of a puzzle. And it's a puzzle we need to solve soon."

Across the desert, late afternoon had already brought a measure of cooling to the oasis. Some boys were playing ball outside again, quite vigorously, and some of the shops that had been closed during the heat of the day had already reopened. Amid the various sounds of activity coming back to life around the central pool, a few individuals with exceptional hearing could barely begin to detect a slight but unusual noise far in the distance. As the level of the sound grew, almost imperceptibly at first, more people stopped what they were doing to listen. Every few seconds, even more became aware of it.

Hamid turned to Masoon and said, "Listen!"

Masoon grew perfectly still and quiet for several seconds and said, "Friend or foe?"

"What foe could it be?" Hamid almost whispered.

Layla walked out of her tent and over to where she saw Masoon and Hamid standing very still and looking in the same direction.

"What is it?" she asked.

"Shh. Listen," Hamid answered.

The faint sound grew slightly louder, a faraway buzz not quite like anything in nature, and within half a minute or so, it became a grinding, throaty roar as a small airplane found the oasis and dropped in altitude, lower and lower until, with what now seemed to be a thunderous din, it passed low overhead. Countless individuals of all ages in the oasis who were unfamiliar with the sound went down to their knees in positions of protection. The camels groused loudly and the horses jumped and whinnied, testing the ropes that held them safely in place. The shadow of the plane passed over all those who were in the center of the trees and small buildings. And any who were brave enough to look up saw something white fall from it as it quickly moved beyond them and then became smaller to the eye and fainter to the ear. It clearly tilted on its side and turned to the right and seemed to circle back toward the direction from which it had come.

An airplane! Few had ever seen such a thing, and one had just passed over all of them. It was a scary experience for many, an exciting one for others. Hamid and Masoon caught a glimpse of the pilot, who was wearing a leather helmet and had a bright red scarf around his neck. As he passed and banked right, many eyes followed him through the sky and watched him recede into the distance until the plane was just a speck in the endless blue of the next adventure, and no sound of its engine could be heard.

As soon as Omari saw the white flash come out of the plane from up at the front where the pilot sat, he began to run toward the area beneath its trajectory. As something now drifted down through the sky, he scrambled and ran all out, at top speed. He cleared the trees and could barely see at first what he thought was an object up ahead in the sand, and as he grew closer he could tell that it was indeed a small box, colored red, and attached by thin long cords to a much larger white piece of fabric—a parachute. He had heard of such things, but had never seen one. He continued to move toward the object, but began to slow his pace a bit and, when he got to it, he stopped and bent down and looked it over. There was a white label on each side that said, in large lettering, "For Walid or Masoon in the Military Caravan." Each label had the same message. Omari picked up the box. It was light. He gathered up the parachute to take it along with the box to his friends, and began to make his way quickly back toward the encampment, where he knew Masoon had been talking with Hamid.

Coming into sight of them, he yelled out, "Masoon! Hamid! I have a package from the plane!"

They began to walk in his direction and could easily see the red box in his hands and the white parachute that was still attached to it trailing behind. "What is it?" Masoon called out.

"A package addressed to Walid, or you," Omari shouted back.

Masoon turned to Hamid and said, "Could you find our friend, and bring him to me?"

"Certainly," Hamid said and quickly went over to the tent the prince was using, but saw that he wasn't there.

"Where's Walid?" Hamid called out toward Rumi and Bhati, who were standing a bit farther down, on the other side of their own tent.

"He went into the middle of the oasis a while ago," Bhati called back. Hamid nodded and began to walk quickly in the direction of the pool.

On the way, he came across his old friend Bamur and asked, "Have you seen Walid—the one the lady of the pool calls the golden boy?"

"Yes, he was on the far side, speaking to some men from the other caravan a few minutes ago," Bamur replied, gesturing toward the north end of the oasis. But just then, Walid and Mafulla came around the nearest building, in full stride toward their own encampment.

Hamid called out, "Walid, there's a package for you. Special Delivery. Air Mail."

"What?" The prince looked perplexed.

"The plane—a package was dropped from it, addressed to you or Masoon," Hamid explained. "Masoon didn't want to open it without you. He's waiting. Come, quickly." On hearing that, the boys walked faster and followed Hamid to where Masoon was standing with the box in his hands.

"Walid, come with me, please," Masoon said. Hamid and Mafulla stayed where they were now, leaving the others with the mystery box, which Masoon carried to his tent.

"What do you think this is about?" Walid asked the older man right away.

"I think the king has sent us something important," he answered.

"The king?"

"No one else would have access to an airplane that could reach this oasis and return to its home base on the fuel that it carries."

"Oh. I didn't know the king has an airplane."

"We actually have several in service to the military, in case they're ever needed. We just recently purchased them and had them brought to us."

"I didn't know."

"It was one of the matters I help take care of in my duties over the military. Let's open the box," Masoon said, while ripping off some string that tied it around all sides. He then slowly lifted off its top.

"Is it … empty?" Walid asked.

"No, no, it seems that there's something in the very bottom," Masoon said. And then he added, "Well, this is a surprise."

23

The Message

A message can either enlighten or confound its recipient, depending on its nature, the recipient's mindset, and the circumstances under which it arrives. A perplexing one had just come into the palace. Bancom listened to it on the radio, jotted it down in the notebook he always kept handy, and took the written version up to the Ali's office.

Kular greeted him and went to check on the king's availability. He was just finishing up on some paperwork, and so Bancom had to wait for only about five minutes and he was admitted into the office.

"Hello, my friend. Come in. What do you have for me?" the king said.

"A message from Naqid," Bancom replied and, looking down at his notebook, he said, "It starts with this: All but one of the groups have reported in, and none of the suspects were found where they were supposed to be. They had all vanished."

"Vanished?" the king said.

"Yes. It goes on to say that the professor was not in his office, even though the group of operatives covering the university arrived to apprehend him during his regular office hours, and his chairman assured one of our officers that he had arrived for the day and would be there. We have someone posted nearby, in case he reappears."

The king nodded his approval. "Good."

"Then the group that raided the Wasa office found no one there."

"Interesting."

"And the men who had followed Mansur Arobi to the apartment building couldn't locate him there, either."

"Did they search thoroughly?"

"They say they did."

"Very strange," the king said. "Do you suppose someone alerted them about our intentions?"

"That's possible, Your Majesty, but I have no idea who would do such a thing. Our operations people are very loyal and well trained. And they're careful. But each group did have a city policeman along to make the arrest an official matter for the police department."

"Have Naqid check into those officers. And have him find out who else knew of the operation in advance. He should get the names and backgrounds of everyone who could have tipped off the criminals."

"Yes, Majesty," Bancom said, as he wrote quickly in his notebook.

"And what of the clinic? Is the observation team in place?"

"That group hasn't reported in yet."

"Let me know as soon as you hear from them or about them."

"Yes, Your Majesty, immediately."

"Thank you, Bancom, as always," the king said.

"You're welcome," Bancom said and then bowed and left the king to return to the communications room and contact Naqid.

Several miles away, Haji and Malik had walked for more than thirty minutes, with Malik's dog on a leash trotting along beside them.

Haji said, "Are you really sure about this?"

"Well, no, I'm not absolutely sure, but it's something we can do."

"The king's probably got people already watching the place," Haji replied.

"Yeah, from the outside, but this way we can check it out from the inside." Malik reminded Haji of why they were doing this in the first place. "Admit it, we've been sort of benched or sidelined, left out of the main action since the king sent guys to keep an eye on the other places. I never heard him say anything much about this place, but even if he already has men watching, they can see only what goes on around the buildings, not where the real action might be. And that's what we can check out."

"Yeah, I got it," Haji said. "I just sort of wonder if we should have told someone we were going to do this."

"They would have come up with a reason we shouldn't—it's too risky, it's not safe, and so on."

"Well, maybe they would have been right," Haji said, with a tone of tentative caution.

"Hey, nobody around here knows we're the Wild Camel and the Silver Sabre. The guys who do—Walid and Mafulla—told us to take care of things while they were gone. So the question is: Would they do something like this to help the investigation, or not?"

"Yeah, they would, I bet," Haji said.

"So, that should settle it for us," Malik concluded.

"I guess you're right."

"Ok, there it is. Now, let me do the talking," Malik said.

"Sure thing," Haji replied. "You're the boss."

The boys walked up the path to the front door of the main building and entered under a sign that said Cairo Veterinary Clinic.

Just outside the desert oasis, Masoon had sat down on the sand with the red box in front of him. He was still peering into it and said, "It looks like an official palace envelope for a document or letter. But there's a bulge, a lump in one corner."

"Really?" Walid was puzzled.

"The envelope has on its front our names again—the two of us." He reached into the box and lifted out the inner envelope.

Opening it carefully, he slid into his hand a small object wrapped in cloth.

"The Stone of Giza," Walid nearly whispered. Masoon unwrapped it and indeed the brilliant green emerald now sat in the palm of his hand, sparkling like the legend that it was and long had been. "I wonder why Uncle Ali sent this?"

"There's also a letter here—a very long one in the king's handwriting," Masoon said. "It goes on for several pages. I suppose it will explain this for us." Dusk was filtering out the last light of day as the general sat on the sand with the letter in his hands. "Do you mind if I read aloud for both of us?"

"Please do."

"Ok. Here we go." Masoon looked up at Walid and then back down at the pages in his hands.

"My Dear Walid and Masoon: I have addressed this letter to you so that you will be the first to read it. I would like you then to share it also with Rumi, Bhati, Hamid, Layla, Mafulla, Kissa, Hasina, and Omari, as soon as you finish your initial reading. One of you may want to gather them for a second reading, aloud. But otherwise, its contents should be kept confidential from all the others.

"I recently sent Reela to Algiers, Tunis, and Tripoli, the capitals of some of our neighboring nations, to see whether they had been experiencing the crime of animal abduction that has been so sudden and pervasive in our own city. He has conveyed to me the news that they have seen the same things. Further, we now have reason to believe that all this activity is being coordinated from our kingdom, and that the main hub of the ongoing criminal enterprise is right here in Cairo.

"As I write, our agents are seeking to round up several suspects, including a man who visited the Cairo Detective Agency to gain assistance with an investigation. Leem and Ibrahim brought his requests to my attention. He was seeking to learn the identity of the person who had been asking in the other capitals about the crimes we're determined to stop. There is also another man, who apparently was brought in to the operation because of his academic specialty and now is playing a leading role in these activities. He's a professor of philosophy and religion at the university, and his specialty is the role of animals in human belief and ritual, focused on religious contexts. His inclusion in this group, along with his apparently current prominence in it, has led me to some realizations.

"Hoda entered my sitting room the other day with an urgent request, saying that Layla was facing something very difficult and needed our help. We joined together and, as you know, with Walid's help, were able to turn back a fierce storm of some sort that was being sent your way. It was impinging on Layla's spirit directly, as she took on the burden initially of seeking to resist it and turn it back. She was fighting at full force when we joined her in spirit and augmented her efforts. I'm pleased that, together, we were able to prevail quickly over what can only be described as a mysterious power that was seeking to keep you from completing your trip to visit the village. If she had known what force she faced, our friend may have been able to defeat it alone. But since it took her by surprise, it was important for several of us to be involved in its defeat.

"The strange nature of the power we encountered in this bout of what can only be called 'spiritual warfare' alerted me to the fact that something of vital importance is playing out and, whatever it is, the force at the center of it does not want your caravan anywhere near our old village. Why? Possibly because Walid is there, representing the power of the monarchy. But I think it's, most likely, another reason. There are, of course, several Phi in the caravan, and I suspect that this individual can detect your presence and growing proximity to where, I'm guessing, he must be located. What we felt can only be called a malicious force, a monstrosity, and that seems to be exactly what it is. Further, I believe that this is connected with all the animal abductions. But I should explain this conclusion, backed up as it is by both a bit of evidence and some strong intuition.

"First, you may wonder why an expert on the role of animals in human belief and ritual through history is engaged in a current rash of animal abductions on a large scale. I believe that our hidden adversary, our monster, if I may call him that, the source of the malicious energy we had to fight together, is seeking to increase his unusual and already formidable powers through the use of some of these animals that are being gathered together, ultimately, in some place near Dromeda, I would venture.

"There's an ancient philosophical notion, derived from the Greek neoplatonists, called 'The Great Chain of Being.' It's the idea that all of creation represents a hierarchy of value, spirituality, and fullness of being. Nearest to God are the angels, and even within this category, there is a gradation of types and individuals. Below the angels is humankind. Below us, in turn, are the animals, then the plants, then simpler life forms, all the way down to the inorganic, and then farther down to the most basic forms of existence imaginable. What is higher, according to this view, is nobler, more complete, and more akin to the divine spirit, and it's endowed with a greater, richer, and more powerful form of existence. We have bodies like animals but spirits like angels. We are thus between animal and angel in our essential form. We are most of the way up the scale between dirt and divinity, if I may put it that way, but still are of a lesser being and power than is available within the full sweep of the created realm.

"Philosophers influenced by this vision of reality, this conception of a Great Chain of Being, have traditionally denigrated the role of animals in the world. Such creatures are here, it's thought, to serve us, at best, to help feed and cloth us and toil for us, or at worst, to act as our adversaries and obstacles, in conflict with whom we may try ourselves, test our skills, and enhance our bodies and souls, cultivating strength and courage and boldness, along with such other qualities as perseverance, and focus. We consume animal and vegetable alike, and take them into ourselves for sustenance and growth and health. They must die so that we may live and flourish. When a philosopher like René Descartes concluded wrongly that animals do not have souls, some of his followers reasoned then that they must not be able to experience real pain, having only behavior that simulates the outward consequences of that range of sensations for a real mind, without involving the actual experience, in their particular case.

"But, there is a very different, and actually much older philosophical tradition—one that views animals more profoundly and wisely. It's the tradition behind the practice in our kingdom's history of representing gods in forms that are composed of both animal and human features. The animal is thus seen as capable of conveying and expressing, in its own vital way, something deeply important about the divine.

"In traditional cosmologies, the entirety of creation was thought to spring from the hand of God, or in more sophisticated expressions, the mind of God. In the western tradition, there was believed to have been a creation of our overall environment, fully formed, and then our ancestors, as a special work of divine art. In humans, the divine creation gave birth to the potential for a special form and keen level of self-awareness and understanding from within the created realm—an outpost of deeply self-reflective spirit arising in a universe of matter.

"But in the march of modern science, we've been presented most recently with a very different vision. The Source of All, in this conception, whatever it might be, has created directly the smallest and simplest of nonorganic entities, the most basic fundamentals of matter or energy, and it's from these elusive beginnings that all else has then come to be—including atoms, molecules, and then ultimately such things as microbes, plants, animals, and humans—or to put it more precisely: the various life forms and animals other than humans, and finally, most recently, we human animals. On this view, the nonhuman animals are, in the main, as species, a step closer to the ultimate origin of things than we are. But, regardless of such considerations of temporal precedence, when you refuse to dichotomize the human and nonhuman, allowing for greater continuities of spirit and soul and mind, you find that you may live in a very different world from what had long been supposed.

"Consider the religious practice of animal sacrifice, something that no longer occurs in most developed cultures, but that was quite common in the infancy of the race. Human beings sought to placate, appease, or satisfy the divine by shedding the blood of animals, ceremonially. But: why? How was this supposed to work? What did it say about the view of animals underlying the ritual? Some have thought that only a Cartesian could justify such a thing, a person following the philosophy of Descartes, holding that animals are without souls, spirits, or minds. But, in fact, those who engaged in such practices were as far removed from that mindset as possible. What conceivable impact on the divine could anyone think might result from the equivalent of breaking a rock, or even cutting down a weed? On a Cartesian view, animal sacrifice would make just as little sense. It would involve the destruction of a physical object in the hope that, somehow, the mechanism by which it was done, or the divine economy in which it took place, would bring about the transformation of that act into a message or gift that would be pleasing to God and, as such, then either turn away divine wrath, or curry providential favor, resulting in something good for the humans performing the ritual.

"Traditional or primal religions viewed all this quite differently. They saw the animals as their neighbors, fellow spiritual beings with souls and minds and their own distinctive closeness to God. When those ancient members of the human family hunted animals and killed for food, they did so with a sense of the sacred nature of the life they had to take in order to save and preserve their own. They understood and appreciated deeply the sacrifice of the animal's existence here on earth for what they hoped and believed was a greater good, the perpetuation and strengthening of their own lives and the lives of their dearest loved ones. They sincerely, in their hearts, asked the animal to make this sacrifice. Indeed, they initiated the sacrifice prayerfully and in a spirit of deep gratitude, believing that it would have a necessary benefit, or perhaps, a collection of benefits, and perhaps even for the animal spirit, beyond the obviously tragic element of it all.

"The same thing is found in ritual sacrifice within the context of many ancient traditional religions. Human beings ask their animal neighbors to make a sacrifice that they are convinced will have a specific and encompassing benefit for themselves and the victim. They believe the value of the benefit will compensate for the tragic element of the killing itself, in the case of the creature whose life is taken, and the other animals around him from whom his life is ripped. This mindset views life on this earth as something quite temporary, in any case, but the higher life awaiting us all as something eternal. They take the biological life of the animal away from this plane of existence, as God will one day take their own. They send the creature into another world closer to God and, by thus recreating this divine transitional act, moving a spirit from this world to the next, they enter into a sacredness that's more than merely symbolic, but that partakes of, and brings down to their own space and time, the proper prerogative of the divine. It's something that they believe empowers them in a unique way, and frees them from certain constraints of creatureliness that they experience as otherwise holding them back.

"I go into this detail merely to paint in broad strokes a picture against which to understand what's happening in our kingdom and beyond. I've come to believe that there is an individual, or group of individuals, who think of animals as having a connection to the divine that's both different from and beyond the best connection that humans alone can have. This man, let's say, has cultivated himself and his powers to the greatest extent that he can as a merely human being. He's perhaps as gifted as a senior Phi in terms of his mental and physical capacities. But, suppose there's a moral vacuum at his core. All he wants is power, or revenge, or personal ascendancy. There is a legend known by all senior Phi about what's called simply, 'The Monster,' and it tells such a story. It is, I believe, this sort of monster that we may now confront. He could be gathering animals of all kinds to see if there is some way he can exploit them to access resources or gain power from the realm of the spirit that would not otherwise be available to him. He wants to be an unstoppable force.

"There is a story in the ancient world of a man and his family who survived an enormous flood by building a large boat and taking into it many animals, two of every kind. It's usually supposed by readers or hearers of the story that the point was simply to save the male and female of each species and thus propagate their kind into the future, beyond the event of the flood. And this makes sense, within the classic narrative. But suppose there was another purpose, or at least an additional one: Perhaps the animals were gathered for spiritual support and power, to help assist the humans in connecting with the divine source more fully and deeply, without which they might have weakened and despaired as they awaited the cessation of the long storm extensive flood. Water is often a spiritual symbol. That element of the story is akin to what's needed in rituals of cleansing. Animals are also often a spiritual symbol.

"Our adversary—and I do think that's how he must be considered—is seeking something similar, but with his own supreme power, rather than the survival of any looming catastrophe, on his mind. The only disaster will be what results if he accomplishes his goals, which would bring along in their wake a flood of difficulty and even destruction that the rest of us would have to face.

"I wanted you to know all this before you get any closer to Dromeda. I will not ask or suggest that you seek to engage this individual directly at present and in person, in case he is near your destination. We may need to know more and create a careful strategy for his permanent defeat. But you may want to locate him, if that's possible, and learn what you can. Just proceed with great caution and immense care.

"I tell you all this only to warn you, to caution you, about something that's likely going on in proximity to our old village, so that you can be suitably circumspect and well-informed and can return here safe, in accordance with your schedule. If, however, you must face this enemy, you won't do so alone, but your collective power will be greatly augmented from here and Alexandria and Giza and Luxor, as well as from other spots in the region. Masoon can explain more. I've enclosed our special stone for you, in case anyone in the group might have need of it. Protect it, as it will safeguard you. Bring it home safe, as you bring each other home, as well.

"Please share this message and go forward with your souls full of strength, calm, hope, love, and confidence.

"With a Heart Full for All of You, Ali."

At the outskirts of Cairo, Malik and Haji walked to the front counter of the large veterinary clinic, and a man looked up from a desk not far behind it. "May I help you young men?"

"Yes, I hope so," Malik said. "My dog is having trouble this week."

The man stood up and came over to the counter and peered down at the animal. "What seems to be the problem?"

"He's tired all the time, lethargic, and he's not sleeping well at night."

"And this is new?"

"Yes, it's just not like him at all."

"How old is he?"

"He's about eight years old."

The man nodded his head in response, and then walked around the edge of the counter, joining the boys in the reception area to get a closer look. "Good boy," he said to the dog. "What's his name?"

"Giza," Malik said.

"If you'd like to wait, I have a moment now. I can take Giza back to an examination room and have a good look at him."

"What will an examination involve?" Malik asked, warily.

"Nothing intrusive," the man replied. "I'll take his weight, measure his height and length, look at his eyes, into his mouth, his ears, walk him around a bit, do a gentle manual examination of his entire body to see if there are any large tumors or growths inside him, and, if I think it's necessary, I may have to take a bit of blood to do more of a workup on him."

"Does that hurt?"

"Not really. It's just a little sting. And I may not think it's necessary, after all the other tests."

"Oh, Ok. What should my friend and I do while you're busy with the examination?"

"You can wait right here."

"How long will it take?"

"Oh, probably ten to fifteen minutes, perhaps a bit longer."

"That's fine, then."

"Well, we do have another animal back there now who is being examined by one of my colleagues. So we may have to put him in a holding room for five minutes first. But you'll likely have to wait no more than twenty minutes or so, at the most."

"Good. That's good."

"You boys can pay for this?" The man asked.

"How much will it be?" Malik responded.

"Five dollars, cash."

"Ouch. I didn't realize that. But … he's important to the family. I have the money, so go ahead," Malik said with a weak smile.

"You can pay right after the exam?" the man asked.

"Yes, I have it with me."

"Ok, fine. You boys can wait out here. I'll have the dog back to you within about twenty minutes at the most."

"It's a nice morning," Haji spoke up and said. "Is it Ok, if we go outside a bit while we wait?"

"Sure, sure, just stay close so we can alert you if you don't see us bring the dog back out here."

The boys agreed and then, as the man took Giza down a hallway toward the back, they both slipped out the front door and walked briskly down the side of the building and over toward a second large structure behind it. Some sort of noise was coming from the building, but it was faint and muffled, like it was being made behind thick, sound proof walls. There was a door into the building that was near them. Malik tried it, but it was locked. There were also three windows near where they stood, but they were all boarded up from the inside. Haji quickly examined each one. "There's a crack, a gap in the boards over here," he said, pointing at one of the windows. "Give me a boost and I think I'll be able to see into it."

Malik put his hands together and boosted Haji up about three feet and leaned him against the side of the building, where he found a handhold against the window casing. "Oh, man!" he whispered.

"What is it?"

"Lots and lots of animals of all kinds, in pens and enclosures."

"Just what we suspected," Malik said.

"There's another door at the back of the building. I can see it from here. It's a double door, I think. Maybe it's not locked," Haji said, as he jumped down from Malik's hands.

"Excuse me, boys, is there something I can do for you?"

They hadn't seen the man coming up behind them while Haji had been peering into the window. At the sound of his voice, both boys jerked around and were shocked to see, not twenty feet away from them, the bushy bearded professor. Their hearts jumped into their throats and their minds temporarily went completely blank.

24

Village Mysteries

Masoon and Walid gathered their fellow Phi together, along with Walid's parents, Rumi and Bhati. At this point, the darkness of the evening had descended fully over the oasis, and the small group sat around a little campfire that Hamid had started for the sake of the reading and conversational light it would provide. Masoon had explained to the other travelers that the Shabeezar family and their close friends needed to make some personal plans for their time in the village, in consultation with him and Hamid. He also asked Baldoor and Dubin again to oversee the operations of the security detail while this was going on, and they were happy to do so.

When they were alone around the fire, Masoon told everyone about the box from the airplane and what was in it. Then he asked Walid to read aloud the letter from the king. Everyone listened intently and the reading was followed by an extensive discussion, basically led by Masoon and Rumi, who both knew a lot about the philosophies and religious practices mentioned in the king's letter.

"Is this guy doing something like animal sacrifices?" Mafulla asked, right away, in a tone of shock mixed with dismay.

Rumi said, "Well, there's no compelling reason to think that's his approach. It's possible, but I'd wager he's assembling the animals around him, almost like you might construct a large radio antenna out of many smaller antennas, clustered together and wired to the same receiver. He's likely trying to access something that he thinks their nearness will help effectuate."

"Like one big psychic collector of spiritual signals?" Mafulla asked.

"Yes, he's apparently looking for a large harvest of spiritual power, something far beyond what he thinks he can gather in alone. And he hopes all the animals can help."

"This is certainly unusual," Kissa said. "Has it ever been tried before?"

"Well, the king did mention that possible interpretation of the famous flood story," Rumi replied. "And some other old religious writings represent shepherds as especially privy to divine messages or revelations, individuals who lived in close proximity to herds of sheep or goats. Perhaps it's a mere coincidence, and maybe not. It's often been observed that atheism tends to be an urban phenomenon, a thing of large cities, whereas spiritual life and belief tends to flourish best in more rural settings, closer to nature, and in proximity to many domesticated and wild animals. Plus, several ancient traditions see one animal or another as especially sacred, or representative of the divine. But I don't know whether any individual, at least in modern times, has ever attempted quite what this man is apparently doing. I actually doubt it. It's too far outside most modern thought. And if any such thing had ever before been done successfully by such a person, we would surely have heard about it."

"Like we've heard the flood story, and the accounts of ancient shepherds," Hasina said.

"Exactly. Look how long those stories have been told," Rumi pointed out. He added, "If there had been anyone before like our currently mysterious adversary who tried this and had success, we might already be living under the constraints of his enhanced power and authority. And fortunately, we're not."

"Do you actually think this crazy scheme might work?" Walid asked.

"Strange things can happen," Rumi said. "We all know the oddness of the world in which we live. Consider the stone the king sent to us in his package. Who can begin to understand what it really is and how it works? We have no hint of any known process or procedure that would give it such power as it seems to have. But we've seen its effects, several times over."

"That's a good point," Walid said.

Rumi then summed it all up. "We live in a land of mysteries, within a world of enigmas, placed in a universe that's in a vast number of ways unimaginably strange."

Heads nodded around the fire. Then someone else asked a question. Masoon offered an answer. Hasina spoke several times, as did Layla, and Mafulla. Their discussion carried on for another thirty minutes or so, and then they broke out of their small group session and rejoined their other fellow travelers and friends. A short time later, everyone had a nice dinner together, and they all enjoyed their last evening at the oasis as much as they could, with what they had on their minds.

Some of their new and old friends from this special place of rest in the western desert brought them desserts that had been baked that afternoon especially for them. They talked and laughed with these good people who had provided them with an oasis for the spirit as well as the body in this place, and eventually they all retired for the evening. Mafulla had his dream again about a man in a boat, but thought little of it, since there was no water nearby that could float a boat. After a good refreshing night's sleep for most, they all rose early, ate breakfast quickly, and left the oasis before dawn, with their faces now turned fully toward their next and ultimate destination, the village of Dromeda.

The day of travel passed uneventfully. A lower temperature and a nice breeze gave them even more time to travel than they had planned. They stopped for a much shorter rest in the middle of the day and, as a result, made more progress. The second day passed in just as pleasant and productive a way. Walid was thrilled not to be experiencing in this final period of travel any of the blistering heat he had encountered on his first and only trip across the desert before this. Mafulla had become good friends with his camel, Clyde. Walid was also enjoying his time with Cammo, and both Kissa and Hasina had gotten into the rhythms of desert travel as well as any novices could. Much of the soreness they experienced early in the trip had also gone away by this point, and that made the day easier, as well.

The king had been wise to send them all on this journey together, not just for the reason of security, but because they were getting to know each other better every day, through questions and stories and jokes and open conversations where they talked about their childhoods, as well as their dreams and hopes for the future.

Several times, Malik and Haji had crossed Walid's mind. And on a couple of occasions when he was alone with Mafulla in their tent during the mid-day rest or at the end of the day, Walid mentioned them and expressed a wish that they were doing Ok, and getting some good things accomplished as new members of The League of Crime Fighters, International. Mafulla would agree, and almost always crack some sort of joke.

Because of the lower temperatures, they made much better time crossing this stretch of sand than they had expected. On the morning of the third day away from the oasis, they realized that if they skipped the mid-day rest entirely, they could enter the village by early afternoon. And that's what they decided to do.

At exactly 1:48 PM, Reverso Time, according to Walid's watch, the lead riders called back the first sight of their destination. Everyone was so excited to be arriving. The word 'Dromeda' echoed along the camel train and a great sense of relief filled the hearts of the riders. Everyone was ready for a good bath, a nice meal, and no travel for a few days. They were finally where all this could happen and they could take some time to explore the village. And nothing had stopped them or warned them further not to approach, which was a bit odd, but a welcome fact to all. Despite their form of dress, this was not meant to be anything like a real military expedition into a war zone, an incursion into enemy territory, but simply a practical trip back home for some, and an educational experience for others.

They wasted no time when they arrived, but set up their tents quickly in a comfortable space where visiting caravans camped. Right away, those who had lived here in the past could tell that something was different. Arriving groups usually drew lots of curious children and friendly older people who would stop by for a chat. And always there would be some vendors and beggars and dogs. But the town seemed strangely quiet on this day. There was literally no one who came to their encampment to see who they were or to ask from where they had come. Maybe it was because of their military uniforms, and the appearance that they were traveling on official business. That certainly crossed Walid's mind. But, as he described to Mafulla what a visiting camel train usually attracted in its first few minutes, he actually became increasingly surprised at the contrast they were experiencing, or, to put it another way, at how much they weren't at all experiencing.

Their one greeter, after several minutes, was a limping dog, the town's official mascot, adopted by all—a homely but sweet pooch of indeterminate age, not visibly old, who had a moderate limp, likely from some accident long ago. Walid saw him wagging his way toward them and bouncing a bit as he walked, and he called out, "Hey! Gimpy! It's me! Walid!"

At that, the dog did the closest approximation available to him of a run, bounding in Walid's direction in a not-so-straight line. "Gimpy?" Mafulla said.

"Yes, the Gimp! My Gimpster! The Chief Gimpologist! His GimpMajesty! The town's most special dog!"

The little guy made it to Walid, who bent down and patted and stroked him and buried himself in the short hair of the happy beast, who was, in turn, now whining and licking and twisting back and forth and repeatedly putting out his front right paw to his old friend.

"The tail is wagging the dog!" Mafulla exclaimed. "I didn't think it was actually possible."

"Gimp! You're going to wag yourself into two dogs!" Walid laughed.

"How did this funny creature get these even funnier names?" Mafulla asked as he bent deep to pat him as well, and then squatted down, and Gimpy nearly knocked him over with enthusiasm.

"When he was young and I was too, an American, visiting with a caravan, saw him and named him on the spot. He said 'Gimpy' was an American slang term for lame or limping." Kissa and Hasina had just walked over in time to hear this explanation.

"His name is Gimpy?" Kissa asked.

"Yes, among many other derivative and variously flamboyant interpretive improvisations on that core characterization," Walid said, still laughing at the dog's antics.

"Boy! He sure remembers you!" Mafulla was impressed.

"Well, I have to admit that it's not all high-minded sentimentality," Walid confessed. "I often snuck him treats. You know, the sort of deal I have with you."

At that, Mafulla and both the girls laughed, and Hasina said, "That explains why he's such a wag."

"The secret's out!" Mafulla said.

Kissa said, "A wag?"

"A person who makes jokes, silly."

"Or a person who makes silly jokes?" Walid offered. "I think it's an old meaning of the word."

Kissa said, "Oh! That's a good play on the other sense that's most appropriate to The Great Tale of Mafulla." And at that, everyone laughed again.

Kissa then looked around and said, "So, Gimpy is our full welcoming committee today?"

"Apparently," Walid answered. "Only the best for visiting dignitaries."

"Maybe it's our uniforms," Mafulla suggested.

"Maybe so," Walid agreed.

Mafulla explained, "It could be that he was attracted because he wants to join the army so that he can claim his limp came from an old war wound and, you know, impress the lady dogs in the area."

"Ha! Well, he's already getting a lot out of the limp. That's part of what snags him so many treats."

After a few more moments of exultant celebration at this unexpected reunion, Walid suddenly thought for a second that Gimpy's dark brown eyes were looking right into his in a way that was both imploring and relieved and happy, but at the same time, sad. On the surface, that didn't make much sense. But in the short time their eyes met, Walid registered something deep, as if this animal was trying to communicate a feeling or need or wish that was important.

Minutes later, Rumi came over with word that he and Bhati wanted to invite Walid, Mafulla, Kissa, Hasina, Masoon, Omari, and Hamid to walk with them to their former home, which was not far away, on this south side of town. The group of them then made their way through a wide opening in the low wall that marked the outer border of the village on this side, and walked by several other small homes on their way to their old house that had been closed up all this time.

There wasn't much activity on the street, but that was not so unusual, since it was still the time of early afternoon when people normally rested inside, away from the heat of the day. But things should pick up any minute, Walid thought. It wasn't very hot, and the villagers would normally be out and about soon enough. He and his friends were going to visit the general store and the bookshop as well, a bit later. But both those stores lay beyond their home, from the side on which they were approaching, so they'd stop by the house first and then later drop in to the businesses that had supported their family for so long and, of course, had also provided the gathering place where Ali's former plans for political revolution were initially developed.

As they drew near the area of their old home, Bhati caught sight of a neighbor, an older lady who lived across the street from them and down a few houses. She called out, "Mrs. Maayuf! How are you?"

The lady squinted and shaded her eyes to see. "Bhati? Is that my Bhati? And Rumi? Yes! Yes, it's you! And Walid!"

"We're all here!"

"My goodness! Have you all joined the army?"

Bhati laughed and said, "No, no, we're just traveling in disguise to come and see you, and to do some things at the old house and our village shops."

"Oh, my goodness! Oh, my gracious! You're the most important people ever to visit our village!"

Bhati laughed and said, "You'll remember that we long lived here."

"Yes, but we had no idea! No idea that Ali and Walid would leave us that day not so long ago and go straight to Cairo and the palace and begin to rule the land. I mean, of course, we hoped it would happen eventually, but we had no idea it would take place so soon. And so we have our former neighbors now serving as the king and prince. And you and Rumi are now officially the most royal family."

"Yes, it's all true."

"We heard the news, of course, right after it happened. And we were so happy that it was accomplished so quickly and peacefully. We were all aglow. Plus, the village suddenly became important. Did you know that? People visiting were always asking about you." She turned and looked back at her house, then again at Bhati and said, "Please, wait just a second." Then she looked back toward the house again and shouted as loud as she could, "Sab! Sab! Come quickly!"

An older man appeared in the door, saying "What? What is it, my wife?"

"The prince is here!"

"What did you say?"

"The prince and the royal family are here! In front of our house!"

"Who?"

"Look at who's here to see us!"

"Oh! Oh! What a surprise! Welcome to you, Rumi and Bhati! And young Walid, and your friends! Welcome to you!" Sab looked around and said, "Where's the king? Where's Ali?"

"He had business in Cairo," Bhati said. "He sends his warmest regards."

"Oh! Well! Warm regards right back! Now, all those of you who didn't have business in Cairo and so were free to travel to my doorstep: Please, come into my humble home and visit a while!" The old man came walking toward them with arms wide open. There were then many hugs, first with Rumi, then Bhati, and then he didn't quite know what to do with Walid, but bowed to him first and said, "The Prince of the Kingdom!" And he threw his arms around him and hugged him.

Bhati introduced all the others to their old neighbors and they stood and talked a bit and then, at the further insistence of Sab, she said they'd all be honored to come into the house and visit for a few more minutes, before they would need to get on with the work they had come to do, both at their old house, and at the shops.

After much more gushing and exclaiming and a quick preparation of tea, some cookies and snacks were miraculously produced for this small crowd of nine unexpected guests. They all sat, somehow, in the front room, and drank their tea and talked about the past year. At first, the Maayufs were asking about the palace and the capital and what their lives were like now. Then, they wanted to know all about Mafulla and Kissa and Hasina. Everyone talked and laughed. Finally, Bhati began to ask about the village and their other neighbors. She first said to her old friend, "I'm sorry that so many people had to move from the area to the capital city to help Ali reorganize the kingdom."

"Oh, we understood completely. We were so sorry to see each of them go—like you, Masoon, and you, Hamid—but we knew that Ali would need the assistance of his best friends. Still, we miss you all. But we know you're doing important things for the good of many. So, we carry on." She smiled and nodded her head and gestured with her hands, in the universal 'what can you do?' motion.

Rumi asked, "How else has the village changed since we've been gone? Have any other things been different here?"

Meskhenet, or Mrs. Maayuf, looked at her husband, and he at her. "Well," he said, "there have been some mysterious changes around here recently, things we don't quite understand—some unusual developments that have given us pause."

"Of what sort?" Hamid asked.

"Tell them," Meskhenet said to her husband.

Sab thought for a second and explained. "Many people began visiting the village after Ali took power. We had more guests coming through here than ever before. And yet, most would just stay a day or two and move on. But then some new people moved into the area and began to shop in town, some Spaniards and a few men from other nations that we don't otherwise tend to see much in this area. Of course, we welcomed them all with the hospitality that's so important to us. They were cordial enough in town, but strangely evasive about where exactly they had come to live and what work they did—the work that apparently brought them here. Whenever they were asked, they would say that they lived 'outside of town a bit,' and that they were engaged in 'various scientific studies and research of an experimental sort,' but they never clarified what they meant by either of these vague generalities. It would leave us scratching our heads. They must have thought we all had lice in our hair."

"Don't say such a thing!" Meskhenet scolded him.

Sab laughed at his own joke for a moment, and continued. "Then, a few animals in the village began to just disappear. Nothing like this had ever happened before. A dog, a cat, a horse, a mule, a camel or two, and even a goat! Poof! Gone!"

"Really?" Walid said.

"Yes! It was so strange! People would go through town looking for their lost animal, calling for them, asking neighbors. Nothing! They had simply vanished! But only healthy looking specimens disappeared, never the scrawny or old or injured ones." He turned to the prince and said, "Your Highness, I saw you had Gimpy beside you outside."

"Yes, sir. He met us right after we arrived."

"He's been fine. No one's touched him. He's not run off, or been dognapped, or anything."

"Do you think it's because he's lame?"

"Yes. To be quite frank, I think someone is stealing the animals, but only the healthy ones." He lowered his voice at this point, adding, "And, if you want my opinion, I would bet it's the Spaniards and some of the others."

"I see."

"My husband! You shouldn't speak of the new people like that!" Meskhenet was embarrassed by Sab's remark, but it was simply his candid opinion.

"Don't be hard on your fine man," Bhati said, with a warm smile. "What he's expressing may be the truth."

"Why? Do you think he's right? Do you know something about this? Bhati, dear friend, please, tell me. Many of our neighbors—good people, kind people—are so sad at losing their pets and favorite animals. And some have also lost an importance source of milk or cheese, on which they had depended. It's just terrible in so many ways. What can you tell us?"

"We don't know much," Bhati said, "but what you've seen here is more widespread than you might imagine."

"What do you mean?"

"It's going on all over," Walid said.

"I don't understand."

Bhati said, "There have been numerous animal disappearances in Cairo and in the capital cities of three nearby countries in recent days. Someone is taking healthy and beautiful animals away from their homes and owners."

"Oh, my. So, it's not just here in the village?"

"No, it's in many places."

Hamid added, "This may sound exceedingly strange, but we think someone is doing this in order to surround themselves with animal minds who may be more sensitive to, or connected with, the spiritual realm of existence in ways that we humans alone could never access." As he spoke these words of explanation, the younger people looked over at him with great surprise that he would reveal this fact. And their elderly hosts had expressions on their faces of what could be either perplexity or great concern.

"So," Sab said, "they take the beautiful animals and leave behind the lame, and what they consider ordinary, like Gimpy."

"Yes."

"Have these people never heard of the deaf and blind and crippled individuals throughout history who have been at the forefront of the arts and sciences, among our great composers and artists and writers and poets, not to mention inventors and great thinkers?"

"Apparently not." Hamid said.

"And so they leave alone poor Gimpy, who may have much more going on in his head and soul than the criminals themselves."

"I think I saw a flash of that today, Mr. Maayuf," Walid said.

"Tell me." Maayuf looked at Walid with interest.

"Gimpy welcomed us to town and we were rubbing and scratching him and it was all crazy and wonderful for a couple of minutes and then he looked into my eyes and I saw something I'd not expected."

"Yes?

"I mean, there was a real connection that went deep, and I could tell he needed me to understand something."

"It's this," Sab said. "It's what's been going on in and near our village. His friends have disappeared, and he hurts for them. I can tell."

"Where do you think these new people live?" Masoon asked.

"I believe they live to the north, but where exactly, I have no idea."

"We'll try to look into this while we're here," Masoon replied, as Hamid nodded his agreement.

"Has there been anything else going on?" Masoon this time asked.

"Well, and this is going to sound very silly," Sab said, "but several people I know in town have told me they've dreamed of a man in a boat, and as the boat floats down the water, it grows. Some have had this dream repeated several times, and no one has a clue what it means."

"I've had that dream!" Mafulla said. "At two different times."

"Why didn't you say anything about it?" Walid asked him.

"What could I say?" Mafulla replied. "There's a man in a blue boat going down a river. The boat gets bigger: End of story. It doesn't seem to signify anything beyond itself. Are we near water? No. Are we likely to go near water on this trip? No. So I've just basically forgotten about it each time I've dreamed it."

"Well, apparently, something's going on," Hamid said. "And I'm guessing it's something we need to understand. It's a warning of some kind, or our unconscious minds are picking up on something we need to attend to. Thank you for telling us this, Sab."

Everyone sat and thought for a moment. Meskhenet said, "Strange things often come in groups. The disappearances, the dreams—what else is next?"

"That's what I want to know," Sab said.

"As do I," Masoon replied and added, "and the rest of us, I'm sure."

Then Bhati said, "Well, we have to make our own disappearance, at least for now. We need to open up the house, and then get to the stores. But we'll see you later on, again."

"Ok. If you must go." Sab smiled.

"Yes, but just for now. It's been so lovely to visit with you both like this, but we can't allow ourselves to overstay our welcome."

"You know you're always welcome," Sab said.

"Thank you. You're always so sweet to us. I just think that, perhaps, we should get going for the moment. There's so much we have to accomplish in only a few days, and I need to visit three more places before dark."

"Do you really have to leave now?" Meskhenet asked.

"I'm afraid so. We'll see you more and talk more, later," Bhati replied, but there are some things we must do this afternoon."

"I understand."

"Yes, go and do what you need to do," Sab said with a smile.

Bhati replied, "Thank you so much for your gracious hospitality and warm welcome, and of course, for your candid and open conversation, which has been helpful."

"You know we love your entire family and want the best for you in all things, as well as for our humble village," Meskhenet said.

"Yes. And we cherish any time we can have with you," Sab said. "But we know you have much to accomplish on a short visit. So please, let me walk you out, and offer you our open invitation and open hearts while you're here."

There were then goodbyes all around, affirmations of friendship and gratitude, and the group of visitors left, with the Maayuf couple standing at their open doorway, waiving to their old and new friends. None of them had any idea of the shocking disappearance that was about to happen, or that it would be like the wildest dream imaginable—and yet both real and revelatory.

25

A Clinic, a Store, and a Bookshop

Things had just taken an unexpected turn at the Cairo Veterinary Clinic. The boys were caught. Trapped. Cornered. Malik finally got his brain to unfreeze and blurted out, "What?"

It wasn't the most original response. The man with the bushy beard said, "I saw you boys just now looking into that window. I was wondering if I can help you find something."

"My dog."

"Your dog?"

"My dog is in with the vet right now having an examination, and it was taking longer than we thought. And we were just looking around while we waited, to see … where you keep sick animals, or those who are having exams. I thought maybe we'd see my dog. And really, we're both thinking about the possibility of becoming vets one day, and we were just curious to see what all these buildings are."

"You have many answers for my one question."

"Yes."

"The buildings here contain animals that need to be seen, or animals that have been seen and perhaps need to be kept a few days for observation," the man stated, in an almost surly voice. He stared at them for a moment, and then said, "Have I run across you two somewhere before?"

"No, I don't think so," Haji said. "You would be easy for me to remember."

"Why is that?" the man asked.

"Because of your … very distinguished looking beard," Haji said. "It's very distinctive and dignified."

"Yes. I have seen you boys. I remember. It was in the Falafel Stop the other day, one of the very few times I've been there recently. You came in and sat at the next booth and had tea or something." His face grew even more ominous as he spoke these words.

"Oh. Ok. Yeah. Sure. We go there a lot," Malik said. "It has great food and isn't far from where we live."

"What were you really doing there—and now, here?"

"Well, like I said, we live not far from the café, and today, my dog's having an examination."

"It's a big coincidence to run into each other again, then, is it?"

"What? Oh, I don't know," Malik quickly answered. "Maybe … we were supposed to meet you at this stage in our lives. I sort of believe in destiny, don't you? I mean, since we're both thinking about becoming vets. And I'm guessing you're a vet. Maybe we need to talk to you."

"I'm no vet."

"Oh. Then, do you work here in some other capacity?" Haji asked. "Are you the owner, or maybe an assistant?"

The man stared at Malik a second more, and turned to Haji, who then felt like his eyes were boring through him. The man slowly said, "I study animals, the history of animals, and animal behavior. I don't do physical examinations, or give shots, or clean out cages. I'm a scholar, of some repute."

Just then, a voice called out, "Hashman! Hashman!" and a figure came around the corner of the building. It was Mansur Arobi. Malik and Haji both fought the natural reaction of surprise, so that it would not appear on their faces, just as it was about to leap up into their features and totally give them away. Their heart rates shot up, as they now felt trapped, indeed.

"What is this?" Arobi said in a stern tone. Then, glaring at the boys, he said, "Who are you two? And what are you doing here?"

Dr. Arib answered, "It's likely nothing. They're just boys with a sick dog who are wandering around while he's being examined. I've seen them before, though."

Arobi looked at the boys carefully and then spoke again. "Well, this part of the clinic compound is off limits for visitors. I suggest you go back to the waiting room to pick up your dog. You can't be back here. There are some very sick animals in this building and you could be endangered by getting too close."

"What?" the professor now said.

"We just learned that many of them have a bad virus that's contagious to humans, and they're all going to be shipped to another, more remote clinic within the hour, to be cured of their illness so that they can be returned to their owners—mostly farmers and food producers in the area. So you boys, for your own safety, must get away from this building. We've been vaccinated, but you've not been, and any exposure would be dangerous.."

"Oh, thank you," Malik said. "We'll go back to the front of the main building right away. Thank you for your consideration." And he led his friend quickly along the side of the building, back toward the front.

"Oh, man," Haji muttered. "I thought we were goners."

"Yeah, me, too," Malik mumbled in response, head down and walking briskly beside his friend.

"I can't believe he recognized us and we still got away!" Haji said.

"Yeah," Malik agreed. "That was a close call."

"Well, it was your quick thinking that saved us," Haji admitted.

"It just came to me, what to say," Malik replied. "And now, I can breathe again."

"Me, too. Have you ever really thought about being a vet?"

"Yeah, actually I have."

"Me, too."

"Really? I didn't know that. It's wild. So, I spoke the truth even though I didn't realize it at the time. I was just saying what came to me."

"Crazy." The boys got to the front entrance once more, and Malik opened the door for Haji to go through first. They both took seats in the reception area, again alone, as they awaited the return of Giza.

Minutes later, the vet came out from the back and said, "Your dog seems fine, but there's one thing that came to light during the examination. If you would both come back here, I'd like to show you while I explain."

"Both of us?"

"Well, you may have to do something for him that will take two pairs of hands, if you don't mind."

"But he's fine?"

"Yes, and he can be even better if I show you a little technique. Come on back with me."

"Oh, Ok," Malik said and got out of his chair, as did Haji, and they followed the vet down the hall and to the examination room while the man, still in the hallway, held open the door for them. But they were quickly confused as they entered. The room was empty. The dog wasn't there. And just as they realized this, they heard the door closed and locked behind them. Click.

In the village of Dromeda, Rumi and Bhati had now opened up their house, and Walid's friends got a chance to see where he had grown up. He gave them the full, yet abbreviated, tour that was appropriate for such a small home, and then took them out back to see where he had played as a child.

Bhati showed Layla, Hasina, and Kissa her old garden area in the back, behind the house, as Walid and Mafulla stood silently for a minute at the door, watching them. Walid took a deep breath and said, "As you can see, it was a big change from this place to life in the palace."

"You had almost as much room in The Kidnappers Hotel," joked Mafulla.

"Yeah, really," Walid agreed.

"Not while you were still in the enclosed arrival box, of course, which was merely your transportation, as distinct from your lodging, but I mean to reference what was all yours once I had opened the box and welcomed you into the larger, more spacious suite that we shared for so short a time."

Walid chuckled and said, "It was a pretty short time."

"Fortunately," Mafulla added, "although the centrality of the location and the view from our window were both quite impressive features of the place, despite the unfortunate placement of the window."

Walid laughed again and said, "Yeah, one of us had to pretty much stand on the other to see out at all."

"And then there was the awkward fact that the door was locked from the outside. And the window had bars. I did truly mean to write up those things in a letter of complaint to the management."

"Somebody should have," Walid said.

Just then, Rumi came up and said, "Boys, we need to go down to the store and visit with the manager. I have some business to attend to for my brother. Would you like to stay here or come with us?"

"Could we go into the bookshop and look around while you have the meeting, and maybe see if my old friend's there?"

"Sure, that's fine," Rumi answered. He looked at Mafulla and said, "The man who runs the general store, it's his son who's in charge of the bookshop and works there most days. He and Walid are old buddies. I think you'll enjoy him." He then looked back at the prince and said, "I'll get the ladies."

He called out to Bhati, Layla and the girls that it was time for them all to walk down into the center of the village. Hamid was going to visit the small medical clinic farther down the street and look up his old colleague there, to catch up on what was going on and make some plans for the future. And Masoon was going to accompany the group to the store, at first, and then, assuming that the situation was all calm and secure, join Hamid at the clinic for a bit.

Omari stayed at the house to begin an inventory of everything there, at Bhati's request, and even do a little cleaning, if that was needed, while checking over all the doors and windows for their continued integrity. Everyone else walked down the hard-packed, sandy street toward the general store, long owned by the Shabeezar family and run now by a man named Aleph Noni. Various former neighbors and friends stopped to greet them on the way, and so the brief walk took about five times longer than normal, or more. But Bhati and Rumi assured everyone they'd be around for a few days, and that they'd make sure to have plenty of time for more visiting with everyone.

Aleph was outside, sweeping the threshold at the front door of the popular store. He stopped mid-sweep and peered intently in their direction, as they ambled up the street toward him. "What? What is this? Can I believe my eyes? Bhati? Rumi? My favorite customers! And Masoon! And … Walid? You've grown so! Come over here and give your favorite Aleph a big hug! How have you all been?"

"Very well," Rumi said. "We hope you are!"

"Yes, very well, indeed," Aleph said. "I'm so pleased to see you!"

"It's good to see you," Masoon said, and stepped up to shake the man's hand, right after Rumi had done so.

"I didn't know you were all coming! What a nice surprise this is!"

"We miss you and the village a lot," Bhati added, as they now stood in front of the shop.

"And we all miss you!" Aleph exclaimed. "But once the well-kept secret of your identity was out for all the world to know, we realized that you wouldn't be able to come back again any time soon. So this visit is wonderful."

"It's been far too long and it's so good to see you again!" Walid said, and gave him that hug he had requested—in a very manly way, of course. Then the prince introduced Aleph to those in the group who didn't already know and love him, and he in turn pleasantly greeted each of them with a hearty welcome to the village and to the store.

"As I like to say to everyone who visits: 'Please, come into my shop!' Of course, I'm but a loyal steward for your great family, and not the owner. And it's my great honor to have been entrusted with my role here. So I do treat your place as if it were my own—in all the best ways."

"I can tell," Rumi said. "You've always been a top notch manager, and that's what we're here to commend you for and speak with you about. We think you've proven your worth to this enterprise, over and over, for many years now, and would like to make you an offer that we think you may welcome."

"Oh, that's so kind of you! And, please, do come into my—which is to say, your—fine shop!" With a big smile and a grand gesture, Aleph motioned them all through the door. Masoon explained briefly that he could stay only for a minute and would then have to go, for now, to take care of some other business, but that he'd be back later to visit more. And Aleph replied that he'd be welcome any time, while also intimating that he had some new merchandise that might interest even a man from the big city.

The store was larger than Mafulla had expected. Walid explained that this was because it had to be stocked not just for the small population of the village and surrounding area, but also for all the travelers who would stop here and visit as they crossed the kingdom. It had become a well-known hub of commercial activity, for a place that in geography and population was relatively small. Being just off the main camel trail that crossed the vast desert and in an area not as desert-like as the expanse to the east, made it a great stop for people traveling west from Cairo or southwest from Alexandria. The village even got a lot of north to south, and south to north travelers, as well. In that sense, it was a bit like an oasis, but a good deal bigger. There was no pool of water nearby, but there were good deep wells that could serve both locals and travelers. The general store was very close to one of the largest and most used sources of water. It was quite popular and had to be well supplied with all sorts of items that visitors and local people might need or want. As the manager, Aleph had a big responsibility and employed several helpers from town to work with him in the shop.

The boys walked around with Layla, Hasina, and Kissa for a few minutes just to take it all in and admire the various things they saw. Aleph had increased the range of merchandise in stock, and had some very high quality items as well as simple and practical goods. Then, after a while, Walid and Mafulla said they were going to duck into the adjoining bookshop run by Aleph's son, a young man named Zet. Kissa and Hasina promised they'd join them shortly, after maybe trying on some nice ladies' clothes that weren't military issue and sampling a few perfumes in stock that were actually from Paris.

When Walid led Mafulla through the bookshop door, Zet was sitting at his desk, reading. "Welcome to the shop. Please help yourself and ask me if you have any questions," he said, without even looking up from the page under his nose, but just hearing them enter.

"The problem is that I need a book on how to be a prince," Walid said.

Zet's head jerked up from the pages in front of him, and he had the funniest and most shocked look on his face. Walid laughed out loud. "Oh! No, no, no, no, no! It can't be! I'm dreaming! It's a vision, a hallucination! Did I fall into this book about Cairo and end up there? But it still looks like my humble shop around me! And yet, there's royalty here!" Zet jumped up from his desk, twisted around the end of it, and gave Walid a huge hug and multiple pats on the back. "What are you doing here, Walid—Prince Walid—Your Highness, My Highness, Everybody's Highness, royal buddy, old friend? What's going on?" Then he bowed quickly three times, and Walid laughed.

"Didn't your dad tell you I was coming? My father wrote him about the trip some time ago."

"No! The scoundrel kept it a secret!"

Walid had to laugh more, and even Mafulla, though he had never met Zet before, couldn't help but laugh as well, because of the very funny look on the young man's face and the hilarious tone of his voice. Walid said to Zet, "This is my best friend who lives in the palace, Mafulla Adi. We were kidnapped and met as fellow prisoners, as soon as I got to Cairo."

"You were kidnapped?"

"Yes," Mafulla answered. "The criminals apparently confused

me with someone important, and wasted a perfectly good kidnapping on me. And then, a short time later, I was joined by a prince-in-a-box."

"It was a stifling box that I had been shoved into—almost like a coffin—from which Mafulla quickly freed me," Walid said.

"I've heard nothing about any of this!" Zet exclaimed, and fanned himself quickly with his hand. "It's far too exciting!"

Walid and Mafulla then told him the entire story, to his shock and endless delight. And his dramatic, almost theatrical reactions to everything fueled their storytelling abilities to a new level. Mafulla started re-enacting things about their efforts to escape, and the rescue, and the assault team, and the dropped gun on the stairs, and how scared they all were, and how it ended with Bancom almost shooting Masoon and Masoon almost shooting Bancom and everybody almost shooting everybody else, right there on the stairs to The Kidnappers Hotel.

Zet had his hands over his mouth during some of the big revelations, and he was slapping himself on the face during others. He was the perfect audience for such a dramatic tale. Now and then, he would yell out, "No!" or "O-My-Gosh!" or make a screech or squawking sound that made Mafulla laugh. And Mafulla then ended the story with his own theatrical flourish and a very funny line that had his new acquaintance doubled over with laughter to the extent that he actually slid down the side of the desk and was sitting on the floor snorting and squealing, with both hands on his bouncing stomach, until he just fell over and lay on his back, saying "Stop! Stop! No more! I can't take it! I can't breathe!"

That had Mafulla laughing again, and he turned to Walid and said, with as straight a face as he could manage, "I like your old friend a lot. He just needs to loosen up a bit and learn how to enjoy himself."

Also laughing at this point, Walid bent down and helped his old friend off the floor, and Zet then reached around to a cup of water that he had on the desk, and began to take a big sip.

"Would you like a more exciting story?" Mafulla asked him.

"Or should we all enjoy a quiet, relaxed intermission with snacks first, and then get on to something really dramatic?"

At that, Zet dramatically spewed out the water in his mouth, and they all nearly collapsed in a heap of laughter.

Somehow, the boys managed to calm down and ask Zet about what was new around the village these days. And in response, he told them quite a tale of mystery and strange events—beginning with things that started happening shortly after Rumi and Bhati had left to go to Cairo, following the restoration of the rightful monarchy. Walid peppered his old pal with a lot of questions, to get as clear as he could on what these mysteries were and who was being affected.

"We see a lot of the new people in the store and here in the bookshop," Zet said. "Some of them are Spanish."

"Yeah, we heard something about Spaniards," Walid said. "What do you know about them?"

"They keep to themselves, much more than camel train visitors ever do. They're very quiet around us locals. But sometimes I hear things. I'm always reading, and it often seems like people don't realize I can still hear what they're saying to each other, if I want to. And maybe it's in part my age. I'm a few years older than you guys, but I'm still not considered by many to be a responsible adult yet. They often don't even continue to notice me here after they've caught a glimpse of me and noted my youth. I'm the famous fly on the wall, the invisible observer. As a result, I overhear things."

"What have you overheard?"

"Ah. You know, that's an interesting concept. Have you noticed how different overhearing is from overlooking, and even from overseeing?" Zet sounded and looked perplexed, but in a semi-comical way.

"I suppose so, but let's overlook that matter right now."

"And why is there no over-smelling, or over-tasting, or even over-feeling? But I don't mean here to be over-bearing."

"Zet! What have you heard?" Walid insisted.

"Oh! Ok. I've heard whispered remarks about a Santiago many

times. At first, since they seemed to be Spanish, I thought they were talking about the capital of the country of Chile, in South America, settled long ago by their countrymen. But then, I realized it was a person they were discussing, and always, in low voices. Finally, I came to understand that it was a man who is somehow their boss, and who also lives somewhere nearby, or at least not too far away. I once even asked, although at that point I knew the answer, 'Are you gentlemen talking about the capital of Chile?' and one of them just said, 'No, you misunderstood,' and walked away."

"Santiago? Any other name?" Walid asked.

"No, just Santiago, and now and then the phrase, 'The Master,' like it was a name, and, apparently, referring to the same person."

"That sounds almost religious," Mafulla said.

"I thought so, too," Zet replied. "And twice, I've overheard the words, 'ruler of all.' That seemed very strange, outside a clearly political or religious context. And there was a time when I heard one of the men speak of 'the professor,' which also seemed odd, since there's no college or university around here."

Walid nodded and asked, "Do these men buy books when they come in?"

"Yes and they sometimes special-order books, strange ones—books on the ancient enterprise known as alchemy, along with some volumes on religion, and even a few publications about animals in history."

"Animals?"

"Yeah. And several of the books they've wanted are rare ones. Most are out of print. But I have catalogues here from many places and have been able, for the most part, to order and get what they're looking for. I wish I knew the purpose."

Walid looked at Mafulla and then thought for a second. He lowered his voice and said, "Be careful with these men and around them, my friend. Don't show too much interest in what they're doing or who they are. We have some reason to believe that their boss is not a good person at all, and in fact may have nefarious purposes in his work."

"Am I in danger? Is my father, or the shop?"

"Not that we know," Walid said. "There's no special reason for you to fear this man, but just be cautious around his people. The king is aware that something's going on, and he's moving to learn more, and then we'll be able to deal with it. But do tell us if you happen to see or hear anything else that might even remotely be connected to all this."

"You've heard of the animal disappearances?"

"Yes, and they're going on in the capital city as well."

"Oh. I see. So it's not just here?"

"No, it's more widespread. We just got a message from the king that these things are taking place in Tunis, Algiers, and Tripoli, as well."

"My goodness. What's this all about?"

"We're not sure yet, but we think it's all part of a strange, mystical effort to accumulate power."

"Strange is right."

"I can explain more when I'm more sure of what I'm talking about," Walid said. "But," he added, "just be careful. Promise me, Ok?"

"Don't worry about me, old buddy—I mean, Your Highness! I promise to be cautious."

"Good."

"I wouldn't want to end up like some people I know … kidnapped." He almost hissed out this last word and Walid knew, as a result, that he was all right, and would be fine. He was, in a way, the opposite of Mafulla in his use of humor. He joked when he felt good. And it was nice to see this in action. Zet looked less worried already, at that moment, as if he was convinced that the king and Walid and the others would be able to handle anything that was going on. And the fact that he could once again joke, so soon after this discussion, was a very good sign of his equilibrium, and emotional resilience.

"Hey, being kidnapped isn't always so bad," Mafulla said, with a grin. "When it happened to me, I ended up as a duke or an earl or a satrap or something, living in a palace, and having all my food prepared, dishes washed, and clothing provided and cleaned for me. And, oh, yeah, people even sometimes sort of bow to me, after they've bowed to the you-know-who here."

"Really? This is quite impressive," Zet said and immediately bowed to Mafulla, making him laugh again.

Suddenly a voice called out, "Zet! Could you come in here for a moment? Bring your friends!" It was Aleph.

"Sure! Just a second." Zet did a silly grin to the other two boys.

The three of them then walked toward the sound of the call and saw Aleph standing with Rumi and Bhati. He had a big smile that lit up the room. "The most wonderful thing has happened," he said.

"What is it?"

"These incredibly gracious people, Rumi and Bhati, have conveyed to me their wishes and the king's that I should be granted a part ownership in the store, a whopping thirty percent, in addition to a higher ongoing salary, as a reward for my stewardship over the enterprise, both while they were here and since they left."

"Father, that's wonderful!" Zet said.

"It is, indeed!

Zet went up to him and hugged him. Then he turned to Rumi and Bhati and, doing something like a bow, said, "Thank you both so much, and please thank the king! It's a great honor for us."

"You're welcome," Bhati said. "But there's one more thing you should know."

"What's that?"

"You're also being granted the same ownership stake in the bookshop, in addition to your normal salary, starting today."

"What?"

"You're now officially one of the owners of The Dromeda Bookshop. You'll be getting profits as well as your normal pay for work that you do here."

"This is unbelievable!"

They all laughed and Rumi said, "It's true, so you'd better believe it!"

"My son, the businessman! The owner!" Aleph exclaimed in his own surprise, and they hugged again.

"Well, I'm not exactly a tycoon, at least, not yet," Zet replied. "But I can aspire. And I thank you all very, very much."

In a locked room at the edge of Cairo, far away, Walid and Mafulla's close friends and new comrades in masked escapades had just experienced another shock. Malik looked at Haji and whispered, "Look, no matter what happens next, unless our lives are immediately threatened in the most severe way, don't fight back. Look weak. Look confused. Be docile. Be complaisant. Act scared. Be just an ordinary kid. Go along with whatever they do and say."

"But."

"I know you want to unleash all the fury of Masoon, junior, on anyone that opens the door, but don't."

"Why?"

"They'll expect resistance now, and it's best for them to get it when they don't expect it. The element of surprise is crucial. We don't know how many we're up against. And we don't know where Giza is. We need more information and a plan before we act—or at least a big element of surprise and some clear options."

"Ok, Ok, you're right. I get it. I promise."

They knew the door would most likely open soon, given that they were hearing more footsteps and a muffled conversation out in the hallway. But they had no idea what would happen right after that.

The next sound was a loud rattle and a click.

26

Animals In Our Midst

First, there was the sound of a key in a lock that it didn't quite fit. It made a rattle as it was twisted around. Then the door was unlocked. That was the click. Immediately, it swung open and two very large men came through it. Each of them grabbed one of the boys by the shoulders. "Come with us," one of them barked, and added the command, "Now!"

"Ow! What's going on?" Malik protested verbally, in a humble voice of sheer perplexity, and he didn't physically resist at all, as he and Haji were shoved forward toward the now open door. They let themselves be pushed by their new escorts and then roughly pulled down the hallway to the back of the building.

At the end of the hall, the professor was holding a door open. "Take them to Building Two," Arib said in a brusque voice. "Tie them up and we'll move them out with the animals."

"Why not just get rid of them?" One of the men paused and asked, as he stared at the professor.

"The Master's orders. He wants to see any guys caught poking around here and have the chance to talk to them first and learn what they know. He has ways of convincing these poor saps to tell him anything, mysterious ways that always produce the truth." The man grunted in response and pushed Haji again toward the building they had been peeking into earlier. The boy tripped and almost fell.

Malik said, still in a tone of confusion, "You guys didn't want us to even look into this building a few minutes ago, and now you're taking us inside to see everything? I don't get it."

"Oh, you're gonna get it soon enough, kid," his own personal bad guy barked out, and then he shoved Malik up against the wall of the building next to the door while he took out a key to unlock it. He said, "Don't move or you'll get it where you stand. The big boss wants you alive, but I can still mess you up real bad." The other man had a death-grip on Haji and was standing there silently, waiting for the moment when he could shove him forward once more. The men were intent on showing off their strength and making the boys fear them. They had no idea the true effect they were having with their actions, or what would soon result.

The door opened and the boys were both again pushed roughly through it and into the second, much larger, building. Haji said, "Ouch! You hurt me!" And Malik was impressed.

They now saw clearly all the animals they earlier had glimpsed, in stalls and pens and cages. It looked like an acre or more of animals in one building, creatures of different types and vastly different sizes. Just as they were pushed again into what seemed to be a horse stall on the right, Malik saw his dog being led by at a distance on a leash. "Giza!" Malik yelled out. "Giza!"

The dog turned and barked twice. And then he let out a loud yelp. "Shut up! No talk from you," the man growled, who was still holding Malik's arm.

"That's my dog!"

"Maybe it was your dog," the man said. "It's somebody else's dog now." Haji looked at Malik and he saw and barely moved his head to the side and back, in the most subtle communication of the answer 'no' that he was capable of giving. The man said, "Hold your hands behind you, and if you move I'll kill you here and explain it later." Malik complied with the command, holding his hands loosely together, and the man tied them with a rough piece of rope. He could tell by the feel of it on his skin that it wasn't a tight weave or made of good material. The same thing was then done to Haji, who looked over at Malik again, as if to say that maybe we ought to move now, but Malik gave a small frowning rebuff of the unspoken suggestion.

Of course, Haji had in mind the eminently sensible principle that it's easier to act with your hands untied than it is with them bound together. And Malik knew this was what he was thinking. But there are things in life that are more important than the issue of what's easy. Malik was sticking to his strategy for dealing with this situation. Knowing that the rope binding their hands was not very strong had helped him to stay consistent with his intent for handling all this.

"Now, both you boys sit down and stay there until we come and grab you. No getting up. Do as you're told and you might live, after all." The main loudmouth gave this instruction while forcing Malik to sit by shoving down on his shoulders. The boy again passively complied. He even said, "Ow! Stop it!" The man smirked and thought to himself how weak this kid is. Malik had learned well that you often have to let your enemy think he's winning and in control. That creates a mindset that helps allow for the coming turnaround.

When the men had left and were gone for a little more than about half a minute, Haji turned to his friend and said, "So, it sounds like we're going to get shipped off with all the animals to have a chat with the main bad guy."

"So it seems," Malik said. "Or, at least, that's their plan."

"Do we have one?"

"One what?"

"A plan."

"The only thing that's definite right now is that we should wait until an obvious opportunity presents itself."

"Oh, Ok. I've already felt a couple of those come and go and wave goodbye," Haji said with a little sigh.

"Yeah, I know," Malik replied with a slight smile. "Thanks for asking first, each time."

"Well, you do seem to be my superior on most matters of strategy," Haji said. "So I deferred gladly—although, not with enthusiasm, I must admit, as I was feeling the rope being tied around my wrists."

"Yeah, good thing it's pretty shoddy rope," Malik responded.

"My thought, too," Haji said and wiggled his arms behind him. "And the tie isn't tight. I did the hand thing, of course. They must think we're really idiots and total wimps."

"Then, we're good actors," Malik said. "That's what we want them to think."

"Well, I'm ready to pull this play down over their stupid heads, and pretty dramatically," Haji replied.

"Be patient a little longer."

"Yeah, I know, until one of us really feels it, but especially you."

"That's right."

The general noise level in the building was pretty intense. Someone had worked hard to sound proof all this from the outside, so the animal noises couldn't be heard a mile away, or even right outside the walls. But inside, it was a loud cacophony of sound. The boys could talk as much as they wanted and as loudly as they had to, and no one was likely to hear what they were saying unless they were right at the opening to the stall they were in.

Every now and then a loose animal meandered by the door of their stall. That door had not been closed completely, and so the boys could see the occasional strollers wander by. First, there was a goat, then a large pig, then a dog they didn't recognize, and then a real first-class surprise.

"Haji. Look over across toward the stall in front of us and to the right."

He leaned and twisted around to see a little better. "No way!" He stared again and then said. "Is that?"

"Yeah, I think so."

"Oh, man! I can't believe it!"

"Well, we could be wrong but let's try. Manni? Manni? Hey, Manni!"

There was a small sound of "E, E, E," and they saw the little monkey who was sauntering by on the ground turn his head, look their way and do the monkey version of a double take. "E?" This was quickly followed by "Ah! Ah! Ah! Ah!" as their simian friend ran over toward them. He came scampering through the door of the stall, and jumped onto Malik's right shoulder, grabbing his hair, but gently, and making a whole array of happy monkey sounds.

"Manni!" Malik said.

"You old monkey, you!" Haji exclaimed, and then added the question of the moment: "Where's Jabari?"

At the name of his owner, Manni jumped off Malik's shoulder and started twirling in a circle and jumping up and down, and running around the stall. He was a whirling dervish all of a sudden, and went flying across the straw that was underneath them, screeching.

"Whoa!" Haji said. "What have I unleashed here?"

"Wait, wait, wait!" Malik whispered loudly. "Good monkey! Good monkey!" He looked over at Haji and said, "He must have been stolen away from Ja … from his owner!"

"Poor Ja … guy!" Haji responded. "That's terrible!"

"Yeah, really."

"Hey look at the piece of paper on his collar. It looks like today's date is written on it."

"You think he just got here?"

"Maybe he was just taken."

"Ja … the rightful owner will be frantic."

"Yeah, for sure. Now we really have to do something."

Just then, Malik noticed that in his wild running and twirling on hearing his owner's name, Manni had spread the straw in the stall all around. Where there had been a pile, it was now partly flat. The straw had been thrown over a larger area, and in one spot where it had been thinned out, the boys could now see the very end of a pitchfork, hidden until the wild monkey dance, and it was lying on its side, near the wall. It had been buried under the straw not four feet from where Haji was sitting.

"Ok, then," Malik said. "There's our way out. Thanks, Manni!"

He scooted over and used the sharp point on one of the metal tines to cut through the rope that had been binding his hands. And as he did so, he said, "Sloppy, sloppy captive management. These criminals are scoring pretty poorly today on bad guy skills." Then he said, "Now, you," to Haji, who moved over and repeated the process. Meanwhile, Malik peeked around the edge of the stall door to see what was going on elsewhere in the building.

"There seem to be some trucks outside. There's a big double door and it looks like they're going to start loading the animals any minute, and I'm guessing we're not far behind."

"Get them into the first truck! I want them in the first truck out!" A man's voice, yelling very loudly, could clearly be heard in the stall. It was Mansur Arobi, as sure as anything. And he was close to them.

"Quick, sit like you were when they left us here," Malik said to Haji. "I think our time for action has arrived. Get Manni in your lap if you can, or right behind you."

Haji took hold of Manni and placed him in the straw right behind his back and looked at him in the eyes and softly but firmly said, "Manni, stay here and wait. Good monkey. Stay."

Not five seconds later, one of the original tough guys walked to the open door of the stall and said, "You two stand up. You're going for a little ride."

"I can't stand. I have a bad leg cramp." Haji almost whined.

"What?"

"Ouch! You have to help me," Haji pretended to get up and fell back.

"Yeah, I'll help, you little jerk," the man said as he approached him and grabbed his arm roughly, not seeing the small monkey just behind him. "Get up!" he yelled.

That was all it took to send Manni into his best jungle attack mode. The boys had almost forgotten how loud the screech could be. It was nearly mind numbing in its intensity and volume as the little monkey practically flew from the straw behind Haji onto the guy's head, grabbing his ears, and then his eyes. The man howled in shock and pain as he was assaulted by claws and teeth that seemed to be coming from twelve animals, not one. "Stop it! Stop! Stop! Owwwwwwwww!" The man fell over, tripping on Malik's feet as he backed up, and he fell and hit his head hard on the wall of the stall. He was out cold in a split second.

"That was too easy," Malik said and smiled. Haji was standing up at this point, with Manni whirling around at his feet and shouting something at the unconscious man, a call that sounded like "Chee! Chee! Chee! Chee!"

Haji laughed and said, "That must be the victory song. He's taunting his downed opponent."

"What the?" A man with a rifle had just walked into the stall. In that instant, he saw his colleague lying down and Haji standing up, and he swung his gun around to aim at the boy. But his focus on Haji at that moment didn't allow him to see Malik's one smooth motion of springing up forcefully from his seated position, using all the power in his legs, and with the pitch fork now in his hands, a terribly lethal tool that he swung around so hard, the man had no time to dodge it. But then, due to the violent reaction of the man's body to what hit him and ripped through his flesh, his finger accidentally pulled the trigger and the resulting loud POW tore through the stall.

Far away from there, the day in Dromeda had been a full one. Baldoor and Dubin had already lined up potential buyers for each of their village homes. And Baldoor retrieved some personal property that he had stashed away long before, including a box that Dubin swore must be full of medals and awards that the man had purchased over the years. Baldoor of course pretended to be completely incensed by the suggestion. He denied that he would ever think of such a thing, and added that he had more awards and medals already than he could ever display, so it made absolutely no sense that he would stoop to acquire a single extra one in a commercial transaction, of all things. It was totally absurd, he insisted.

Baldoor was too easy a target, and as everyone knew, Dubin loved poking fun at him. Dubin was in any case already in a good mood, because, in addition to his small house, he also had a flock of goats to sell, animals that had been well cared for in his absence, and it looked like a successful transaction with them was imminent, as well.

Rumi and Bhati had visited more friends and neighbors after their long stop at the general store. They already had an interested buyer for their house, or a renter, if they preferred. A newly married couple needed their own place. Meanwhile, Hamid had enjoyed a good visit to the health clinic that he had run for years with Rumi. His former partner had even broken away for a while to join him there during part of his visit. In the middle of a great conversation with the two experienced medics who were now running the facility, they both were actually able to help with an emergency that came in—cleaning some wounds, stitching some deep cuts, and bandaging up a couple of local farmers who had sought help right after suffering a fairly serious accident. Hamid and Rumi had them patched up quickly, and it was just like old times, with one notable exception.

"You have to hold this pouch in your hand while I stitch your wounds," Rumi told the older man of the two, who had a very deep cut, long and painful, that needed to be closed. "Squeeze it firmly before my needle touches your skin and keep squeezing until I finish. Try to contract the muscles all over your body."

"Why?" the old man had asked. "What is this?"

"It's a new technique I'm trying," Rumi said. "It helps block pain. The tension in your muscles will help."

The man did as he had been instructed, and when Rumi was finished, the surprised patient looked at the good doctor with a measure of wonder on his face. He said, "I never felt even a twinge, for the whole time you were sewing me up. It's the strangest thing. I thought it was going to hurt badly."

Rumi said, "Good! My new technique was a success!"

The man just looked at his repaired arm and fully stitched up leg and said, "What was I holding? What's in the little bag?"

"Just an object of precisely the right size, shape, and substance.

It's something I'm trying out lately. The full explanation is too long and complicated. I'm just glad it worked so well for you."

"You bet it worked! I feel no pain at all. I'm not even sore."

"You should be as good as new very soon, and maybe even better," Rumi assured him. The man and his friend were both grateful for the treatment, and the doctors waived off their efforts to pay, saying only, "Bring your friends in for all their medical needs, and have them pay the other doctor what they can. That's the best reward for us!"

"You bet!" the older man said, as his friend nodded and expressed his own appreciation.

Later in the afternoon, right before dinnertime, all the inner circle of palace friends were back at the Shabeezar home, sitting around and talking. After detailing their adventures throughout the day, the conversation turned to the mysteries of the village and the surrounding area. Walid and Mafulla shared with the others what Zet had told them about the new people in the area who had been coming into the bookshop, and what he had overheard them saying.

At one point, Walid said, "I understand animal intelligence, I mean, that they have much more of it than most people think and that they have feelings and souls like we do, but I'm still not sure I really get the whole big picture of what exactly this Santiago is trying to accomplish, and how he thinks it's going to work."

Masoon spoke up. "Has Hamid ever told you his story about his son and the strange dog? It may shed some light."

Walid said, "I don't think so."

"It might help."

So the prince turned toward Hamid and asked, "What's the story about the dog and Malik?"

Hamid said, "Well, it illustrates an important fact about the world. It shows in a concrete way how there are animals among us who are quite sensitive to the realm of spirit and mind."

"This sounds good," Mafulla commented.

"Is it a story about Giza?" Layla asked. She knew Malik's dog well.

"No, no, years ago, another dog, and not one we owned," Hamid said and slightly grimaced. "First I should ask. Do any of you know about Malik's bad experience with a dog when he was younger, years ago? He was maybe seven at the time."

People around the room shook their heads to indicate that they hadn't heard anything about it. Hasina said, "No, what happened?"

"We were visiting relatives in another village, a much larger place, and Malik was at play with some children. They had all wandered off down the street, kicking a ball, and some of them were older and they ended up maybe a mile away from the house. While playing in the street in that location, Malik was running to get the ball, and suddenly he was chased and bitten deeply by an angry dog. The animal took a chomp out of his leg and then ran off."

"That's terrible," Kissa said.

"Yes, it was. Poor Malik was totally shocked by it and limped all the way back to the house, crying, and told us what had happened. Our older relatives there didn't recognize the description of the animal, and they said he must be a dog who lived on the far side of the village. When I heard about it, I knew that the creature could possibly be rabid, and that if he was, my son would be in danger and could need some painful shots. The only way to avoid the procedure would be to find the dog, put him into quarantine for a time and, if he was Ok, then the shots wouldn't have to be administered. Poor Malik would be spared great pain."

"What a traumatic thing for a child to go through," Bhati said with feeling, as she looked around at the young people there.

"Yes. Well, I got all the information I could from Malik and cleaned his wound and stitched him up. Then I went to the approximate spot where he had been attacked, and I began to walk around the area. I asked some neighbors about the animal, giving them the best description of the dog that I could. At first, no one seemed to know anything. Still, I found him about an hour later, some distance away, and recognized him from what Malik had told me."

"So, what did you do?" Walid asked.

"As I walked toward the animal, a large breed, he started barking ferociously and baring his teeth, hair bristling. There was even a feel of violence in the air. At that moment, a man passed by who knew of the dog and he said to me, 'Please, for the sake of your health and safety, don't go near that animal. He's dangerous.' But I told him the dog had just bitten my son and had to be taken into quarantine to make sure he wasn't rabid. He asked me, 'How in the world are you going to get control of such a beast and take him into quarantine?' I said I didn't know but had to do it. The man wished me good luck, told me to be careful, and then quickly walked away, not offering to help, or to go get any assistance for me."

"That's awful. What's wrong with people?" Layla commented.

"I know," Hamid said. "So, I began approaching the dog and he started backing up, nearly foaming at the mouth in his fury, which was not a good sign. And he was going crazy with the loudest barking I'd ever heard. If there ever was a truly vicious dog, this was it."

"Yikes," Mafulla said.

Hamid went on, "Well, I continued to walk forward, and the dog was at that point backed up against a house. And certainly, you know what they say—never back an angry dog up to where he has no means of escape. The desperation will cause him to attack. But, that's exactly what I did. What choice did I have? And yet, at that moment, I began to talk to the dog, mentally. I know this sounds strange, but I calmly told the dog in my thoughts that I was going to have to take him with me, either alive or dead, and that the choice was up to him to make."

"Did you have a weapon?" Mafulla was very concerned.

"No, but I had some rope with me. That's all."

"So you projected your thoughts to the dog?" Walid asked.

"Yes, as best I could. I just spoke silently as if to the dog directly. I repeated myself once more with total concentration and calm sincerity, and then the strangest thing happened."

"What?" Three of his four young listeners spoke simultaneously.

"The dog suddenly lay down where he had stood. He stopped his vicious barking that very second. He was just breathing rapidly."

"No way," Mafulla said.

"Yes. It was instant. He then grew quiet and even whimpered once or twice. I approached him slowly and he let me put the rope around his neck and lead him back across town to where he could be safely confined and fed and watched for two weeks."

"Wow," Mafulla said. "That's amazing."

"Yeah," Walid said. "So, was the dog rabid?"

"Fortunately, no. And because we had found out, Malik didn't have to get the painful shots. And the dog was then released back to his owner, with serious instructions from the local authorities to train or confine the animal so that this would never happen again."

"That's quite a story," Walid said. "You communicated in some detail to a dog without vocalizing aloud or using hand signals, or anything external, but just with your mind."

"Yes."

"Remarkable."

"And it's deeply relevant to understanding what animals can be like, on a mental and spiritual level."

Mafulla then said, "Why do dogs ever attack a person?"

Hamid replied, "There are different reasons. Sometimes, it's as simple as the predator-prey instinct. A small boy is running and a dog gives chase, as he would pursue any prey in the wild. He doesn't think. He just reacts. Mere motion sets it off. But other times, it's more interesting. If the dog is basically good and sees you trying to do something bad, he may act to stop you. I've seen it happen. And if he senses that you fear him, a good creature, he understands that you must be bad, and so attacks either out of what is actually something like a first-strike move of self-defense, or the knowledge that this is likely what it will take to prevent you from doing wrong. But then, if he, the animal, however, is somehow violent by disposition, which often comes out of fear in his own heart, and he senses that you fear him, he reasons that you must be weak, and so he attacks out of his vicious nature, and sometimes in an irrational form of what's still intended as a form of self-protection. Domesticated animals rarely bite or harm people who have no bad intentions or fear. Sometimes, it happens. And in those cases, the animal is out of touch with his own deeper nature. He's blocked and acts unreasonably."

"So, what about with the dog and Malik?" Walid said.

"I suspect it was simple predatory instinct, and the dog had his higher sensibilities turned off until I showed up and sparked them back to life. Or it could be that he once had been attacked by a stranger and was acting in what he considered to be self-defense. There was no real way to know."

"So there can sometimes be a lot more going on in the mind of a dog, or another kind of animal, than we realize." Walid drew the conclusion that was exactly what Hamid had wanted to express.

"Yes. And things can be conveyed, spirit-to-spirit. Matters can be sensed, and there's reason to believe, as in my experience, that complex thoughts can be communicated through something like psychic means. But, as in the case with people, there's probably a large spectrum of intellect, feeling, and spiritual sensitivity represented among our animal friends," Hamid added.

Masoon then said, "So this is what our monster, Santiago, is likely hoping to exploit for his purposes—the spiritual attunement, and the openness, of certain animals. There is, indeed, as the king has often pointed out, a battle of good and evil going on in the world. This man is forcibly recruiting into his cause animals who may grasp nothing of his ultimate intent, despite their otherwise keen intelligence."

"Yes, it's tragic," Hamid responded.

Masoon nodded and said, "There's a complexity of conceptual resources that may be, at some level, available only to us human beings, at least among all the creatures of earth we know. And these resources can, of course, like everything else, be used for great good or terrible ill. They allow for our monster to hatch ambitious plans with devious intent and exploit other creatures, human or otherwise, for his purposes.

"Shouldn't we do something about him?" Walid asked Masoon, and then looked at Hamid and Layla. "I mean, we're here, and if he's really somewhere nearby, maybe it's our job to stop him."

"He could be very powerful, and much more so than you might imagine," Masoon said. He then added, "And I'm sure the king wants to plan a strategy first."

"I understand," Walid replied. "But that's for defeating the man once and for all and ending his monstrous doings. Maybe we can stop just this one aspect of what he's up to, and leave the big battle for later."

"I see what you're saying," Masoon responded.

"It could be that there is something we can do," Hamid said.

"Yes, perhaps so," Layla added. "But we'd have to think it over carefully. And first, of course, we'd have to find the man's base of operations."

27

A Surprise Development

Total chaos was about to break out in the large animal confinement building at the Cairo Veterinary Clinic.

The side effects and unexpected consequences of our actions can sometimes hurt us, but on other occasions, they can help us in unanticipated ways. Fortunately, the surprising turn of events that had just now transpired in Malik and Haji's temporary confined quarters as a result of their initiative would shortly have a fortuitous effect and set in motion what was soon to become an avalanche of events.

The most immediate large-scale result of the accidental gunshot that had just rung out in the small, otherwise empty horse stall that the boys and Manni now occupied was to create a split second of near silence in the cavernous building, then something like pandemonium. As soon as the shooter went down, Haji grabbed his rifle and a large knife he also found on him. Malik bent over and looked through the clothing of the other man who had been knocked unconscious, thanks to Manni, and located a revolver with all six cylinders loaded.

A few more men immediately came running into the building from various directions, but because of the now thunderous noises of the terrified animals in their pens and other enclosures, along with the few who were loose, they couldn't communicate well with each other. Malik looked around the edge of their stall and saw that the animals who had been wandering around earlier were now running here and there in a panic that was creating additional problems for the men now entering the building. That gave him an idea. "Haji! We should open the cages and stalls, now, as many as we can!"

Haji understood instantly and dashed out from their enclosure, flicking latches on as many pens and cages and other stalls as he could. Malik ran out to do the same. And even Manni, seeing what they were doing, surprised them both by mimicking their actions and opening a couple of cages himself while screeching, of course, which, the boys guessed, must be his ongoing battle cry at this point. The larger animals now freed from their enclosures began frantically charging out in all directions and stirring up dust clouds from the dirt floor of the building, making it harder to see. And, fortunately, the biggest cloud of dust was between the door where several men had just entered the building at its far end and the part of the space where the boys were still fast at work, springing loose more captives.

The men were diverted into a desperate effort to catch and stop the animals that were nearly stampeding toward the wide and now open double doors on the back end of the building where several trucks had pulled up outside. There were dozens and dozens of animals loose and running and barking and whinnying and howling and screeching and making an even louder racket than before. Malik and Haji continued their efforts at the fastest pace they could maintain, creating more chaos by the moment and an even thicker cloud of dust thrown up by the frightened and excited animals.

Malik then heard a loud voice suddenly yell out, "Get the boys!" Manni was six feet away, and the first thing Malik did was to run over and grab him in a hug, picking him up and dashing toward his friend.

"Haji! We have to get out of here!"

Just then a man appeared out of the whitish brown, almost choking dust with a look of contorted fury on his face. He spotted Haji and yelled, "You!" and rushed toward him. Haji nimbly ducked his effort to grab him and immediately came up behind the man with a rifle butt to the head that he didn't at all expect. Malik and Manni were closing in to the spot where Haji had just dropped the guy, out cold on the floor, when professor bushy beard suddenly appeared, brandishing his own revolver that was pointed now toward Haji.

There was just something about that big, thick, full beard that seemed to push a button in Manni's simian brain and shot him out of Malik's arms like a cannon ball from a cannon. And with two bounds across the floor and a high leap onto that large collection of facial hair, which was an ideal hirsute handhold, a direct frontal monkey assault of the most vicious sort imaginable began. Again, nails and teeth flying, Manni did his thing and had the evil professor screaming and dropping his weapon to the floor within three or four seconds.

Malik, momentarily watching this unfold, was caught by surprise from behind and knocked forward. He stumbled over some loose animal at his feet and fell headfirst toward the professor's sandals. Catching himself with his left hand, just as he heard the expert in animal history scream, "I'll kill you," he found himself temporarily face down, looking right at the man's sandaled right foot. He quickly swung the barrel of the revolver in his right hand to a spot between the toes and arch of that foot and rolled his face away while he pulled the trigger.

BLAM! Malik didn't know what was louder, the extraordinary report of the gun at such close range, right at the floor, and now beside his head, or the deep and primal scream that came from the mouth of the professor, who dropped and rolled over, twitching and jerking and howling in agony. Manni leapt free of him at this point and jumped back over to Malik. Haji had scooped up the man's pistol and now had it in his possession, along with the rifle, weapons that he was otherwise hesitating to use because of all the innocent animals that were everywhere around them, running here and there.

More of the animals were finding their way to the open double doors in the back of the building and pouring out of the big exit, running for their lives. Malik grabbed Manni again and Haji joined them, running in the same direction and opening a few more cages along the way. At the door in front of them, as they now ran as fast as the melee of creatures would allow them to, three men appeared with guns raised right at them. Malik and Haji lifted up their own, but before they could aim or fire, there was a loud sound at a distance and the three men all twisted violently, doubled over and went down, without discharging a single one of their weapons, as if they had been shot from some vantage point outside the building.

As close to the door as they were now, Malik and Haji could suddenly hear shouting out beyond the door, near where the trucks were gathered and waiting: "Egyptian Agents! Put Down Your Weapons! Agents of the King, Drop Your Guns! Hands Up!" As they emerged into the sunlight, they saw several men near the trucks laying rifles and handguns down in the sand and raising their arms. Four men in street clothes held guns on them.

One of them noticed Malik and Haji and yelled to his colleagues the word "Guns!" and as he did, he whipped his rifle over and pointed it toward them. "Stop! Drop Your Weapons!" he shouted at the boys.

"Masoon and Hamid's sons! I'm General Masoon's son, Haji!" the boy yelled. "And Hamid's son Malik!" as he held his revolvers out in front of him, barrels down, barely gripped by fingers and thumb so they could not be seen as threats. Malik did the same with the rifle he had been carrying. They both knelt down and placed their weapons on the ground, as animals continued to run by them, escaping from their confinement. Malik still held on to Manni, and he was squirming in his friend's arms and chattering, but no longer screeching.

"What did you say?" The man called to them.

That moment, another individual was brought around the corner of the building at gunpoint, with his hands in the air, and seeing the animals loose and escaping in droves, he shouted, "Three months of work! Three months wasted! Three months lost!" It was Mansur Baram Arobi.

"Quiet!" His captor shouted.

"It's you!" he said as soon as he saw Malik and Haji! "You did this! I'll kill you for this!" "I'll ..." but that was his last word, because the man who had been holding a gun on him now used it to swat the back of his head with a sickening thud, and he grunted and crumpled to the ground, unconscious.

"Haji! Malik! Please stand!" This agent yelled out, and then turned to the others and said, "These are boys from the palace, the school, the sons of General Masoon and Doctor Hamid!"

"That's what I thought they said," another man replied. "But I didn't know!"

"Up, up!" the first agent repeated, and the boys got to their feet.

The other man said, "We're so sorry we didn't all recognize you right away. It's been chaotic. We had to be careful!"

"No problem! We're glad to see you!" Malik said. "But how did you guys get here?"

"We're the king's observation team, posted across the road in thick cover. Our orders were just to watch the place, but then trucks started arriving and we heard a gunshot, and then another one, and we had to act. And then, coming across the road, we saw large numbers of animals beginning to run away. There were men with guns who had already shot toward us, and then turned into the building and either couldn't hear our commands or ignored them, and we had to take them down. Are you both Ok?"

"Yes! Thanks! It was a little crazy in there," Haji said, "and there are three men down, at least, bad guys, and two of them may need serious medical attention before you haul them off to jail."

As the men who had been captured were being tied up and gagged, the agent who recognized the boys came closer and said,

"I work often with your fathers. I'm Rubi An'am. I'm pleased to be at your service."

"Nice to meet you," Malik said, and Haji nodded.

"How did you boys get into the middle of all this? We saw you earlier walk into the front door of the clinic, and I was certainly surprised, but I had no idea you'd end up in such a mess."

"We thought there'd likely be an observation team watching the place from on the outside, but we figured we could get inside if we brought my dog …" Malik suddenly looked panicked and turned around toward the building and called out, "Giza! Giza! Here, Giza! Good dog! Giza!" As he shouted over the continuing noise, he said, "Excuse me for a second," and began walking back toward the doors, now with Haji right behind him, and he called out to Rubi that they would be right back. The boys then walked through the open doors, from the side, just as most of the animals seemed to have cleared the structure. "Giza!"

"Oh. Is this your dog?" An angry, hostile voice growled out the words, and Malik and Haji both turned to the left to see the man who had fallen in the stall, knocked out, the first one down, now back on his feet with a leash in his hand and Giza on the other end of it. And now, the dog had a revolver held to his head.

"Let him go!"

"No! We've lost all our animals, so it's only right for you to lose your little mutt!" The man looked down, so that he could see and enjoy fully what he was about to do.

"Don't!" Malik's insides froze. He could hardly believe what he was about to witness. Giza was his first and only dog. He had come into the family when Malik was just five years old, and had been an ideal companion for him all throughout his childhood. He met the boy every day after school with a wildly wagging tail and extravagant licks and was always eager to play. He'd chase a ball and, even at his relatively advanced current age, he'd often stand up on his back feet and beg for attention, and Malik would always give it to him. He and his owner and friend had a bond unlike any other in the boy's life.

BLAM! Before Malik or Haji could move, the last gunshot of the day was fired. The shock they felt could not possibly have been greater. That second, three armed agents came running through the door yelling, "Stop! Freeze!" with their guns at the ready and aimed right at the man who had the end of the leash to Malik's poor dog wrapped around his hand. Time seemed in that moment to die a sudden and violent death.

Across the kingdom, in the small western village of Dromeda, Walid, Mafulla, and Masoon had spent the night in the Shabeezar home, along with Rumi, Bhati, and the other three ladies—Layla, Kissa, and Hasina. It was quite a crowd for a small house, but the men made sure the ladies were able to sleep on the real beds. The guys had brought extra bedding in from the encampment for the night, and were more comfortable in the house than they would have been on the sand at the edge of town. Two tents had been set up in the backyard where eight of the soldiers in the general security detail were taking turns in groups of four, alternately sleeping or watching the house.

The family and friends in the house slept later than they had been able to in the desert. There were no stirring camels and horses, and there wasn't any urgency to wake up and get going before the heat of the day began to build to its peak. This morning would allow more of a leisurely pace. But still, much was to be done. Things had to be accomplished.

Plenty of food had been brought back from the general store, and breakfast was made for everyone in the house, as well as for the soldiers outside. Their old neighbors, Sab and Meskhenet Maayuf came over to bring even more food, "for lunch, later," they said. Gimpy the dog had sniffed the air as soon as they left home with the large baskets of goodies and had followed them all the way to the Shabeezar house, where he was appropriately treated like a king, and given a lavish assortment of snacks.

"I think Gimpy likes me," Mafulla said, as he shared yet another tidbit of tasty food with his new friend, out behind the house.

"You're a likable guy, especially with treats in your hand," Walid replied. "And you two have a lot in common. You both love food more than anybody else I know, except of course, Bafur and his dad."

"Actually, you're right, I think. We do have a lot in common. From the moment he wagged up to us, I felt a kinship with the little mongrel, who, despite it all, has about him a nearly royal air."

"Well," Walid laughed, "he often does have about him an air, but I've never quite thought of it as royal."

"Come on. There's a whiff of special dignity in the old boy."

"Ok. Maybe. And I do think he's really glad we're here."

"Yeah, can you imagine what it's like for him? I mean, first all you guys move away, and then, when he finally adjusted to that, he sees his friends dognapped, and he gets left behind again. I bet he feels a real ambivalence about it—you know—relief on the one hand that he wasn't taken, mixed with a wonder of why not, blended with sadness at the loss of friends, combined with a good measure of what they call survivor's guilt. It's all enough to make a little dog a little down."

"Yeah, knowing Gimp, he probably does have all that going on inside him. I'd feel good if we could help him while we're here. It'd be great to get his friends back for him."

"Even if that means going up against a super-anti-Phi monster of major proportions?"

"Hey, we have to do what we have to do, and I really believe we don't get called to do something unless we're the ones for the job."

"Yeah, I guess you're right. Here, boy, have another treat."

They spent a little more time with Gimpy and in the conversation that his presence naturally evoked. Then they went back inside to confer with the others as to what was planned for the day. The news was good. This was the day for which Walid had hoped. He and his friends were going to have a lot of free time, and he would use it well.

He got to show Kissa the many places he played and the things he did as a child when he was growing up here. He walked her around after breakfast and told her stories of his childhood memories that he thought would fill in the picture for her. Mafulla and Hasina came along as well and asked lots of questions. They were particularly fascinated by hearing about all the camel trains or caravans that came through the area, and how the people visiting the village had long brought news of what was happening all over the region and the world. Walid explained that some of the desert nomads would even carry messages from town to town and were often the lifeblood of communication out here in the more remote parts of the kingdom.

Morning and mid-day were passed in fun, pleasant activities, but always in the back of Walid's mind, and Mafulla's, was a nagging concern about the serious problem that might lie just outside of town, and what they should do about it. There had been serious attempts to scare them off from this visit and prevent their coming. But they had ignored the warnings and, apparently, turned back the threat. And yet, it was still troubling why there had been no further effort to stop them, and why they were being left alone now. Had their adversary given up? Or had he changed plans, now lulling them into a false sense of security right before springing a big trap? But these thoughts never lasted long. The diversions of the day would reel them back in, and something would rivet the boys' attention to the present moment, and whatever they were seeing or doing.

Later on, about mid-afternoon, Masoon and Hamid took Walid and Mafulla outside the edge of town and a little beyond the caravan encampment to give them a training session together that was extremely advanced, beyond anything they had done in the past. Layla also used the same time, but a different location, to train Kissa and Hasina at a new level of intensity. Was something coming up that they were being prepared to meet? Did Masoon or Hamid or Layla have Phi hints or plans they had not yet shared with the students?

Nothing more was said about it at dinner. Walid and Mafulla had decided to just let the older Phi call the shots about this, and leave it to them when it would next be brought up as an item of conversation. Plus, they were both tired and already a little sore from their workout.

Dinner, as it turned out, was a time of family stories and reflections. Everyone enjoyed listening to Rumi and Bhati tell of days past in Dromeda and its area of the kingdom. The Maayufs came over to join in with all the talk, and they told some stories on Rumi and Bhati that had everyone laughing. When he closed the bookshop, Zet also came by for a visit, and not too long afterwards, his father Aleph wandered by and stopped in as well. Merriment was abounding.

It was just the kind of time they had all needed. In fact, the talk was so much fun and entertaining that thoughts of evil and trouble and a monster lurking somewhere out in the darkness didn't intrude into their minds at all. The evening was filled with joy and laughter and friendship and remembrance.

They were all a bit late to bed because of the spontaneous party. And when they woke up, they could smell breakfast already cooking outside. Two of the soldiers were sitting at a roaring fire, with Masoon and Hamid and five other men who were dressed in the garb of desert nomads, whose head wraps and tunics were distinctive and colorful. Walid went by himself out the door and across the sand to ask if they needed anything from inside. There was plenty of food available for all these men to have a hearty start to the day, including the new visitors, and as much as they might need could be brought out to augment whatever they already had.

The prince was always concerned about the soldiers and security people. He believed that he should take good care of the men whose job it was to take good care of him. And visitors should always be shown hospitality. It was the way of the desert, and it was something Walid had grown up believing.

Masoon saw Walid emerge from the house, and he immediately stood up and moved in his direction. He smiled and waved, and then a serious look came over his face. He put up his hand as if to signal the boy to stop for a moment. And the prince complied.

The general approached and spoke to him in a low voice. "Walid. There's an important new development. In fact, there are several." He stepped up closer, putting his hand lightly on the boy's arm where he now stood, well short of the group talking around the fire. "Could we step over here and speak for a minute?" He motioned to a spot off to the side and actually back toward a corner of the house.

"Sure, what's up?" Walid said in almost a whisper, and followed his friend.

In a voice just above a whisper, Masoon quickly began to tell the basic story of what had been going on in the capital city with Leem and Ibrahim and Malik and Haji. He shared with Walid all that he now knew about Mansur Arobi and Professor Hashman Arib and the Wasa Import and Export people, and how Walid's friends had helped locate them, and the raids that had just happened, only to find that the key people who had been targeted for arrest were gone. He then dramatically recounted the entire tale of Malik and Haji as it had now been reported to him, and how they had ventured out on their own, without telling the king what their plan was. And he rapidly went through the basic details of how it had unfolded in surprising ways.

At the crucial moment, near the conclusion of the story, Walid said, "Wait. At the very end of all that, one jerk shot and killed Malik's dog, Giza?"

"No, no, no," Masoon replied. "The gunshot came from our agent, Rubi An'am, who had followed them close behind and had emerged at just the right second through the door. He has great instincts and lightning fast reflexes. He cut down the evil man before he could even start to pull the trigger. The jerk, as you call him, appropriately, was dead on the ground before he ever realized what was happening, with the leash still wrapped around his hand."

"Oh, man. Was Giza Ok?"

Masoon answered: "He was frightened badly, and fouled with a bit of the man's blood, from the sudden violence of his untimely end, which he brought on himself, by his own terrible actions. But the dog basically was fine, and was cleaned up quickly and comforted."

"And Malik and Haji?"

"They were both fine, too, once they got over the emotional shock of what they almost had to see. And, of course, they were the heroes of the day. They broke up the entire operation there at the veterinary clinic, freeing all the animals that had been abducted from four national capitals and brought together in that one place, before they would be transported to their ultimate destination. Of course, it took everyone quite a while to find all the animals again and even start to locate, and get them back to, their rightful owners. That's a process that will still have to play out over a period of time. But we intend that all of them will be returned to their homes."

"Oh, my goodness," Walid said. "This is just amazing." Then he asked, "What did the king say to Malik and Haji? Was he mad at them for going off and taking action without consulting him? Or was he proud of them and what they accomplished?"

"I need to ask one of our visitors, the man who brought all this news to us."

"Oh, Ok."

Masoon turned and in a louder voice said to the backs of the nomads, but apparently to one in particular, "Sir, I'm sorry. I have a question."

"Yes, ask anything," the brightly dressed man replied, as he turned around.

Walid's mouth fell open. "Oh my! What are you doing here, Uncle?"

28

Plans and Movement

"My boy!" King Ali had a big smile across his face for his favorite young man.

"Why are you here? How did you get here?" Walid was overcome with perplexity, which was then tinged with a passing touch of something almost like fear.

"I decided to bring a few friends to help do a job that needs to be done." At those words, two of the other nomads turned toward Walid, so that he could see their faces.

"Paki! Amon! I'm nearly without the power to speak!"

"Hi, Prince," Paki said.

"Your Highness," Amon replied.

Two of the other guests also turned toward the prince, and they had faces that were vaguely familiar to Walid, but he couldn't quite place them. Ali then said, "I also brought a couple of our good friends from Alexandria, the two most senior Phi there. You may recognize them from the hotel lobby during the class trip."

"Yes, yes, I do now," Walid replied. "Greetings, and welcome to you all. But this is a little overwhelming. What's going on?"

"Come, sit," the king said. Walid walked over, bent down and gave the king a hug, and then sat beside him on the still cool sand. Ali answered the prince by saying, "Before I sent my note of warning and information by air mail the other day, I had already realized that I needed to come and join you here, so I alerted these friends and immediately prepositioned groups of fast horses along the way, through the help of our extensive military resources. There's also a heavily armed, major strike team from the army that's now about to arrive and camp to the north of where the man Santiago most likely is located, several miles outside of the village, to our north and west. Within a couple of hours, they will have sent scouts to search for the place that we think is his dwelling and the home of all his operations."

"So, there's going to be an attack on him?" Walid surmised.

"Yes, well, in a sense."

"What do you mean?"

"We have several senior Phi now here. He's one powerfully developed adversary, and we're many. We also have advanced Phi who aren't yet strictly considered to be senior, but are far along in their development, as you know, and we have you younger Phi—and you've already proved yourselves many times in difficult situations. We plan to advance on him and, perhaps, stop what he's been doing. The army unit will keep a tight noose around him, once we've made our initial approach—but we don't plan, first and foremost, a military style assault, only an armed intervention and an arrest, if we find him. Whether things go differently from that plan will be up to him."

"Why do we want so many Phi involved?"

"It could well be that the right individual senior Phi could do the job alone, but we don't know that, and we're not sure what this monster would be prepared to do to innocent others, for example, here in the village, if he's not sufficiently contained from the very first moment of confrontation. And with such stakes in play, I prefer to have an abundance of power available to bring to the situation, because of an equal abundance of caution."

"If this is to be a big Phi operation, why isn't Hoda here, too?"

"She's at home during the vacation, tending to some extended family matters, still, and having an unusual amount of needed time with her sons, who work so hard for the palace every day. She's actively served us in difficult situations so often, as in the defense of the palace, that I decided to ask her to stay in Cairo, with the family there, and to assist us on this occasion from that location."

"Who's in charge in the palace?"

"I've taken care of all that. I've been in touch by radio along the way, when possible. I learned of Malik and Haji's adventures that way, and commended them. In terms of day-to-day decisions, I've asked Mafulla's uncle Reela to help out, now that he's freshly back in Cairo, because of his foreign policy experience and many connections, a few of which are active now. And a couple of other senior and trusted advisors are assisting as well, with Hoda and Khalid also available for consultation, as needed."

"Really?"

"Yes. So, all's well at the palace."

"With both Hoda and Khalid helping?"

"Yes, their knowledge and judgment could become crucial in certain issues. But they're serving in only an advisory capacity."

"Ok. So, what are we going to do now?"

"We'll do the rest of our planning today. Tomorrow, we'll advance on the location where we believe Santiago to be hiding."

"How do we know where he is?"

"I have ways. And so we already suspect much. We're just learning a bit more before we make our move."

"Ok."

"The combined resources of seventeen Phi, augmented by the strike force and the security team that's already with you, can take care of the situation, regardless of how it develops. Our friends here in the village should all be safe."

"Wait. Seventeen?" Walid silently counted. "I get thirteen, including our two Alexandrian friends here, and fourteen if we count Hoda."

"There are also three more who will be helping out in their own ways."

Walid was surprised, and wanted to ask who they were and what they were going to do, but decided to remain silent and trust that the king knew what he was doing, as he always did. He and Mafulla had talked about the fact that not all Phi identities were known to junior Phi, and even to those who were more advanced, and at what might be called an intermediate stage. Only senior Phi had access to The Book of Phi, identifying all officially trained Phi in the kingdom and in a few other parts of the world. Walid had benefited from many secrets in the book that the king had shared with him and Mafulla, but he also respected the lines that were drawn regarding full access.

The king asked Masoon to gather all the Phi present. They would meet in the house for a briefing. Of course, the rest of those who had come on the caravan were as surprised as Walid had been that the king had arrived. Ali spoke to Kissa alone for a few minutes about her mother's absence on this occasion, and then, with everyone wedged closely into the largest room in this relatively small house, he gave his overall report on what had happened and would yet transpire over the next twenty-four to thirty-six hours.

There was suddenly a knocking at the door, at first soft, and then growing louder. Ali was wrapping up his briefing but was not quite finished, so Rumi, who was sitting close to the door, got up opened it to see who was there. It was Zet Noni.

"Hi, Dr. Shabeezar. Walid told me he wanted to hear any news I might have about certain out-of-towners who shop in the store, and I got here as soon as I could."

"Yes, Zet, certainly. Wait just a moment, if you would."

The king spoke a few more words and looked up at Rumi, who was still standing near the door. "Zet's here, from the bookshop, with some new information for us, about the mystery people."

"Please, ask him in," the king said.

Rumi opened the door again and said, "Please, join us."

As Zet slipped into the room, he looked surprised at how many people were sitting on the floor. And then his eyes grew big as he realized who was standing across the room.

"Hello, Zet, my friend."

"Ali! I mean, King Ali! Your Majesty! I didn't know you were here! What a surprise!"

"I just arrived."

"It's so good to see you! But I didn't mean to interrupt your gathering here with everyone."

"It's quite all right. We were in a little meeting, but it just ended. You have news for us?" The king said.

"Yes, I do, and it may be important."

"Would you mind telling us all?"

Zet looked at Walid, who nodded and smiled. And so he said, "Oh, Ok. Sure." But then he seemed momentary lost in thought.

"Go ahead," the king said with a smile.

"Oh, yes. Ok, this morning, really early, I went to the shop with dad, much earlier than we usually open up. He was going to do a bit of inventory and restocking, and I thought I'd help out. But when we got to the store, five men were already there, waiting for us. All of them were Spaniards, men from outside town. They said they had a need for supplies this morning and would pay double if we'd let them in right then to gather what they needed. Double! So, of course, we allowed them to shop and get anything they wanted."

"What did they buy?" the king asked.

"Lots of food, mostly. They often come in about this time of the week for groceries, but not this early in the morning. And they also bought a number of other supplies—some, it seemed, for travel, and lots of ammunition, bullets for rifles and pistols. They took all that we had out on the shelves. And then they asked if there was any more. Dad was suspicious at that point and just said that we put it out on the shelves as soon as it comes in, which is true, but we do also have a private stash in the back, just in case, which he didn't mention."

"Are these men still in the store, or have they left?"

"They left about half an hour ago on horseback, all of them. I waited a bit to come tell you about it, because I didn't want to barge in too early this morning while you were still having your breakfast."

"It was kind of you to wait," the king said, and then he added, "You mentioned that there were five of them?"

"Yes, sir. I mean, yes, Your Majesty."

"Are they the men who always come in for supplies or books?"

"Well, I don't think I've seen all five of them in together before, but individually, and in groups of two or three, these men have been in several times when I was there."

"Have any other Spaniards or foreign looking individuals come in to shop and buy for the same place?"

"Yes, two men that I can think of."

"And no others?"

"No, sir."

"So, you've seen a total of seven such men over time come into the store or into town."

"Yes, sir. Oh. You said also into town, and not just into the store?"

"Yes, I did."

"There was one other man, in the company of several of these guys, months ago, who came into town, but not into the store or the bookshop. He seemed to be just looking around. I didn't see him speak to anyone who lives in the village, but he was here for a short time and then he left."

"Do you remember anything about him?"

"He was a little taller than the others. He had dark hair and a beard. He seemed to be about the age of Masoon or Hamid, or a little older. But I didn't see him up close. He sort of gave me the creeps, even at a distance. I don't know why. Do you think maybe it was the mystery man, that guy Santiago?"

"It could have been."

"Wow. I never really thought about it at the time."

"You've been very helpful. Thank you so much, Zet, for coming by. If you'll excuse us now, I think I have a few more things to share with the group before we fully adjourn our little family meeting."

"Oh, yes sir, surely. It's good to see you all! Please come visit the shop again while you're here, if you can."

There were many voices in reply saying things like "Thank you, Zet," and "See you later," and "We appreciate it."

The king summed up. "So, we now know of eight individuals, and it sounds like our mystery man might have been the visitor who didn't go into the general store or bookshop, but just had a good look around. We don't know by this information that there are only eight people at the location outside town, of course, but simply, that there are likely at least this many."

He continued. "I want to ask all of you, individually, to go and find a quiet place in the next few minutes where you can spend some time in complete meditation, in absolute inner quiet and openness. I want you to empty out all your thoughts and concerns and feelings. Set them down beside you on the floor, or in the sand, and let go of them. And then, just be. A few minutes for relaxing your mind and calming your spirit will be crucial for you—for all of us. We can reassemble here in exactly three hours for lunch and more talk."

Everyone got up and stretched and there were many conversations around the room between Phi who then walked outside or into other rooms of the house. Hasina and Kissa were talking to Layla right afterwards, and Mafulla came up to Walid and asked, in a very low voice, "Why aren't we in hot pursuit of the guys who were here?"

"I don't know," Walid answered. "There must be a reason. I wish I knew more about what the king has in mind."

"Yeah, well, remember, he's read the whole, entire Book of Phi, and studied it. And he knows a lot that we don't, and we just need to have a little faith that what he's doing is right, and also the best for us." Mafulla gave an arm and hand gesture like "What else can you do?"

"Yeah, you're right," Walid admitted. "I just always want to be a step ahead of where I am."

"Don't we all, unless of course we're standing in front of an angry lion, then most of us would love to be at least a few steps back, if not more."

Walid looked impressed. "Maybe that's not such a silly image, in our present circumstances, as I was at first going to suggest."

"Yeah, maybe. Look, there could come a time when you and I have to be the guys standing right up in the jaws of the angry lion, between him and everybody else, and it'll be up to us what happens. But, for now, it's the king and the senior Phi, and I'm really glad."

"That's a good way to put it," Walid replied. "Did anyone ever tell you that you can sometimes be quite a philosopher?"

"No, but my mother's often said I was a big thinker."

"Are you sure she wasn't saying 'big stinker'?"

"Hmm. Given at least several of the original contexts that immediately leap to mind, I can see what you're saying, but no, I'm sure that it was my thinking she was commenting on, and with praise for the quality of the cogitation."

"Ok."

"Plus, you know me and cologne, so it couldn't be the other possibility—no way." With that, Mafulla gave Walid a facial expression that made him laugh, even under the circumstances.

"Yes, I do know you and cologne," Walid said. "And that's why … oh, never mind!"

Layla came over at that point and said, "Walid, Mafulla, would you like to come outside with us ladies for our meditation time? I think we can find quiet spots."

"Yeah, that's a good idea. The house is a little crowded," Walid replied, glancing around.

"I'd like to go out, too," Mafulla added. "I've been inside since I woke up, and the day needs greeting. You know, the old 'Hello Sun, Good Morning Sky, How's It Going, Sand' routine. They've really come to expect it from me, and I'm afraid I'm a bit late, already. They'll be worried."

Layla looked at Walid with a smile and just shook her head. The five of them then walked out behind the house and found individual spots in the yard, a distance from the embers of the outdoor breakfast fire and from the soldiers' tents, where they could sit and be calm. Layla quickly explained to the guards what they would be doing, and the men understood. Masoon had created a military culture where the inner side of warfare and preparedness was nearly as appreciated as the outer and more obvious side.

Layla led the students through a preparation for deep meditation, coaching them on their breathing and bodily postures, as well as on how to relax their muscles throughout, sequentially beginning with their toes and feet and working upward to their ears and the tops of their heads. By the time she finished, in her soft, quiet voice, everything was still and soundless. Within thirty seconds, each of the younger people was at least on the verge of a deeply meditative mind. The seconds passed and then several minutes.

Hasina had a vision of an arid landscape, almost like a desert but not quite so austere, and a wall and some buildings. The buildings seemed familiar. Later, she found out that Kissa had roughly the same picture come into her mind.

After a time, Mafulla had the image that he had seen in his dreams enter his otherwise empty consciousness. But it had an additional part now. He saw the man in the blue boat, in a river, and the boat, as it made its way forward, grew bigger, much bigger, until its sides were almost touching the banks of the river. This he had seen before. But now, the boat started to shrink and grow ever smaller, until it returned to its original size.

Walid saw a vision of Layla sitting again in the desert, where she had been when he helped her fight the storm. He could also feel Hoda again near him, behind him, and the king was there. And they were all looking in the same direction. But nothing was to be seen. And when he realized this, no emotion arose at all. And then he noticed, far away and off to the side, a small storm, a speck of darkness. It was moving away, for now. And then there was a very bright flash, so powerful that it bleached out the entire sky. Walid thought: "That was strange." Then he released the thought and returned to restfulness.

Within about three minutes of each other, Walid, Mafulla, Kissa, and Hasina came out of their meditative states and back to their more ordinary consciousness. Layla was still in deep. The younger people got up from their places and motioned to each other that they were ready to go back inside. But when they got there, they realized that all the senior Phi there were still in deep meditation, like Layla. Walid gestured for the rest of them to follow him, and they walked out the front door behind him, which he had silently opened and then closed.

"I have a feeling we should go down the street and visit with Zet for a few minutes," he whispered.

"Are you sure we should leave?" Mafulla seemed uneasy.

"Well, the older Phi are in deep, it looks like."

"Shouldn't we tell them we're going?"

"I don't want to interrupt anyone, but—look—we can tell one of the guards and he can pass it on when they get up."

"Ok, I guess that makes sense," Mafulla said.

"There's really nothing else I know of that we should be doing," Kissa said.

"True," Hasina repeated.

"But, did anyone see anything in your mind's eye while we were in meditation?" Kissa thought to ask.

"I saw some place—it was almost like desert but not quite, and a wall, and some buildings," Hasina offered. "It sort of looked familiar."

"I saw the exact same thing," Kissa said, looking surprised. "Did you see people?"

Hasina shook her head. "No, there were no people."

"I saw that thing that I've seen in my dreams a couple of times, but it was a little different this time," Mafulla said.

"What thing?" Hasina asked.

"You know, the boat thing from my dreams. Some guy is in a boat in a river and as the boat moves along, it gets bigger and bigger until it's almost the width of the entire river. But just now, I saw all that, and then also something I've never seen before. The boat at a certain point started getting smaller again, until it returned to its original size."

"Very strange," Walid said.

Mafulla looked over at him and asked, "How about you?"

"I saw you getting bigger and bigger because of all that you're eating here in the village," Walid said. "I was thinking that if you got on your dream boat, it might sink."

"Hey."

Then he said, "No, I'm kidding. I actually saw the same desert scene that I saw when I helped Layla and Hoda and the king fight off that storm of some sort that was heading our way the other day. But there was no oncoming storm this time, only a very small speck of dark clouds on the horizon and moving away from us. And then there was a really super bright flash."

"That seems like a good sign," Kissa said. "Except maybe for the flash, and I don't know about that."

"Yeah, I guess it's mostly positive, aside for the fact that there's still a storm, however small, and then there's the flash."

"Interesting," Hasina commented.

"What do you think it all means?" Walid asked.

"Well," Kissa reflected, "Mafulla's boat may represent the Noah's Ark type of thing. The Santiago guy was collecting animals and his boat was getting bigger. But now, it's getting smaller and smaller again. Maybe that has to do with Malik and Haji freeing all the animals back in Cairo."

"Wow. That was a good potential interpretation," Mafulla said. "Impressive."

"And, Hassi and I seeing the same thing—maybe that's Santiago's compound nearby, and it's empty."

"Really?" Mafulla said. "You mean, like nobody there, as in, they've all left?"

"Maybe," Kissa replied. Then she said, "And Walid's vision that the storm is passing, that all fits in as well. But the flash, I don't know. Maybe it's just an exclamation point to the end of something."

"So, are we going to find this guy or not?" Mafulla asked. "Is there going to be a storm in our future or not?"

Kissa looked over at Walid, and so did Hasina. "I guess we'll find out soon," he said.

But he couldn't know yet that the most important thing they'd find out, or discover, or experience, very soon, would be in a flash—a huge, destructively explosive flash beyond anything they'd ever imagined.

29

A Conversation

Rumi and Bhati hosted the king and all the other visiting members of Phi for lunch in their home. They sat around on the floor in subdued conversation for most of the meal. At one point, toward the end, Walid asked the king a question.

"Your Majesty, on our journey here, because of something that happened along the way, Layla told us about the old story that's called the legend of the monster."

"Yes, she's informed me of the circumstances."

"According to the legend, it was said of the man who became the monster that perceived insults during his youth caused a terrible reaction in him, a burning desire for revenge, and not only against those who had offended him, but against the world."

"Yes, that's correct."

"Well, now we've heard about this Santiago fellow, and his life might reflect the legend. But I've been wondering about why people get so worked up by what they see as insults. I know it's common, but I'm a little puzzled about why. And, there's another side of my question. The greater a person is, the less they seem to be bothered by the comments of others. I've noticed that with Phi. Nobody who's senior Phi ever seems insulted or offended. And then, on the other hand, the weaker a person is, or the less mature, the more easily they're insulted and offended by things. Why is this?"

"You've asked me some good philosophical and psychological questions," the king said. "If everyone's interested, we might reflect on this for a moment." He looked around the room and saw many heads nod and so he said, "Good."

"Wait. Your Majesty, first, could I ask a sort of preliminary question?" Hasina spoke up.

"You certainly may," the king replied.

"You just used the words 'philosophical' and 'psychological' together. These concepts are so close in some ways that I think many people confuse them, or use them interchangeably. Could you say what the difference is, really, from your point of view, between philosophy and psychology?"

All the older people appeared like they might have some sort of answer, but they all looked to the king to see what he would say. Ali smiled. "Very good. It's a fine question," he said. "For most of the history of human thought, what's now known as psychology, the study of the psyche, or soul, or mind, was a proper part of philosophy, which had two main branches: natural philosophy, and moral philosophy. Natural philosophy was an investigation into the nature of physical things in our world—what's above our heads, in and around our bodies, and also beneath our feet. And as different studies within that overarching category began to develop distinctive and more precise methods and tools for research, they began to break out as the various natural sciences we now know—such as astronomy, physics, chemistry, biology, botany, geology, and psychology. So, natural philosophy gave birth to the modern sciences. Moral philosophy, in that ancient scheme, broadly encompassed most of what's now thought under the heading of philosophy—issues of being, knowing, feeling, and doing that are in some sense deeper than the typical questions of science, more fundamental, and are somehow either assumed, or else otherwise untouched, by the natural sciences, with their precise empirical methods."

"Could you say more about that?" Hasina was obviously in a deep state of concentrating hard on his words.

"Yes. Let me put the point like this, for the sake of simplicity. Philosophy is a broader enterprise, overall, but both philosophy and psychology study human thought and action, and issues concerning our nature and place in the world. Philosophy takes on many topics, such as the basic nature of being itself, which is the subject of metaphysics; and the proper roles of community and governance in human life, which is the realm of social and political philosophy; the rules for gaining and preserving truth in our thought, which is logic; the nature of belief and knowledge, called epistemology, from the Greek word for knowledge; ethics then examines right and wrong, good and evil, virtue and vice; and then there is aesthetics—the study of beauty and art as objective matters, as well as in their subjective side."

"That's a lot," Walid said.

"Yes, it is. And there's more, such as the philosophy of language and of science. But let's now focus on the overlap between what are currently recognized as distinct disciplines in our universities, despite the fact that they seem to have great common ground: the study of what's human. I can put it like this. Psychology wants to understand how human thought and behavior works. It can study what's deemed defective, or abnormal, or what's thought of as optimally functional, or anything in between. Philosophy, on the other hand, ponders largely how human thought and behavior *ought* to work—whether in the disciplines of ethics, logic, or in social and political matters, among other things. Philosophy examines *what is* in order to discover *what should be*, as well as speculating on *what could be*, charting out the realm of possibility and necessity as well as the most fundamental aspects of actuality. A psychological question is always related in some way to how our minds in fact do work—whether badly or well. A philosophical question can in principle range far afield, such as in the most basic concern regarding why there is something rather than nothing, or whether we ought to care at all about ethics, and even the very concept of ought, or obligation to be found in ethical thought."

He looked around the room, then at Hasina, and said, "I realize how complicated this can sound. Does it make sense, and help at all?"

"Yes, Your Majesty, I think so," she said. "And so, in Walid's question about Santiago, and people generally, there's room for both the psychological and the philosophical?"

"Yes, indeed," the king responded. And then he said, "Now, Walid, allow me to address your question."

"Great," the prince responded.

"The concept of an insult and the concept of an offense—these are interesting things, and they have a fascinating history. As Aristotle saw, we are social, or political beings, and as such, we need to be liked and appreciated and accepted. We need to feel that we have influence, and the regard of others. We care about that because we can flourish only in community. An insult, first and foremost, in its perceived impact, distances us from the safe and positive role we want to have among others. It threatens to make us, or to reveal us as, outsiders—in a sense, shunned, or exiled from the community."

"Wow. I'd never thought about it like that," Walid said.

"Furthermore, and this is where it gets very interesting, there's a firm connection in some of the most primitive parts of our brains between insult, offense, and violence."

"Why is that, Your Majesty?"

The king replied, "In human prehistory, and throughout much of our subsequent history, an insult against an individual was a provocation or a threat, a sign that he was not respected or feared by the person or group from which the insult arose, and this had to be recognized as a territorial danger that could compromise survival."

"Really?" Walid spoke up again because he was always eager to understand as fully as he could.

"It's actually simple," the king said. "In primal circumstances, where there's no reliable governance of law, anyone who doesn't respect or fear you is naturally seen as a potential threat to your territory and your life. He's more likely to seek to take your resources for his own use and claim the area where you hunt, or gather, or farm, or even directly eliminate you as an obstacle to his own aims, treating you as an unwanted competitor for the limited available sources of nutrition, shelter, and reproductive opportunities in your mutual environment."

"That's very interesting," Mafulla spoke up and said.

"It is," Walid agreed.

"Yes. So we've been hardwired to recognize such a person, one who issues an insult, as a threat to our survival. And this is a realization that's been encoded into the mental repertoire of successful survivors for thousands of years, with, of course, a behavioral consequence that would have to follow."

"What's that?" Mafulla now asked.

The king replied, "In such primal conditions, it was ordinarily of survival value to be on the lookout for insults, because they would help you to identify threats and dangers. It was a sort of early warning signal for danger. It also then facilitated survival if a perceived insult gave emotional offense to the insulted person, a perception of harm tinged with a strong negative feeling, and for that feeling of offense to generate a form of anger that easily grew into something more like rage, or fury, and finally would beget preemptive violence."

"Could you say more about that?" Walid asked.

"Yes. You see, for most people, something like anger, rage, and certainly fury are the emotions that alone can create the wave of energy necessary to motivate the most extreme form of physical action that may be required to end a mortal threat of the most serious sort. When reason isn't strong enough, passion has to do the hard work. Those who naturally reacted to an insult or the threat implied by it with a strong sense of offense and anger would then be more likely to take action to fight and remove the threat. Passion is often a blind guide, so these actions wouldn't always be effective. But, still, for basic survival value, action is normally more effective than inaction in the face of a potentially serious threat and a possibly mortal danger."

"I see," Walid said.

The king continued: "This set of connections has been, for millennia of human life, no more or less than a natural protection needed for survival in a world of dire challenges."

"So, the tendency to be offended by insults became widespread among people," Walid said.

"Yes, because they were the descendants of the survivors who reacted like that, and so had been themselves primed, by nature or nurture or both, to be the same. And, like everything else, this reaction is more extreme in some than in others. There's a spectrum. There's almost always a spectrum. But you'll all notice right away that your Phi training is very different from this. You're taught to deal with threats and even violence from a core of calm and peace, augmented by courage and skill. That gives you a tremendous advantage over the person who may attack out of anger or rage. Remember the Triple Double and the forms of control it specifies."

"The king speaks with deep wisdom, as is his way," Masoon said, looking at the younger Phi. "This has always been one of his great advantages, the cool head and calm heart, and those same things have made my successful work possible, as well."

"So, wait. Let me get this straight," Mafulla interrupted. "For general survival purposes, anger is better than nothing. But a calm and focused use of force against an enemy is much better than anger."

The king nodded his agreement, and went on to say, "Yes. That's correct. A calm core of emotion is best. But a person who's incapable of rising to the level of calm and focused control most often depends on anger to motivate him. That's an initially easier motivation, which requires no spiritual discipline. And in fact, it functions most freely in the absence of such discipline."

"I see." Mafulla nodded his understanding of the point.

The king said, "So, this is the brief history of the basic psychology of insult and anger. But then, with the passage of time, the notions of insult and offense began to grow more sophisticated, and became detached and separate from this original context, along with their entire conceptual neighborhood of ideas like honor and respect. They eventually became completely distinct from the originating dynamic of physical threat and response. And over the past two thousand years, many philosophers have made an interesting observation about these concepts, in their developed forms."

"What's that?" Walid asked.

"People often speak loosely of those who might insult a great person of the past, a great nation, or a great religion. And they sometimes grow very angry over a perceived insult to someone or something they hold in honor. But the philosophers have seen into this more deeply." The king paused and said, "And here's the surprising insight. It's literally impossible to genuinely insult or offend, demean, or disparage a truly great man or woman, or nation, religion, or group of people. You can hurl invectives, make comments that are intended to demean or disparage, verbally attack, and seek to ridicule, but true greatness is not affected. It's untouched. We might vividly say that the insults bounce off their target. The deprecations don't stick. The invective fails to wound."

Mafulla looked puzzled. He said, "What do you mean, Your Majesty? I'm not sure I understand. People seem to think that the greater a person or nation is, the worse an insult is—not that it's impossible!"

"Ah, yes. But think about it for a moment. There is an old proverb: 'The lordly lion ignores the yapping of small dogs.' This is an image of the philosophical insight we're discussing. Greatness has within itself its own intrinsic honor and worthiness of respect. When it's badly disparaged, or disrespected, harm is indeed done—there's no doubt about that—but not to the great person, or group, or movement, but both by and to and in the one showing the disrespect."

"There's even a childhood song about this," Mafulla said. "You know: 'Sticks and stones may break my bones, but words can never hurt me.' And yet, we're often very much hurt by the words of others."

"You're right. And when that happens, it's because we're not living and feeling the wisdom of the ages on this point. There is a long history of reflection behind this insight I'm bringing to your attention. Socrates believed that others could harm us only physically—that's where we get the part about sticks and stones. We alone are capable of harming ourselves inwardly and spiritually, in our souls—and that's why the rhyme has the part about words. The great philosopher was convinced that the worst efforts of lesser men could never do genuine harm to the souls of greater men or women, however they might contrive and attempt to inflict that damage."

"Wow. That's amazing." Hasina spoke up. Ali acknowledged her, and then continued.

"No matter how noxious and demeaning a person's comments or actions might be intended to be, he can't in any manner truly harm a great person, a great religion, or a great people. He's not capable, in his own actions, of literally giving offense in that way. But lesser people, those who are less developed spiritually, can take offense from what he offers. That's their freedom. And yet, it's a freedom to do what's wrong and confused—the same freedom that the person hurling the insult has abused, thereby harming directly his own soul, and the only one he has the full power to harm. In each case, the damage happens to the one who misuses a particular freedom."

"I've never thought of it like that," Walid commented. "It's sort of a revolutionary way of viewing all this."

"The best philosophy often is. And this is a powerful realization," The king said. He then continued, "We sometimes come across people who think that their great tribe or religion, or leader or prophet, or teacher has been insulted, and they feel they must get even and take violent revenge against the offender. But they don't understand what's really going on. The dynamic of revenge, retaliation, and retributive justice, as it's invoked and played out most of the time around the world, is merely a rationalization, a masking of the ancient reflex to protect position and property and personal life. An insult allowed to stand is thought of as a chink in the armor, a weakening in the wall, an invitation to push me, or us as a group, aside. That's the perspective that can give rise to an endless cycle of violence. And in our modern world, it still operates with power."

Walid then suddenly raised his hand as he would in class. The king smiled and nodded to him, and he said, "But shouldn't we come to the defense of any who are wrongly attacked, even if it's just verbally? I've read in history that, many times, when there was an insult to a people or a king, those who felt they had been insulted, or had seen their monarch insulted, rose up in arms to defend themselves or their sovereign. And they were praised for it."

The king replied, "People do it, that's true, but it's not right—they ought not to do it. And this is what philosophy teaches. Those who seek so strenuously to defend greatness miss the big point. Arrows shot toward a greatly distant target never reach their goal. They fall to the ground. They miss the mark. So it is with words of insult aimed at any form of true greatness. They miss their target. They fall to the ground. We should just let them lie there, and not be provoked to counter-attack by either words or weapons. On any occasion when no territory is being taken by force, when no valuable resources are in imminent danger of being stolen, and when no one is under threat with immediate bodily harm or death, the proper attitude for anyone to take toward an attempted insult against greatness is simply to pity the one hurling the curse. And you might perhaps seek to educate him with kindness, but not to rise up in armed defense of the great one toward whom the invective or deprecation was directed."

"Why do so many people do that? Why do they tend to get really violent in defending the honor of someone or something they consider great, whenever there's a perceived insult?" Mafulla was working hard to get his head around all this.

"To do that, to act violently, is to try to frighten people into showing respect. And that's to confuse the distinct attitudes of respect and fear, which are entirely different things. The concept of respect, as it's properly developed, is not at all tied to fear. It's connected rather with the notions of honor, value, and worthiness of respect."

There was a nodding of heads in agreement all around the room among the older Phi, as the king went on. "Consider the most extraordinarily kind and saintly of people. They're honored and respected by those who know of them and their deeds because they're worthy of that honor and respect. There's no fear involved in any way. And of course, there can conversely be fear in situations where there's no genuine honor, or true respect of any kind. The notions of fear and respect are just different and unconnected concepts, in their logically developed forms."

He let this point sink in for a bit, then said, "Here's the ultimate payoff for all this philosophy. Most human beings have no notion of their own inner spiritual greatness. If they did, they would not be so easily insulted and offended by the careless or even calculated remarks of others. In fact, if they appropriated all the tremendous greatness that's properly theirs in the realm of the spirit, they could not be insulted or offended, or ever demeaned. And, likewise, anyone who understands this won't try to insult or disparage any other person—because they would know that, ultimately, they would be wrong and would be harming themselves."

"But it's not disparaging and wrong to think that an evil guy is evil, or to say that such a man is bad," Mafulla said tentatively.

"No. Not at all—as long as that's a well considered conclusion and not an attempt at insult. Everyone is born with inner greatness, but they can ignore it, and erode it, and live in such a way as to tarnish or diminish it. Even the worst of humanity are fallen or displaced royalty. They could have developed differently from a deep core of spiritual value. And I always seek to find a kernel of possibility yet in them."

The king let this point hang in the air for a moment and then said, "This is relevant to how we should all strive to live, in full recognition of the true greatness often invisible to the casual glance, the glory and honor and dignity with which all human beings, at their core, are endowed. They can fail to recognize it. They can even act to disavow and destroy it. And this is why there are so many things that are sad and tragic about the legend of the monster, and perhaps the story of Santiago, from what we know so far. There was no reason for anyone to insult the young boy. He was different. That's all. There was no reason for him to feel insulted and demeaned. He was born with the inner greatness that we all bring into the world. But we're also flawed, in that we fail to recognize and embody that greatness properly, and keep it in view. We fail to act from its resources. And too many people, as a result, become some version, however minor or major, of the monster of legend."

These words from the king left everyone in silence, reflecting on the immense depth and importance of what he had just said.

Walid finally spoke. "And those who do recognize this are in what we often call the fellowship of the mind."

"Yes. That's correct. We Phi are the spearhead for the fellowship of the mind, the vanguard, and often we're at the core. It's important for us to invite others into the fellowship, whatever their talents and abilities might be. They're worthy. Everyone deep down begins this life as worthy."

"Even the monster?" Kissa asked.

"Even the monster," the king replied, "although he's ultimately free to renounce that worthiness, and erode it by his actions through time. But that's a long process. And the wise are divided on whether it ever fully has its way, and extinguishes every small glowing ember of worthiness that might otherwise remain within. That's why I'm always hesitant to say of anyone simply that he's evil. He may be living in service to the wrong values, even perverse ideals, and abandoning his true nature by his actions; he may have layers of terrible habits of thought and action in him, but there always may still be a core, a speck, however small, of the original nature and intent of his life."

They all sat in silence for a few moments, pondering this weighty point. "Now," the king said, clapping his hands twice, "I think that's enough philosophy for the moment. We should stand up and stretch, lest we lose the circulation and suppleness we all so greatly need in our bodies as well as in our souls." He then smiled and said, "Walid, I thank you for the question. Also, I thank you, Hasina, for yours. And I thank the rest of you for your patience with my lengthy answers."

As they stood, most of the group gave the king a little bit of light friendly applause, and various words of verbal acclamation and appreciation for his time and his thoughts.

But still, no one knew exactly what would happen next—until the king spoke briefly again.

"Oh. There's one more thing, my friends, I think it's nearing the time when we need to go look for our Santiago, or at least the animals that are his captives. I plan to send out Amon and one of our soldiers on two fast horses to alert the strike force to the north of the village. And then we can approach the likely area of his secret compound from two sides."

"Do we know where he is?" Walid asked.

"We still don't yet know the exact location of the man and his followers, along with all the worthy creatures they're detaining. And we need to learn it now."

"The pilot of the plane that dropped our package at the oasis could have done an extensive flyover to find them," Walid said.

"Yes, and he actually did search in that direction," the king replied. "But from his flight path, dictated by his extremely limited fuel, he couldn't see anything except sand and brush. And yet, I have my own sense of direction that should be able to guide us, as do both Masoon and Hamid." He then looked around the room and said to everyone, "We should all, at present, return to the camp and arm ourselves well for any unpleasantness along the way. In some time spent with Zet this morning, after his visit to us here, Walid picked up a few helpful pieces of information that I'll share later in camp."

In Cairo, Malik and Haji were still having a hard time relaxing after all the excitement and action at the Cairo Veterinary Clinic. The king's men who had come to the rescue and taken out the last threats the boys faced had also escorted them back to the palace, where a debriefing was held, with Reela Adi leading the session, along with Naqid, Leem, and Ibrahim in attendance. Bancom was also present so that he could get word to the king about anything else that might had happened, while he was in transit, traveling toward the village with his friends on fast horses, but stopping briefly at the same military bases the larger group had visited.

After relating their entire story, the two boys felt, oddly, at the same time both exhausted and energized. At the end of the session, Leem could tell it would be best to invite them out to a café so they could get something to eat and continue to absorb and discuss all they had experienced. That way, they wouldn't have to go straight to their homes where relatives were visiting to be of help while their fathers were away, on the trip to Dromeda. The detective knew they still needed to talk about all they had been through. And he even had some additional questions to discuss with them. There might still be several loose ends to be tied up in town.

Mansur Arobi and the professor were both under arrest and in custody, and were being treated for their injuries. The man who answered the phone at Wasa Imports and Exports was also in jail. He had been at the veterinary clinic at the time of all the action, as well. The king's men had somehow managed to recapture all the escaped animals with the help of local police. And information was being gathered from the various national capitals about which animals were missing from each country, along with full descriptions and contact details, where those were available. The hope was that they would all soon be returned to their homes.

Already, some of the Egyptian animals had been brought back to their grateful owners in the Cairo area. First on the list, of course, was Manni, whose reunion with Jabari was a thing to see. In fact, after their time in the café with Leem and Ibrahim, Malik and Haji personally delivered the little monkey to his home and to his relieved and ecstatic owner, telling Jabari the whole story, while Manni punctuated their narrative with his own chirps, tweets, and occasional screeches. When he first saw his owner, Manni jumped on him and bounced up and down and then hit the floor, did a happy dance, and leaped back up into the arms of the grateful boy.

By dusk, Malik and Haji were still walking around the city and talking about the day. Malik reminded Haji of the decision they had made earlier that this had to be considered an official Wild Camel and Silver Sabre success in crime fighting. And Haji now fully agreed, with enthusiasm, right away. He had no doubts about it at this point, masks or no masks. It was nice to have a victory for the new League of Crime Fighters, International while the true founders, The Golden Viper and Windstorm, were away. In fact, the boys felt like they had a huge accomplishment under their belts with this one, and they were right. The Viper and the Storm would be very proud. And, they both knew, so would their dads.

They had not yet told their fathers about the masked crime fighter stuff, but after the conversation about it with Walid and Mafulla, some time back, they decided that maybe this would be best. It would be a topic to bring up when Masoon and Hamid got back from Dromeda, now that the boys had experienced such extraordinary success in helping to shut down a major criminal operation. Their confidence was riding high. Who could argue with that kind of success?

Up ahead, Haji spotted two familiar figures. "Look, Malik! It's Khalid and Hoda! Let's say hello!"

"Yeah, good idea," Malik replied.

"Hey, Khalid!" Haji shouted out and waved. "Hoda!"

The two of them were across the street, nearly a block away, approaching the front entrance of the Grand Hotel. Khalid gave the boys a small, dignified, half-wave, and Hoda did hers much more enthusiastically, with a big smile.

As the boys drew closer and now crossed over the street, Haji said, "It's good to see you, Khalid, especially when there are no assignments or homework that we should be doing!"

Khalid laughed and said, "I could give you an assignment right now. I have something in mind."

"No, no, please don't trouble yourself. We're fine."

"You look a little tired."

"Yeah. We've had a busy and exciting day."

"Oh?" Hoda said. "What have you boys been up to?"

Malik answered, "A little work down at the Cairo Veterinary Clinic, across town."

"Really?" Hoda commented. "What in the world were you doing there?"

"Just cleaning up a bit," Malik said, and the boys both laughed.

"Ok, what's going on?" Khalid knew when the boys were joking around, as well as when they were hiding something.

"Nothing, really," Haji replied.

"There's something. I can tell."

"Ok. You're right. It's just that, through a series of fortuitous circumstances, we ended up being in a position to help break up a major crime ring that was stealing animals throughout the city, and we were personally able to liberate the animals, and they're in the process of being reunited with their owners. But other than that, it was just a normal vacation day."

"What in the world?" Hoda was so surprised.

"You're kidding, right?" Khalid said.

"Nope. It was quite a scene. Just me and Malik here against a big bunch of bad guys, and we were taking them down, one by one, when some of the king's men showed up, shot a few of the criminals on the spot, and then handcuffed the rest and hauled them off to jail."

"Oh, my."

"Yeah, you should have seen it!" Malik said with a huge grin. "It was pure madness! Guys were coming after us with guns and we fought back at first with nothing more than a pitchfork and a maniac monkey on our side! I mean, until we took their guns, and then that helped a lot. But, without the monkey, who knows what would have happened!"

"Manni, again?" Hoda said, still looking perplexed.

"Yes!"

"How?"

"We didn't know it, but the animal thieves had just stolen him from Jabari."

"Oh, my."

"And, well, that was a mistake of major proportions, because when we found him, he was so important in helping us to bring down the whole enterprise from the inside."

"At the big clinic?"

"Yeah. Those guys were using the clinic as a cover, and they were storing stolen animals out back in a huge building, animals from four countries."

"And you brought them down and stopped it all?" Khalid said, in a bit of awe.

"Yes, sir, we did!" Haji said. "Extra credit?"

Khalid laughed and said, "Maybe extra credit! You know, they tried to steal our dog."

"Shibby?"

"Yes, but Kissa and Hasina and Hoda stopped the three men who were involved and were able to get them to jail, where now I imagine they're having a nice reunion with their friends and associates."

"Man! We didn't know that," Malik said.

"So it's a good thing you helped get rid of the rest of their operation," Hoda remarked. "We're very proud of you two, like usual."

"Thanks," Haji said, and then Malik said the same thing.

"What are you guys doing here at the hotel?" Malik asked.

"Dinner with an old friend," Hoda replied, "One of my oldest friends, a lady who's been a real mentor to me."

"That's great. Well, we'll let you guys go. Enjoy your evening."

"Yeah," Haji added. "Have fun!"

"We promise!" Hoda playfully responded, adding, "And you two crime fighters, get some rest."

"We promise," Haji said. Then the boys grinned, said goodbye, and walked off into the night.

Within a few seconds, Haji turned to Malik and said in a low voice, "She called us crime fighters."

"Yeah," Malik said. "If she only knew."

What she did know was that she was about to have dinner

with one of the biggest crime fighting resources in all of Egypt, an older lady who had come in from Luxor, at Hoda's request and the king's, precisely for a dinner conversation this evening that would prepare Hoda to fight crime in a most powerful way, and in a very short time. It was a conversation that was going to have a huge impact.

30

An Attack

Khalid had walked with Hoda to the hotel for the dinner, even though they were planning to dine separately. She was there to meet one of her oldest friends. He would sit across the dining room with another teacher, a man he had known for years, and they would likely talk philosophy and politics the whole time. He wanted to give Hoda and her mentor, a lady named Theta, the time alone they might need. And they made the most of the opportunity.

The dinner had been light. The conversation, by contrast, had been heavy. Hoda shared everything with Theta that the king recently had told her. Her mentor had taken it all in and had offered some reflections and opinions as to what might be coming and how best to defend against it. After dinner, Khalid had rejoined his wife and had enjoyed some small talk with her older friend before they had to part. They had gotten together like this at least once a year, for many years now. Khalid understood how much the time meant to Hoda.

It was now the next morning. Hoda and Khalid were waking up from a sporadic night's slumber. "How was your rest?" Khalid asked, as he rolled over and saw that Hoda was awake.

"Troubled," she replied.

"Oh?"

"I had times of deep sleep, but long bouts of wakefulness. I think that today, the king will make his move."

"I thought that was likely to be tomorrow," Khalid said.

"Yes, that was the plan. But you know plans. It's a bad one that can't change. Something has happened, or will soon happen—something to alert the king. He'll move up his schedule, or already has. Things will happen quickly."

"How do you feel about it?"

"Concerned, and alert, but not worried," Hoda responded.

Khalid paused for a moment and then asked, "After some sleep, however fitful, and now that your unconscious mind was free to process the time you had with Theta, how do you feel about that?"

"It was very helpful. She sees the inner side of everything. I'm grateful to have her in my life," Hoda responded. "The many possibilities she laid out were, of course, troubling, but forewarned is forearmed. You can't prepare for something you can't anticipate, and this is such a different, and even unparalleled situation."

"Yes, the ancient legend may have taken on the form of a real life."

"That's what's so troubling about it," Hoda admitted. "We have here not just an adversary, but perhaps the one of legend, about whom we've been warned for centuries. And there's Kissa, our sweet Kissa, far away on the edge of the vast desert, close to the monster of myth and lore, and likely about to go forth against him, without me there to protect her."

Khalid reached over and touched Hoda's arm and said, "She's with the king and Masoon, and Hamid, and Layla and Walid, and others who have great wisdom and power."

"Yes. And we're here. I'm just glad Theta's staying an extra day or two. I need her support and insight."

"That was good of her," Khalid said. "There's something about physical proximity."

"Yes," Hoda agreed. "Wherever two or three of us are gathered, something unique happens."

"Remember that this is also true for Kissa," Khalid said.

"Yes. I will. Mothers always have a special form of concern, but I know and I appreciate your words of reminder."

"Most of what I can say in reassurance, I've learned from you."

Across town, some time later, Malik and Haji woke up from a long and deep night's sleep. They had been more exhausted than they realized and had slept late. Malik had decided to stay over at Haji's so that they could talk more about the day they had lived through before their need for sleep would inevitably catch up with them. There seemed to be endless things to diagnose and analyze about what they had experienced. And some things just needed to be repeated, several times, for the full emotional processing they deserved. It had been a wild experience.

The boys got up and had a nice late breakfast and, while eating, decided to go over to Jabari's house at some point to visit with him and Manni, just to see them both again. But Malik had an idea for something he wanted to do first. "Haji, let's go by the library at the university this morning, and see if the professor has written anything they might have in their collection."

"You mean evil professor bushy beard?"

"Yeah. But we might not use that name with the librarian."

"Ha! So: What do you have in mind?" Haji asked.

"Well, he's the intellectual of the group, right? And if he's published anything about animals and religions and philosophy, maybe we can get some deeper insight into what he was doing and why he was doing it."

"Yeah, I guess being a jerk and a criminal and getting paid for it is probably not a profound enough characterization to fully explain what he was up to."

Malik laughed and said, "You're right. And I think that, who knows, he may have written something, even years ago, that could give us a clue as to what's really going on, and whether something else might happen that we'll need to face. In fact, the guy he's working for may have found him originally through an essay or a book of his and, you know, then made him an offer he couldn't refuse."

"Ok. That makes sense. Sounds good to me," Haji said. "Let's go."

The boys cleaned up a bit and then took off for the library, where they were in for some strange surprises. Dr. Hashman Arib, from the Department of Philosophy and Religion at Cairo University, it turned out, had written and published both academic essays, one scholarly book, and a work of fiction that purported to present the text of an ancient manuscript, long ago discovered, buried deep in the sands of Giza near the Sphinx, and kept safe by a small group of religious monastics ever since. The setup of the novel was that a natural disaster had destroyed their small monastery, killed all the monks, and left the manuscript damaged, but not destroyed. Arib, or his fictional narrator—it wasn't clear—claimed to have rediscovered the text and restored it, and that he was presenting it in this book.

Malik read in it as fast as he could, while Haji skimmed over some of the journal articles and short writings that were on topics of religion and philosophy, involving animals and their images through history. Haji was heard to utter several times, "This is pretty dry and boring."

And Malik was heard to say, even more times, "This is really strange."

Then Haji offered, "Why don't I do the strange, and you do the dry and boring?"

"We need to stick with what we're on, for our continuity of understanding, as Khalid would say."

"Yeah, Ok, sure, and continuity of total boredom. The guy is a pretty tedious writer. It's like, all right, come on, already. He quotes a French philosopher, then a German scholar, then an author from Argentina, and then a Norwegian anthropologist. It's just pretty convoluted stuff."

"Hey, you picked it."

"Yeah. Big mistake." After a bit more reading and skimming, they took a break, and whispered to each other about what they had each read so far and what they made of it. The fictional book was so much more bizarre than even the strangest accounts of animals in the scholarly essays on real religious belief and ritual, that the boys finally decided to both start up where Malik had left off in the novel.

Four hours later, they got to a point where they realized they needed to stop and have some lunch. There was a café near the library that allowed them to grab something quick and get back to the book, which they had left with the librarian to hold for them during their break. Their lunchtime conversation had made them even more eager to dive back into the reading they were doing together. And so they both dove back into the novel.

By mid-afternoon, their heads were swimming from the arcane and esoteric details of the story they were encountering. There were shamans and magi and talking animals and strange rituals and focused powers, and some story about the pyramids being built originally as big shields against antagonistic energy. There were two cats in the story, one black and white with long hair and bushy whiskers and eyebrows, and another with light and darker broken, orange-tan stripes. It was starting to look like the people in this tale thought that, as humans, they were in charge of the course of events, but it was really the cats who were making everything happen.

When the boys now first read something indirectly implying that, Haji looked up at Malik and said, "This is very odd."

"Yeah," Malik replied succinctly.

"Is it the black and white cat that people are talking about when they say the name Odysseus, and the name Odie?"

"I think so."

"And the other cat gets called Mister Wes?"

"Yeah, it's really bizarre."

Haji yawned and said, "Look, I'm getting a little tired. Do you think we can leave the book again with the librarian, to hold it for us, and go see Jabari now?"

Malik yawned also and stretched. "Yeah, I think you're right. Let's take off for now. We do need a rest and a visit. The cats would want it that way."

"Ha." That was all Haji said, as he stood up and grabbed the book.

The boys took it up to the librarian and explained to him their need to take a break and come back later, or even the next day. They asked if he could hold the book for them with a bookmark in the place they had gotten to, and he pleasantly agreed. It's not like there were a lot of people in the library and a big, pent up demand for this particular book, but they just wanted to be careful and make sure it would be available for them if they needed it any more. There was just something about this book.

It took about fifteen minutes to get to Jabari's house by foot. His mom let them in and told them again how happy they all were to get Manni back. She hugged them both twice and was so nice about what they had done. Then she told them to go back to Jabari's room where they could find both boy and monkey.

It was, again, a great reunion, and Manni screeched out his greetings as Jabari jumped up off his bed to hug his friends and thank them once more for the heroic things they'd done. He also wanted to hear the whole story over again, as did Manni, so Haji and Malik took turns giving the most dramatic rendition of it that they could. Jabari asked a question now and then, and actually helped the boys to reflect on some of the lessons they had learned. Manni chirped whenever his name was mentioned. And he did one well-timed twirl.

On this retelling of the tale, they finally realized that it would have been great to have some sort of backup from the start of their undercover operation, something the king had always been stressing to Walid and Mafulla. But until you experience great danger, you never really appreciate how bad it can get, and how suddenly and unexpectedly in some situations it can turn much worse. And even then, when you've actually lived through such a challenge, it's easy at some level to forget the real intensity of it, once enough time has passed. Backup is always a good idea, whenever it's available. And this was a lesson they were explicitly discussing with Jabari.

Right in the middle of their conversation, Manni, who now had been messing around on the floor and playing with some small monkey toys, suddenly let out an ear-piercing screech that shocked all three of them. Malik said, "Whoa!"

Haji said, "Yikes!"

Jabari looked shocked and said, "Are you Ok, buddy?"

It even brought Jabari's mother running into the room, saying, "Is everything all right? Is Manni Ok?"

A second or two after he let out the screech, which really sounded like a scream, he started frantically running and jumping all over the room, like he had been terribly frightened or badly hurt by something. But the moment Jabari's mom walked into the room, the little guy started to slow down and moan and whirl in a circle and bend over and make a little coughing sound. Jabari moved over to pick him up and he went limp on the floor with a glassy look in his eyes, and his arms and legs started trembling, and he was breathing in a fast and shallow way that was just not like him. Everyone was stunned at it all.

"Oh, no!" Jabari said. "Something's really wrong with Manni!"

"What happened to him?" Jabari's mother asked, as she bent down to look at him.

"Nothing that we could see," Jabari said.

"We were just talking," Malik added, "and he was playing and suddenly he did that scream and started running around the room screeching, and then this. We didn't see anything touch him or happen to him at all."

"Yeah, that's how it looked to me, too," Haji said.

Just then they heard a voice calling out from a distance. "Ama? Ama? Are you home? Jabari?"

"Is that Hoda?" Haji said.

"It sounds like her," Malik replied.

"It's Hoda?" Jabari said.

"Hoda? Hoda, Come in! We're back here in the back," Ama al-Sout, Jabari's mom, called back toward the front of the house.

Hoda walked quickly to Jabari's room and as she came to the door she said, "I have to talk to you about Manni."

"He's just had an attack of some kind," Jabari told her.

"What do you mean? What happened?" Hoda asked, as she also bent down to look at the poor monkey, now almost motionless and quietly breathing in that fast and shallow way.

Jabari gave her a quick rundown on what had happened. She said, "He looks bad." Then she turned to them and said, "There's only one thing we can do."

"But, what's going on?" Malik said.

"I'll explain in more detail later. Manni is being attacked inwardly, through his spirit, as strange as that may sound. I think it will be happening in some way to every animal that was in captivity. But, I'm afraid that Malik and Haji and I have only a few minutes to do what we need to do, right now, and you also, Jabari, and Ama, if you'll indulge me for a few minutes."

"Will it help Manni?"

"It's the only thing that can," Hoda said.

"But how do you know?"

"I can't explain right now, but I just do. We all need to put our hands on Manni, gently, lightly, and close our eyes and try our best to move into a meditative state, calming ourselves from our emotions and quieting the chatter that's running loose in our thoughts. You need to let go of what just happened, what you just saw, try to release it, and make your mind as much of a blank as you can. Would you begin now?" As they nodded or agreed in a word or two, she said, "I'll lead you through a process and a visualization that's necessary for Manni and the rest of us."

She looked at each of them, and their eyes were all now closed, so Hoda closed hers as well and said, "Breathe in, and hold it for just a few more seconds … and now breathe out. And now do this again, breathing in, and holding it, until I say otherwise … and now breathe out. Repeat this for me a few more times, with the same slowness of timing, and now shed everything in your thoughts and feelings. Release your worry. Feel it dropping away. You're at rest. We're safe. Everything will be fine. You'll be fine. We'll all be fine, including Manni. But we first must rest our minds and hearts."

After twenty seconds of silence, Hoda said, very softly, "Now, we should all imagine something. We're surrounded by a solid, thick, impenetrable wall of stone in front of us, and one behind us, and one to our left, and to our right. The stones are huge and massive and dense. The walls stand some distance out from where we are. We have plenty of room. And we're safe. The walls will protect us. They will protect Manni. Now, in your mind, build those walls up, higher than your head, much higher, towering over us, higher than ten people, then twenty, and now taper them in, angled inward, and have them come together, four walls getting more narrow as they go up, and merging into a point high above us. From the outside, imagine that our fortress looks like the great pyramid, and from the inside it will shield and protect us. Sense the immense thickness of the walls, and know with certainty that everything negative is turned back by the force of those walls and the shape of the structure."

"Hoda!" Haji whispered loudly. "Hoda, my head! It's hurting!"

"Did you break the meditation?"

"Just for a second. Today we read something about pyramids and I was thinking … Ow! Oh!"

"Not now. Concentrate, Haji."

"Ok. Ow! Oh, man."

"Concentrate on what we're doing. Ignore any other thoughts. Ignore the pain. See your pyramid. Only it can block the pain." Hoda spoke in a low but emphatic voice. "Don't be distracted now. Think of nothing else but what I say. See the walls and your pyramid of power and protection. Clearly and vividly visualize it all in this moment. See it only from the inside now. Feel it. You're in it. You're protected. Great power is with you. It will block the source of the pain. This is the only way. It can protect you from much worse. You're helping me to create the protection against the pain, for you and us and Manni."

Across the desert, two hours earlier, King Ali and Masoon had led the group of Phi out of their camp, around the village, and to the north, along with eleven soldiers who stayed a short distance behind them. Half the soldiers who had come along on the trip as security had been assigned to stay in town, in case the villagers might need any protection beyond what they themselves could provide. And four armed men would remain posted around the encampment to guard all their belongings that were still there.

As the group led by the king got just out of sight of the village, a single horseman approached them from a distance up ahead. He was riding at a fast pace. The soldiers grew wary. But as he drew closer, they could see that it was Amon. When he was near, he shouted out, "Your Majesty! The strike force has been unable to locate the compound we seek, so they're going to wait for you roughly two miles to the north and four miles to the west of where we are now."

The king pointed up ahead and said, "There's a crossroads a bit north of here that you've just passed. We'll take the western road from there. I believe that's how we can find our destination." And, at his lead, they began once more to ride.

The king and his top associates, Masoon and Hamid, were on horses, as was Amon, for his special service, and each of the ladies at this point, in case they needed for defensive purposes to move quickly. Everyone else was on camels as they progressed up the road toward the place where they would turn to the west.

Walid and Mafulla knew that the Triple Double was now in effect in the minds of all the more advanced Phi and that they, too, should be reviewing and applying its components. In fact, something moved Walid at that point to actually say to Mafulla, in a low voice, "Triple Double."

And Mafulla responded with the same two words, "Triple Double," nodding his understanding. Then the prince turned around to look at Hasina and Kissa, and said the same thing.

Hasina then repeated aloud, but just loud enough for her three close friends to hear, "Prepare, perceive; anticipate, avoid; concentrate, and control."

Twenty minutes later, they were at the crossroads where they went west, and after another roughly equal period of time, the king motioned for them to stop, and he signaled for quiet. There were scrub bushes and tall clumps of thin grass on both sides of the road, and some trees, but they were sparse. The group was fairly open and exposed on this stretch of road, as they would be on most roads in this part of the kingdom. There was a slight hill, a bit of a ridge a distance up ahead of them on the right, set back maybe twenty yards, or a little more, from the road. Moments after the king had signaled for them to stop and be silent, Walid and Mafulla at the same time both felt something—an ill-defined uneasiness, a disturbance, or a vague perturbation within, not anything focused, clear, or easy to describe at all, but a definite perception of some sort. Maybe it could best be captured as an intuitive, almost instinctual, awareness of danger in the area, or a nearby looming threat of harm.

Through a series of hand gestures, Masoon positioned five of the soldiers to continue on down the road on their camels, while he directed the other six to loop back around, on foot and off the road, to the flank and back of the hill that the men on the road would be passing. Their camels would be led forward with the group that stayed on the road. The king and Masoon and their Alexandrian friends had a third path to take. They turned around and began to ride a short distance back down the road, and then off the path to the northwest to, in turn, flank and get behind the soldiers who would be moving around the hill, as a sort of second wave of protective backup.

Hamid then led Layla, the students, and the intermediate Phi—Amon, Paki, and Omari—around on a parallel track to the left or south side of the road, off into the surrounding sand and grasses, some distance back, so that they would be at a greater remove from the road and the hill than anyone else, and if that was indeed where the danger was going to erupt, they could judge from their more remote vantage point how to reinforce any group that might need it. Weapons were now out and ready for everyone.

The group that, at this stage, began once more to ride slowly down the road knew that it was their job to lure out any adversaries who might lie in wait to ambush the group. If any such enemies showed their presence behind the hill or at the top of it, the soldiers behind flanking them would attack and seek to prevent them from getting off any shots at the group on the road. But they, as backup, would be able to remain undetected only if those going down the road were making enough noise to draw the focused attention of any armed attackers who might lie in wait for them. Then, the flanking group could get into position with a good chance of being unseen and unheard. The king and his top men would be too far back from the hill and the road for there to be much likelihood that they would be observed, even though they were on horseback. But that mode of their conveyance would allow a rapid response on their part to anything that might happen.

The trap was set, and all the groups maneuvered as they had planned. The target group of soldiers were all talking loudly and clanging metal objects in their packs as if they were just badly stored. And this noise was effective, but a bit sooner than their backup had expected. When the road soldiers drew near to where the small hill sat back from the road, there was a sudden sound of gunfire from several weapons. It was indeed coming from the hill, as expected. The king's men on the road fired back immediately but were a bit too much out in the open to have any secure protection for an extended fight. However, they did have something planned, as a contingency. They threw their large packs into the road and dove behind them for cover while returning fire.

Fortunately, within less than twenty seconds the flanking group of soldiers drew close enough to open fire from slightly behind the ridge, catching the men who were launching the ambush in a cross fire of bullets they didn't at all anticipate. This, in turn, though, brought out a hidden, second wave of assailants, who were dug in behind a smaller second ridge that rose up nearly thirty yards or so behind, or to the north of, the first one. As they began shooting at the flanking soldiers who were firing on their comrades, the king and his men on horses swooped in from farther to the north behind them, in order to stop their supporting attack. And no one could shoot with the speed and precision of the king and Masoon. Their assault was quick and deadly, finding their targets at first from a great distance. The fact that they were on horseback and moving fast didn't at all diminish their lethal effectiveness.

However, something else that was completely unanticipated suddenly happened. There were at least four more adversaries who had buried themselves with coverings of sand on the opposite, south side of the road, lying flat and observing it all not fifteen yards back from the king's men on the road who were under ambush. At that moment, they rose up from their places of hiding, and from low and kneeling positions began firing at anyone they could spot. It was a good thing they didn't see Hamid, Layla, and the rest of the group behind them. Hamid and the three ladies, all on horseback, galloped from their position toward the backs of the four snipers. Layla shot first and took down one of the men. She got him through the upper back near his right shoulder. Hamid then instantly took out a second, shooting also from his fast moving horse. The other two twisted around and began to return fire toward the two of them, and then toward Kissa and Hasina, who were right behind them.

Walid and Mafulla were farther back at the moment and couldn't get a clear shot around their friends, so they began to urge their much slower and now reluctant camels off to the side, so as to gain a better angle of fire. But before they could move into position, Kissa and Hasina had both shot the same adversary, who went down flat on his face. The remaining sniper took aim at Kissa, in response, and began to squeeze the trigger. He had perfect aim and led her just enough for the headshot to be dead on. Hamid took him out the split second after his bullet was leaving his gun, on its way. But he was not fast enough to stop that one shot.

Walid and Mafulla could both see what was happening, and even before the man pulled his trigger, they both yelled, "NO!" Walid jumped off his now frightened camel and began to run toward Kissa as gunfire was still ringing out all around them. Mafulla heard a bullet whiz by his left ear and, turning, saw the shooter standing now on the close-by hilltop and, without thinking, and while jumping down off his camel to follow his friend, turned his gun, fired with only an instinctive aim, and without even pausing to see the result, doubled the man over, dropping him on the spot.

Walid and Mafulla were now both running at full speed and looking straight at Kissa, who was at a distance up ahead of them on her horse. They saw when she suddenly jerked to the right, twisting, and fell off her horse and sprawled into the sand. Time seemed to slow at that moment and almost stop as her body dropped those few feet to hit the hard ground below her. Walid ran the fastest he had ever run and not even Mafulla could catch up to him, as he bent over and nearly dived down to Kissa and called out her name and touched her now unmoving body, holding her shoulder and turning her over to find where she had been shot.

He didn't expect to see anything like what he now saw.

31

A Terrible Loss

In Cairo, things were happening fast. Everyone in Jabari's room had their hands on Manni. Haji's headache was splitting and throbbing and he was starting to get dizzy and nauseous at the same time. He even felt like he was going to throw up. But he listened to Hoda and fought to concentrate, and then the pain and awful sickness began to subside, gradually at first, and then more quickly. He had thought that if it got any worse, he would pass out and die on the spot.

Malik had also developed a bit of a headache and a sick feeling when Haji interrupted Hoda to speak about what they had read earlier in the day. He even had a strange taste in his mouth, almost metallic. But then Hoda took over and stopped Haji from drifting any further, and that also put Malik back on course. And his pain, which he could tell was on the verge of becoming intense, began right then to withdraw and diminish.

Hoda kept them meditating and visualizing vividly the position of being safely inside a solid pyramid of power and protection, and they did so for nearly twenty minutes. Haji's pain eventually vanished completely, but it left him feeling wasted—empty, and exhausted. He didn't have a clue what had just happened to him, or why.

When she was sure that her protective work had been fully accomplished in league with the others, Hoda said softly, "Continue in these thoughts for a bit longer until I invite you out of them, and feel now that the sun is shining brightly on our pyramid, reflecting light and power off its surface and making it glow for all to see." Then she silently turned her attention to Manni's situation. She moved her hands just a bit and touched his head, and with a total mental focus that was redirected toward him alone at this moment, she conveyed healing power into his little body and soul.

Some distance away, in The Grand Hotel, Hoda's old friend Theta had been sitting in a comfortable armchair and reading when she first felt the disruption and knew that someone dear to Hoda was in trouble, and then that Hoda was with that person. In the next moment, she got up and moved into the middle of the room and sat down on the floor and began to fight her own battle with the forces she felt, adding her seasoned skills and pure heart to the mix. And, as it turned out, she and Hoda were able together to carry much of the weight of the situation, at least initially, constructing a mental and spiritual fortress of protection, but she could tell that their efforts were being greatly augmented by other good and powerful sources linking up with them as the moments passed. In addition to the protection, there was a reversal of spiritual energies going on that transformed the situation and completely extinguished the particular threat.

Hoda opened her eyes and noticed Manni blink four times and heard him groan and saw him quickly scramble into a sitting position. He took a sudden and deep breath. Everyone else felt his movement and resisted opening their eyes for just a second until they heard Hoda say, "Open your eyes now and see." The little monkey squirmed out of the many hands that had been touching him and jumped onto Jabari's shoulder, now making little chirps and noises almost like purrs. He seemed totally normal again.

"Manni's Ok," Hoda said. "Is everyone else all right?"

Haji said, "Oh, man, Hoda, I thought my head was going to explode for a while there. I felt sick and nauseous. I thought I was going to just drop dead."

"My head started really hurting, too," Malik added. "And I was feeling sick in my stomach just a second after my concentration was broken."

"Yeah it was me, talking," Haji said. "It was totally my fault. I'm really sorry. When I realized we were mentally building a pyramid of protection, it just hit me that we had read a story today about that, in a book written by the professor who's in with the bad guys."

"Oh?" Hoda said. "Say more."

"Yeah, a novel the guy wrote years ago, where he makes up a story that there's an ancient text, long lost, and now rediscovered that describes all kinds of strange things, and there are these two powerful animals, cats, and it just all gets really weird, but there's stuff in there about the protective function of the pyramids at Giza, and why they were built long ago, to ward off bad power."

"I'd like to see this book," Hoda said.

"Ok, we'll take you to the library and show you," Malik replied. "The librarian said he would hold it for us."

"Sorry, Hoda, and guys, but is Manni really Ok now?" Jabari asked.

"Yes, he is, Jabari. I'm so sorry for your worry, and that we got off on this other issue. He's fine now."

"What happened to him?"

"It's a long story, but there's a man with great power who has been behind all the thefts of animals, including Manni. And our friends Malik and Haji helped to destroy his operation here in Cairo, where he was holding a lot of animals that he was about to move to a compound far to the west of here, near Dromeda, I think, where our friends are now, and where Kissa is visiting. He wants to use the animals in some way to magnify his spiritual power and his intent is only for what he thinks of as his own ultimate good."

"This man had something to do with what Manni and Malik and Haji just experienced?" Jabari asked.

"Yes. I think so. He must have the attitude that if he can't have these animals, then no one else can either. And now he can't keep them, so he's sought to destroy them in the only way he can at this point, with a very strange and powerful mental, or spiritual, energy that he's directing toward them, and toward anyone who was involved in thwarting his plans. And this means that Manni, Malik, and Haji were all targets just now."

"Oh, man. I don't know what you did, Hoda, or how the pyramid stuff worked, but I'm so glad that you were here to help us," Jabari said. "Thank you so much."

"Yeah, really, thanks Hoda," Haji said. "You may have saved my life."

Malik added, "I don't know what we would have done if you hadn't come in."

"I just had a feeling earlier that I should check in on Jabari and Manni," Hoda said. "It's good for us to trust our deeper feelings."

"But what about all the king's guys who helped us at the clinic?" Malik suddenly asked. "Have they just been attacked, too?"

"I would imagine so," Hoda replied. "But I made sure to build our pyramid around them, too. And I feel certain they're safe. They may have felt various pains like you boys did, and probably for longer, but they're fine now, and most likely have no clue what just happened."

Jabari's mother had been quiet all this time and just listening, but now she said, "Hoda, my dear friend, this is all so strange to me, as you must know."

"Yes, I'm sure."

"I believe in the mind and in the spirit, but I must say that, in many ways, I have no idea what just went on here. And yet, I can see that the result is good for Manni and the boys, and so … thank you so very much, for … whatever you did, and helped us to do."

"You're welcome, Ama. I have a long history of training in these things—in psychology and philosophy, and spirituality. I don't know everything, either, for sure, and sometimes I feel like I know very little, but I do know more than most. And I can do a few things to offer protection against those who would seek to harm others, abusing the true powers of the mind and spirit."

"You're a gifted and good woman, Hoda," Ama said, and she leaned over to hug her.

"Thanks, Ama. You are, too," Hoda replied. "It was meant for us all to be together right now."

"I have one question, though."

"Sure, ask anything."

"Will this happen again?" she said, with a look of great concern.

"I don't believe so," Hoda replied, cautiously. "I have no reason to think that the man directing such energy at Manni and the boys knows that we blocked his attack. He probably thinks the job is done, and that he's accomplished his goal."

"What about all the other poor animals?" Jabari asked.

"I tried to protect them, too," Hoda replied. "And I think they, and you, have had more protectors, as well. I don't know for sure, but I feel there's reason for hope. If the man who wishes them all harm now has had his way, it will be a terrible loss of life and kindred spirits. I couldn't prevent it alone, not everything that was intended, and we in this room couldn't, together, but I think the king and others may have known and may have been acting, or will do so quite soon, to defend the many creatures other than Manni who may be targeted. And I feel that my oldest mentor, a lady of truly immense ability, has helped out in this regard as well, in just these few minutes."

"The lady you met last night?" Malik asked.

"Yes."

A bit earlier, and not far from the edge of the desert, gunshots were still ringing out and many shouts could be heard in the distance—but not by the prince or his best friend, or the young lady who was loved by the remarkable golden boy from Dromeda.

Walid had run to Kissa as she lay on the ground, now motionless, and he had just looked at her face, with his heart as cold as ice from fear and his throat closed tight. His insides were paralyzed, with an inability to even think, as he saw her mouth lying open and her eyes still and partly open, but without focus. And he just stared at her for the longest moment the world has ever known.

And then, a sudden sound came into the muffled silence of his panic and fear and emptiness. He heard something beyond him almost like a rushing wind and then the words, "Oh. That hurt." It took a split second for him to process and understand what he had just seen and heard.

"You're alive? You're alive!" Walid nearly yelled out, with his hands gripped tightly on Kissa's arms.

"Too loud," she said. "Quieter. Please. My head's pounding."

"But, you got shot!" he said.

"I did?"

"I saw you fall off your horse!"

"No, no, that was … on purpose."

"What?"

"I felt the bullet … coming through the air—my sense of, you know, extended proprioception—and I knew, I had to turn sideways quick and flip off the … horse, so it … would miss, and I didn't land very well, and I think I got knocked out for a minute. And, wow, that hurt. It sort of knocked the breath out of me, too."

"Wait. You didn't get shot?"

"I don't think so."

"But it looked so much like you did."

"Oh, my head hurts."

At that point, Walid became aware that Mafulla was beside him and he said, "She's Ok! She's alive! She didn't get shot!"

"I can't believe it!" Mafulla said. "I thought for sure …"

Walid looked straight into her eyes and brought his face close to hers and said, "Don't ever, ever get shot. I love you." And then he gave her a quick kiss.

And she was stunned. But she said to him, "I love you, too."

Mafulla missed that part because, as soon as he saw that Kissa was alive, it occurred to him that he didn't know where Hasina was, and he realized right then, at that moment, that if she was Ok, she would have already been here with Kissa, too, checking on her best friend ever. He felt a sudden shiver of fear and jumped up and turned around and saw her horse a distance away. But she wasn't on it, and there was Layla's horse, but it was standing alone, too.

And it was almost as if his hearing was instantly turned back on and he realized that he heard gunfire. He instinctively began to run toward the two horses and as he did, he could suddenly see Hasina and Layla, both lying on the ground.

They were on their stomachs, flat on the sand. That's the first thing he saw. And he thought: No. Then he broadened his focus and took in more of the scene and noticed that their rifles were in front of them, propped up, and they were shooting at someone on the hill. It took three shots—pop, pop, pop—but the man in their aim went down hard and then lay unmoving, and as soon as he saw this, Mafulla's heart did a flip, and he dove down beside them.

And not even realizing that Mafulla had gotten up, not noticing anything outside the bubble of magical feeling he was in, and a sense almost of resurrection and renewal that now surrounded him and Kissa, Walid said to her, "I don't deserve you. But nobody does. And I don't ever want to lose you, so don't ever scare me like that again."

"I don't deserve you, either," Kissa said. "But, help me up." She stirred and began to lift herself off the sand, brushing the hard grains off her face where they were nearly embedded. "Where's my gun? It's not over yet." They now could hear the three shots from Hasina and Layla, and then one more shot rang out, and after it, no more were heard.

"Or maybe now, it is over," Walid said. He listened intently.

And there was silence, aside from a blowing wind. And then there were some scattered camel noises. A distance away, two of the soldiers on the road were lying in the sand, wounded. One of the men who had been involved in the flanking maneuver had also been shot in the leg. He was sitting on the ground, holding his wound. And a bullet had just barely grazed Paki's arm. Dodging another, that one got him, but only in the most superficial way. And he, Hamid, Omari, and Amon were already at work, walking about quickly and tending to those who had been hurt.

Layla jumped up from her position and looked over toward Kissa and Walid and called out, "Is she all right?"

"Yeah!" Walid shouted back. "She eluded the lead once again!"

"I'm fine," Kissa said in as loud a voice as she could muster, while waving her hand. The king rode up with Masoon to check on them.

"Everyone?"

"We're all fine. How's everybody else?" Layla asked Ali.

"Three wounded soldiers, nothing bad," the king said to her, "and Paki was lightly grazed on the arm. But he's fine."

"How many attackers were there?" Layla wanted to know.

"Twenty. Two lived through their assault and are being questioned by our Alexandrian friends, right now."

"Do we know anything yet?"

"Yes, that their compound is only a mile and a half farther down and just fifteen minutes north of the main road. There's a smaller road that will take us there. Santiago, their leader, has already left, they said, unfortunately, with more of his men. But we still need to go there and see if there's anything we should do. Before we continue on, though, we need to have an inner circle meeting, like we had this morning. As soon as the wounded are patched up and the stone is passed around among them, I want us to take a few minutes alone. Then, we can go on to do our job."

"Good idea," Layla said. "I'll find a spot that's conducive."

The king nodded and said, "Excellent," and rode off to round up all the Phi and post the remaining unwounded soldiers both on the road to the east and west of their current position, and also on the hill, where they could spot anyone approaching.

Mafulla saw Paki's torn sleeve and noticed him rubbing his upper arm. He said, "What happened?"

"I got grazed."

Mafulla gave him a strange look and said, "Proprioception, man."

"Yeah, I know. I avoided one, but in the process, I got just a little distracted."

Within a couple more minutes, all the Phi gathered in a circle, seated on the sand. The king was the last to join the group. He sat down in a space between Masoon and Hamid and looked around at everyone there. He then began by saying, "I'm grateful for your courage and skill in repelling this attack that we all, in a sense, expected. As ever, I'm saddened that we had to be put in a position where meeting deadly violence with similar force was our only option. But our motives and purposes here are pure. And we had no good, available options, given the circumstances. While we should always regret the loss of life and the injuries inflicted, and I'm sure you do, we should also be glad of the result that we survive in good health to carry on with our mission, to the extent that it's still available to us."

"What do you mean?" Walid asked.

"I'm sorry to report, if you haven't heard it already, that Santiago has apparently left his compound. We're still going to it and should reach it within the next hour, at the latest. I've called this meeting because one of the surviving men who was questioned a few minutes ago has told us that Santiago knows of the loss he's incurred in Cairo, the loss of all the animals."

"But how?" Mafulla said, and then added, "Never mind."

The king continued, "And he seems to have the point of view, not at all surprising, that if he can't have them, then no one else should have them. So he plans to attack and destroy all of them. He's too far away to do so by physical force before they're all dispersed and returned to their homes. So he'll be attacking them with his formidable mind and all the spiritual powers to which he already has access. We don't know exactly when this will happen, or precisely what form it will take, but it's my feeling that it will likely be soon, if it hasn't already started. We need to act now to counter his aggression, and seek to save those many innocent lives. There's some reason to think he'll also be attacking any who freed the animals, so they'll need our protection as well."

Mafulla looked over at Walid, who looked back at him, greatly concerned for Malik and Haji. "Your Majesty, how can we do this?" Hasina asked, now much bolder than she had been in the past, and eager to help in any way she could.

"It is all in The Book of Phi, in the previously unreadable passages," the king said. "I'll lead you now through a meditation and projection of power that will turn back his efforts."

"Your Majesty, Hoda also needs us right now," Layla said calmly, but with a sense of urgency in her voice. "I can feel it."

"Yes, I can as well," the king replied, and then looked around the circle. "Senior Phi, you know how to come to her aid. Do so this instant, please."

Kissa said, "Is Mom in danger?"

Layla replied quickly, "No, don't worry, Kissa. She's fine, and is in no personal danger, but she's right now using her mind and spirit to try and stop the torture and potential death of at least three other good individuals, and I think, even more. With our immediate help, it can be prevented most quickly and fully, and with minimal to no negative consequences."

The king turned to his most advanced colleagues and said, "All of you senior Phi, go apart now and gather to help our friend."

Masoon, Hamid, and Layla then stood up, along with the Alexandrian Phi, and they walked off to a spot not far away and sat down together there, in immediately still, meditative positions. Masoon began leading them through whatever it was that they were going to do.

As soon as they had gotten up to walk away, the king turned and said to the more intermediate and junior Phi, "Friends, we'll relax our minds now and start with the broader emergency that's ours to help meet. The others will join us as they can. The particular need that Hoda has for their focused services is more pressing for them at the moment, but we also must be underway with the broader task at the same time. We need to prevent a terrible loss of innocent life on a large scale, and we should also begin, this moment, in order to do so. We can encompass Hoda's need, but go with our spirits to help more broadly, as well."

The many palace guards and policemen and veterinarians from other animal clinics that were now working at the site of The Cairo Veterinary Clinic had just begun to hear sounds of distress coming from all over the building that was housing the many animals. Screeches, howls, yelps, and what have to be called screams sounded out suddenly from all directions. Animals began to run around in their cages and pens. Even birds outside the enclosures started to fly rapidly about in seemingly random patterns, as if attempting to flee something terrible that they couldn't escape.

In some houses and farms nearby, animals that had already been taken back into the custody of their families and rightful owners began experiencing the same thing, like what Manni had endured. Their owners who were in a position to see and hear what was going on were shocked and distraught—not knowing, or even having a clue as to what might be happening. They tried in various ways to comfort or help their animals. But it was to no avail. They couldn't stop whatever was underway. The sounds of pain and suffering were emotionally wrenching and terribly difficult for them to hear. A strong puzzlement and even panic beset everyone who had charge of these clearly distressed animals.

And then cries went up, around Cairo and beyond, from the humans in whose lives these animals were so important. Children sobbed and shrieked and called out to their parents for help. Adults were just as distraught. "What's happening?" "What's wrong?" "Oh, my! Please, help me!" The howls and bellows of the animals were almost too hard to take. It was heartbreaking to hear. And animals of various kinds soon began to fall. They contorted and froze and had seizures and spasms. They lost all control of their bodies, and many went silent where they collapsed and lay.

But it was at that instant that the collective power of the gathered Phi began to have its effect. A few men and women on a stretch of sand near a remote road in western Egypt, with their concentrated efforts, began to make a crucial difference throughout Cairo and beyond. Seconds before death was to come to a great many of the animals, their positive energy began to arrive and prevail and turn back the onslaught that one very powerful man had unleashed, in his blind rage and attempted revenge. But they were able to block his work, together, and force his dark energies back and break them up, and dilute their power to the point that they were no more.

At first, there was diminished noise, and then an eerie silence at every scene where an attack had been underway. At the clinic and in homes and farms, in barns and in back yards and indoors, the badly stricken animals at first grew subdued, and then silent and still. And then, two seconds later, they twitched again and jerked to pick themselves up, and they variously shook off what had just happened, and took tentative steps, and then walked and moved normally.

The king knew the moment it happened. So did all the other senior Phi. And Walid had a feeling of total relief a split second before anyone else said anything. Boys and girls all around Cairo were at that moment shouting out to parents and running to say things like, "Mama! Papa! The kitten is all right! The dog is fine! The horse is back on his feet! The goats look normal!"

Farmers were uttering prayers of thanks. Old men were holding the cat or dog they thought they had almost lost to some strange and sudden disorder. Shock, fear, and panic were giving way to relief and joy and a confused gladness at what now had happened.

At The Cairo Veterinary Clinic's large outbuilding, fifteen stunned guards, veterinarians, and animal keepers who had just experienced moments of panic and confusion now stood suddenly speechless as they watched what, moments before, had been scores of inexplicably and severely stricken animals begin to come back to life and return quickly to their normal behavior.

Rubi An'am, the seasoned government agent who was at this point in charge of the entire operation at the clinic, had seen the animals stricken and then had been attacked, himself, seconds later. He had experienced the most severe pain of his life, far worse than a gunshot wound or vicious knife attack, with a hot, blistering, searing sensation in his head that had rendered him temporarily unconscious and on the ground. It was now that he also came to, and realized what was happening all around him. He turned to the guard next to him and said, "What is it, my friend, that we've all just witnessed and experienced?"

"I don't know," the man had said, barely able to speak at all.

Rubi said, "Incredibly intense pain and moments of something like a plague have been erased as if by a miracle!"

What could have been a terrible loss was powerfully prevented. It indeed appeared that a miracle had intervened and saved many lives from a fate that otherwise had seemed imminent. And a miracle just as big, or bigger, would soon be needed back in the open country near Dromeda where even more would soon be at stake.

32

The Strangest Thing

The king was right. It took less than an hour for the group of Phi and their accompanying soldiers to get to the edge of what had to be Santiago's compound. There was a gate across the small road and a wall topped with barbed wire stretching out a great distance to the east and west. They broke two locks and opened the large gate and began to move forward, passing by scrub trees and bushes, along with berms of sand on each side of the private road that now allowed their entrance. There was a small building, like a guardhouse, inside the gate. A quick inspection showed it to be empty and recently abandoned. There were many twists and turns of the road, possibly to slow down any visitors and also, most likely, to impede any view of what lay ahead.

Around the last curve and between the sand berms, the strangest thing came into view. As the king signaled for all to stop, they could now see what seemed to be an abandoned village, a cluster of buildings that looked … exactly like Dromeda, but perhaps on a slightly smaller scale. There were the same houses, and what looked like the same shops—a copy of the general store and the bookshop and the leather and sandal shop, and even a public well just like the one at the center of their village. There was a replica of the medical clinic that Rumi and Hamid had set up long ago. An additional oddity was that the buildings all looked to be as old as the originals, which, of course, couldn't have been true. It was an eerie reflection of their home, a near duplicate of the community where the current monarch and senior member of Phi, and the young prince and others, had lived in exile for so many years. A strange feeling overtook everyone.

Ali and the others were silent for a few moments, taking it all in as far, at least, as their current positions along the road would allow them to see. "Search building by building, inside each structure" the king then told the soldiers. "Split into two groups and go up both sides of the road at the same time. And at each building, once you've confirmed no one there, mark a zero on the front near the door, and put a vertical slash through it, so it won't be mistaken by anyone for a simple circle—Is that clear?" Walid looked at Mafulla and he met the prince's glance. The king was clearly sending a message to anyone who might come here later, and especially to any of the recent residents who could possibly return in the coming days.

The soldiers nodded their understanding of the king's instructions. Their top officer said, "Yes, Your Majesty!" and then he turned and assigned the men to two groups. He led one group, and his second in command led the other, respectively, to each of the first two houses.

"Masoon, I'll proceed straight down the road with our Alexandrian friends. You take Layla, Omari, Mafulla, and Hasina around behind the buildings on the left. Hamid, you can take Walid, Kissa, Paki, and Amon with you around and behind the buildings to the right. We're searching for people or animals, or anything to give us more of a sense of what this place is, why it's here, and what's been going on in it. Be careful, in case any hostile forces are still around."

Walid came up close to the king and quietly said, "Your Majesty, as you know, I tend to work really well with Mafulla."

"Yes, you do," the king replied. "And that's important. But it's also vital for you to become accustomed to working closely with others in a situation of uncertainty like this. And the two of you help to balance the two groups."

"Yes, sir." Walid nodded his understanding and went back to

join Hamid. And so the search began. There was an odd and complete silence in the mysterious village as they first began to move through it. It was almost as if the wind was afraid to blow. They could see and hear no signs of life at all. But then, as the king and his senior Phi friends rode slowly down the center road, after a couple of minutes, a few slight, very faint and muffled sounds from the distance began to peel back the otherwise enveloping quiet.

Walid turned to Paki and in a low voice, he said, "This is so weird. They've replicated our village. They've made a copy of it in pretty much every detail." He pointed and said, "I mean, there's my house, looking just like my house looks, and we just passed a duplicate of the Maayuf home. I can see Hamid's house down the way—an exact copy of it. What in the world have these people been doing, and why have they been doing it?"

"This is indeed puzzling, and even disturbing," Paki said. "It's like everyone's privacy has been violated in the strangest possible way. It's eerie."

"I had the same thought," Walid agreed.

Paki then added, "It's almost as if someone was seeking to perform a dark magic here, and we're intervening before it could be fully completed—or at least, that's what I hope."

Mafulla, a distance away at this point, out of sight, and in Masoon's group, said to Hasina, "I have no idea what's going on here, but it looks like somebody picked up Dromeda and put it back down in this spooky, isolated place."

"Yeah," Hasina said. "It's just the strangest thing. It makes me feel really weird."

The search went on, as quickly as it could be carried out, while still being thorough. No sign of anyone was detected anywhere. The king and his small group rode to the far end of the village and saw that beyond what was the northern edge of town back in Dromeda, there were here several large buildings unlike anything in the original site. The closest of them was just across a low stonewall that marked something like the natural border of the replica village, and located a bit farther back. These structures were the source of the sounds that the king and his senior Phi had barely been hearing, now and then. And as they drew near, the noises grew a bit louder, but they were still heavily muffled.

The king dismounted, and so did his colleagues. They approached the first and largest structure cautiously and very slowly. Before they got all the way there, Masoon had appeared a short distance away on their left with his group, and Hamid was moving up on the right, from behind them, followed closely by Walid and Paki. Kissa was taking her horse around the front, or south side of the building, toward Hasina and Layla. The two groups of soldiers were also emerging from the last of the homes in the village, with their report ready that there had been no people or any signs of ongoing occupation to be seen in any of the structures. The soldiers had, unfortunately, missed something important that had been left behind, in many of the buildings, but that had been so well hidden as to escape any quick detection.

Amon rode up toward the king and dismounted as Ali had, but then quickly jogged to where the king now stood, very close to the building. "Your Majesty!"

"Yes?"

"Please approach this structure with caution."

"I will, just as we've moved through the entire village so far," the king said.

"No, Your Majesty, I mean with even extra caution," Amon said. "I just sense something awaiting us."

The king looked at him inquiringly, and the seasoned veteran explained, "Remember that this man, Santiago, just tried to kill all the animals in and around Cairo that he couldn't have. Now, it sounds like we're about to discover other animals, here in these buildings. He wouldn't want us to have those, either. And, unlike the ones in Cairo, he had physical access to these."

"But they sound very much alive," the king said.

"Yes, for now, and perhaps that was meant to continue, in case his men had stopped us on the road. But if we seek to open the building, he may have something planned for killing them all, and likely us along with them. And, having personally experienced what I once suffered by being the first to walk through a doorway that had been rigged with a bomb, I know that it will pay us to be extremely careful about how we open and seek to enter this building."

"This is a very good point, Amon, and I thank you for reminding us at a crucial moment, before any of us might have blundered into such a predicament. Your unfortunate experience now serves us well."

This discussion was taking place now on the right, or eastern side, of the building. Because of where the king and Amon stood, they didn't have a good view of the left, or western, side, and hadn't seen Mafulla, Kissa, and Hasina, now on foot, approaching the structure.

Hasina said, "Mafulla, there are animals in there—I can tell there are a lot of them—and it sounds like they're in some sort of agitation or even distress. We should do something."

"Yeah. You're right."

"There's a door over there. I can just see it behind that pile of hay. It might not be locked."

Kissa interrupted. "I think we should let the king decide what to do."

"Yes, definitely, but you know he'd never want any creatures to suffer unnecessarily," Hasina replied. She then whispered, "Listen!" They all became quiet and heard what sounded like a small dog in pain right inside the door.

Mafulla grimaced and said, "The rest of the group may have already entered the building from the other side, so maybe it won't be wrong for us to take a little initiative and stop whatever's going on right inside this door. It could be that a poor dog is caught on something."

"He's yelping and howling like he's in pain," Hasina said with urgency in her voice.

Kissa turned and looked back at Masoon and Layla, who had, at this point, walked back a distance to examine something at the side of the closest village building, probably about twenty yards from them. She said, "Let me first get Layla," and she moved away toward where Layla and Masoon were standing together, bent over now and looking at something. She didn't realize that Mafulla and Hasina had not heard her clearly. And with her back turned to them now, she couldn't see that they were already walking up to the door in question, and then moving some of the bales of hay that were in front of it. Within seconds, it was unobstructed.

The king was thinking about what Amon has just said, and was waiting for Hamid and Paki to make their way to where they now stood. Paki had the most experience with explosives and potentially booby-trapped situations. But as Ali stood there, his mouth suddenly became dry. A strong sensation instantly swept through his mind and heart—a sense of something like dire urgency and the strong possibility of impending disaster and death. Without a conscious thought in his mind, and with no time for questions or emotions that would not be of any help here, he reached up and grabbed a thin chain that had been around his neck, inconspicuously, all day long.

In Cairo, right after they left Jabari's house together, Malik and Haji had walked with Hoda to the university library and retrieved from the librarian the book that had been written by Professor Arib. They all sat down at a large table in a quiet area with no one else around, and Hoda began to read as quickly as she could. The boys couldn't believe how fast she seemed able to take in each page. In a very short time, she had caught up to where they had left off and was going much farther into the book. Her intense focus had made this remarkable speed of reading and understanding possible.

Meanwhile, Malik and Haji, at her request, had found the professor's other book and the articles they had looked over, earlier. She put the two of them back on the task of searching there for anything that might be helpful and could possibly shed more light on what was being planned by their adversaries. After about thirty more minutes of speed-reading, Hoda looked up at the boys and said, "The cats weren't really running things, but they seemed to be at one point because they were the most intelligent of the animals that are going to play a part in this story. But the important thing is that the book, at the point I've gotten to, has now alluded to an ancient story known as the legend of the monster."

She briefly told the boys the story. And they were amazed. "This book tells that story?" Malik asked.

"It alludes to it in many ways," Hoda said. "And it talks about a man who will seek to exploit the mental and spiritual openness of animals. He will gather them around him in large numbers and try to find a way for them to magnify his power."

"How could anyone do that?" Haji now asked.

Hoda said, "The power we're talking about is a spiritual power, an ability to draw on spiritual resources, and in this case, without moral constraint, to raise yourself in the world and impose your will on others. This is what the monster of legend seeks, so that he can have his revenge on those who hurt and offended him—and on everyone else."

"Why everyone else?" Haji asked.

"It's apparently for the simple sin of not stopping his tormentors when he was young and, more broadly, just for being—in his opinion—exactly like them."

"Oh."

"This book makes it clear, as far as I've read, that once the monster adopts such a strategy, he won't let anyone stand in his way. And we're seeing such a thing reflected in our experience. That's why you were attacked today."

"Wait. You mean that the professor was writing in this book about that old legend, and the legend has now come true, at least in part, and there really is such a man behind all the crimes that have been taking place?"

"Yes. That's what I think," Hoda intimated. "That's the power we were up against earlier, and to turn it back, we got help from strong forces, the king and Layla and their friends, I believe."

"Oh, man," Malik said. "So, we've made a powerful monster mad?"

"Yes. But what was the alternative?"

"Good point."

"We do what we have to do to resist evil, and that sometimes puts us into a vulnerable position; but, so be it," she stated. "Personal safety is important, but it's not the only important thing in the world. We sometimes have to make ourselves vulnerable in order to protect or save those who are more vulnerable."

"What else does the book say in the parts we didn't get to?"

"Only what I already suspected, that the person who's doing this will never allow his animal spirits to be taken from him and remain alive in this world. If he can't have them, no one can. Plus, he'll seek to kill anyone who stands in the way of his plans."

"Ok, that's bad," Malik said.

"What's really bad is that it's now clear the legend as a whole has always been a prophecy. We have reason to believe that the monster has come to life in all the relevant details, fully real, after all the centuries through which the story has been told. The monster now does in fact exist. He's been behind all the animal abductions. He's collected many of them at a remote place far from here. And that place is where Kissa and your friends are, right now. And they may have to stand up to him, physically and spiritually."

"Really?" Haji said.

"The monster has a compound somewhere near Dromeda," Hoda explained, "And our friends are going to go there, or are already there and are trying to stop him. And he plans to kill all of them."

"What can we do?" Malik asked.

"Is there anything?" Haji said.

"Yes, there is, and I feel that it's needed soon, any second now, so please, where we sit, join me in sending a message to the king, with your minds, a message of warning and protection."

"How should we do it?"

"Concentrate with your whole being. Project thoughts of protection toward the king and Walid and Kissa and Hasina and the others."

"Ok. We can do that."

"Focus with all your whole mind and heart."

At the large building just beyond the mysterious village, Mafulla reached toward the door handle, intent on saving whatever animal was in such distress, and pulled on it. It wasn't locked. But it was attached by a wire to a very large explosive device sitting next to several big fuel tanks full of gasoline, sufficient to kill in a large radius anyone who was so unfortunate as to be near. The entire building would shortly turn into one huge detonating bomb, eliminating all life in it or near it. And, in addition, there were other fuel tanks, and secondary incendiary and explosive devices, in the other buildings close by. Nothing short of a complete and utter devastation had been planned and orchestrated here by the previous main resident, all prepared for and awaiting the moment when someone would open a door to one of these buildings in order to rescue their residents.

Time and space are interesting dimensions for life in the world. We're often separated from people who need our help—by one or the other, or both—and it's up to us somehow to bridge that distance. We do what we can. We pray. We send thoughts of love and comfort. We even seek to commune and assist, spirit to spirit. But we typically lack the knowledge or the skill to intervene directly across these cosmic dimensional chasms that seem to separate us.

At the precise moment that Mafulla touched the door handle and exerted the very beginning of force on it, in order to pull it open, Walid began to call out his name. King Ali quickly pulled up the slender silver chain that was around his neck and slipped his finger through the white gold and platinum ring that was on it. And, in the same rapid movement, he twisted the double braided movable bands in the middle of the ring.

At this point, the king knew how to use the famous and widely feared ring without necessarily incurring terrible consequences as a result. Secret passages within The Book of Phi that he had finally been able to decipher had recently taught him. Without these secrets, any use of the ring could be disastrous for the user, despite the fact that it was almost certain to secure any other intent that he or she might have focused on. But by using the secret instructions, it was at least possible that a heavy cost for its use might be avoided.

And yet, the king still didn't know what precisely would result. He knew, or at least suspected that in some way, time would be stopped or at least vastly slowed, and that physical space and distance would mean almost nothing—or at least something quite different from what they normally mean. He had to trust that, when the Ring of Phi was used, it would allow him to avert the impending disaster, and the catastrophic death of his friends. And in that moment, to that extent, he believed it would help to preserve the order of goodness that's always struggling to prevail in our world and that, he was convinced, one day will ascend and envelop all.

For Mafulla, the next sliver of a moment bore within itself the single most extraordinary experience of his life. As he pulled a bit more on the door to the large building in front of him, his normal everyday consciousness vanished in the blink of an eye. It was as if a mighty windstorm surrounded his soul and plunged him into an inner darkness, and caught him up in a swirling vortex of power that lifted him out of the matrix of normal reality. He felt no emotions in that instant except that, in what would have seemed to be a mere echo or shadow of his soul, there was a curious objective noting of this unparalleled feeling and the movement it involved. Then, there was nothing. Nothing.

Right behind him, Hasina's full, alert consciousness was instantly extinguished without any shred of a shadow, or of any immediate intervening experience. Just like when a light switch is flipped, the light of her eyes and mind were shut off.

Kissa had not made it far enough away to escape the exact same thing. But even if she had gotten all the way to Layla and Masoon, it would have made no difference, for they too were swept up and blinked out in that first twinkling of a moment. Walid never got the entirety of Mafulla's name out of his mouth, which he was in the process of shouting, without even really knowing why. His senses simultaneously shut off, and his conscious thoughts were no more.

The king experienced something similar to what Mafulla had felt in that initial instant, but for him there was a long drawn out moment, pulled and stretched like the most flexible taffy. And during that enormously elongated instant, he was able somehow to see a swirl of bodies all around him, and he watched them as they seemed to disintegrate and vanish in front of his eyes, blinked from the contents of reality and yet, despite the evidence of this seemingly apocalyptic event, he remained strong and calm and focused, and even strangely confident and at peace.

If an airplane had been flying overhead, the pilot would have witnessed an enormous flash and a fireball unlike anything that had ever been seen in the entire north of Africa, or even across the globe, throughout the preceding centuries, or in fact during the entire multi-millennial sweep of history up until that moment. If the plane itself could have survived the event, the now stunned pilot would have been able to see nothing but utter devastation and debris and fires scattered about where buildings and stores and roads and homes had been. And there would be no trace of any people or animals, alive or dead, nearby—not even the ashes of their existence.

There are many unknowns in death. There are just as many in life. The entire sphere of existence is much more complex and surprising and extraordinary than our daily habits of thought and emotion ever allow us to glimpse. One aspect of the fellowship of the mind that Walid and Mafulla had experienced for a little more than a year with King Ali and all the Phi they had come to know, was that they had often caught hints, now and then, of this vastness and complexity. They appreciated that it was there. And they believed that there are forces to be drawn upon that are far greater than any that might ever be widely manifest in the total sweep of what we call normal life.

If we could only draw on these forces, fully and completely, they had each thought, on one occasion or another, imagine the tremendous things that could happen. We need to learn how to do so. We need to discover how to harness all the incredible resources that are always deeply available to us.

The mysterious village as a whole had disappeared into tiny shards of splintered and burning rubble. The intensity of the fireball had even melted things that the average observer would have thought incapable of such a state. Sand had turned into glass in many places and now under the still glaring sun of the day it blindingly reflected the shocking absence of what most recently had been.

But the strangest thing of all was that this one moment whose very first touch had ignited all of this, and had itself as a result been melted and stretched and pulled into something unexpected, would also have to come to an end, as all moments in time eventually do. And the next moment would be history's judgment on what Mafulla had done, and what the king, in turn, had attempted in his anticipatory response.

It's difficult to find words for what the consequence was in that next moment. Not even the king could have anticipated it. But, as the American philosopher Ralph Waldo Emerson had written, years before, "Life is full of surprises."

33

The Aftermath

There was a warp within the overall weave of cosmic space-time, an opening and interruption, a gap or delay of sorts, and it allowed for an abrupt transformation akin, in terms of its qualitative extremity, to what had been sought in the wildest dreams of alchemists throughout the centuries. But this metaphysical mutation was in a different mode and on a vastly bigger scale than anything the ancient spiritual quest of the extraordinary had ever envisioned. A hole in the space-time continuum had just opened up, for the least particle of a moment, and something radical was happening in and through it.

This is not supposed to be possible. But that's judging it from what we currently have as a purely physical point of view, and more than known physics was now in play. The deepest spiritual realm had intervened. And as a result, strange and radical things happened.

Very few people on earth would be able in any way to sense this going on, but every Phi alive felt something at that instant, however subtle or startling. Even a few other spiritually sensitive people detected something. Hoda, sitting at the library table in Cairo, had a sensation like a quick electric current pass through her body and soul at that precise point in time. Her eyelids jumped open, wide. Her mind was on high alert. Her heart rate shot up. She reached out and gently grabbed the hands of Malik and Haji. They both looked at her, startled, and were struck with an inner jab of confusion.

Rumi and Bhati were standing in the house in Dromeda, the real Dromeda, and he reached out to hold her shoulder. Their eyes met and they each had the strangest sensation either had ever felt. Bhati said, "What is it?" But Rumi couldn't answer. He just listened with all his body and soul, as if to hear. His spirit reached out. And then he heard. And she did, too.

Outside their home, the little dog had just barked twice. He got up slowly from the sand where he had lay down to rest, and he began to trot unsteadily up the road to the north end of the village. He was limping forward about as fast as he could go. Gimpy somehow knew.

Hoda's old friend Theta felt it strongly as she sat in meditation. Her experience of the anomaly was akin to seeing a blazing sun suddenly appear for a second, pop out of existence in the next moment, and then just as fully reappear. Her eyes opened. But her heartbeat stayed soft and slow and measured. Otherwise without bodily reaction, she turned over her hands, resting now open and facing upward on her knees.

The moment was experienced in various widely different ways by other Phi in the kingdom and beyond. Some felt emotions. Others just found themselves suddenly stopping whatever they were doing and spontaneously saying, in their innermost thoughts, "Something just happened." But at once, all senior Phi sent forceful thoughts of support and protection out to wherever they were needed. Prayers were uttered. Power was invoked. A cushion of goodness was provided.

Reela Adi was in the middle of writing a letter and suddenly jerked his fountain pen up from the thick white sheet of paper on the desk pad in front of him and quickly glanced out the window near where he sat, as if he'd be able to see something outside. But he knew that nothing in the immediate environment had just grabbed his attention. He sensed the cosmic shift as it occurred and felt that something completely unparalleled had just happened. He had no idea what. There was no emotion or alarm in his soul. He merely sat for a moment, motionless, soaking in the gravity of something's just having transpired on the level and monumental scale that this thing, whatever it was, must be.

At the remote area in the far west of the kingdom where the normal fabric of reality was briefly pulled asunder, it was almost as if everyone in the king's group had ceased to be for the merest speck of time and then immediately ... came back, and with full, complete consciousness, almost as if nothing had happened. Their fleeting, utter loss of awareness and sensations of any kind had not altered their bodily positions or ongoing movements in the least, which continued on for a flash as they had been in the previous, thinnest slice of an instant. But then, at the next hint of time's elapse, anyone who had been in motion now found that he or she had stopped, still, almost as if temporarily frozen in place.

There was a moment of utter astonishment followed by a near total confusion. Everything felt the same as in the instant before. And yet, there were no buildings in front of them, or anywhere near them. Mafulla's hand was out to pull a door open that was no longer there. He could see the king standing on what had just before been the other side of the building that now didn't exist. They were in open land, but between Mafulla and the king, and stretching to Mafulla's left, there were lots of animals of many kinds—standing, or lying, or sitting as they presumably had been in the previous moment, in the building that was no longer around them. There was a small dog near Mafulla, three feet in front of him, who had just yelped, but now stopped short of continuing with any noise, through sheer shock and fright. He was looking quickly around and breathing fast.

"What?" is all that Mafulla could say in the complete disorientation of this newly minted moment. The sound of his one word was followed by the distinctive concussive roar and noise of a gigantic explosion in the far distance, somehow itself composed of many large explosions, together creating a huge storm and rumble that rolled through the air and across the sand and brought its unique aural signature forcefully to their ears. For a split second, in a brilliant flash, the level of already bright daylight around them seemed to increase. And the ground shook under their feet.

Juan Santiago was too far away by this time to hear the explosion as they had, but he still knew when it happened. He simply sensed it. And yet, what he thought would bring him a sharp, sweet sense of vengeance had no such effect at all. Instead, his reaction to the knowledge that the giant network of explosive devices throughout his village had been activated was marred by a sense that something was deeply, and from his point of view, terribly wrong. Right before knowing of the explosion, he had felt a twinge of realization that something outside the realm of his power had taken place at a fundamental level, and his immediate reaction was to suspect that this, somehow, would not be good for him or his plans or hopes in any way at all.

It took everyone within sight of the king a couple of seconds to realize that they were all standing exactly as they had been right before whatever just happened, with their horses and camels near them, but that there were no longer any large buildings in front of them. The big structures that had just dominated their attention and interest, and that had muffled the sounds of many captive animals, did not now seem to exist. They had simply disappeared.

All the animals that had been in the buildings right outside the mysterious village were now standing, lying, and sitting on the sand, out in the open, but just as they had been inside the buildings where they had been kept for a time as sequestered prisoners. Most of the group with the king looked around quickly to appraise their situation, and those who turned their heads toward the village could now see the village trees and all its buildings a short distance away, still standing, looking normal. And at a distance, in various parts of the village, they could now see some people outside, gazing west, northwest, in the direction of the flash and rumble that had just been created, and then within seconds, walking on, some talking, and others apparently going about their business after a moment's perplexity and paused curiosity.

The people in the village for some reason apparently had not yet noticed the exceedingly odd sight slightly to their north and east that consisted of some very confused Phi and a number of shocked military men, now standing silently a short distance beyond the village with a great number and variety of strangely quiet animals in their immediate proximity. And, mere seconds before, there would have been no such things there to see. It had been just open land, devoid of people and animals, featuring only featureless sand.

The king slowly smiled and raised his right hand toward the animals, scores of them near to him, and he said aloud, "Peace. Be still." He then slid the Ring of Phi off his finger and tucked it under his clothing once more. He looked around him and visually checked on each of his colleagues. "Is everyone all right?" he asked, in a louder voice.

"What … just happened?" Mafulla responded, with an extreme degree of puzzlement in his tone.

"Your Majesty," Masoon said, now taking Layla by the arm and walking with her quickly in the king's direction. As he approached Kissa, he also took her by the arm and steered the ladies toward the king. Then he remembered and turned back and waved to the stunned soldiers to come over and join them. Those men were looking about with utter bafflement on their faces but, following his signaled command, they too walked slowly in the direction of Ali.

Walid could hardly think, he was so muddled and thrown off kilter by all that he was now seeing, and what he had just experienced. Hamid touched his arm and so did Paki, and they led him closer to the king, who was still standing beside Amon.

Mafulla now approached with Hasina. When everyone had gathered near the king, Ali said, "Friends. A blessed and extraordinary thing has just happened and has saved us all from a conflagration of immense magnitude, and an untimely departure from this world. Amon warned me seconds ago, as we stood by the large building outside the mysterious replica village, that it was likely booby-trapped and filled with explosives. And from what we've just seen and heard, he was right."

"But what's going on?" Walid said in a tone of perplexity, and almost to no one in particular.

"It was me, again!" Mafulla exclaimed, hardly even able to believe that, once more, he had been responsible for setting off a major explosion, and this time a truly monumental one, from what they had just heard and felt.

"You acted to save an animal in distress," the king replied.

"How did you know?"

"I just did. And I knew that you didn't anticipate the trap. I had only a part of a moment to act to save that animal, and all the animals, and you, and the rest of us, as well. So I did."

The soldiers at this point looked like they didn't understand in the least what they were hearing, but they were silent, as they felt they should be in the presence of the king. Ali turned in their direction. "I must now speak for a moment to you men who serve in our military. There are forces in this world that go far beyond what we normally encounter, experience, and understand. I'm greatly blessed. I've been taught about these things from my childhood, and introduced to them, and trained in their access and benevolent use. I ask you to trust me in what I'm about to say, just as you would in more ordinary times." He paused for a moment to look around at their faces.

"I can tell you and explain to you only that the power and knowledge granted to me, as a result of my lifelong training, was just now used to prevent a great wrong, and to save all our lives. I would ask further that you not seek to know everything behind this event—or talk about the more unusual aspects of it that we have just lived through. Who would believe you, or any of us? Please consider it to be something like a national security secret. Your lives have been saved, and your part now is to keep in your heart, and preserve within you, whatever you have seen of the secret manner by which that has happened."

The king again paused and examined the faces of the stunned

soldiers. He went on. "You may tell anyone the truth that we fought violent enemies today and found our adversary Santiago's compound, and that we are now back. You can even describe what you saw there—to any of your friends and loved ones, if you like. And you may tell them that we were able to rescue all the animals that were being kept there, before explosives that the man had set destroyed the entire compound and village. And you can say that we brought the animals quickly back to Dromeda to be cared for until they can be restored to their proper owners and families."

He gestured to the nearby houses and stores and road and said, "This … is the real Dromeda that we left hours ago, in case you haven't realized that already. It's not the mysterious village we were just visiting. We've returned, rather suddenly." He smiled. "And we've come back in an unusual way. But we're here. We're indeed back. And I can assure you that the village of Santiago's compound, and the animal containment buildings there, have been totally destroyed, absolutely obliterated, to the extent that no one will be able to put together the puzzle of what once was there, if they had not already seen it."

Everyone continued to stay quiet and listen. Ali now placed his hands together. He said, "I give thanks that we've been brought safely back to this special place where our friends await us. You've served bravely today. I will ask you, our military men, to go now, get your colleagues who remained here, and ask them to help you find places in and around the village for these animals to be kept, for the present. I know that we'll receive plenty of assistance in town to care for them until they can be returned to their proper homes. And some belong here." The soldiers responded to the king's instruction, and at an inviting motion of his hand, they turned to walk together back into the village, speaking softly among themselves about the wonders that had just, somehow, come to be.

Ali then turned his attention back to his Phi friends and said, "The rest of you, dear friends, please walk with me now among the animals. They will be very quiet and sedate for a time, yet, and that will allow us to move between them without disturbing their rest. I've asked them to be calm for us, and they know they're our beneficiaries, and are grateful for what's been done to save them, so I'm sure they'll comply. We need to count them. We need to know how many species we have here, and how many of each, and we need a total number. I'll ask all of you to begin to look over them while I consult for a moment with Walid. Take a deep breath now and clear your heads. And I thank you, again, for your vital role in today's challenging events."

Masoon began to lead the ladies and Mafulla to walk through all the resting animals. And Hamid did the same with the Alexandrians, and Paki and Omari.

Walid moved in close to the king and asked in a very low voice, "Did you use the ring?"

"Yes, I did. And it was instantly effective in a most surprising way."

"That's for sure," Walid replied.

And, at that second, Mafulla changed direction and walked quickly back over to where he had initially been standing when he went to open the door of the animal building. He looked more closely at the little dog, now lying down and facing away from him, the animal whose yelps and cries had set all this into motion.

"Hey buddy," Mafulla said, as he looked down at him. You don't seem injured or hurt in any way at all. Are you Ok?" Then he stepped toward the dog's face and bent down a little and stared for a second and said, "Wait. No way. I mean, really. It can't be. Is it … you?"

The little dog whimpered what Mafulla could only interpret as a yes. Then he bent down more toward the animal and, to his further astonishment, the small cur let out a low, nasty sounding growl.

Mafulla stood there, completely stunned, for a moment more. Then he turned toward his best friend, who was now a bit of a distance away.

"Walid!" The prince looked over. Mafulla pointed down, and shouted, "We found … Yippers!" And Walid couldn't help but laugh, big and long, in a new sort of astonishment.

APPENDIX

The Diary of Walid Shabeezar
Animals and Kindred Spirits

I've been better about keeping my diary recently. But I've also realized that to use journaling or diary writing well, you don't necessarily have to do it every day—just when you have something worth writing down. But never let a good insight pass without recording it. That's the secret. Then, over time, you get better about having more new insights. It's like your mind realizes, "Hey, I take this wisdom stuff seriously enough to write it down!" And then the unconscious shares with the conscious mind more freely. Or at least, that's the way it seems to work for me.

Δ Δ Δ

Life is like a puzzle. The sooner you begin to figure it out, the better off you are. Many situations are like that, too: puzzles within the bigger puzzle. Pay attention to the details and patterns emerge.

A friend can bring you support and fun, deliverance and delight.

Creativity costs nothing and adds value to everything.

Nothing has quite the dramatic effect of a great pair of sunglasses.

Sometimes, a small gift can have big consequences.

Working out hard is paying off plenty. I can tell I'm getting stronger almost every week. There are a few guarantees in life like that: Work your muscles, and you make them stronger. Leave them alone, and they get weaker. I guess your mind is the same—intellect, imagination, and memory. Work it all to grow it all. And work hard!

Maybe every friendship is like that, too. You're either making it stronger or weaker by what you do or don't do. Remember that. Everything makes a difference.

I've heard older people say, as a sort of joke, that there are two things you can always count on: death and taxes. Maybe crime is a third. Stupidity might be a fourth, and it could be that greed is a fifth. There are lots of interconnections here.

ΔΔΔ

When you want to do something good, it's often useful to get help.

Many minds and hands share the load and ease the burden. An old proverb says, "Like iron sparks iron, so one man sparks another." That, of course, holds for women, too. Partners can inspire us.

Mafulla gave me a couple of great early birthday presents by enlisting the help of the king, Darwishi, Mahmood, Paki, and some guy who knows some other guy in New Jersey. Who would have guessed? Help comes from surprising places. But you have to ask.

The Law of Unintended Consequences: Our actions often have unexpected results, and sometimes these surprises can undermine what we were trying to make happen.

The best way to avoid unintended consequences is to think things through as carefully and well as you can before taking major action.

A Good General Rule is this: Think through it before you do it!

Animal friends may be just as important in life as human friends, and we often take them for granted. There's a lot they can give us and teach us.

My old friend Cammo the camel recognized me today. And we had a great ride, despite a little excitement with some outlaws.

Mafulla was funny on our adventure, saying "Good camel" over and over to his ride whose name was Clyde. And later, I was thinking, Clyde ended up being a good camel. Maybe, if we want other people to be good and strong, we should communicate to them that this is what we believe they already are, deep inside.

Build people up. Don't tear people down: Words and actions matter.

∆ ∆ ∆

Trust your instincts. You have them for a reason. They're not guaranteed to be right. But they can teach you something important about yourself, and often about the world around you.

The Triple Double for Dealing with Trouble always helps! Prepare, Perceive; Anticipate, Avoid; Concentrate, Control.

Not every good plan works. But a good plan is better than no plan.

Some actions have consequences that can never be undone. Be extra cautious before launching into one of them.

Never rush forward on first appearances when you don't have to. And remember that you rarely have to.

Situations can seem urgent when they're not. Don't let pressure call the shots when you should be doing that yourself.

Stress can make a mess. Don't let it. Give yourself the gift of inner calm.

∆ ∆ ∆

Friends come into our lives for many reasons and bring us many benefits. We need to be grateful for every real friend we have.

A good friend is a source of guidance and strength.

Emotions can block, muddy, or even hijack our deeper intuitions. Calmness allows for clarity.

Our feelings can blind us to the obvious. They can also open us up. How we use them is key.

We always want to know. And that's generally good. But sometimes, not knowing may be exactly what we need. It's only within a cloud of confusion, or under a veil of ignorance, that we're forced to dig deep and develop some qualities of character that make us stronger.

Remember to remember what you know. Remember also to remember what you don't.

△ △ △

The fabric of life is woven through with a bright thread of surprise.

There are other guys out there doing what I do. There are others fighting crime in masks. If they're good, then we're all better off.

Be careful building a road in the desert. You give yourself an endless job. That's a nice metaphor. Some goals, if achieved, will create much more work for you than you might imagine. Think it through.

Men and women often seem to approach life differently. But that's fine. We need to hear different opinions to make sure we're not missing an important perspective.

I hope that, if one day I become a father, I can laugh as much, and have as much fun, as Mafulla's dad. He's a really good example.

Δ Δ Δ

Malik helped me realize something today. Animals have a lot more intelligence and emotional life than most people think.

Animals suffer stress and trauma just like humans. They need kindness and consideration, just like we do.

We should always act so as to honor our fellow creatures.

The earth is not ours, alone. We share it with all the species of living creatures. We have a duty to them as well as ourselves to keep the world in good shape.

Good housekeeping is important at every level of life, from your room to your world.

There's much more mind and soul in nature than we think. In fact, mind may undergird and somehow touch almost everything.

Δ Δ Δ

Girls can take care of business. Some guys tried to steal Shibby, Kissa's dog, and Kissa and Hasina stopped them cold.

Never underestimate girl power.

I have to admit that I sometimes forget what the women Phi can do. They're definitely equal partners with the guys. And they have their own strengths that we may never be able to match.

△△△

Dualists believe that both minds and bodies exist, mental and material stuff. Monists think that only one sort of stuff is real: typically either matter or mind. There are a lot more materialists in the written history of philosophy, perhaps, than idealists (the mind monists). But matter isn't at all like what they thought it was in the ancient world, and even until recently. Maybe matter is more like the mental and mind is more like the material than anyone ever realized. And, yeah, this all gets a little complicated.

Wouldn't it be wild if, at the deepest levels, there is very little difference between mind and matter, if ideas and energies are more alike than we think? Or maybe they're quite different, but strangely and powerfully compatible, and more closely linked than we imagine, so that mind is more pervasive and active in the physical universe than we think. It could be that matter is more permeable by mind than most people would ever guess. There's a lot to think about here.

Are the dimensions of space and time objectively real, or dependent somehow on something else that is matter, or mind, or God?

Proof and truth don't always walk hand-in-hand. Some truth may elude proof forever. And that might be because of the nature of each.

It amazes me how much our minds can understand, and that we still have limits beyond which understanding likely can't go. We all live within limits. But they make us what we are, within what's limitless. Everything alive is circumscribed.

Artificial limits confine us. Real limits define us. We need to break through all the false barriers in order to get to our true nature.

We may have very few real limits. But there are endless false ones. Telling the difference is crucial.

We can ask questions that we can't answer. And even when we can come up with answers, they're most often harder to formulate than the questions were. It takes hard work and persistence. I think I've thought about this before. But I need the reminder. Maybe we all do.

Maffie and I had a funny conversation about his cologne today that reminded me of the two things I recently read about that were inscribed in marble at the holiest spot in ancient Greece, the Oracle of Delphi: "Know Yourself," and "Nothing in Excess." I'll have to remind Maffie about the second one. I can use that.

Δ Δ Δ

My birthday party was amazing. So far, I think I'm going to like being 14. I guess every age, like every day, has its distinctiveness.

There was a time when I thought birthday parties were frivolous. But now that I've experienced a great one, I realize how nice it was to get together and celebrate with my friends. They were celebrating me, and I was celebrating them!

Having such friends is always a gift worth celebrating!

There are many things to celebrate in life. We should find at least one every day.

Parties are like anything else: Their value lies in how they're done and what role they play in your life.

The king sprang some big stuff on Maffie and me tonight. I maybe shouldn't write down the details, since they came from a coded passage in a secret book, but the basic idea is simple. We tend to think of the material, physical world as huge, and of the realm of the spirit as almost thin by comparison, but the opposite is true.

Spirit is the overarching, undergirding reality enveloping all.

Mind is greater than matter. The spiritual has the most substance. What's personal can prevail over what's physical. The reverse often seems true in the world, but again appearances mislead.

The Golden Ratio, Phi, is found in unexpected places.

We live within mysteries.

Δ Δ Δ

The resources of the mind and spirit are greater than we imagine.

Hope is a bridge to help you get to your real self.

The mere existence of hope may be a sign that we're supported deep down by what's most real.

Those with good intent need to draw deeply on their mental and spiritual resources, and for many reasons. One of those reasons is that individuals with ill intent may do so, and need to be stopped.

What can be used for great good can be used for great harm.

We should adapt and change with changing times, while staying also true to our essence.

Age takes away some things, but it can give you others, if you're spiritually flexible and alert.

The story of Beowulf is a great cautionary tale for powerful people.

Partnership is a key to success. Lone individuals can do much, but collaborations are necessary for meeting major challenges. That's a big lesson from the Beowulf story.

∆ ∆ ∆

When The Wild Camel and The Silver Sabre showed up to help The Golden Viper and Windstorm today, I felt at first like I couldn't have been more surprised. That's what I thought, until I found out who they are. Then, I was even more surprised. They had been so inspired by the Viper and the Storm that I felt bad about having to reveal that those legendary crime fighters were in fact just Maffie and me. I didn't want to take away their inspiration!

Today's Lesson: We can be an inspiration to others in many different ways. Sometimes our deeds can be the most inspiring when we don't take noisy credit for them but do them quietly, or even anonymously. We don't have to leave big footprints in order to do great good.

Today, we started a new collaboration of four friends. I hope we can accomplish surprising things with it.

∆ ∆ ∆

Good humor helps people relax and enjoy themselves. Especially when you're a little nervous at the outset of a new adventure, a little joking never hurts. Baldoor and Dubin reminded me of that today, although Maffie is my ongoing teacher in the psychological uses of jocularity.

A nice ride on a slow camel is great. But sometimes a fast truck is even greater, bumpy though it might be. We should be grateful for the gifts of nature, and for those of technology as well.

Sometimes slow is best. At other times fast is needed. We can't get hooked on one speed or the other. We need to flex to the situation.

There are times when rich experience needs to give way to reasonable efficiency. But then, that's true only when the efficiency ultimately allows in some way for a better and richer experience in the end.

When you think you've seen it all, know this: You haven't.

We had a super strange thing happen tonight. A big fire blazing high suddenly went out, just vanishing, and then a short time later, it burst back into flames. No one had ever seen anything like it before. It could be a warning. In any case, whenever you're in contact with anything unparalleled or unique, caution is often a good guide.

△ △ △

There's an old mystical tradition that says an interrupted fire is a bad omen. A fire on earth has its integrity, however long it lasts, and it undergoes a natural progression. Any time this is violated, powerful forces have to be in play.

Tonight, Layla told us The Legend of the Monster. It was pretty scary—appropriately enough.

The greatest monster is an individual who is on fire with negative, destructive thoughts and feelings, like resentment and hatred, and seeks to use all the knowledge and power he can gain to establish control over others and get revenge.

The monster cares only about power and status and destruction.

△ △ △

Don't worry about what you don't understand. We're always surrounded by what we don't understand. Act on what you do know.

Masoon said something really funny today: "Sometimes I feel like it's raining idiots, and I'm just glad I brought my umbrella."

While watching the camels and horses for a while, an insight really impressed itself on me. We can learn a lot from our animal neighbors if we'll just pay attention and listen, and contemplate what we see and hear. Maybe that's why the ancient writer Aesop used animals in his famous fables. They can be great and vivid teachers.

∆ ∆ ∆

The first time you engage in a demanding physical activity, your body gets sore. The first time you engage in a demanding intellectual activity, your mind gets numb. But this is all necessary for growth. You become stronger and more able through the process.

You can't get big results without tackling big challenges.

We're sometimes called on to be of help and turn back evil, without even knowing exactly what we're to do or how we're to do it. But if we've cultivated our deepest intuitions, we can usually trust how they prompt and guide us to act in the moment, when the moment comes.

I had a very strange experience today, as of fighting back a storm of some sort. It took four of us using our inner power together, as partners, and somehow we did it. It was another lesson in partnership.

Some storms we just have to endure. Others, we can avoid.

Corrupt people can't work well together. Individuals who depart from a moral framework of thought eliminate from their lives certain important inner and outer forms of harmony.

ΔΔΔ

The oasis today reminded me of the trip across the desert with Uncle Ali when the two of us began to talk seriously about life and the mind. On that trip, he told me that I'm a prince and I thought he was just joking. This was the place where it all began.

I talked to the older lady today at the oasis who spoke mysteriously to me on my first camel train. She sometimes sees into the future. Of course, we have no idea how that works, but it does. They call her the lady of the pool, naming her for the nice pool of water, the small pond in the oasis that gives such great refreshment to weary travelers. And that's good because she's given a deep sort of refreshment to me.

The lady predicted that Kissa's dog Shibby will have two healthy boy puppies and two healthy girl puppies. I'm writing this prediction down to remember it and see if it comes true!

ΔΔΔ

The lady of the pool also said to me today: "You will do what you were born to do." I wonder what that is? She added, "Never despair or fear." And I guess that's a good sign, although it does imply dangers.

She also said: "You will always have a choice, even when it seems you don't. Use your power of choice wisely."

I got a message that was dropped from an airplane today. Strange things happen all the time. And then the message was stranger than the delivery of it.

Δ Δ Δ

I've been thinking about Uncle Ali's long letter and what he said about The Great Chain of Being. We like to think of ourselves as the center of the universe and the top of a big chain of value, but this is a gross distortion of reality. To see that and correct it is not in any way to diminish human worth, but is rather to appreciate it more accurately.

I never have to devalue others in order to value myself. In fact, the more I value others properly and see myself in connection with them, the more I'll understand my true value and place in the world.

We are distinctive without being discontinuous with the rest of reality.

We are made of earth, air, fire, and water, just like the animals around us. But we embody these elements in a unique way. And that's true for each of the other creatures, as well.

Δ Δ Δ

It's possible to communicate with animals, mind-to-mind and even heart-to-heart. Few people try it, and even fewer do it, but it can be done, and it can sometimes be important to do. It's my feeling that the animals can also communicate with us, if we're properly receptive. When souls are aligned, there is communion. And the deeper the alignment is, the deeper the communion can be.

Δ Δ Δ

Good friends can be trusted to do good things. When we reach out to them in a spirit of partnership, the results can surprise us.

The story I heard about Malik and Haji today was amazing. They have far surpassed even my wildest dreams about what The Wild

Camel and The Silver Sabre can accomplish. I'm really proud of them. Maybe we can do something that they'll be proud of, too.

The best of friends spur each other to grow and get better.

It pays off to associate with people who inspire you to good deeds and who motivate you to reach higher. Even if there's a little competition in it, that's perfectly Ok. When a relationship is positive and good, friendly competition can be healthy. It drives achievement.

∆ ∆ ∆

Sometimes you just have to trust the people you believe in. It can be hard in certain situations when you'd really rather know and decide for yourself what should happen, but you need to be able to trust the trustworthy at crucial junctures. That's what trust is all about. It's what the idea really means. It's not about believing in people just when it's easy, but especially when it's hard.

We all want to fit in and belong and be appreciated. Insults and harsh put-downs can seem to threaten our social status and sense of belonging. They can also be signals of a deeper danger. So people react to such things with anger, and sometimes violence. But the more spiritually developed we are, the less we're moved or bothered by negative words that are directed at us.

True confidence comes from within. It's a spiritual condition.

Genuinely great people can't be insulted or offended. They're sure of themselves, and of their value. They move through life above the approval or disapproval of the crowd. Their level of attainment is obvious, but it's also without any hint of arrogance.

Those who are easily insulted are not sure of themselves at all. Their self-esteem depends too much on others. They need to find their value within themselves, and in connection with deeper realities.

Most people have no idea of their own inner spiritual greatness. We all have a heritage of infinite value that's ours to claim. When we do claim it, we can be calm and properly self-assured.

∆ ∆ ∆

Preparing to give or receive important help with a difficulty doesn't necessary prevent the challenge or diminish it. But it positions us to make the best of what yet confronts us.

An ambush is an opportunity for creative thinking and courage under fire. Unexpected onslaughts can be met and turned back, but typically, this is done best by cool heads using well-developed skills.

Believing your eyes always involves believing your mind as well. We seldom have raw, pure conscious experience that's untouched and unfiltered by the lens of expectation, prejudice, and interpretation. Because of this, we should not be too quick to accept what our eyes seem to show us, if there's any chance our filter may have distorted what we see. And emotions can be the most distorting forces of all.

I thought I saw that Kissa was shot. I feared she was dead. And she was alive and unharmed, except for being momentarily dazed. The memory makes me shudder and then fills me with relief.

We should never be quick to jump to conclusions.

∆ ∆ ∆

Just when you think that nothing can surprise you, something does.

Avoid intellectual arrogance forever. We know only a fraction of a percentage of what we think we know. But still, we know enough to do what we need to do.

One thing we need to do is stay humble, and open to new light.

We'll never understand everything. And that's Ok. Really, it is.

I'm convinced that understanding one thing is enough to get us through anything: In the end, love conquers all.

Acknowledgments

I'm continually thankful for the process that led to this book. I suspect that many people think of creativity as an iffy or onerous challenge, and perhaps difficult out of all proportion to the ordinary course of work. But it can actually be the easiest thing in the world, once you've mastered a lot of stuff that already exists out there to be known. At its best, creativity is a flow of something outside your conscious mind into the stream of consciousness that we think of as normal thought. It happens like a gift. It's free, when it comes. And it's a great blessing. And so, for it, I'm grateful. I enjoy living with these characters, these people, every day.

I want to thank again everyone who has helped me stay happy and balanced and sociable during the otherwise solitary process of transcribing the ongoing movie in my head that has played for over eighteen months now—and then the light editing that has gone on for years. Especially, thanks to the guys in the gym: Don, Ed, Tom, Michael, Paul, John, and Pam and my many other co-sufferers in the local cathedral of bodily exertion. The exercise of the mind must be balanced each day with that of the body. You guys sure help.

Thanks again to my family and especially Sara Morris for her great cover design work, and to Abigail Chiaramonte for all the other great design elements she brings to these books. I've benefitted from the expert editing advice of Ed Hearn and Bruce May, and from the many philosophical comments of early readers.

I also want to thank my cats, my dogs, and the wild creatures of the land, water, and air around my home for their contribution to the great scheme of things here, as usual. Woof, meow, chirp, tweet, splash and wiggle to you guys, too.

Tom Morris
Wilmington, NC

Afterword

Beyond *The Mysterious Village*

First, there was *The Oasis Within*, a short tale about a series of deep conversations and surprising events that took place as a group of men and camels crossed the desert in Egypt in 1934. Then there was *The Golden Palace*, the official Book One to a series of subsequent stories about these remarkable individuals collectively entitled:

Walid and the Mysteries of Phi

Then came *The Stone of Giza*. Next was *The Viper and The Storm*. Then, *The King and Prince*. This is Book Five in the series. If you've read *The Oasis Within*, or you've enjoyed *The Golden Palace*, *The Stone of Giza*, *The Viper and The Storm*, *The King and Prince*, and the current book, you'll likely love the books to come. All together, they present a sprawling epic account of action, adventure, and ideas set in and around a reimagined Cairo, Egypt in 1934 and 1935, with a few sojourns farther abroad. They will all contain captivating tales about life, death, meaning, love, friendship, the deepest secrets behind everyday events, and the extraordinary power of a well-focused mind. The events they relate will interact with many classics of philosophy and literature. With unexpected humor and continual intrigue, you'll gradually discover in these books the outlines of a powerful worldview and a profound philosophy of life. To find out more, visit **www.TomVMorris.com/novels** or go to **www.TheOasisWithin.com.**

The prologue and companion book to the series, *The Oasis Within*, as well as any book in the series, will be available for large group purchases at special discounts. To find out more, contact the author through his oldest and most reliable email, **TomVMorris@aol.com** or through his website. Tom is also available to speak with book groups via email, Skype, or any other means that would help in the discussion of these stories. Make a request, and talk to the author.

About the Author

Tom Morris is one of the most active public philosophers and business speakers in the world. A native of North Carolina, he's a graduate of The University of North Carolina (Chapel Hill), where he was a Morehead-Cain Scholar, and he holds a Ph.D. in both Philosophy and Religious Studies from Yale University. For fifteen years, he served as a Professor of Philosophy at the University of Notre Dame, where he was one of their most popular teachers. You can find him online anytime at **www.TomVMorris.com.**

Tom has been honored with the University of North Carolina's Distinguished Young Alumnus Award, as well as with honorary doctorates in recognition of his work. He has been a George A. and Eliza Gardner Howard Foundation Fellow, through Brown University, and a Fellow with the National Endowment for the Humanities.

Tom is also the author of over twenty-two pioneering books. His twelfth book, *True Success: A New Philosophy of Excellence*, launched him into an ongoing adventure as a philosopher working and speaking throughout the world. His audiences have included a great many of the Fortune 500 companies and dozens of the largest national and international trade associations. His work has been mentioned, commented on, or covered by NBC, ABC,

CNN, CNBC, NPR, and in most major newspapers and news magazines. He's also the author of the highly acclaimed books *If Aristotle Ran General Motors, Philosophy for Dummies, The Art of Achievement, The Stoic Art of Living, Twisdom, Superheroes and Philosophy,* and *If Harry Potter Ran General Electric: Leadership Wisdom from the World of the Wizards,* as well as many others. His most recent books include the philosophical prologue to the current series, *The Oasis Within,* and the subsequent books, *The Golden Palace, The Stone of Giza, The Viper and The Storm,* and *The King and Prince,* as well as the current volume. He just may be the world's happiest philosopher.

An Ode for Odie

If you want to know
how good a cat
he was in this world:
It would be my great honor
to clean his litter box
twice a day
in eternity,
forever.

www.ingramcontent.com/pod-product-compliance
Lightning Source LLC
Chambersburg PA
CBHW031957040826
48979CB00043B/1523/J
* 9 7 8 0 9 9 9 3 5 2 4 7 2 *